EPIPHANY

Rashid Darden

Old Gold Soul   Washington, DC

Old Gold Soul
810 Kennedy Street NW
Suite 305
Washington, DC 20011

www.oldgoldsoul.com

www.facebook.com/rashiddarden

Epiphany is a work of fiction. Any references to real people, events, establishments, organizations, or locales are intended only to give the fiction a sense of reality and authenticity. Other names, characters, and incidents are either the product of the author's imagination or are used fictitiously.

First Edition

Cover Design by Neil Wade

ISBN 0-9765986-4-7

For

Alice Dixon
Wendy Holmes
and
Ahmatah Paul Love

Acknowledgements

Sincere thanks go to God for helping me remember my passion and my destiny.

Thank you to Carolyn Darden-Stutely, my mother.

Thank you to my friends, brothers, and sisters: Liz Burr, Liz Collins, Kimya Dennis, Jeffrey Hill, Warren Jones, Tracy Joseph, Lana Johnson, Gena LeBlanc, Carey McCray, Chris Moore, Charles Murray, James Reed, Pontip Rasavong, Krista Robertson, Andre Rosario, Muhammad Salaam, Felicia Thomas, Dominique Tillman, Kwame Ulmer, and Elyshe Voorhees.

Thank you also to The Guild, LLC.

Thank you especially to all of the readers of *Lazarus* and *Covenant* who have supported me through the years, through my website and as my Facebook friends.

Thank you most of all to my cover designer, my buddy, my friend, my partner in crime, and my constant. Neil Wade: I love you.

EPIPHANY

Part One:
Winter Break

Christmas Eve

I'm crazy, she thought. *That's all.*

Once again, she was curled in the fetal position, not allowing even the promise of Christmas morning to bring her out of bed.

She stretched out on her back and stared at the ceiling, letting herself slip into a familiar stupor. Twin tears slithered out of her eyes, past her jaw line and down her neck, warming and then cooling two identical paths on her face.

I'm going to be okay, she thought. She sat up in bed and looked around her room, that of a modern-day princess. Although she was a bit too old for the pink ruffled décor, it was still the only place where she found peace.

She reached for the Raggedy Ann doll that she had owned for as long as she could remember and hugged it tightly, rocking slowly back and forth.

Tears streamed down her face silently as she tried not to think about what she had seen.

Chapter 1:
Christmas Morning

It wasn't so much that I was concerned about the mean old lady who glared at me as I stroked my boyfriend's sleeping head. He dozed in my lap as the Amtrak train rolled north to Baltimore. No, the caramel-colored lady with the scrunched-up face and the beady little gray eyes and mustache to match didn't really upset me. She just annoyed the hell out of me. So I stroked his head some more and watched the lady smolder and cringe at my public display of homosexual affection.

Isaiah— my man— was letting his hair grow out a little bit, so the natural waves were really popping out more than usual. I knew that he was at peace because of the ease with which he rested his head on my shoulder when we first took our seats on the sparsely populated train car. By the time the wheels began turning, he slid his head from my shoulder to my lap and made himself comfortable. Mere minutes outside of the Washington city limits, he was asleep. A hint of a smile decorated his face.

I had no choice but to also be put at ease, even though we were about to do the unthinkable: enjoy Christmas day at his mother's house. Just one day before, I found myself nauseated at the idea of him meeting my mom and me meeting his. As much as we had been through in the previous months, however, we both knew that life could be much worse than dealing with mothers and holidays and questions and looks.

We were in love. We had to be. Why else would I let a 200-something pound, extra-tall basketball player lay in my lap like I was made to be his pillow? Yeah… I loved him. I loved the way his hair felt beneath my palm as I let my hand slide over the waves on his scalp. I loved feeling the weight of his heavy noggin in my lap, threatening to make my thighs fall asleep. I loved knowing that he loved me as much as I loved him. All that I did for Isaiah was returned to me, sometimes three-fold. He could be a possessive sonofabitch sometimes, but I didn't mind. It was nice having someone who would fight for me— someone who talked the talk and walked the walk when it came to being with me.

So to hell with the old lady who didn't approve of two black men loving each other. Nothing was going to stop this train. I turned on my MP3 player, closed my eyes, and tuned the woman out.

Forty-five minutes later, as the train slowed down upon our entry to Baltimore, I tapped him lightly on the forehead. He opened his eyes slowly and blinked a few times.

"Huh?" he asked, still in a fog from his deep sleep.

"We're almost here," I said. "Get up."

Isaiah slowly rose from my lap and stretched his arms high above his head, tickling the light fixture above us. He rubbed the sleep out of his eyes and gazed out of the window. We were slowly coming to a stop at Baltimore's Penn Station. The skies above us were the same calming shade of gray as they were in DC. He turned around and smiled.

Within five minutes, the train had come to a complete stop. I grabbed my bag from the overhead compartment and placed it in my seat. I then handed Isaiah the brand new duffle bag that I had gotten him for Christmas.

"I still can't get over how nice this is, Adrian," he said.

"Whatever," I shrugged. "You know you needed it."

"Just like you needed that MP3 player. You like it, right?"

"Love it."

Isaiah walked down the aisle first and didn't notice our grouchy neighbor giving him the evil eye.

"God bless you!" I said sweetly and loudly to the woman. She looked at me in utter shock. I winked my eye and kept walking.

"What was that about?" Isaiah asked as he stepped carefully off of the train and onto the platform.

"Nah, nothing really," I said. "That old lady was mean-mugging us the whole ride up here."

"Word?" Isaiah laughed. "Leave them old ladies alone, Adrian. They ain't ready for you."

I smiled at him. Isaiah was wearing his traditional winter uniform, which consisted of baggy blue jeans, tan Timberland boots, and a black North Face jacket. A lean, muscular body hid beneath the bulkiness of his winter clothes. He wore a black knit hat that fit him like a skully. He knew he'd better put it on while he was in Baltimore— his mom would be able to sense that he wasn't protecting his head from the cold. His duffle bag, with the initials ICA, Isaiah Christopher Aiken, embroidered on the side, was slung over his shoulder effortlessly. As though he knew I was still staring at him as we walked, he turned around and winked his brown eye and flashed a toothy grin in my direction. He knew me all too well.

We were quite a pair, the frat boy and the athlete. By the looks of things, we were just two college chums coming home for the holiday. Only a few people really knew what we were to each other. The term "boyfriend" was so trite sometimes, yet so scary to say aloud, especially when you were a black man from DC or Baltimore. "Lover" was one of those words that sounded even worse than "boyfriend." It had this connotation of an illicit affair in my mind. For me, "my man" was good enough. Since there were so few people who even knew of our relationship, "my man" was a phrase I didn't have to use very often.

The cab ride to Isaiah's house was brief— no more than ten minutes— so aside from downtown Baltimore, I didn't get a good sense of the essence of the city. The place we ended up couldn't have been one of the best neighborhoods in the city, but it wasn't the worst I'd ever seen, either. All of the houses on the block were uniform, with small front yards and porches that were in need of a paint job. As was the tradition in most places I had known, the Christmas lights were turned on even in the daylight hours.

"Christmas comes to Coppin Heights," Isaiah mused as the cab came to a stop. "We home, baby."

I smiled and stepped out of the taxi, onto the curb. As far as my eye could see were two-level homes on a long, flat street. It was quiet, almost like the set of a movie before the director yells "Action!"

His house looked just like all the others, plain and in need of some superficial repair on the pale blue porch. A few sandy colored bricks were missing from the façade as well. But this was his home— I was determined to take in this whole experience with an open mind.

Before the taxi had time to speed away, the front door of this North Warwick Avenue house flung open.

"My baby!" the woman said.

"Ma!" Isaiah shouted. He dropped his bag to the sidewalk and jogged up the stairs to his small porch. Without hesitation, I picked up his bag and walked slowly to the stairs. Isaiah and his mom held each other and rocked from side to side. I still hadn't had a good look at her since Isaiah's huge frame eclipsed her.

"I'm so glad you're home," she said, though her voice was muffled by Isaiah's North Face jacket.

"Me too," he said.

"Let me look atcha, boy," she said. Releasing her son from her embrace, she stood back a few steps and looked at him. Her face was lit up with unadulterated joy.

"Well, you still look good," she said.

"Thanks," Isaiah said. "Ma, I want you to meet Adrian."

Isaiah turned and beckoned me up the porch stairs with his outstretched arm. Each step I took up those stairs felt like twenty years.

Isaiah's mother was a diva. She was as fair skinned as her son, but her features were round and soft where Isaiah's were sharp. She was a tall woman indeed – I judged her to be six feet even by the time I got to the porch. Her nails and hair were *done*— French tip manicure and weave for days. The good Beyonce weave, though, not the cheap stuff. She was a young looking woman, too. I was convinced she couldn't have been more than forty years old.

"Hi, Ms. Aiken," I said humbly, stretching out my hand to her.

"Boy, you better go 'way from here with that 'Ms. Aiken' stuff!" she said. "You practically family— you better call me Gloria and give me a hug!"

Without warning, I found myself in Gloria Aiken's embrace. From the corner of my eye, I saw Isaiah smiling at us both.

"I heard so much about you!" she said, finally letting me go.

"All good things, I hope," I said sheepishly.

"Mmm hmm," she said. "Handsome as you wanna be, too!"
My brown skin blushed.

"Mmm hmm, and shy, too! Well, y'all better come on up in here out of this cold air. My baby can't be catching pneumonia during the season." She turned around and led us into the house. She wore a Columbia blue jogging suit with white trim and zippers. It fit her form in ways that most mothers wouldn't dare to think about, much less try for themselves. She was a fine woman, and judging by the switch in her walk, she knew as much.

The Aiken house was immaculate on the inside. The hardwood floors shined as bright as the gloss on Ms. Aiken's manicure. The walls of the foyer were adorned with pictures of her "baby" and others in the family. There were too many to survey in the brief moments we stood there. She took the bags and set them down near the door.

"Go ahead and make yourself at home, Adrian," she said. "It's space set up for you in the basement. Don't worry, it's got plenty of heat and a big old comfy sofa-bed for you."

"Thanks a lot," I said. "I can't wait to meet the rest of your family."

"Boo, they are gonna love you!" she squealed. "Of course, they are gonna love seeing the baby, too."

"Ma, I ain't no baby," Isaiah interjected as he had a seat at the kitchen table. I followed Gloria into the kitchen and watched the two interact.

"You always gonna be the baby," she said. "All there is to it. You been the baby since you were born. Your grandma still calls you the baby. You're her youngest's youngest. So, you the baby."

"You have siblings, Ms.-" I began.

"Boy, you better call me Gloria!" she said. "And yes, I have two sisters and a brother. Isaiah's Aunt Gillian and Aunt Grace and Uncle George."

"Uncle Greg died, though," Isaiah added.

"Yeah," Gloria said. "Greg done gone on away from here."

There was an awkward silence before Isaiah broke it.

"So when do we eat?" he asked.

"Boy, it's only just now eleven in the morning! You better sit your tall self down somewhere, get a bowl of cereal, and watch some cartoons. Ain't nobody thinkin' about no real meal until it's time for dinner."

"Well when's that?!" Isaiah asked in earnest.

"Three o'clock like it always is, boo-boo! Now 'gone, get out of here so I can get back to cookin'. Shoot. I *still* got cooking to do. Now scram!" Gloria smiled at us, but still shooed us away.

"Uh-uh, Ma, how you gonna do us like that? I just got back!"

"And? We got a few days, you'll be aight. Now get outta here. And put your things upstairs in your room so it won't be in nobody's way."

We chuckled on the way up the stairs.

"Your mom is a trip," I said.

"Ain't she?" he said. Isaiah's room was toward the back of the house. It was small, but I reckoned it was just the right size for a high school senior. That was the last time he'd spent any extended period living at his mother's house. I couldn't tell what color the walls were since they were literally covered with a collage of posters: Michael Jordan, Larry Bird, Scottie Pippen, and Dennis Rodman. Every inch of shelf space was taken by trophies and medals. This was truly an athlete's room. We tossed our coats and bags on the bed and headed back down the stairs.

The basement had wood paneling and a deep red carpet straight out of the late 70s. There was a big screen television at one end of the room, and a big, plaid sofa on the other end. There were space heaters in two corners of the room as well.

"Well... you're here," I said, looking into Isaiah's eyes. "How does it feel?"

"It feels great, baby," he said. He eased toward me and met his lips to mine. We kissed and then he held me in his arms. He always knew exactly how to put me at ease.

"I think my mom likes you," he said.

"You think so?" I said.

"Yup. But I knew she would. Yo, you want something to eat? Some cereal or something?"

"That would be nice," I said. "Whatever y'all have is fine."

"Bet," he said. "I'll be right back. And get comfortable, baby. Take them shoes off. You home now."

He winked at me and darted up the stairs. Isaiah looked like the happiest man in the world. He was with his mom and soon the rest of his family for Christmas dinner. He was with his man— wow, that's still me, huh? And most of all, he wasn't stuck at Potomac University playing basketball.

I turned on the television and quickly found *The Teen Titans*. Isaiah came back down the stairs within a few minutes, carefully balancing a tray with two bowls of cereal.

"Teen Titans?" he asked me with wide eyes.

"Yup," I said. "What we got?"

"Frosted Flakes," he said, gently placing the tray on the floor in front of the sofa. He gave me a bowl in my hands and I eagerly accepted it, having not eaten all day. He sat on the floor near me and devoured his cereal.

"This was good," I said a few minutes later.

"Mmm-hmm," he replied. I put my bowl back on the tray and Isaiah slid it to the side.

"You cold, baby?" he asked.

"Yeah, it's jive chilly," I said. Without hesitation, Isaiah turned on the two space heaters in the room. Soon, the temperature rose to a much more comfortable level.

He sat on the end of the couch and took his boots off. I did the same. He rested one leg on the sofa and the other on the ground and beckoned me to him. I obliged. In the space he created between his legs, I rested - my back to him and my eyes on the television.

"I'm tired," he mumbled, circling his arms around me. As he exhaled, the breath that left his lungs traced a path around my neck before it dissipated into the air.

"You been 'sleep all day," I said.

"But we were up all night," he said, holding me tighter.

I chuckled.

"Is like… your whole family gonna be here?" I asked.

"Yeah," he said. "Pretty much."

"Oh."

"You ain't freaked out, are you?"

"Naw. Just nervous."

"Baby, you ain't got nothin' to worry about. My mom is the only one I told. She's the only one that matters anyway."

"I'm not worried about them knowing we get down. It's just, you know, kinda overwhelming. You just met my mom last night and that was stressful enough. Now I'm meeting your mom and your entire family."

"Adrian, you will be fine, I promise you. You are the type of person who can handle any kind of situation. You know that."

"I guess."

"I know," Isaiah concluded.

My mind wandered as the cartoons played on. Soon, Isaiah was asleep again, his snoring lightly tickling the back of my neck. I felt restless, though.

I slid out of his arms and stood up. Damn, he was beautiful. And he was mine.

I left the television on and tip-toed upstairs with the tray and empty bowls to visit with Gloria, if she'd have me. I didn't want to just feel like "Isaiah's little friend" the whole time I was there. I wanted to know this woman.

I placed the bowls into the sink and began washing them.

"Fell asleep, didn't he?" Gloria asked as she emerged from the dining room.

"Yeah," I said. "He was out like a light no sooner than he finished the cereal."

"Mmm-hmm," she said. "Been that way since he was five. Sleep in on Saturdays, wake up late to watch cartoons, have some cereal and fall right back to sleep. Y'all didn't even get your presents from under the tree yet."

"Y'all?" I asked. "You mean Isaiah, right?"

"Now how do I look having Isaiah's... friend... in my house and not getting him anything for the holidays?"

"You're too nice, Gloria," I said. "For real."

"It's no problem, baby! You might as well be family!"

She gave me a great big hug for the second time that day. Hesitantly, I hugged her back.

"Aight, what's wrong?" she asked with furrowed brows.

"Nothing's wrong," I said, forcing a grin.

"Mmm-mmm," she said. "We need to talk."

She walked toward the back door of her kitchen and unlocked the deadbolt.

"Come on," she ordered. "See, cuz we need to talk."

I obeyed. She swung the door open and led me to a back porch that was enclosed by storm windows. Through the screens I could see the backs of other homes just like this one. There were no yards, just plots of concrete that had patches of grass springing up through the cracks. There were a few cars there, some junked. Isaiah had told me that he played at the elementary school which was a block or so away, but I never thought it was because he was surrounded by concrete everywhere else that he went.

"Lovely view, huh?" she laughed.

I smiled uncomfortably as she had a seat on an old sofa that looked like it was on its way to the alley for the trash man, but gave up at the back porch instead.

"Loosen up, boy. I ain't gonna bite you. Do you smoke?"

"No," I said.

"Good," she said, whipping out a pack of Kool Milds. "This is bad for you. Never start smoking."

I gazed out of the screen some more while I heard the click of Gloria's lighter and smelled the funk of burning tobacco.

"This isn't easy for me," I said, trying to break the uneasy silence.

"Shit -- I mean shoot," she said. "Who you tellin'? My only son is gay."

My heart froze in my chest.

"How can you welcome me into your home so easily?" I asked.

"Because my gay son loves him some Adrian Collins, that's why. And I knew if I wanted to keep him in my life, I'd have to accept you, too."

"If you're not comfortable with me being here, I don't have to stay," I said.

"Adrian, sit down and listen for a minute. That's not what I'm sayin' at all."

I walked over to the sofa and sat near her.

"When Isaiah came home for Thanksgiving, I knew something was on his mind. He was different. All day he'd look scared, sad, happy, all these different emotions wrapped up into one. And I'd ask him about it, and he'd say 'Nothin's wrong, ma' and I'd leave it alone. But when we went over to my mom's for Thanksgiving, he was beside himself. Really depressed and irritable. It was real obvious that something was on his mind. So when we came back here I sat him right down in that living room and asked what he needed to say."

"Uh-huh," I responded. Isaiah had never told me all the gruesome details of how he came out to his mother, but I sensed that Gloria would leave no stone unturned when it came to this story.

"And he said 'Ma, there's something I need to tell you' and I say 'what?' and he's all 'Ma, you gotta promise not to get mad at me' and we go back and forth like that until I start to get pissed off. And finally he's like 'I met somebody.' And, of course, I'm like relieved because I really couldn't stand that saditty little thing he was with... what's her name... Tina? Tiajuana?"

"Taina," I said.

"Yeah. *That* heffa. So I ask what happened to her and he says that he broke up with her. So I'm like okay, what's the new girl's name? And says, all serious, 'His name is Adrian.'"

"He told me he said it like that," I said.

"Mmm-hmm," Gloria continued. "I bet. So I say to him 'His? Whatchu mean, "his?" What are you trying to tell me, boy?' And of course, he says 'I'm gay, ma.'"

"Wow," I said.

"Exactly. So we had this huge fight like you wouldn't believe, chile. I was crying, he was crying, I threatened to put him out, he threatened to walk out and never speak to me again, I'm fallin' out, he's fallin' out. Just drama." She chuckled.

"He didn't tell me all of that," I said.

"That don't surprise me," she said. "Isaiah don't like anybody to think he isn't in control. He knows exactly what he's saying and doing at any moment. But when he gets mad... Honey, just stay out of his way. Just can't control him. That's why I made sure I kept his butt in basketball. You can't walk around in the streets with a rage like that. Basketball saved his life by keeping him out the street. But anyway, Adrian, that's not my point. I'm telling you all this because... because I want you to know that Isaiah and I done had our drama. He knows that all this is gonna take some getting used to for me. But he knows that I love him and I'm always gonna love him. I know I raised him right. That boy is in college for free— and he smart, too! Even if he couldn't play ball, I have no doubt in my mind that he would still be at Potomac."

"That's for damn sure," I said. "Isaiah puts me to shame with the grades that he gets."

She smiled. "That's my boy. But Adrian, as hard as it is for me to say... my son loves you. He *loves* you. He ain't never in his life been as passionate about something like... well, he just digs you, that's all I'm saying."

"Thank you," I said.

"No, thank you," she began. "Because..."

That's when the tears started. I knew that Isaiah's mom and my mom were two entirely different people. My mom was more refined, quiet, and prone to internalizing her emotions. There was no discussion about who Isaiah was to me. Yet, she knew. I knew she knew. And nothing more needed to be said.

But Gloria needed to say it all. She wouldn't be content until everything was out of her system, including one good cry.

"Because," she repeated, her voice cracking. "All I got is my baby and all my baby got is me. He ain't had no daddy in a long time. I wish every day that he hadn't seen what happened down there on that playground. But he did, and I know that changed him. And I can't do nothin' about that but be there for him."

"He loves you for that, Gloria," I said. I sat nearer to her on the sofa and awkwardly put my arm around her shoulder. She wept.

"Isaiah told me what happened to his father," I said. "He told me how he saw him get shot that day on the basketball court. But he is strong. Your son has been nothing but strong the whole time I've known him. He's been there for me. Look... I know it can't be easy living with the fact that Isaiah likes guys. But... he's still the same man you raised. He always will be."

Gloria stopped weeping and wiped her eyes.

"I see why he likes you, boy," she said. "You know all the right things to say."

I smiled.

"I could say the same thing about him," I replied.

"How did your mom take it when you told her?" she asked.

"Well... I never really told her," I admitted. "Me and my mom don't have a really close relationship. I'm pretty sure she knows, though. I'm not hiding it from her, but it also never came up."

"I see," she said. "And your dad?"

"He has no clue," I said. "But until recently he hadn't been part of my life. So we've got other things to work through. The gay thing can wait."

"I'm sure they'll be proud of you regardless," she said.

"Just like you're proud of Isaiah," I said. "It's kinda wild. Your son is probably going to be a professional basketball star. At least, that's what all the papers are saying."

She beamed.

"Yeah," she said. "All his dreams are coming true. But I know he's going to stay in school and get his degree first. Leaving early's not even an option."

"So you're not gonna let him enter the draft early?" I asked.

"Hell no," she said. "Education first. Plus, he ain't ready. He needs to gain some weight and hone some skills. Don't get it twisted, boo-boo. Isaiah is great on the court. But he need to be greater than great if he wants to get drafted in the first round next year."

"Well, basketball's not one of my favorite sports, believe it or not, so I'll take your word for it."

"You don't like basketball?" she asked.

"I mean, it's okay," I said. "Isaiah is getting me some tickets to some games so maybe I'll start liking it more."

"Shoot, you better," she said. "Gone ahead and get used to being at those games. From the way Isaiah been talking, you gonna have courtside seats for life no matter where he's playin'."

I smiled.

"I like him a lot. It's just so weird for both of us. Neither of us is like… I dunno… we're not the typical gay men."

"Aren't you though?"

"What do you mean?"

"You ain't hardly lived yet, Adrian. Gay people look like you and Isaiah and a whole bunch of other people."

"Well, I know that, but still."

"But still, nothin'. You and Isaiah act like y'all the first gay black men that ever walked the earth. Not even 21 yet and acting like life is so hard. Hmph. Gay black men and women been everywhere since before you was a twinkle in your grandma's eye."

"You're right," I said. "I guess everyone has their own experiences. I never thought… well, I never thought I'd be talking so openly with my boyfriend's mother about this."

"No shit," she said. "Well until a month ago, I ain't think I would either. But I thought I better get used to it."

"Thank you for talking to me, Gloria. If you ever need me, want to talk or, I dunno, come visit in DC…"

"I feel you," she smiled. "You a good kid."

She hugged me again.

"Well, let me go get ready. Family will start trickling in soon. Maybe an hour or so. Tell Isaiah I need him to get me some ice when he wakes up."

"Okay," I said. And just as swiftly as it had begun, Gloria's emotional rollercoaster ended.

***

"I gotta get Ma out of Coppin Heights," Isaiah confessed as we walked to the end of the block. The sky was still overcast, even in the middle of the afternoon, making it look like we were walking through an old black and white movie. The street was still; the only sound was that of the far off traffic.

"It's not so bad, Isaiah," I said. "I've seen much worse."

"But she deserves much better," he quickly responded. "This neighborhood is the fucking pits. When I make it big, I'm gonna buy her one of them big ass houses in Roland Park."

"Where is that?" I asked.

"North side of town. It might look real quiet around here today but don't be fooled. I do not like my mom living over here with these winos and dope fiends."

"I hear you."

"I just want her to live nice, like your mom does."

"You think we live nice?" I asked.

"Your neighborhood is real quiet and your house is big," he said. "The whole time I've known you, you've never mentioned anything real bad about your childhood. Of course you live nice."

"I guess," I said. We were at the corner store ready to walk in when he stopped abruptly and looked around the corner. Halfway down the block to the right was a tall chain link fence that bounded an asphalt basketball court. He was drawn to this court like an iron filing to a magnet.

"Walk with me down here," he asked. Before I could suggest that he didn't have to go to that spot, he was already walking. I knew exactly where he was going. It was the same dreaded place that he had told me about the previous summer, the place where his father fell in a hail of bullets from an angry thug.

"Are you coming?" he asked. All emotion was gone from his face.

"Yes," I said.

It didn't take long to get to the spot. I looked down to the sidewalk, illogically afraid that I would see Isaiah's father lying there in a pool of blood. This was the place of tears and pain and lost innocence. This was the place that Isaiah remembered as he sobbed in my arms last summer, recounting the final moments of his father's life.

I looked up at him.

"Are you okay?" I asked. He nodded, never breaking his stare. I wanted him to look at me and not into the oblivion of his past. There was nothing for him in that asphalt behind the fence; just a basketball court, a school, and memories that deserved to be forgotten. In that moment, he was at his most beautiful, even as the first tear began to form in his eye.

"Look," he said.

"I am," I replied.

"No. Look out there," he demanded. I inhaled the cold December air deeply into my lungs and turned to the basketball courts. Nothing sinister cluttered my vision except for a stray piece of paper the wind had tossed to the court.

"This is where I stood," he said. "And that's where it happened."

I tried my best to put my arm around his shoulders but the most I could do was gently touch him. Sometimes he was just too tall for me to comfort him like I wanted.

"I miss him so much," Isaiah choked. His hands clenched the chain link fence and he finally broke his gaze from the scene of the crime, over a decade old by now, but obviously just as fresh in Isaiah's mind as though it had happened yesterday. He looked down to the ground.

"I know," I said, still rubbing his shoulder through his coat. "It's okay."

He raised his head and looked at me. Tears streamed from both of his eyes and his perfect mouth was turned into a painful frown. My heart broke into thousands of pieces as I saw him at his most vulnerable.

I did the only thing I could. I slowly raised my arms and took Isaiah into my embrace. He wrapped his arms tightly around me, burying his head into my coat and shaking me with each pained sob.

"It's going to be okay. He knows you miss him. He's here. He's here," I said.

I held him for centuries, trying to transmit to him what little strength I had. He wept and I held. And he held and I wept. Around us the neighborhood remained quiet, devoid of even a child playing with a new bike. It was as if Coppin Heights itself had given Isaiah space to grieve and time to heal.

"I love you, Adrian," he said. "Don't ever leave me."

"I ain't going nowhere," I replied. "I'm right here."

Chapter 2:
Christmas Night

"So tell me, Adrian," Cousin Yvonne began. "What brings you to Baltimore for Christmas? Didn't I hear Isaiah say you were from DC?"

"Mind your business, cuz," Cousin Prince said. "If the man wants to come spend the holiday with his boy, let him."

"I'm just making conversation, dang!" she said. "It's just unusual to see people not spending Christmas with their own families."

"Actually," I began while finishing off a piece of sweet potato pie, "We were at my mom's yesterday. We came into Baltimore this morning."

"Oh, really?" Yvonne said. "Well isn't that special."

Cousin Prince rolled his eyes. Both were in their mid to late twenties and shared the same fair complexion and keen features of their cousins Isaiah and Gloria Aiken. The night had been entertaining, to say the least, with over a dozen of Isaiah's relatives crammed into every single room of the house. With a family this size, you couldn't just eat around the dinner table. You just fixed yourself a plate and took it wherever there was a place to sit. For me, Yvonne, Prince, and Isaiah that happened to be Isaiah's old room, which was doubling as the coat room for the evening.

"When you gonna leave that raggedy ass school and go pro?" Prince asked Isaiah unexpectedly. Even with his zig-zag cornrows and extra pounds, he still resembled Isaiah.

"Potomac ain't raggedy," Isaiah said, defending his our school. "And I ain't leaving until I graduate. I got a year and a half before that happens."

"Man, don't you know folks are expecting you to go pro? Especially if your sorry little team makes it to the Sweet Sixteen."

"That's cool," Isaiah said. "But I'm not going pro yet. I'm getting my degree."

"Aight, son," Prince said. "You always talkin' about how you wanna get Aunt Gloria out of Coppin Heights. Well, now's the fucking time, nigga."

"I'ma get her out of Coppin Heights, but I'm no good to anybody if I don't get my degree," Isaiah said.

"Backwards ass nigga," Prince said. "You go to college so you can get a good paying job. You can get one of those right now. Why risk a year playing for free and getting injured?"

"Are you finished?" Isaiah asked.

"I guess," Prince replied.

"How's your daughter these days?" Isaiah asked, changing the subject.

"She fine," Prince said quickly and quietly. It seemed as though Isaiah knew exactly what to say to get his cousin off his back.

"How old is she now, eight?" Isaiah asked.

"Ten," Prince responded.

"You have a ten year old?" I asked incredulously.

"Yeah," he said. "She's my baby."

"How old are *you*?" I asked.

"Twenty-six," he said.

"Wow," I said. "So you had her when..."

"He was fifteen, going on sixteen," Yvonne interjected. "Broke his mother's heart."

Prince stood up abruptly and glared at Isaiah.

"Yeah... I made my mom a grandmother. But at least she can *be* one."

"What's that supposed to mean?" Isaiah asked.

"I always been on your side, cuz," he growled. Isaiah rolled his eyes as his cousin stormed out of the room.

"Well..." I began.

"Dang, Isaiah, you ain't have to go there," Yvonne said. "You know that nigga ain't seen his daughter in months."

"That ain't my fault," Isaiah said. "That nigga older than I am, still out runnin' the streets. Don't make no sense. He got a daughter to provide for."

"That's his business though, ain't it?" Yvonne asked.

"He shoulda thought about that before he got in mine."

"Man, you know he just wants the best for you," Yvonne said.

"Whatever," Isaiah scoffed.

"Well, how is everybody?" a soft voice asked. We looked up and saw Isaiah's grandmother in the doorway. She was a thick woman, but like her daughter Gloria, you couldn't tell her that she didn't have it going on, even with the brown cane that she used to steady herself.

"Come on and sit down, grandma," Yvonne said, rising from her chair.

"Thanks, baby." Mrs. Ella Martin shuffled slowly across the room and sat in the chair that was nearest to the window. Yvonne leaned against the wall and Isaiah and I stood up and walked closer to her. I noticed that she had a photo album in her free hand.

"Are those pictures?" I asked.

"They sure are," Ella said.

"Oh no, Grandma!" Isaiah exclaimed. "Why you wanna go and do that for?"

"Naw, grandma, you ain't embarrassing me like that, I will see you downstairs," Yvonne said. She quickly left the room.

"You kids are a trip," Ella said. "Every time I bring these pictures around, you scatter like little mice."

"Cuz grandma, these are embarrassing!" Isaiah whined.

"Boy, you better look at these pictures with me and Adrian or sit on that bed and be quiet," she laughed. She looked at me and beckoned me over with her eyes. I stood behind her as Isaiah threw himself onto the bed and covered his face with his hands.

I loved seeing the family. Ella explained each and every photograph to me, from the first ones of her interracial parents (the white dock worker Richard Smith and his washer woman wife, Clara, both dead) to her late husband William Martin; from her five children (Gillian, Grace, George, Gregory, and Gloria) to the nearly dozen grandchildren. Ella went on and on… and on. I should have pulled up a chair.

"And here's Isaiah," she said finally, after twenty minutes. My ears and eyes perked up and I looked into the album to scope the shots of my man.

"Ain't he cute?" Ella asked. I smiled and said nothing. Isaiah was cute but he looked like a little white Gerber baby. Richard Smith's European genes ran strong in this family. Isaiah stood up and walked over to me, hoping that he could intercept any embarrassing pictures before they reached my eyeballs.

"Grandma, why don't you go ahead and let me..." He reached for the album, but Ella quickly snatched it back.

"Don't play with me boy! Me and Adrian are getting along just fine, thank you!"

She turned the page and showed me a picture of a child whose world was frozen in an instant. A four-year-old Isaiah Aiken was walking toward the camera wearing nothing but an oversized white t-shirt adorned with a pearl necklace and his grandmother's purple church hat. His face demonstrated the utmost innocence and joy at dressing in his grandmother's drag. I looked at Isaiah with my mouth agape. He looked so ashamed.

"Why you do that, grandma?" he asked. I smiled.

"It's cute," I said. "Don't worry."

"Isaiah, now why you get all upset?" Ella asked. "Ain't nothing wrong with a little boy playing around in his grandma's things."

Isaiah sighed.

It's okay, I mouthed. He put his hand on my shoulder and we both continued to look at the pictures.

"Well, that's the family," Ella announced after ten more minutes went by. "How'd you like your orientation?"

"It was nice, Mrs. Martin," I laughed.

"Why'd you call it 'orientation' grandma?" Isaiah asked. Ella closed the album and slowly stood up. Isaiah and I helped her.

"Well..." she began. "Seems to me like Adrian here... is going to be around for a while."

"Whoa, grandma, what are you talking about?" Isaiah asked. I stepped back once she was safely to her feet.

"I'm not trying to be in your business boy," she began. "But me and your mama talk."

"So, what are you saying?" he asked. "You... know?"

She nodded.

"Lord, Jesus," he said. "Why did she do that? Can't keep nothin' secret around here."

"Isaiah, it's not that bad. I'm fine with it. And your mama is fine with it... now."

"That's not the point, grandma," he said.

"I'm going to go downstairs," I announced.

"Don't," Isaiah said.

"Thanks, baby," Ella said, giving me the one-eyebrowed look that said *I think you best leave for a little while.*

"I won't be long," I reassured Isaiah. He nodded and closed the door as I walked away.

It made sense that Gloria would tell her mother that her only son was gay. I mean, come on. That's a big deal. But I couldn't imagine what was going through Isaiah's mind at the time. We were so used to me being the "out" one. I had gone to the club meetings in school. I had dealt with homophobic frat brothers. I was the one who was used to the slings and arrows of the "out" life, not Isaiah. Yet, Isaiah was the one dealing with his family knowing about him and wanting to talk about it. His family was big, touchy-feely, and emotive. My family was just me and my mom and we never talked much about anything. Everyone had their own path, I supposed. This was Isaiah's path and all I could do was stand at his side—not lead him.

The family was crammed into the living room, just laughing and having a great time. Although I was introduced to each and every one of them, I wouldn't dare try to recall all their names. Gloria beckoned for me to come over to the couch and sit on its arm.

"Where's my mom?" she asked.

"Upstairs talking to Isaiah," I said. Gloria's eyes widened and showed me a hint of fear.

"Is everything okay?" she asked.

"I think so," I said. She nodded in response.

"You never opened your present," she said. "Yvonne, pass me that present in the blue and gold paper, please."

Her niece complied, handling the package with care. Gloria then handed it to me. I paused, admiring the paper.

"Negro, open the daggone present!" Gloria said.

I smiled and obliged. Underneath the wrapping paper was a box of Curve cologne, which I had never worn before. I smiled again.

"I ain't know what you wear, but I figured most guys would like Curve."

"Thanks, Gloria," I said, hugging her tight. As I scanned the room, taking in the personalities of each and every one of the family members, I noticed that everyone's topic of conversation was more or less the same: Isaiah.

Why he should forgo his senior year and go to the NBA.

Why he should stay in school.

How much money he could make if he went pro.

Where he should play.

What coach would be best for him.

I could tell that everyone in the room cared about him to some degree, but it was also clear that nobody truly understood him, save his mother, who remained largely silent when it came to her son's intentions. Gloria's face showed nothing but the soft glow of a mother's love and the Christmas spirit.

A few moments went by and Isaiah and his grandmother came down the stairs. He had a slight smirk on his face and nodded in my direction as he positioned himself in front of his family.

"Aight, everybody," he began. "Listen up. I want all of you all to know I love you very much. But I've been listening to everybody for the past five minutes from upstairs, and I just gotta say a few things."

I glanced at Gloria, who just continued to beam.

"I know I'm a good basketball player," he continued. "But I came to Potomac University for an education. And basketball ensures that I get that education for free. I am letting you know, right here and now, that I will not be entering the NBA draft this year and that I fully intend to stay at Potomac and receive my degree. I know most of you feel that playing basketball is a way out of the 'hood, and you're right—it is. But my mother also told me that my mind will be sharp for years after basketball. If I don't get drafted next year, I'm going to grad school for education—I want to be a teacher if basketball doesn't work out."

"A teacher?" Prince asked incredulously. "Teachers don't make any kind of loot! What the hell are you talking about?"

"I want to be a teacher," Isaiah repeated. "And that's all there is to it. I will play basketball for as long as I can, but as soon as it's over, teaching is the profession I will enter. Now I want to enjoy the rest of my Christmas break and not have to talk about basketball anymore."

His impromptu press conference was over and there was no room for further questions. The man—my man—had made his decision and could finally enjoy the rest of his vacation in peace, even if it meant scornful looks from all of his cousins, uncles, and aunts for the rest of the evening.

"What can I say?" Gloria whispered. "That's my boy."

I clinked a glass of eggnog against hers.

"Amen," I said quietly.

Chapter Three:
December 29

"I love this time of year!" Nina Bradley exclaimed as we walked down U Street in DC. "All the dumb tourists are gone and it's just real natives in the streets. Ugh, I love this place!" Nina was my best friend, my ace boon coon, my homie from day one at college.

"If you love it so much, tell me again why you're leaving?" I asked wistfully. "You don't even like Austrians for real, for real."

Isaiah smiled and his roommate, Hodari Hudgins looked on. We made quite an interesting foursome: two basketball players well over six feet tall with leather jackets and loose-fitting jeans on, the sexy, tall, chocolate-brown sister with the fierce suede coat, and me, the regular height, kind of skinny college kid with the pea coat on. Until I pledged Beta, I had no clue just how comfortable and warm pea coats could be.

"Honey, I barely like Americans. Time to see what the Austrians are working with." She winked at me and I smiled.

"Do you have to know any German for this program?" Hodari said in his deep baritone voice.

"Yeah, I've been taking it the whole time I've been at Potomac, so it's going to help. But you know how all these study abroad programs are. Basically an easy 'A' overseas, especially from the Potomac-sponsored programs," she said.

"I dunno about that," I said. "I mean, it's still college, right?"

"Yeah," she said, as we stopped on the always-busy intersection of 13th and U Streets. There was a Starbucks was on one corner, a cluster of restaurants across the street, and a women's boutique cattycorner to us. Beyond each corner were rows of brownstone houses and short apartment buildings, except for the tall building the restaurants were housed in. The Ellington Apartments were the newest addition to U Street, a high-rise of apartments and condos seemingly designed for DC's wealthiest yuppies.

"It's still college," she continued. "But everyone's telling me not to worry. So... I'm not going to worry. It's only for a semester."

"True," I said. "So… Alero or Sala Thai?"

"I want Thai," Isaiah said.

"I'm good with whatever," Hodari added.

"What do you want?" I asked Nina. "It's your going-away dinner."

She paused, put her finger on her chin, and thought about it.

"Sala Thai," she decided. "And drinks at Alero after dinner."

"Good plan," Hodari said with a smile. As we crossed the street, I checked Hodari out for the first time in a while. Nina was sort of walking with him, but not terribly close. He was an extremely handsome dude, with features nearly polar opposite to Isaiah's. Hodari had shoulder-length dreadlocks, deep brown skin, and a round face. He was as tall as Isaiah, but had at least 30 pounds on him. He was the stocky center to Isaiah's wiry power forward.

Hodari seemed like the kind of dude that Nina should be with, at least on the surface. He was not only handsome but nice, too; he had a bright future ahead of him, most likely as a professional basketball player, but whether he would be drafted remained to be seen. Like Isaiah, his intentions were to get his degree first and let the rest unfold as it may.

In the two and half years we had been at Potomac, Nina only dated guys occasionally. She never had a serious boyfriend. I never thought that between the two of us, I'd be the one who already had two serious relationships in college. It was my hope that going on this farewell outing might spark something between the two of them.

Don't get me wrong, Nina didn't *need* a man. But there was nothing wrong with her having a little more fun with a dude who was good enough for her.

We were seated pretty quickly by a tall, slender Asian dude no more than 20 years old. I remembered him from a few other times Nina and I had been to Sala Thai. He smiled at us and led us to a square table at the front of the restaurant. Nina sat down first, then Hodari sat to her left. Isaiah and I sat on the other sides of the table. As we sat, our knees slightly hit one another.

"Sorry," I said.

Isaiah smirked in reply and lightly touched my knee with his palm. He let it linger.

"So, how's the season looking?" Nina asked Hodari.

"It's going well. We're dominating in the low post on the offensive end. We definitely gotta improve our team defense once we get into the conference schedule though. We're not gonna be able to just outscore teams like are are now. But you wouldn't know anything about that," Hodari said with a smirk.

"Oh, for real?" Nina replied, not missing a beat. "Well if y'all would take Billy Abbott off the bench, maybe defense wouldn't be as big a concern. You know there's nobody better on defense and transition than him."

Hodari's round eyes widened.

"What makes you say that?" he asked.

"His three-pointers would open up things in the paint for you, too. Not to mention he was one of the most sought after high school shooting guards in the country last year."

"Damn girl," Hodari said. "Adrian ain't tell me you was a color commentator in a previous life!" We laughed.

"What can I say?" she asked. "I'm a Renaissance woman."

"I see," he said, sipping his water.

"You coming to the game Saturday, right?" Isaiah asked me quietly.

"Yup," I said. "Tommy's coming with me, if that's cool."

"Your frat, Tommy? Sure, fine with me. Mom dukes ain't want to come?"

"Uh..." I chuckled. "You know she's a diva, she can't be bothered with such things as college basketball games."

"You ain't ask her," he said with a smile. I shook my head.

"Mmmm, mmmm, mmmph," he said, expressing faux shame. "One of these days, we're gonna just kick it with you, me, and Mama Collins."

"Good luck with that!" I laughed, taking a sip of water. I noticed that Hodari was shifting in his seat a bit and looked quickly away from Isaiah and I. A thought popped into my head.

Nina began to engage Hodari further while they browsed the menu. Isaiah quietly did the same, until I nudged his foot with mine. He looked up and smiled at me.

"Does he know?" I mouthed to him.

"Know what?" Isaiah mouthed back.

"About us!" I silently said, eyes wide and emphatic. He shrugged in response. I rolled my eyes, annoyed.

He tapped my foot and I looked up at him. He winked at me.

I got that warm feeling in my chest again.

Damn, he loves me, I thought.

We all chit-chatted throughout dinner, and as expected, Nina and Hodari dominated the conversation. For every quip Hodari had, Nina came back just as strong. For every time Nina tried to brush Hodari off as corny, he turned a 180 and charmed her. Isaiah and I watched in awe as both of our Type A personality friends hit it off well with each other.

Before we knew it, dinner was over. Alero was right next door to Sala Thai and by the time we got there, it was pretty crowded. It was some sort of Mexican fusion place with recessed lights of blue and red. Plenty of people enjoyed the good food and liquor.

They were strict about carding, so we weren't pressed to have any alcohol. Isaiah and I wouldn't turn 21 until that summer anyway.

In a few moments, the four of us were able to gain seats in a corner booth, recently vacated by four white chicks wearing tube tops (in winter, no less) and fuck-me pants. Being from the area, I was accustomed to DC being a black city, even in the suburbs. I found it oddly disconcerting that the four of us were the only black people at a restaurant in the heart of U Street.

Nina and Hodari sat next to each other and immediately started running their mouths again. The zingers, the one-liners—they just flowed so easily between them. Isaiah and I quietly watched and only weighed in on occasion. Meanwhile, Isaiah inched closer and closer to me. His arms rested on the back of the seats casually. He brushed his hand on my head casually when he thought no one was looking. We ordered flan as dessert and a round of sodas.

Before we knew it, our evening was winding down.

"It's after midnight, y'all… we need to go. Nina has a plane to catch tomorrow!"

We put on our coats and braved the cold air, walking as slowly as we could to Nina's car. These were our last few moments together for a long time and we wanted them to linger.

"What are you pushin'?" Isaiah asked.

"Just my aunt's minivan over here on the right. She lives out by Dulles, so I'm staying with her for the night."

"That's cool," Isaiah replied. "Girl, we're sure gonna miss you."

"Aww, you're so sweet! Hey, let me holla at you for a minute though," she said, grabbing Isaiah by the arm. She quickly walked ahead of Hodari and I. When they got more than a few paces ahead of us, I looked up at Hodari.

"She's pretty awesome, isn't she?" I asked.

"I can't lie man," he said. "Shawty is fly. Just wish I had gotten to know her before now."

"Yeah. Sucks that she's going overseas… like, tomorrow."

"Hell yeah," he said. "But yo, on the real? I always thought she was your girl."

"Shit man, *everybody* thinks that—to this day! No matter what I do, no matter how many dudes I date… I mean, dudes *she* dates." I laughed nervously as Hodari raised his eyebrow.

"Well, y'all kind of always just be… together. Ya dig? Except when you be with Isaiah."

"She's my homegirl. Best friend, really. You know how it is."

"Yeah, I guess." I could tell that the gears in his head were starting to turn. Bits and pieces of our conversation started to come together, bonded by the non-verbal communication I had with Isaiah all night. Touching a shoulder, giving a side-eye. Hodari was a cool dude but I could tell he was getting uneasy with our intimacy.

Isaiah was so reckless these days. I could appreciate his desire to just be out, but we needed to talk these things through first before we put our friends in these situations. I loathed creating a scene when it came to coming out, but wouldn't it make more sense to just take five minutes and tell somebody rather than letting them assume?

Then again, wasn't I one to talk? Volumes could be written about my inability to be upfront with the people closest to me: my mom, my fraternity brothers. At least those days were mostly behind me. I was more confident in myself than I ever had been. Coming out was no longer an issue of deciding who to tell, but when to tell them, and whether it would be in my best interest to do so in that moment.

Isaiah suddenly laughed heartily and hugged Nina, lifting her up off the ground. She smiled and giggled as he gently placed her back on the ground.

"Hodari, come holla at your girl," he said in between laughs. Hodari walked away from me and past Isaiah to say his farewells.

"What the heck are you laughing so hard at?" I asked.

"Come here," he said. He pulled me into a huge embrace. "It's cold out here, ain't it?"

He kissed me on the forehead.

"Isaiah, what are you *doing*, man?" I asked.

"Loving you fearlessly," he replied.

I froze.

"Well… damn." was all I could muster before I saw Nina kissing Hodari goodbye.

"Hit me up on Facebook when you get settled in, aight?" he requested.

"Bet on that," she replied. Still stunned by Isaiah's boldness, I walked over to Nina.

"You look like you just got your mind blown," she said.

"I kinda did… what did you say to him?"

"Never mind all that," she said. "Listen. I want you to have fun this spring. Go to every last party, step show, poetry slam, whatever. I want to hear that you're enjoying everything I'm missing, okay?"

"I got you," I said. And it finally hit me: my girl was leaving the entire country for six months!

"You better not start crying, bitch!" she said, stifling her own sniffle.

"I'm not," I smiled.

"I want you to have fun. I want you to enjoy yourself. Your

frat. Your friendships. Cat, Samirah, and Morris all love you and look up to you. And I love you."

"I love you, too, girl," I said, holding her tight.

"And I know Isaiah cares about you. Just be safe. Keep your heart safe."

"I will. Hey… you be safe in Vienna, okay? I don't have no bail money for you and you better not come back with no half-black, half-Austrian babies."

She laughed and embraced me one more time. Exhaling slowly, she let her hands slide down the length of my arms until she held each of my hands in hers.

"This is it," she said.

"Go on," I said. "Get out of here."

She unlocked her door and got into the driver's seat as Isaiah and Hodari stepped forward. Isaiah placed his arm around my shoulders. Nina placed the key in the ignition and started the engine. She waved at us one more time and drove away, down 13th Street toward downtown, across the river to Virginia, to her aunt's house, and ultimately, to Dulles airport.

I tried my best to hold back my emotions, but the tighter Isaiah gripped my shoulder, the more I felt the tears welling up in my eyes.

"You aight?" he asked. It was all I needed for the tears to fall from each eye. Although I nodded my head to affirm to him that I would be okay, he pulled me into his arms anyway.

It wasn't that I didn't want her to leave; I was happy she had the opportunity to study abroad. But it was hard letting go of one of the few people who knew me—the real me—from the first day of freshman year up until that very moment. Nina was my sister.

Isaiah let me go and cupped my face in his hands.

"She'll be back before you know it," he said. I smiled and nodded.

"I know," I whispered. "I know."

"Let's get a cab back home," he said. We walked to the corner of 13th and U, slightly behind Hodari. Within moments, we were in a Yellow Cab heading back to Potomac. I was sandwiched between two handsome ballers. On any other day, I would have considered my life to be complete. Instead, I situated my body closer to Isaiah's side and rested my head on his shoulder. I closed my eyes and felt Isaiah's hand rest on my knee.

About fifteen minutes later, we were on campus walking toward Isaiah and Hodari's dorm, where I planned to crash on the floor for the night and go back home to my mom's in Silver Spring in the morning. Since Hodari still didn't know, I didn't mind the minor inconvenience.

We got to the front door of the dorm when Hodari stopped and spun around to face us.

"Listen y'all... real talk," he said.

"What up?" Isaiah asked.

"Y'all fuckin'," he said matter-of-factly. I didn't know whether my chest would explode from the surge of fear and panic or from the largest stifled laugh in the known universe.

"What?" Isaiah asked incredulously.

"Y'all fuckin'," Hodari repeated. "Right?"

"Something like that," Isaiah replied, calmly and coolly.

"Aight then," he concluded, turning around to slide his ID through the card reader on the dorm's front door.

"We good?" Isaiah asked.

"Yeah, we good."

"Aight."

Isaiah followed Hodari into the building and held the door open for me. I was stuck where I stood, slightly in shock about everything that had happened.

"You comin'?" he asked me.

"Dude... is that it? You just fuckin' came out to your roommate and there's no drama? No fight? No anger? Fear? Just 'you fuckin'?' and 'yeah' and 'aight den'? What the hell kind of Twilight Zone am I living in?"

"Babe... why are you mad?" He allowed the door to close and he walked to me.

"I'm not mad," I insisted. "I'm just... surprised."

"Relax. Hodari is my boy. I mean, I wouldn't call him my best friend, but we been roommates and teammates since day one. He makes me look good, I make him look good. We got nothin' but love for each other. We might not be as tight as you and Nina, but he's what I got."

"Trust me, I'm not angry or upset or anything like that," I said. "I've just never seen the kind of acceptance that you're having. Doesn't that concern you? Aren't you afraid of losing your friends? Family?"

"Adrian. You been to my house. My mom knows. Hell, my fucking grandma knows. Now my roommate knows. Nina knows. I don't have the same networks that you do. Yes, these feelings I got are scary as hell, but you know what I got?"

"What?" I asked.

"I got you." I smiled. "Naw, for real though. I've been with you for six months Adrian. You make me feel better than good. You make me feel right. I've known you since we were freshmen, but if I had taken the time to really know you? Shit man, I would have never wasted two years of my life with Taina. I got mad love for her, but you know what? I am gay. I was gay before her, I was gay when I was with her, and I'm gay now. I like dudes. I like you. And I ain't never, ever gonna do anything to fuck up what we got going. You heard me?"

"I feel you," I said. "Come here."

I got on my tip-toes and put my arms around his neck.

"I love you," I said. We kissed.

"But one more thing," I said.

"What?"

"Nigga, we have not been together for six months! What the hell kinda math you doin?"

"You moved in with me in May of last year, and that's when it was on and poppin! It's December now, so it's actually longer than six months."

"Isaiah, we were not 'together' in May, hell, we weren't even 'together' by August! Let's not forget you didn't really break up with Taina good until a month ago. I'll give you one month, not six."

"One month?! Boy, boo."

I laughed.

"Boy, boo?" I laughed some more. "Dude, when did you get so gay? Did you go to gay charm school?"

"Shut the hell up, nigga," he laughed.

I grabbed his hand.

"No, for real though. I'm proud of you. I get to know a little bit more of you every day. And I'm a little envious that you're able to slide into this life so easily. I just really hope it stays this easy for you. I just don't want anything we do to jeopardize anything else. I'm just a regular dude. But you play Division I basketball for the Potomac Pirates. I know you know how much that means. And I know how you feel about me, but I want you to be sure that this is the way you want to go about things. I have your back no matter what you decide."

"Adrian, listen. I know you have my back. That's why I *can* do this. My teammates? Eh, fuck em. Some of them won't care. Some of them will. It's my coach that I'm worried about. A little bit, at least. He's old. He won't get it. And yeah, if the media got hold of this, there could be repercussions. But guess what? I don't care. I am a damn good basketball player with good grades. If basketball doesn't work out, I still have a future."

I nodded.

"You scared?" he asked. I thought about it for a moment.

"If you're trying to love me fearlessly, then I'm just going to have to love you back fearlessly. Right?"

"Sounds like a plan to me," he smiled. "Let's go to bed."

Still hand-in-hand, we went into the dorm and fell asleep, Isaiah and I spooning in one bed and Hodari softly snoring in the other.

Chapter Four:
December 31

"Ma?" I called upstairs.

"Yes?" she answered.

"Are you ready to go?"

"I'm coming," she said. She turned out the light in our upstairs hallway and came down the stairs. No matter how hard she tried to be casual, she looked like a diva anyway. Her twists were held back with a purple headband to match her Potomac Pirates sweatshirt. She wore jeans and winter boots to set off the ensemble. She reminded me of Diahann Carroll with natural hair, both in her dress and in her demeanor. I'm glad that Isaiah teased me into bringing her to the game, even if it meant rescheduling with my frat brother for a later time. I wouldn't see her much when the semester started, so it wouldn't kill me to spend some time with her.

I guess she agreed. She didn't give me a hard time about giving up a few hours of her Saturday to be with me. That was nice.

"So there's parking down there, right?" she asked.

'Well, it's downtown on a Saturday, Ma... I'm not sure how close we'll be able to get."

"Think there's valet parking?" she asked.

"Maybe," I said. "Never thought about it before."

"Well, we'll just see, won't we?" she smiled. I handed her a long leather coat from the closet, as I layered myself in a Potomac hoodie and my crossing jacket.

The day was cool, but sunny and warmer than when I last saw Nina. She had sent me a Facebook message letting me know she was safe and sound and ready to ring the new year in with the other internationals staying in her dorm in Vienna. I knew she'd quickly make friends.

Although me and my mom still didn't have a lot to say to each other, there was more peace between us. Something about Isaiah's presence in my life not only made me feel right inside, it made things right between people I needed to get right with. Me and my mom would still have a long way to go before we'd have the type of relationship a mother and son should, but I was confident that we'd be alright.

"Is Isaiah a good player?" my mom asked suddenly as we drove down Georgia Avenue toward downtown.

"He's okay," I said. "To be honest mom, this will be my first game since freshman year. I watch them on television from time to time. More so this year."

"Of course," she said. "Well I guess you'd better start paying closer attention."

"Why do you say that?" We rolled to a stop at Howard University, with the huge red-brick school of business to our left and the old Miner Teacher's College building just beyond it. In the clear winter air, we could see almost all the way to the convention center from this hilltop.

"He's your friend, right?" she asked. "A special... friend?"

"Mother, are you asking me if Isaiah is my boyfriend?"

"I don't believe I'm asking you anything really. It's just quite apparent that you two are pretty close. And pretty quickly, too."

"We've known each other since freshman year, mom."

"And you started dating when?"

"Mom, ugh, awkward..."

"I'm just trying to get to know the brother better, that's all. Maybe even get to know you better, too."

"I'm sorry mom. I just never talked to you about him like that before. Or about me... being gay. It's just like all of a sudden, you knew."

"Baby, I could tell by the way you looked at each other that he was your man."

"For real, mom?" With little traffic, we neared the Verizon Center quickly.

"Adrian, this is Mommy you're talking to."

I laughed.

"No, seriously. It's been you and me for this long. And I know we grew distant, but I still know you. I knew you were gay before you knew. But I raised you right. So I know you weren't going to pick no dummy. Did you?"

"Of course not, Mom! Isaiah's a pretty amazing guy."

"So what do I have to be afraid of?"

"Nothing, I guess."

"You're right. So my son is gay. Yeah, it sucks that you have to be gay in a world that isn't so welcoming to you. And yeah, I'll never have a daughter-in-law to go shopping with or grandbabies to spoil."

"I can still be a parent one day, mom. I could adopt."

"Eh. It's not the same. But whatever you want to do is fine with me. In fact, you should put off parenthood for a good ten, twenty years if you can. Mommy is far too young to be a grandmother, you hear me?"

"Mom, you are a mess!" I laughed. "Well, what do you know—Verizon Center does have valet parking."

We pulled up to the curb and stepped out of my mom's car. I couldn't believe it—we had actually had a bonding moment. I had come out to her, she was accepting, and everything was going to be just fine. Now I knew what Isaiah felt like coming out to his people. Even though his mom had confessed that there were many tears at Thanksgiving, by Christmas, everything was fine.

Whose life was this, anyway? The next thing you know, I'd be getting straight 'A's and a Rhodes Scholarship.

We truly had some of the best seats in the house, even better than the student seats behind the baskets. We found our seats at center court, only four rows back, as Potomac was warming up. For home games, Potomac wore white uniforms with purple and silver lettering and borders. The twelve men on the team were pretty amazing to see all at once. They were all black men—nothing at all like the composition of the campus. The coach—Mr. Andrew Kalinowski—was a white guy of about sixty years and even from across the arena, you could tell that what he didn't have in height, he made up for in personality. It wasn't that he was short; he just looked that way next to his players. Coach Kalinowski was well-loved among the students and alumni, even though his gruff exterior and lack of tact were well known.

As me and my mom had a seat, I felt a tap on my shoulder. I looked up into the aisle to see a tall, fair-skinned woman dressed from head to toe in a purple Potomac jogging suit.

"Hi Gloria!" I exclaimed, rising to embrace her.

"Hey, boo!" she said. "How you doin?"

"I'm fine—didn't expect to see you here! Are you sitting with us?"

"Us? Wait a minute, is this your mom?" she asked, gesturing at the one and only Ms. Collins.

"It sure is," I said. "Gloria, this is my mom, Elizabeth Collins. Mom, this is Isaiah's mother, Gloria Aiken."

My mom rose and extended her hand to Gloria.

"Just Liz, please," my mom said. Before I knew it, Gloria had pulled my mom past me and into the aisle and was squealing and hugging her like she had known her all her life.

My mother, not a "huggy" person, lightly patted Gloria on the back.

"Nice to meet you," she said softy. Gloria let go of her embrace, but held my mom by the hand.

"Nice to meet you too! You have raised such a wonderful son!" I blushed a little.

"Thank you," my mom said. "Isaiah is a perfect gentleman himself."

"Well he just better be!" Gloria exclaimed. "It is hard out here for single mothers today, especially single black mothers, you heard me? Shooooot… but he's book smart and street smart, so I know he will be just okay. And I know Adrian is looking out for him, too. Ain't that right, boo?"

I nodded quietly, gently pulling her toward me so the woman behind her could get through.

"Oh, I'm sorry boo-boo!" Gloria said to the woman.

"Not a problem," she said firmly. I looked directly at the woman to match that deep, syrupy voice to a face. She was overdressed for a basketball game in a black pants suit and a gray shell top. Her pale skin was like porcelain and her long, light red hair cascaded behind her. Her eyes peered over small glasses with black frames as she fidgeted with her mobile device. She barely even noticed us.

As she took her seat in front of us, I suggested to the mothers that we do the same. I sat in between them and as I imagined, Gloria monopolized the conversation. This would be good for my mom—she needed to be around people who took her outside of her comfort zone. It was hilarious—the suburban princess and the around-the-way girl.

The opposing team—the McCotter University Marauders—was introduced first, with a more ethnically diverse and imposing team dressed in black uniforms with old gold lettering. Their coach was a tall black man who looked vaguely familiar to me.

Potomac was introduced next. The starting line up, of course, included Hodari Hudgins, immediately followed by Isaiah Aiken. As he was introduced, he acknowledged the crowd cheering for him, of which Gloria was the loudest. Getting his attention with her cheers and hoots, Isaiah turned his attention to the three of us.

He smiled and gave a thumbs-up. His attention still on us, he winked and then joined his team in a huddle.

The redhead in front of us turned around to see who Isaiah was acknowledging. We locked eyes for the briefest of moments and she smiled, almost knowingly. I smiled back.

Potomac won the game with a final score of 83–72. Isaiah had scored 18 of those points. Basketball was growing on me—now that I had a reason to come to games. And better seats, of course.

That night, I was in another good seat—this time, on a charter bus filled with the men's basketball team and their friends. Isaiah invited me to travel with the team to a New Year's Eve victory party. It was an annual tradition that I hadn't heard of before—I guess because I wasn't part of the "in crowd" before.

I kept my outfit simple: black slacks, black blazer, wine colored shirt with gold cufflinks. Isaiah wore a black shirt with pinstripes which flattered his wide shoulders and thin waist. While it wasn't too tight, his muscles made the fabric fit just right on his body. He went without a blazer.

The bus pulled up to a club called Renard's across the street from the Washington Convention Center in a four-story converted warehouse. As local legend went, Renard's belonged to Renard Charles, youngest brother of Victor "Fats" Charles, the notorious drug kingpin from the 1980s. Even though Renard's was the classiest dance club in DC, everyone assumed it had to be a front of some sort. I had never been there before and never thought I could get in due to the long lines and not quite being 21 yet. In fact, neither was Isaiah, so we'd just have to see whether either of us would really get in, much less drink.

The line to the club extended all the way to the corner. The neon lights extended from the ground all the way up to the top floor. This place even had those big Batman-style spotlights twisting and turning into the sky.

"Have you been here before?" I asked Isaiah, who sat next to me in the bus.

"Yup, every year since I been here," he said.

"They let you drink and everything?" I asked.

"Baby," he whispered. "We are the Potomac Pirates. Do you know what that means in this town?"

"Baby," I replied. "I didn't even like basketball before I met you."

I smiled. He groaned.

We got off the bus and hurried into the club through the front door. As security hurried us in, the crowd in the line began screaming and applauding. It was bizarre to me—none of these people went to Potomac and likely knew no one at Potomac. I guess Potomac basketball really was a local legend, like Ben's Chili Bowl and Chuck Brown.

Security ushered us down a long hallway to the back of the building. A freight elevator was waiting for us and most of our party was able to fit on it.

The group was talkative among themselves, but I still didn't know most of the team well so I remained quiet.

The doors of the elevator opened on the fourth floor to reveal an expansive mezzanine with a long bar, a dozen plush couches, and a small dance floor. A guardrail safely separated this floor from the main dance floor below, where the public partied away from us VIPs. The latest tunes on the radio were playing.

"Wow," I mused.

"It's pretty great, isn't it?" Isaiah asked me.

I realized quickly that the people already in the room were the Potomac basketball coaches and a few other people I recognized from the game or around campus. The players dispersed with their dates and other friends.

Coach Kalinowski was sitting on a couch talking to a black guy. Isaiah was certain to make a beeline to his coach first before getting any drinks or dancing.

"Coach K," he said. "I'm sorry for interrupting you, I just wanted to introduce you to my friend Adrian."

I extended my hand to the coach. "It's nice to meet you, sir. I go to Potomac as well."

"Yeah," he grunted. "Nice to meet you, kid."

"And this is—" Isaiah began.

"Renard," the black guy said. "Welcome to my place."

"You're Renard Charles?" I asked, clearly surprised to actually meet the owner.

"Were you expecting someone taller?" he laughed. I laughed with him.

"Not at all, sir," I said. "I just didn't expect to meet the owner. I'm from Silver Spring, so I've heard about your club practically all my life."

"Well it's nice to finally meet another local," he said. "I was beginning to think Kalinowski had something against recruiting the homeboys!"

"If your damned public schools were any good in this town, maybe I could recruit guys who could actually pass Potomac classes," coach said.

"Ouch," I said.

"Don't mind him, kid," Renard said. "He's just an old grouch. What's your name again?"

"Adrian," I said over the music. "Adrian Collins."

"Nice to meet you, Adrian. Go get yourself a drink. On me."

"Wow, thank you Mr. Charles," I said.

"Renard," he said. "Always Renard. Enjoy yourself tonight."

"I will. Thank you." I looked at Isaiah with my eyes open wide. He led me to the bar with his hand on my back.

A few minutes later, with drinks in hand, we went to the guardrail overlooking the third floor of the club.

"Wow," I said. The music was loud and clear where we stood. The third floor had two bars on either side of the room, a DJ booth in the corner, and a small stage on another wall. There seemed to be hundreds of people packed down there. Everyone was enjoying themselves and nobody was acting a fool. It was nothing at all like a college party.

Over the music, the DJ made an announcement for all the revelers.

"Ladies and gentlemen, it's about quarter to midnight and I want to introduce you to the Potomac Pirates men's basketball team!"

The partiers looked up at the mezzanine and began cheering.

"Congratulations on your victory today!" the DJ continued as Isaiah and his teammates waved to the crowd "Let's take it all the way to the championships this year!"

Minutes passed and my drink was long gone. The DJ switched it up on us and played some Baltimore club music.

Isaiah went nuts, becoming a huge mass of arms and legs, rhythmically flailing about the dance floor. In no time, his teammates and others encircled him and watched him go. He was the only Baltimore boy on the basketball team, so he had no problem dancing all by himself to the heavy bass, staccato snare drum, and R&B samples. I wasn't mad at him—I got the same way when I heard DC's own go-go music.

What I didn't expect was for Hodari to nudge me into the circle from behind, pushing me into Isaiah while he danced.

Not missing a beat, Isaiah grabbed my hand and compelled me to do what he did. When he dipped down low, I followed. When he raised his hands in the air, I did the same. And when he did some fancy footwork that involved crisscrossing his legs and falling back on one hand, well... I watched.

I had never seen him so happy. When the song was over, he gave me a huge hug and a kiss on the cheek.

"Haaaa, his ass is drunk like shit," one of the ballers said.

Hodari laughed. "Watch out now, Isaiah," he said, smiling, but most certainly serious.

When Isaiah let me go and the song changed, I turned around to see a stunning woman wearing a tight black tank top and tight black pants. She wore silver jewelry on both hands and silver cuffs on her upper arms. Her straight red hair hit her shoulders perfectly.

"Cute," she said, her small lips cracking into a smirk.

"I know you," I said. "From the basketball game."

"Rebecca!" Isaiah exclaimed. "How are you!?"

"Sober," she said flatly. "Who's your friend?"

"This is my boy," he said over the music. "Adrian. He goes to Potomac."

"It's nice to meet you," I said, extending my hand to her.

"Likewise," she said. "My name is Rebecca Templeton. I work for the basketball program."

"Nice," I said. "Are you a trainer?"

"Not quite," she said. "Let's just say I make sure the basketball program looks good."

"That's... interesting," I said.

"Quite," she said. "Listen, Isaiah. Party hard, but party safe. You got that?"

"I got it, Becky," he smiled.

"Rebecca. Don't play with me," she said. "And Adrian?"

"Yeah?" I asked. She leaned into my ear.

"If you're really his friend," she began. "You'll help him keep his future safe."

I looked at her.

"You got that?" she asked.

"Uh... yeah, I got it."

"Good," she smiled. "Enjoy your evening!"

I looked up at Isaiah, who smiled as Rebecca walked away.

"Isn't she great?" he asked.

"I guess so," I replied. "Kinda bitchy though, ain't she?"

"You jealous?" he laughed. "Come here, boo, don't get mad."

He pulled me into yet another hug.

"I'm not jealous, negro," I said through a nervous laugh. "She's just kind of intense."

"Mmmm, intense. Kinda like how I feel in my shorts right now?"

"Nasty," I replied.

"It's almost midnight y'all!" the DJ shouted. "Grab your champagne and the one you love!"

Isaiah and I grabbed our glasses of champagne from the bar.

"Ten!"

We looked around the room and found the darkest possible corner away from the action.

"Nine!"

The rest of the players hurried to the guardrail to look out at the crowd below.

"Eight!"

Renard Charles and Coach Kalinowski laughed at some unknown joke and rose from their couch.

"Seven!"

Rebecca fiddled with her mobile device as she walked.

"Six!"

Isaiah looked at me and ran his hand over my scalp.

"Five!"

I smiled at him and grabbed his sides.

"Four!"

He giggled. "That tickles."

"Three!"

"Silly."

"Two!"

I got on my toes.

"One!"
We kissed.
"Happy New Year!"
"I love you."

Part Two:
Spring Semester

Chapter Five:
January 6

I lay in his arms wide awake well before the sun came up. The clock said 5:30. It was the Saturday before classes began, and I was still plenty busy. The Brothers of Beta Chi Phi believed that servant-leaders never slept, and the brisk chill of early winter air could never be a deterrent to community service.

But right now, minutes before my alarm would ring, I just laid in bed with my man wrapped around me like a boa constrictor, one huge leg sliding through mine and resting on my manhood, keeping it warm. I rested my head in the crook of one of his arms while the other draped over my chest. He was slightly propped up as though he had stared at me until he fell asleep. Now it was my turn to stare.

I touched his curly-wavy hair. He would be getting a haircut soon. I loved him with length, but the basketball staff preferred their men to be clean-cut. Hodari was the lone exception to this rule, having come to Potomac with many inches of dreadlocks and a fanatical belief that his hair gave him his strength. You couldn't argue with a record-breaking lead scorer and all-American like Hodari.

Isaiah was fine with the rules. He didn't rock the boat. He came to do his job and get an education. Like all of us, he was also looking for his passion. I understood why he wanted to be a teacher—he could just be himself and that's all a classroom full of street-savvy kids would need. He wouldn't have to change himself to get a job, like most black men at Potomac had to do.

In his sleep, he smiled slightly, moving his head in a circular motion with my hand. Waking up slightly, he grabbed my hand and kissed it, keeping it near his face when he was done.

"What chu tryin' to do?" he growled.

"What *chu* tryin' to do?" I growled back, my hand finding its way down his torso and to his rock-hard manhood.

"Let me find out…" he said, thrusting himself into my grip.

Within seconds, we were all over each other, touching, kissing, rubbing, doing anything we needed to do—quietly, of course, as the walls of this collegiate room were thin enough.

Isaiah flipped me onto my stomach and rested his body on mine with his crotch perfectly lined up with my behind, rubbing it slowly and rhythmically.

"You gonna let me hit that?" he asked as he grinded my ass harder and harder.

"Yeah," I whispered. "Go ahead."

He reached his long arm to my desk drawer and pulled out a safe sex packet I had gotten from a Potomac Pride meeting the previous semester. He pulled a condom out, unrolled it, and placed it on his dick. He opened up the small packet of lube with his teeth and spit the top to the side.

He squeezed some of the clear liquid out into his hand and rubbed it over the condom. He squeezed out the rest onto his fingers and then gently applied it to my hole, first inserting one fingertip, then a second. It was sexy, but still scary—Isaiah was huge—but I was hoping this attempt to penetrate me would go better than previous ones.

"You ready?" he whispered.

"Yeah," I exhaled. "Go slow."

"I will, babe," he said. He glided to my hole and placed his tip right on it. He slowly thrust himself forward and began to penetrate me.

"Ow," I said.

"You okay?" he asked.

"Yeah," I said, breathing hard. "Keep going."

He thrust himself forward a little more and the discomfort became acute.

"Ow," I repeated. He kept going forward. "Ow… ow, Isaiah, stop."

He took the head of his penis out of me.

"Are you okay?" he asked.

"Yeah," I said. "It hurts, man."

"I don't want to hurt you," he said.

"I know."

"I just want you to feel good."

"I know."

"I'm not going to do this to you if it hurts."

"We can try again," I reassured him.

"Dude… we don't have to. You and Savion never did, so I'm cool."

"It never even really came up with us," I said. "I mean, it was whatever. We were just fooling around, trying whatever worked."

Isaiah laughed.

"What?" I asked.

"Y'all were dykin'," he said.

"The fuck? Oh, so we were dykin' huh?" I got out of bed.

"Baby, I'm just playing," he said, peeling the condom off his now shrinking piece. "I said I'm just playin'!"

"You got a real nice way of just playing," I said as I grabbed a towel and wrapped it around my waist. "Do you even know what that means?"

"Yeah, I be on the message boards and shit. It's when two bottoms find a way to work it out… you know, sexually."

"And what makes you so sure I'm a bottom?"

Isaiah paused and sat upright in my bed.

"I don't know, babe," he admitted. "I mean… you my baby… I'm bigger than you… I be wantin' to just…"

"Do the shit you did when you were straight?" I asked. "It's not the same."

"I know it's not the same. I just do what feels right, that's all. And what makes you happy. Don't be mad."

"I'm not mad," I exhaled. "Just be patient. And don't be afraid to reverse roles now and then."

"Whoa, what?" Isaiah asked, then laughed. He stood up from the bed and searched for his underwear in the dark.

"Nigga, you ain't too tall for me to climb your back sometimes," I said, folding my arms.

"Yeah, right," Isaiah said. "You know I love you, but I ain't feeling that."

I rolled my eyes as he pulled up his sweatpants and put on his tennis shoes. The clock almost said six in the morning.

"Why you gotta get up so early, anyway?" he asked. "I'm loving the fact that you have the single room of this apartment, but damn."

"You know I gotta do community service with the bros. Wanna come?"

"I'm good. I'm going to enjoy some more sleep soon as I get back to my dorm. Plus the only dudes that go on your service projects are Betas and dudes trying to be Betas. I don't need them thinking you trying to sex me into your gang or something."

"Shut the fuck up," I laughed. "It's not a gang."

"Beat in, sexed in, same difference," Isaiah laughed while putting on his hoodie.

The faggie is gonna drop, plain and simple! You know who you are—get out! You heard what I said. We do not pledge homosexuals in Beta Chi Phi. Leave. Now!

"Adrian?"

"Yeah?" I asked, snapping back from a sudden memory from my pledge process.

"You zoned out for a minute. You good?"

I smiled.

"I'm good. Just thought about something I had almost forgotten. Listen, let me hop in the shower so I can meet the bros at the gates."

"Aight, I'd kiss you, but you know where my mouth has been," he joked. I gave him a hug and he squeezed my ass.

"I'ma get some of that some day," he said with a wink and a smile.

"Yeah, we'll see about that," I said with a smirk.

About half an hour later, my line brother, housemate, and friend Calen Hawkins and I were all set to go to our local soup kitchen. We would be joined by another housemate, Orlando Ford, who was interested in pledging Beta if we had a line that semester.

Orlando was just as tall and muscular as Calen. If you were in an elevator with the both of them, you'd probably think they were taking up all the air. While Calen was a beautiful caramel shade with a face that still seemed round with baby fat, Orlando was coal black and strikingly handsome, like a young version of Blair Underwood. His wavy hair was always cut close and he wore a gold stud in one ear. He was on the quiet side in public, but could be counted on to be the life of the party when he was with his housemates and fellow footballers Calen and Brad.

Orlando walked in silence behind Calen and me as we hurried to the front gates to meet the other Potomac brothers and prospects.

"Who all is coming?" I asked Calen.

"I don't even know, for real," he asked. "All I know is Ed is driving his car. I hope we all fit."

"Especially with y'all big NFL asses," I joked. Calen giggled.

"Yo, the chapter needs to buy a van or something, we're getting mad big, and we got five prospects already," he said.

"Orlando," I quizzed, "Who are the other prospects?"

"Rick Brown, a junior, and Alex Valenzuela, a sophomore," he quickly replied.

"Is that all?" I asked.

"That's all I know," he admitted.

"Looks like you need to keep your eyes and ears open at this soup kitchen, then. There's definitely more than three of you, and they certainly aren't all at Potomac."

"Okay," he replied.

"Damn kid, don't give 'em too much!" Calen laughed. "You gotta live with him, don't make him come smother you with a pillow tonight!"

"Orlando knows what's up," I said seriously. "No skaters."

By the time we got to the front gates, we were about three minutes late. Ed was waiting for us in his four-door sedan.

"Hey frat," Calen said. "Sorry we're late. Somebody wanted to take a long, luxurious shower after a late evening with their partner."

"Oh hell no!" I exclaimed. "You did not just try to play me."

"Just jokes, just jokes," Calen reiterated with a smile. I laughed.

"No for real, sorry about that Ed," I said.

"It's all good, LB!" Ed said. He was probably the happiest Beta in our chapter. He knew that he wasn't among the favorites of our prophytes, so he tried extra hard to show everyone he belonged. He was a little taller than me and one of the stockier guys in the chapter.

"I guess these guys are coming, too?" he asked. I hadn't even noticed that Orlando had went to two other guys who were at the gates, also waiting.

"Hi guys," I said. They quietly greeted me back.

Rick Brown was a junior like me, Calen, and Orlando. He was a shy, quiet kid from Ohio that none of us knew too much about. He had a brown complexion similar to mine, but rather than a close cropped haircut, he had a three or four-inch afro which he often had done in cornrows. Sometimes we just referred to him as "that guy with the cornrows" because he was such a loner that nobody knew his real name.

There were two good things about Rick that I liked. First of all, since he was so quiet, he had no baggage—no possibility for negative attention to the chapter. Unfortunately, that meant there would be few bragging rights if he crossed, like when my line brother Micah, then president of the campus NAACP chapter, finally made it. But who needs a "popular" guy when you can get a nice guy who shows up to do the work of the fraternity?

Alex Valenzuela would cringe if you called him Alejandro, but everyone on campus knew who he was—the angry Latino boy from the Bronx. He was a sophomore, probably best known for his scathing editorials in the Potomac Press campus newspaper, as well as his leadership as the current President of the NAACP, a position that I didn't run for even though people expected me to take up Micah's mantle.

I respected Alex for being unafraid to voice his opinion when it came to the oppression of the people, but that's also what frightened me about him. I wasn't sure if he could ever become humble enough for the Beta pledge process, to actually trust in and submit to the brothers.

He was nice to look at in the meanwhile, though. He was an attractive Puerto Rican dude who generally dressed in jeans and t-shirts, effectively obscuring his intellect from those who took him for a street thug.

"Well, get in!" Ed said. "We got mouths to feed!"

Twenty uncomfortable minutes later, we peeled ourselves out of the car in the parking lot behind the homeless shelter.

"Oh my God," I said, exhaling. "One of us has got to get a car this semester. Four people in one back seat is not the business."

"You got that right," Calen said. "That was like being back on line!"

At that moment, we heard a car horn and turned around. Behind us was a silver Cadillac Escalade that gleamed in the morning light. When the doors opened, out spilled three of my line brothers and two prospects.

It was always a mini-reunion when we met up with our Rock Creek brothers, even though they seemed to be quite different from us.

The driver, an ostentatious southern gentleman with the southern drawl, gray eyes, and curly hair was my Deuce, Ciprian Williams.

"If you went to a real school like Rock Creek, you wouldn't have to pile in the backseat of this... thing," he joked.

"Nice ride, bro," Ed said, choosing to ignore Ciprian's typical nice-nasty comments.

"Thanks bro," he replied, giving Ed the fraternity grip. "Good grades pay off in my family."

"Word?" Calen asked. "Your father, the big time Alpha who nearly had a stroke when his son pledged Beta, got you this?"

"Oh please," Ciprian said. "This is from grandma, the Alpha Chapter AKA. She'll do anything to spite her son-in-law."

"Lord, bro," I said. "Your family..."

"Gotta love em!" he smiled.

I next gripped Peter Grant, the ace of my line.

"Hey frat," he said. "What's the deal?"

"Chillin'," I said. "How you been?"

"Ready to graduate!" he exclaimed. "The countdown begins!"

"I know that's right," Ed chimed. "I'll be right there with you!"

In the rear of the small crowd that had formed was my "back"—the line brother who stood immediately behind me— Mohammed Bilal. I reached past the two prospects to pull my favorite line brother into my arms.

"Hey frat," I said while everyone began talking to each other. "I missed you, man!"

He smiled. He was the only international student on our line. Betas truly came in all shapes and sizes—Mohammed was a tall, lean, pale man with dark features. He was unmistakably North African—Algerian to be exact. He and I had the toughest time on line and probably had the hardest adjustments to fraternity life, me being a gay man still dealing with some lingering homophobia in the chapter, and him dealing with being part of an organization which was uniquely American and took him so far away from his circle of international friends.

"I missed you, too," he said softly. "How was your vacation?"

"Amazing," I said with a wide smile.

"And Isaiah?" he asked.

"He's good. We're real good," I replied.

"I'm glad he finally chose you," he said. My smile started to hurt my face. Mohammed was probably the best brother I'd ever meet and the best friend in the frat I'd ever have. There were so many reasons that we shouldn't get along, but we truly just saw each other for what we were.

"Brothers!"

We stopped all conversation, frozen by the deep bass of our chapter president, Aaron Todd. His voice, along with his bald head and Malcolm X glasses, remained intimidating to me, even though I had come to love him and his leadership style. If I didn't know better, I would have thought he said "pledges" instead of "brothers" from the back door of the shelter.

"And friends," he continued, eyeballing the men trying to join our chapter. "I hate to break up this happy reunion, but we are here to serve. Tommy is already inside in the kitchen. Come inside, divide yourselves up, and let's get to work!"

As true Beta men do, we hopped into action.

There was a lot for us to do to prepare for breakfast and none of it was new to our brothers. We broke into small groups, partially to be more efficient, but mostly to get to know the prospects we hadn't met yet.

Mohammed and I took the two Rock Creek prospects to the main dining hall to wipe down the tables and chairs and place plastic flower arrangements.

"What's your name again?" I asked

"Angel Rosario," he said.

"And you?" I asked the other one.

"Christopher White," he replied.

"And you know my line brother pretty well?" I asked sincerely.

"Pretty well," Angel said. "We lived on the same floor freshman year and we took a few classes together. You know... we hang out."

"Interesting," I said. "And you?"

"Mohammed was my freshman orientation advisor," Christopher smiled. "I've been trying to be like him ever since."

I smiled back.

"He's a cool dude. I'm glad I know him."

"Okay guys, stop it," Mohammed interjected. "I can't take all this attention. Christopher, tell him about all your volunteer work. Angel, tell him how you founded Rock Creek's hip-hop festival."

"Wow, all that?" I asked. "You must be really fond of these guys, Mo."

"They're good men," he said.

"I guess we'll find out," I said cryptically. "Angel, where is Christopher from?"

"New York," he answered quickly.

"Christopher, same question," I asked.

"New Jersey," he replied.

"What part?" I asked, not skipping a beat.

"Uh..." he stalled, looking toward Angel, who was also frozen, not knowing whether to give an assist or let him figure it out.

"Sounds like you don't know each other well at all," I said. "My fraternity is about brotherhood. Start acting like brothers and maybe you can become one for real."

The boys remained in silence and slightly nodded in the spirit of humility. Mohammed looked upward as though he was annoyed, but said nothing.

We wiped the final table clean just as the residents of the shelter filed in. We had this process down to a science: seat, call tables, feed, entertain with a short step routine. The prospects were beckoned to the kitchen and Mohammed and I had some down time.

"Don't be too hard on them, Adrian," Mo said to me.

"I won't," I said. "You think I'm being hard on them?"

"A little."

"Dude, I'm not. This is nothing compared to what we got. Remember last year?"

"I remember," Mohammed said. "We met each other at this service project, in this very room. We got to know the brothers and they got to know us. Don't forget that."

"Where's the attitude coming from man?"

"These are good guys," Mo said. "I want you to know them like I know them. And I want to know the guys from Potomac. Nobody else needs to go through what we went through."

"But *everything* we went through wasn't bad. Listen Mo, I would never let you down. I'm just being myself. I haven't touched these guys and I don't plan to. I might not be Mr. Nice Guy all the time, but I am not going to hurt these guys, okay?"

Mohammed shrugged.

"Okay," he said.

"Hey, look at me," I demanded. "I need you to know that I know where you're coming from. You can trust me. I will always have your back. And check me if you think I'm going too far. But just know that we are going to have different approaches to educating these guys."

"I understand, brother," he said.

"Why don't you and I hang out with some of these guys on our own, okay? Away from the rest of the brothers. One night soon, okay? Armand's? For old time's sake?"

"That sounds like a good idea," he said. "You pick a prospect from my school, and I'll pick one from yours."

"That's an even better plan," I said. "Let's make it happen."

Although I wasn't exactly sure where Mohammed's trepidation came from, I understood that he was always just a little bit different from the rest of us. He certainly went through the same hardships we all did, but more than anything, he was a hard worker and community leader. I wanted to be more like him again—since I crossed I really didn't do much else on campus like I used to. On the other hand, I really did love Beta and only wanted to make it better. With the rest of the brothers around me and the promising prospects we had, I was sure that we'd have a great semester ahead of us.

Chapter Six:
January 15

On the Monday night of a three-day weekend, thanks to Martin Luther King's birthday, I was wearing my suit and overcoat and waiting for a mystery date to begin.

I think we should have a date night, I recalled Isaiah suggesting.

A date night? I asked.

Yeah. I mean, things are already busy with basketball. I'm going to be on the road a lot. And things are going to start heating up with Beta, right? So let's just make sure we have one night out of the week when it's just us. Deal?

Sounds good to me. So, like Mondays?

Mondays are good for me. We never have Monday games. In fact, I have a surprise for you this Monday.

Really?

Yup. All you have to do is meet me at the front gates at seven o'clock. In a suit.

A suit? Are you for real?

Yup. Be there.

And there I was, waiting in the chilly air for whatever was supposed to happen at seven. I was a few minutes early, so I sat on one of the benches with my hands in my pockets.

Potomac was an urban campus in that it was within DC's boundaries, but it was quite an upscale community. Located in the Northwest quadrant of the city, it was convenient to nothing and gated on nearly all sides. A bus stopped at the front gates, and you could walk a few blocks and be on the far side of the Georgetown neighborhood, but all in all it was a quiet campus with its own culture.

"Hey man," I heard a familiar voice say. I looked up and saw my freshman buddy Morris Jordan.

"Hey Morris!" I said, standing up to give him a hug. "How you doin'?"

"Good, how are you?"

"Fine," I replied. He was a dapper little dude with dark brown skin, bushy hair, and a fine moustache growing in.

"I haven't seen you in a while," he said. "You don't call me much anymore."

"Oh, you know," I said. "Been pretty busy."

"Yeah, me too," he said.

The awkward silence of two people who had had a one night stand fell over us all too easily. While students walked around us, it felt like we were stuck in time.

"I miss hanging out with you," he said.

I smiled a little.

"You're a good dude," I said. "But I... you know."

"No, I don't know," he said.

"Oh, Morris." I said, not knowing how to break it to him. "I mean, we only hooked up once, and I told you then I didn't intend for things to be awkward between us after that," he said.

"Right, I feel you. So don't make things awkward," he continued. "I'm a big boy."

"I know," I said. "Morris, I... I'm seeing someone. I should have told you sooner."

"It's all good man," he said. "I'm cool with that."

I nodded.

"That doesn't mean we can't still hang out, you know," he said.

"You're right. And we should hang out more. Hey, did you get Nina's latest email from Austria?"

"Yeah, I did—she's having a blast! Hope she's getting some class work done, too."

"And if she doesn't, I'm sure she'll talk her way into an 'A' anyway," I laughed. Morris laughed with me.

"So who is he?" he asked.

"Who?" I asked, hoping he would drop the question.

"Your boyfriend," he said. "Who's the dude that ruined my chances?"

I smiled.

"I don't know if I should say," I said. I saw Isaiah walking toward us from behind Morris. He, too, was wearing a suit and an overcoat.

"Oh lord, one of these DL brothers?" Morris asked. "Dude, whoever he is, just make sure he treats you right."

Isaiah overhead the last sentence and decided to join in the conversation.

"Treat you right?" he said. "Adrian, what's going on?"

"Isaiah, this is my friend Morris," I said, silently praying that Isaiah wouldn't go into one of his notorious fits of jealousy.

"Hello, Morris," he said, extending his hand. "My name is Isaiah Aiken."

"I know you," Morris said, shaking his hand firmly. "Basketball team."

"I guess the height gave it away," Isaiah joked.

"You're doing really well this season," Morris added. "Keep up the good work."

"Thanks man, I appreciate the support," he said, turning his gaze to me. "I think my biggest score is off the court, though."

"Oh my, look at the time," I said. "Morris, it was really nice seeing you. Let's hang out soon, okay? Okay, see you!"

Isaiah just laughed while Morris looked puzzled.

"See you later I guess?" Morris said.

"Take care, man," Isaiah said. Morris walked away.

"You are crazy!" I said, smiling.

"Crazy... in love!" he shouted.

"Cornball," I retorted. "So what's the big surprise?"

"Turn around," he said. Behind me, parked right at the front gates was a black stretch limousine and a chauffer standing next to an open passenger side door.

"What the...?" I exclaimed. Isaiah beamed.

"You like it?" he asked.

"You bought a limousine?" I asked.

"No, fool! We're taking the limousine to the surprise!"

"Oh... okay, then. Yes, it's hot!" I said.

"Get in then!" I walked toward the door.

"After you," he said.

"Hi," I said to the driver. "I'm Adrian."

"Nice to meet you," he said with a smile.

I got in the limousine, bewildered. The limo had an all black, leather interior and a new-car smell. There was enough room for a good eight or ten people, but it was of course just for me and Isaiah. There was an ice bucket with a bottle of champagne and two glasses hanging over the edge.

"Oh my God, Isaiah, this is crazy!" I said. He smiled, closed the door, and cozied up next to me in the back seat.

"You want some champagne?" he asked, placing a glass in my hand.

"Hell yeah!" I said. As the driver pulled off, Isaiah carefully poured the champagne in my glass and then poured his own.

"So where are we going?" I asked.

"I want to make a toast," he said, ignoring my question. "To the first of many date nights this semester... and beyond."

I clinked my glass against his and sipped my champagne. Still gripping the glass tightly, I stole a kiss on his cheek.

Isaiah closed his eyes and rolled them back in his head with a silly purse-lipped grin on his face like Bill Cosby.

"I would have never known about your funny side if I'd never... you know," I said.

"Never what?"

"You know... if I'd never lived with you. Taken the time to get to know you."

"Ditto," he said. "It's funny how things work out."

"Our life is so crazy. Unexpected," I said.

"Who are you telling?" he asked, finishing up his drink.

"Whoa there buddy, you're tossing them back pretty quick. Do I need to see some ID?" I quipped.

"I'll show you some ID," he said, leaning toward me and giving me a sloppy kiss on my cheek.

"Is my surprise that we're going to make out in a limo for the first time?" I asked.

"Nope, but that's a pretty nice bonus, ain't it?" he asked me as his hand cupped my face. He kissed me all over my lips, my nose, my forehead, my ear.

"I'm taking you to see Alvin Ailey at the Kennedy Center," he finally whispered.

"Are you kidding me?!" I squealed. "I haven't been to the Kennedy Center since like third grade! Oh man, this is the best surprise ever!"

I hugged him tightly and kissed him on the lips.

"You are so fucking awesome," I said.

About ten minutes later, the driver let us out at the Kennedy Center for the Performing Arts, overlooking the Potomac River. The building was long and flat, yet still large and imposing. Its gleaming white marble walls and the golden light from the windows gave the building a heavenly glow. I had never seen the Kennedy Center quite like this.

Isaiah put his arm around my shoulder and led me into the building. We were among people who really knew how to appreciate the arts. I saw old black ladies in their floor-length mink coats with their gray husbands in their tuxedoes. I saw military men in their full dress uniforms. I saw well-behaved young white girls in their best dresses running across the dark carpet and smiling mothers not far behind them.

"I'm glad you told me to wear a suit," I whispered to Isaiah. He just smiled.

We checked our coats and walked around the Hall of States looking at all of the flags and tall mirrors adorning the walls. We peeked around the Grand Foyer and then made our way upstairs to the Opera House, where the Alvin Ailey American Dance Theater would be performing.

The Opera House was a huge, breathtaking room that transported me back to the 1960s. Every seat in the room and every inch of the walls were a warm shade of red that still managed to be shocking in its volume. Isaiah kept walking us forward, closer and closer to the stage.

"Where are our seats, backstage?" I joked. He just smiled. We ultimately found ourselves on or about the tenth row. I couldn't believe he scored us seats so close to the stage. I turned around to look at the rest of the theater, and saw three more tiers of seating behind us. Above us, on the red ceiling, was a huge chandelier which looked like a crystal snowflake.

I closed my eyes and took it all in. This moment, this date, this very hour was the happiest I had ever been in all my life. This memory created by my boyfriend, my man, was so purely from his heart and so daringly unexpected.

Although I knew that I loved him madly and deeply, it was at that moment that I realized that he actually *got* me in ways that nobody else could.

And that was before the hypnotic ballet of Alvin Ailey's finest, who took me through mesmerizing leaps and pirouettes, infused with the gyrations of Africa and the antebellum south. Watching these unabashedly black dancers, both men and women, while holding my man's hand, was something greater than a picnic in the park, chilling in a dorm room, or taking a stroll through Georgetown.

This right here was magic.

After the performance, Isaiah took me out for a quick walk on the terrace of the Kennedy Center. We hadn't gotten our coats yet and it was cold, but we braved it just so we could see the lights dancing in the dark waters of the Potomac River at night. Looking downriver, we saw twisted highways and red lights of slow moving cars across the water in Virginia. If we looked the other way, we could see Georgetown University, and if we strained our eyes more, we could even see the top of Potomac University's highest tower.

"It's pretty out here," Isaiah said.

"It sure is," I said, thrusting my hands deep into my pockets.

"Not cold, is you?" Isaiah said with a smirk. He slid his arms around me and kissed me on my forehead.

"Isaiah... thank you for this evening," I said.

"Anything for my baby... my best friend," he said.

"Promise not to get mad if I ask you something, okay?"

"No problem. What is it?"

"How did you afford all this? The limo, the tickets? It had to cost a grip."

"Will you be mad if I ask you not to ask?"

I thought about what he said for a few moments.

"I wouldn't be mad, but I'd be disappointed that you didn't feel you could tell me."

"Aight, you got me," he said. "I didn't pay for it, but I would have if I needed to."

"So who paid for it, your mom?"

"Hell no, Gloria ain't payin for my dates," he smiled. "No... okay, so please don't tell anybody this. Like, not even Nina. Got it?"

"Got it," I said.

"Sometimes, Potomac gets these freebies to things. When the basketball office gets them, they give them to the coaching staff and the players. We're supposed to be like the celebrities on campus, so they want us to go to stuff and be seen, mix and mingle, whatever."

"Damn, for real?"

"Yeah, for real. And one of those things is season tickets to all the shows at the Kennedy Center. I knew coming to the Kennedy Center would be something you would enjoy, so it was a no-brainer."

"The limo, too?"

"The limo... well, remember Renard Charles from the nightclub?"

"Yeah," I said.

"Well... me and Hodari are his favorite basketball players, so he looks out for us."

"That's really, really nice of him," I said. "He seemed like a really good dude."

"He is, but please don't say anything. We're not supposed to be getting any kind of gifts or compensation for being ballers. It's like illegal or something. Plus, you know all about the Charles family. How is it gonna look that a drug kingpin's brother is hooking us up with free shit?"

"My lips are sealed," I said. "Thank you for trusting me. I won't tell anybody."

"Good," he said. "And I'm glad you don't think I'm cheap because I didn't pay for the tickets."

"Oh," I said, letting go of his embrace. I turned to the door, getting tired of the cold. I looked back over my shoulder and said "We haven't gotten to the part where I see if you're a cheap date or not."

He laughed.

"Boy, you a mess."

Back in the limo, we snuggled together in our coats and said little to each other. We had spent a few too many minutes in the night air, so we were merely trying to get warm again.

We stopped for a late night snack at a greasy spoon in Georgetown, picking up a big basket of French fries to split for the ride back to campus.

"You know what I realized?" he said in between munches.

"What?" I asked.

"I haven't seen Taina since the semester started," he mused.

"You know what? Neither have I. I was kind of worried about that, though."

"Really?" Isaiah asked.

"Of course," I said. "I mean, dude. You broke up with your girl and got with a guy, and you ain't exactly trying to hide it."

"Why should I?" he asked seriously.

"Jeez, Isaiah, why do I feel like we have this conversation every week?" I chuckled.

"Then tell me again, baby," he smiled.

"I'ma break it down to you how your girl Rebecca Templeton whispered in my ear on New Year's Eve. She told me 'if you're really his friend, you'll help keep his future safe.' And I agree with her, man. I don't want to do anything that will jeopardize your future in the NBA."

Isaiah quietly finished his last few French fries.

"Do you want to be with me?" he asked.

"Of course I do, now more than ever," I said quickly.

"Do you believe I have what it takes to play professional basketball?"

"Yes," I said. "But homophobia is real. We've been really open when we're off campus. And I try to be careful, but dude, I'm really into you and I'm starting not to give a fuck who knows."

"Good," he said. "Because I want them to know. I want them to know that I am with you. When I see you walk across campus in your Beta jacket, I be like damn, that's my man. And I want everybody else to say the same thing: that's Isaiah's man. And I want people to see me and be like damn, look at Adrian's man. Coach K only dictates what I do on the court. And although she's hired to do otherwise, Rebecca Templeton is not going to run my life, either."

"What is her job, anyway?"

"To protect the basketball brand, plain and simple. She trains us on how to deal with basketball groupies. How to avoid fights with locals. Which bars and clubs we can trust, and which ones we can't."

"She's going to tell you not to date me," I said somberly.

"And I will tell her to go fuck herself, plain and simple. Baby, how many ways can I say it? I am in this for the long haul. I just want to be successful and happy, and if I'm just happy, I know I'll be successful, basketball or not."

"You know," I said. "You're pretty damn sexy when you're all emphatic and shit."

"Thank you, I learned it from you," he quickly replied. "But all jokes aside, you feel me? This isn't about anybody else but me and you. Fuck what anyone else hears, fuck what they see. At the end of the night, as long as I am doing right by you, my mama, and God, I can sleep easy. Everything else is second."

"I feel you," I said. "I just hope you're prepared to deal with everything that comes along with what you're proposing."

"Oh, I'm not prepared at all," he said. "But every man has to go through this at some point, right? Some slowly, some quickly. But I'm gonna go through it. Ya dig?"

"I can dig it. I'm sorry for bringing it up all the time."

"You don't bring it up all the time—you bring it up when I need to think about it. That's why I love you, you know when to say what I need to hear, in just the right amounts."

"I love you, too," I said.

"Now can I get up in them guts?" he asked sincerely.

"Not tonight dear, I have a headache," I said with a wink.

"Man, you ain't shit," he said.

"If I ain't shit, why you fiendin' for it?" I said. "Come here."

In the back of the limo, I kissed and held him until it was time for our driver to leave. I had to come to terms with the fact that this was it, this was the semester that Isaiah was going to come out, and me along with him. Some people knew about me and some didn't. Some people remembered I might have been with Savion, but others never even met him. But right now, the fraternity man and the varsity basketball player were about to break down the closet door, hand in hand, confirming all remaining rumors of my sexuality and likely stunning the campus with the revelation of who Isaiah prefers in bed.

This was it. There was no turning back now.

Chapter Seven:
January 20

A huge pile of red and goldenrod fliers had been divided between Mohammed and I at the last chapter meeting. Rush was coming—earlier this year than last year, but the neophytes were anxious to get the ball rolling.

In some ways, it was unfortunate that our colors were burgundy and gold, and not just because they matched a pretty sorry football team. We could never find a dark enough shade of red for our fliers when we promoted events, so we were always looking like the Kappas if we just used red. When we added goldenrod, or yellow, we looked like the Pi Chis on campus. Thank goodness our actual line jackets and t-shirts were in the proper colors. It was just one of those things which bothered me as a neophyte. I pledged the burgundy and gold, not the red and goldenrod.

After my date night, I got up early on Tuesday morning and placed the fliers everywhere I could on campus. Our official recruitment guidelines stated that we had to advertise our formal information session at least five days in advance of the event. Sigma chapter always did it at the last possible moment—if we left the fliers up too long, we'd certainly attract the attention of guys we didn't already know, or worse yet, guys we didn't like.

With the roll of tape in hand, I posted a flier outside of the computer lab in the library and hurried away down the hall. By the time I got to the elevator, I noticed Rick leaving the computer lab and walking toward me, passing the bulletin board without looking at it.

"Turn around," I instructed. Puzzled, Rick looked behind him. In bright red and yellow were two rush fliers, side by side—as was the tradition in Sigma chapter.

"Take it," I said sternly while his back was turned. He looked to both sides and quickly snatched the flier down. I got in the elevator and headed to my next destination.

Mission accomplished, I thought to myself. I lied to myself that

I couldn't help it if thirsty prospects were taking down my fliers and hoarding them for themselves. We could be assured that the ones we liked would see them and would tell others who needed to know.

The next day I found myself in English class, one devoted completely to the work of black women writers. As one might expect, it was a predominately African American class with a black professor. We jokingly called it "homeroom" because it was the only time out of the week many people in the community would see each other.

There were also several fellow Greeks in this class, though I was the only Beta. All of us were gearing up for rush, pledging, or intake in the coming weeks. There was a weird feeling in the air. Even though we always spoke to each other, promoted events to one another, and generally chatted and gossiped about Greek life, we were all quiet for a change. I also noticed that all eyes were on us more than usual.

Ashley Thompkins was in this class with me. She was a senior, a former board member of the NAACP with me, and an AKA. She was an English major and on track to enter a Masters program in literature at an Ivy League school. Even though I didn't care for her much as a person, I respected her intellect.

Apparently, so did all the other girls in class who wanted to be AKAs. Seemed like Ashley could barely finish a thought without her prospects cosigning her ideas or starting of a sentence with "To piggyback on what Ashley said…" It was pretty pathetic how bad these girls wanted to be down with the pink and green.

As class let out, I would soon realize just how thirsty the people on my campus were when it came to pledging.

"Excuse me," a voice said. I turned to my left and noticed a short, clean-cut guy wearing gray slacks with a silver belt buckle and a black button-up shirt.

"Hi Mark," I said. He was Mark Ferguson, a sophomore. I didn't really know him well, but considering how small the campus was, I had certainly seen him around.

"How are you?" he asked.

"I'm fine, how are you?" I asked.

"I'm good," he said. "Classes are going okay. I'm really enjoying participating in the NAACP this year."

"Oh, you're in that?" I asked.

"Yeah, I do public relations this year," he said. "You and Micah did an amazing job with the board last year. Doing our work is so easy now because you guys held it down."

"Thanks," I said. "It was a lot of fun. I really ought to get active in that again."

"We'd love to have you," he said.

"Thanks man," I concluded. "Well, nice talking to you."

"Wait," he said. "Before you go, I just wanted to ask you. I noticed that Beta Chi Phi Fraternity, Incorporated, is having a formal informational this Saturday at Rock Creek College."

"Yeah," I said. "We're having rush."

"Well, I was wondering if you could put in a good word for me."

"Put in a good word for you?" I asked.

"Yeah," he continued. "I mean, you know me, you see me on campus..."

"Dude... are you serious?" I asked.

"Yes, I'd really like to be a Beta," Mark continued.

"Man... we have had programs and community service opportunities all year long. I haven't seen you at any. I live on campus and take classes full time—you've never even had a conversation with me before now. So all of a sudden, out of the kindness of my heart, I'm supposed to 'put in a good word' for you. Mark, please."

"I didn't know how I should approach you," Mark said.

"You didn't even have to approach me to express your interest," I said, getting more and more irate. "If you had just come to some of our programs, we would have known. You know what we really hate in my fraternity? When dudes come out the woodwork to express their interest and treat this like an honor society. Just because you look good on paper doesn't make you the right fit for us. If I were you, I'd just wait and try next year—after you spend some time around us."

"I'm sorry, Adrian, I just-"

"Beta doesn't take sorry people," I shot back. "Have a good day, Mark."

He held his head down and walked away quietly. I started to feel a little bad that I had bitten his head off to make my point, but it was no different than what my big brothers had made me endure.

My feelings of guilt began to dissipate when I began to put two and two together. Why was Mark waiting for me outside of my class? How long had he been there? Was he really waiting just for me?

These aspirants at Potomac University were thirsty! I couldn't believe this guy was prepared to practically stalk me for the chance at membership, but wouldn't do the bare basics of coming to our events and getting to know us.

Crazy. If people knew how much harder it was to *be* a Beta than it is to *become* a Beta, they might rethink their whole quest.

Our rush happened without incident but had a much larger turnout than we were hoping for. Sigma Chapter of Beta Chi Phi Fraternity, Incorporated, prided itself on the quality of its members, and not the quantity.

Unfortunately, this notion was in conflict with our membership selection guidelines. When it came to picking quality men, the fraternity had a very objective process that went far beyond a simple chapter vote.

To become a Beta pledge, you had to attend rush, submit a completed application with letters of recommendation attached, and undergo an interview. The application, recommendations, and interview are all assigned points. If an aspirant has above 75 points, he has made line. If he scored under 60 points, he has not made line. If he scores between 60 and 75, the chapter has the right to vote on him. If a chapter really likes a candidate in that gray area, they can save him. But if they don't like him, that's the only time they can vote him out.

The chapters hated this system, but it was nearly impossible to change it on the national level. Fortunately, most of us knew how to work within the system to prevent candidates from moving forward.

Some chapters, like Mu Chapter at Howard, only placed one

flier up on campus to advertise the rush. And just to be extra cautious, they only left the flier up for 20 minutes. We found that to be pretty intense, but it worked for them.

Other chapters had advisors who would allow their selection committee to ask ridiculous questions at the interview with the intent to lower the candidate's score.

Kappa Chapter at the University of Maryland was notorious for "losing" applications.

And we at Sigma Chapter were fairly creative. On the one hand, we had to advertise—we needed people to know that we existed. Certainly, there would be times when we would get interested guys who just didn't know a lot about how to express interest to us prior to rush. But it was so much better when we knew the guys well and could determine if the process would be for them.

So prior to rush, we'd just be bitchy to the guys we didn't like. Some of us chose to be standoffish and ignore questions from aspirants. Others, like me, were masters at the "Are you freaking kidding me?" facial expression.

In addition to deterring guys in advance, we also had an unofficial "smoker" at a brother's house, secretly inviting all the guys who had attended rush. A true smoker is just an informal meeting for prospects to meet brothers—in the old days, there would be cigars.

Our version of a smoker still carried an informal aspect to it, but its true intent was to "smoke out" the prospects we didn't want, and to test the mettle of the ones we did want.

This year there were fifteen guys at rush. There were only five who we really knew and wanted. We had some work to do.

"How many candles, Tommy?" I asked our Dean of Pledges for the semester.

"Still fifteen," he said. I reached into the box and counted out three sets of five small white votive candles. I arranged them haphazardly on the mantle of Ciprian's house. He had moved off campus since last year into a nice dwelling less than three minutes from Rock Creek. It was convenient and large enough for the nearly 30 guys who would be in the room, counting prospects, chapter brothers, and alumni.

"I can't believe that many guys really showed up," I said.

"And Brother Spector was just chatting it up with all of them," Aaron, our chapter president said. "He really doesn't get how we do things. He thinks we're really going out and searching for guys. What a shitty grad advisor."

"I feel so bad for you guys," Micah said. He was my line brother who graduated shortly after he crossed. I was his vice president when he led the campus NAACP chapter and we became quite close.

"I should have asked to become your advisor," he continued. "Y'all need a dude who won't be all up in your business. Sigma Chapter has been good for 21 years. He need to just fall back."

"Well falling back is not something he's going to do," Tommy said. "We just gotta be more careful, more quiet than before."

"Dude, we still pledge above ground!" Deji said. He was visiting DC for the weekend, and like a good prophyte, came to support the rush and smoker. "I don't want Beta to go out like the Kappas, or Alphas, or any of those other pan-hell organizations. We get to do a lot of shit they haven't been allowed to do since the 80s. Our organization is supposed to trust that we ain't out here beatin' niggas to death or drowning them in the ocean."

"We're going to hold it down, frat," Tommy said. "The five dudes we have lined up are on point. And some of the 'surprises' we had come to rush seem like they're down for the program, too."

"Fuck that," Deji said.

"Now dear brother, let's be honest with ourselves for a minute," Ciprian interjected. "I know y'all didn't want me. I know that if I hadn't been one hundred percent on point with my application and interview, I would have been a goner. But here I am. Working hard for Beta anyway. Fact is, we can't predict whether the five we like are gonna be worth a damn any more than a stranger coming through those doors and impressing us."

"Ciprian, you're different," Aaron said. "You were funny. You were engaging. You were a dude we never even looked at because we knew you were an Alpha double-legacy. We gave you a shot. You worked it out. Shit, what more can be said?"

"I'm just saying," Ciprian continued. "I'm trying to give these dudes the same chance that y'all gave me."

"I can dig it," Peter said. "I got my favorites, but I'm gonna keep an open mind."

"Fuck that," Calen said. "I worked hard for mine and I'm not about to let these dudes just run up in my frat without having a clue of what it's all about. We can't be giving it away."

"Word," I said. "That nigga Mark cornered me earlier in the week asking if I would vouch for him. I don't know him from the man in the moon."

"But he came to rush anyway," Mohammed said. "He's trying to prove himself."

"Whatever," I said. "Many have tried. Many have died."

"Brothers, your attention please," Tommy said. We gathered around him and listened intently. We all wore white shirts, burgundy or gold ties, and black slacks. Tommy and Aaron wore black blazers.

"To remind the older bros and tell the younger bros, this is how the smoker will work. Adrian, you can light the fifteen candles now. Each candle represents a prospect. Each and every one of those dudes needs to be asked a question of some sort—not about Beta, but about themselves and their pursuit of Beta."

We all nodded.

"Nobody should walk out of this smoker feeling like they weren't in the hot seat for a minute. Especially not the five dudes we know—this should not be a cakewalk for them. But yo, if you got personal beef with one of these dudes? Leave it at the door. This is not the time to call them out because they stole your girl. Or your boy, Adrian."

"Sheeeeit, I wish a nigga-" Calen covered my mouth and the brothers laughed.

"If you know a dude is weak, wouldn't fit in this chapter, or is the type that would snitch when the heat is brought—that's when you call him out. Tell him straight up you wouldn't vote for him. See how he reacts."

"We play off each other," Aaron added. "If a dude looks shaky, go in for the kill. But if it's a good dude, and he's shaken, come in and be good cop. Bring it back to the brotherhood and the service. Be challenging, but be inspirational."

"Yo, this is your only chance, brothers," Deji added. "If a dude slips into the chapter after this night, then you gotta live with him. Period. End of story. And he will be your brother. Ain't gonna be no talking shit about him. You gotta carry his weight."

"Absolutely," Tommy said. "And finally, bros—please avoid the racial shit and the homosexual shit. No calling niggas niggas, faggots, towelheads, whatever they call Latinos—none of that. Shit that's in good fun for us behind closed doors is grounds for a lawsuit. Ya dig?"

We all nodded again.

"Aight, y'all," Tommy said. "It's 7:59. Let's open the door and bring these motherfuckers in."

Ciprian turned off the house lights and let the glow of the candles fill the room.

Micah opened the doors and the solemn, slightly terrified potential pledges filed into their personal hell for the next two hours.

Chapter Eight
January 29

I sat on the floor between Isaiah's legs as he sat on the sofa of my living room. Calen was in his room working on an assignment for his Business Ethics class. Orlando was hopefully out getting to know his potential line brothers before their first session later that night. My housemate Brad was missing in action as well. Although he hadn't said anything directly to us, we were pretty sure he was pledging Kappa.

Yuck.

So that left Isaiah and I to enjoy another date night. This one was my pick, so we were much more low-key than our previous excursion to the Kennedy Center. The dinner choice was take-out soul food that I picked up from a new spot near Howard University: greens, sweet potatoes, macaroni and cheese, and fried chicken. The entertainment was Isaiah's favorite show: *The Wire*.

Even though the show had long since gone off the air, Isaiah maintained that much of what it depicted was true to life. Maybe not the gay stick-up dude walking down the street in a silk robe, but close to it. I didn't feel afraid in Isaiah's neighborhood, but the streets in *The Wire* did remind me of his block.

His large hands spontaneously gave me a shoulder rub as the credits rolled on the third episode that we watched.

"I think you're right," I said.

"About what?" he asked.

"I really don't think Taina came back."

"Told you," he said.

"Have you tried to contact her?" I asked.

"Hell no!" he said. "Why would I do that? I'm done with her."

"You don't think she dropped out because you quit her, do you?"

"Naw," he said. "That can't be it. Maybe she went abroad at the last minute."

"Maybe she's pledging," I said. "People just disappear when that happens."

"I don't know. Why do you care?"

"I don't know," I said. "I think it's weird when any black person just disappears from Potomac."

"I wouldn't worry about her. Our lives are easier without her around. Can you imagine?"

"Yeah. You're right."

His strong hands never stopped massaging my neck, shoulders, and back.

"That feels good," I said. "I'm gonna need it for this damn session tonight. I swear I do not miss being up at all hours of the night."

He laughed lightly.

"Gonna put a hurtin on them pledges, ain'tcha?" he asked.

"Naw, not really," I said. "I mean, it gets physical, but not dangerous."

"Good," he said. "That it doesn't get dangerous, I mean. You know I would lose my damn mind if anything happened to you."

"I know," I said.

"Hey, I gotta tell you something," Isaiah said, still massaging me.

"What?"

"I'm going to tell Coach K about us."

"That we're dating?" I asked.

"Yup."

"Okay," I said. Already holding on to his legs, I leaned into him just a bit tighter.

"You okay with that?" he asked.

"Other than not being sure if he needs a special announcement about it… I'm fine with it. I mean… we're out. Pretty much. Kinda. So there's nothing new to share. With the public, at least. I guess you're just giving him a heads up, right?"

"Right. The man is my coach. He needs to know. He's the closest thing to a dad I've had. Sorta. If my dad was white. And angry all the time."

I laughed.

"Yup, that's Coach K," I said. I got up to my knees and turned around to face him.

"Boy, if you think this is what you need to do, then I'm down with you. No questions asked. I hope he accepts you just as you are. I think we've both been pretty lucky. Most people who know us don't care that we like dudes."

"I'm hoping he feels the same way," Isaiah said. "If not... well, fuck 'em. I'm still playing the basketball games of my life. That won't change."

"No doubt," I said. I looked at his perfect lips and slowly leaned forward to kiss him.

Suddenly, I heard Calen bound up the stairs to our living room.

"Get a room, ya horny bastards!" he yelled at us with faux indignation.

"Nigga, you know this is date night!" I shouted, throwing a sofa pillow at my line brother as he turned on the lights.

"And it's also the night we put the boys on line! Are you ready? We gotta meet Ed like now! The boys gonna get the call in five minutes!"

Calen was easily the most exuberant of all of my line brothers and eager to lead our boys—now nine in number—to the Beta light.

I looked at my boyfriend and shrugged.

"Thank you for my date," he said, pecking me on the lips as he stood up.

"Thanks for coming," I said. "I'll see you later."

I let him out the door and watched him walk down the pathway toward main campus.

"Aight nigga, get out of all that cute 'I'm on a date and I want to impress my man' shit and put on your black hoodie! We finna get our pledge on!"

"Why are you crazy?" I asked.

"I ain't crazy," Calen said as he pulled his hoodie on over his huge torso. "I'm just excited to not be a neo too much longer!"

I smiled.

"You good with the boys we had to take?" I asked my LB.

"Man..." he paused, changing out of his Jordans and into the black combat boots he got last year just for pledging. "I like the five we already knew we wanted. They're on point. Interviewed well. They know the deal."

"But..." I prodded.

"You know. It was some bullshit how we had to take the extra four! I mean, on the real, I can understand taking Josh Robinson. He's an athlete. We never see him. I get it."

"Man, taking Mark is really bothering me. I told that dude he needed to wait, but he came to rush anyway. I mean, he interviewed well, and he is tight on paper, but he just bogarted his way in. Who does that?" I asked rhetorically.

"Then we got that Nigerian dude with the 4.0 GPA—yeah, like we could really reject him. And then Dexter Rodgers. Who are these people, man?!" By this point, Calen had his black gloves on, pounding one fist into an open palm.

"Whoa there, Gibraltar," I said, calling him by his line name. "We got who we got. You know the game. We just gotta make sure that who we got gets made right. They wanted it this bad, they made it this far. Now we just make sure they know what they need to know and don't make us look bad."

"You think it's that easy?" Calen asked, tossing me my black hoodie. I put it on over my t-shirt.

"No," I finally answered. "But shit, what else are we going to do for the next seven weeks but try to make it work?"

With that, we left my apartment and met the rest of my chapter. That night began a new journey for nine young college men who were certain to be caught by surprise at the trials before them.

Chapter Nine:
February 3

It was early on a Saturday morning that we made our nine boys official pledges of Beta Chi Phi, along with the pledges of all the other chapters in the Washington, DC area. All of our official ceremonies and our membership education classes were conducted on a cluster basis. This saved time and resources and allowed all the chapters the chance to see each other more often. I actually liked this aspect of the process even though most people didn't. It was about the only aspect of pledging Beta that had rhyme and reason.

The unofficial sessions weren't meant to replace the official meetings, but to supplement them. Beta Chi Phi still called its membership process pledging, but it was more like membership intake. The sessions, or sets, hearkened back to the old days of pledging when each chapter was responsible for its own pledges and what they learned. These sessions were how our pledges bonded and got to know the brothers, to hear their stories, and to gain an appreciation of what they were about to join.

About once every other week, our cluster would also have huge sessions with all the different chapters. They, too, were unofficial meetings, but they were usually controlled and uplifting. Nothing bad happened at these meetings, and the highlight was that upon their conclusion, the pledges would "emerge" on whichever campus we were visiting that week. Emergences were not full out probate shows, but more like inviting the public to inspect the line. We almost never let the boys emerge formally without other chapters present—we were far more impressive with 30 or so pledges and 60 visiting brothers than just a handful of pledges and brothers.

The awkward thing about how Beta conducted pledging was that so much of what we did broke the rules, but so few people cared.

Technically, all the pledges had to do was show up for the official meetings and ceremonies and pass the national test. If they knew the rules, they wouldn't even have to dress alike if they didn't want to.

But nobody wanted to be the one who bucked the system. If so many people had done it exactly the same way and nobody had died, why not do it? Beta was also now old enough where legacies like me wanted to go through exactly what their dads and uncles had been through.

We wanted to wear the berets and pea coats.

We wanted to be lined up and recite information.

We hated being put on social probation, but we appreciated the time to reflect on our journey and not be bothered with the outside world for two months.

We appreciated our girlfriends (or boyfriends) so much more for sticking by us through the process. (Assuming that they stuck by—mine didn't.)

We didn't want to be paddled, but we took it for the respect.

We didn't want to be yelled at, but we needed to know that the big brothers cared.

We wanted the stories that led to the creation of our line names and the names of our lines.

We wanted personal big brothers who cared about us.

We wanted the memories that our fraternal ancestors had.

We didn't want anything to make us any different from any other Beta man.

We took it when it was our turn and gave it to keep the traditions going, so that no one after us would feel that we had cheated them out of the most important experience of their college days.

So the cycle continued, as did the song and dance of "hiding" from the advisors.

As was the tradition, we had the pledges out all night in session with us, preparing them mentally for the first major ceremony. We knew that becoming a pledge was little more than a pin, a candle, and a smile, but our boys didn't know that. Part of the session was meant to scare them for the hell of it, but the other part was to instill the respect and solemnity of what they were embarking upon. And yes, perhaps part of the purpose was the hope that one or two of the men would drop—no questions asked and no hard feelings. We always added that part in if we could.

But nobody dropped, and the morning of February 3, 37 men from all of the Beta chapters in the DC area became pledges, including several from the alumni chapter.

They were all tired. In fact, they all looked like crap. The only people who didn't look like crap were the alumni chapter members, especially Brother Spector, who was particularly chipper to the point where it just made you sick.

Me and Calen were sitting with new pledge Christopher White, our number eight from Rock Creek College when Brother Spector came over. We were all going to head to IHOP after the ceremony and we kind of really didn't want him to come along.

"Hello, brothers," he said cheerily.

"Hi Brother Spector," we grumbled.

"Isn't today a great day? These young men have begun the first step in their journey forward to Beta. How do you feel, Christopher?" he asked our pledge.

"Great, sir, thank you," Christopher said, mustering a smile.

"Adrian, why don't you get Sigma Chapter together and we can all go out to brunch?" he suggested.

"Yeah," I said. "I have to go study."

"Me too," Calen said.

"You can't study on an empty stomach," Spector said. "Come on, go get the brothers together."

"No, thank you, maybe another time," I said sternly.

"Let me talk to you over here for a minute, Brother Collins," Spector said to me. I rolled my eyes, stood up, and walked over to the corner with my chapter advisor.

"Yes?" I asked.

"What's going on?" he asked.

"Nothing," I said.

"Nothing?" he mocked. "Seems to me like something is going on. Why are all of you—and your pledges—so tired and haggard?"

"I stayed out late last night," I said. Which was true.

"Doing what?" he demanded.

"Fucking my boyfriend!" I shouted. Down the hallway, Calen laughed. Christopher turned his back to me to avoid laughing in a big brother's face.

"All that isn't even necessary," Brother Spector said. Aaron and Tommy rushed over to us to intercede.

"What's going on?" Aaron asked.

"The chapter advisor here is accusing us of hazing the boys," I said.

"Now that's not what I said," Spector retorted.

"But that's what you meant," I hissed. "Ever since you became our advisor you've just been waiting for us to do something wrong. You never give us props for our programming or having the highest GPA in the region. It's always about the boys, what we're doing to the boys, have we hazed the boys. Well you know what? We ain't touched the boys. You got that?"

"Cool it, bro," Aaron said.

"You know, Brother Spector," Tommy began. "Adrian has a point. We all love Beta—and we know you do, too—and it's hard for us to fathom the level of distrust you seem to have for us. We are a great chapter. Just take the time to get to know us. We follow the rules to the letter. We're not doing anything to make us, the chapter, the frat, or you look bad."

"Wow," Spector said. "I didn't know you felt this way."

"Well, we do," Aaron said. "Can you just trust us, Brother Spector? Can you depend on us to do the right thing—as we always have—and not make you look bad?"

"Yes, brother," he replied. "I trust you. And I'm sorry for how I came off to you, Adrian. I didn't mean it."

He extended his hand to me. My brothers looked at me in anticipation of my reaction.

"Apology accepted," I said, taking the advisor's hand and giving him our fraternal handshake.

The brothers breathed a sigh of relief as I had helped keep the chapter's cover. We later pretended to all go our separate ways, though we really ended up at IHOP, to celebrate the pledges first official ceremony and our continued snow job of our pesky chapter advisor.

After IHOP, a few solid hours in the library, and a nap, I was ready to go out with my man. Date night was early this week and it was his turn. He wanted to celebrate yet another basketball win by going to a club. Not Renard's this time—he wanted something a little more homey, a place where he could wear jeans and just dance.

He also insisted on going to a gay club—so to the Delta Elite we went. I hadn't been in a while, so I was game. The thing about the Delta is that it was easy to get to via cab, but a bitch to get home from since it was in a small, nearly hidden corner of Northeast DC.

Luckily, one of my Lesbian friends on campus had a car. Cat, who was now dating Samirah, was happy to make it a double date.

"So it's true?" she asked me as we walked to her car in the parking lot behind the school. "You're really dating Isaiah Aiken?"

"Yeah," I gushed. "Are people saying that? Is there like gossip about it?"

"Not really," Cat answered. "I only heard about it from Morris. And he wasn't sure, he just suspected. You know, the night he saw you on your way out with Isaiah."

"Oh yeah," I said. "Isaiah made it pretty obvious that night. He's so jealous sometimes."

"Yeah, Samirah can be pretty territorial when she wants to be, too. Thank goodness we're going to the Delta on men's night. She'd be a mess if we went to ladies night."

"I know that's right," I said. "I'm hoping Isaiah won't try to fight for my honor or some dumb shit."

"He's quite a catch, though," Cat admitted. "If I didn't like women so much, please believe-"

"I believe it," I interrupted. "Trust me, I see how these chicks out here look at him. I know we're not hiding it, but I'm not exactly looking forward to the day when the campus as a whole finds out he's with me."

"I feel you," she said. "Well, that's the ride," she said, pointing to her Audi.

"Nice," I said. We got into her car and took the service road behind campus to pick up Samirah behind her dorm. We then pulled up a little further and got Isaiah behind his dorm.

"Sup, baby?" he asked, pecking me on the cheek through my open window before he got in the back seat.

"Hey Cat, hey Samirah," he continued.

"Hey cutie," Cat said. "This your first time coming to the Delta?"

"Not quite," he said. "I used to sneak around and make an appearance or two before."

"It's kinda hard for somebody of your height to sneak anywhere, ain't it?" Samirah asked.

"So now you know why I stopped trying," Isaiah winked.

We arrived at the Delta and parked at the last available space in the small parking lot. It was just after midnight, yet there were dozens of people already in line.

"This is wack," Samirah said. "I thought we were here pretty early, too."

"The line's not that bad," I said. We piled out of the car, got to the back of the line, and started chit-chatting among ourselves.

The line inched forward but that didn't make it any less cold outside.

"We'll be in there soon," Isaiah said, rubbing my back. I grinned.

I happened to catch the eye of one of the bouncers at the door. A big, round dude wearing a bomber jacket and a backward baseball cap, he looked at me, then looked up at Isaiah. He appeared puzzled at first, then somewhat pleased, as though he knew us.

"You know him?" I asked Isaiah.

"Who?" he said.

When I gestured in the direction of the bouncer, he was gone.

"Never mind," I said. Isaiah was easily the tallest person in line. The patrons were mostly men, a handful of real women, and a few transgender women. It wasn't my first time at a gay club, so I was pretty comfortable, even though all eyes seemed to be on Isaiah.

I mean, he's hot. I'd stare too.

A few more moments passed, and the bouncer came back, this time on his cell phone. He walked briskly toward us and stopped just in front of us.

"Aight," he told the person on the phone. "Hold on."

He took the phone away from his face and looked at Isaiah.

"Potomac?" he said.

Isaiah nodded.

"Aight then," the bouncer said as he got back on the phone. "Yeah. It's him. You want me to bring him in? Aight, bet." He ended the call and put the phone back in his pocket.

"How many of y'all is it?" he asked Isaiah.

"Four," he said.

"Aight, come with me," the bouncer said. Confused, I looked up at Isaiah, who had a blank expression on his face. Me, Cat, and Samirah followed him as we trailed the bouncer to the front door of the club.

"Excuse me, fellas," he told the boys waiting to enter the club. They rolled their eyes at him and gave the four of us the evil eye. I looked normal, although I was confused. Nobody knew Isaiah was gay outside of Potomac. How could we be receiving the same treatment at the Delta that we would have at Renard's?

"Welcome to the Delta," the bouncer said. "Couldn't have you waiting in that long ass line."

"Do I know you?" Isaiah asked politely.

"Not really," he said. "But you know my uncle. I do security at his club sometimes. Renard's."

"Renard Charles is your uncle?" I asked.

"Yeah man," he said. "I remember you too, from the New Year's party."

"You know, I thought you looked familiar," I said. "My name is Adrian. These are my friends Cat and Samirah. We all go to Potomac."

"Nice to meet you," he said, shaking all our hands. "My name is Brandon. And good to see you again," he told Isaiah. Isaiah nodded.

"Are you family?" I asked.

"Naw, man," Brandon replied. "I don't mean no harm, but I love the pussy."

"So do I," Samirah said with a laugh. Brandon smiled.

"Anyway, I wanted to bring y'all in out the cold," Brandon said. "I'm sorry we ain't got no VIP area, so you gonna have to slum it with the regular folk."

"It's all good, man," Isaiah said. "That's exactly what we came to do. I appreciate you looking out for us."

"Hey man, my uncle love Potomac, and he love his clubs. When I saw you in line, I had to call him and ask what he wanted me to do. I hope that's cool with you, man," Brandon said.

"You told your uncle?" Isaiah said. "Well shit, it's all good then. I ain't got no secrets."

"No doubt," Brandon said. "And word to the wise. Upstairs is house music. It fucking sucks. Go downstairs for the hip-hop and go-go, aight?"

"Thanks for the advice," Isaiah said, giving Brandon a handshake.

"Oh, one more thing," Brandon said. "Renard said the first round is on him."

"Bet," Isaiah said.

As we went down the dark stairs, I asked Isaiah if he was cool with how everything went down.

"Man, I'm used to it," Isaiah said. "Niggas know who I am wherever I go. At least we got into the club free, and folks are looking out for us."

"And a free drink, holla!" Cat said.

The Delta was a hole-in-the-wall kind of place that looked like somebody's old school, 1960s-era basement with a DJ booth in the corner and wood paneling. Isaiah's head almost touched the ceiling. We all headed to the bar to cash in on our free drinks. Jack and Coke for Isaiah, fuzzy navel for me, and gin and tonic for Samirah. Cat was the designated driver. The good thing about being with Isaiah is that we never got carded.

Cat and Samirah quickly took their drinks and went to the dance floor, leaving Isaiah and I to finish our drinks.

"You're famous," I said, sipping the last bit of my sweet drink.

"I'm not famous," he said. "Some people just know who I am. That bouncer dude is the only one here who knows me."

"You know that's going to change," I said, hugging him at the waist while I leaned into him.

"You're going to get drafted," I continued. "I read the sports blogs, sometimes. They're saying great things about you, that if you left now, you'd do well. But they don't know what I know."

"And what do you know?" he asked, staring down into my eyes.

"That you can do whatever you want to and be good at it," I said simply.

"Thanks, baby," he said. "I needed that."

He hugged me and kissed me, first lightly on the lips then more passionately. I slid my hands up the back of his shirt, then down lower into his pants. My fingertips rested on top of his high ass.

"Fast," he said. "Gloria Aiken warned me about boys like you."

I smiled and squeezed his ass.

"You are going to be famous though," I said. "If you do go pro next year after you graduate, do you think you're ready for that kind of scrutiny?"

"I'll have no choice," he said plainly. "I'm sure the money will make it right."

"Can you imagine?" I asked. "You could be like—a millionaire."

"Don't jinx it," he said. "I just want to take care of you and my mom."

"Me?" I asked. "You're thinking that far ahead?"

"Aren't you?" he asked. "You don't think I'm gonna let you go, do you? I mean shit, you the best thing happened to me. I know you're not thinking about the money. You know what my life is gonna be if I don't go pro and you still with me."

"I mean, everybody deserves to be happy, no matter what their profession is," I said.

"Exactly," he said. "And you love me no matter which road I choose."

"I do," I said, putting my head in his chest.

"Hey!' Cat called out over the music. "Dance, bitches!"

"Aight, girl," Isaiah called back. "I see you!"

We went out to the dance floor hand in hand, jamming to a Black Eyed Peas tune. It wasn't quite hard core hip-hop, but the "children" loved it.

I loved seeing Isaiah this way. He was happy. It was just that simple. When he was with me, he was happy. When he was himself, he was happy. He never smiled a whole lot when he was with his teammates or just by himself on campus.

He was a thinker. Before I met him, I could tell that he was always deep in thought. I used to call him "the finest boy on campus"— at least that was my nickname for him when I was with Nina. At that time, he was just a handsome, mysterious dude. We had sporadic conversations, random participation in a class or two.

Never in a million years would I have thought that I'd be with a man who was so gentle, yet so ferociously protective of me.

I did my best to be realistic because I didn't want to be hurt again. I once thought Savion Cortez was the love of my life, but the pledging process wasn't something either of us could weather. He never believed in the process and I wanted more than anything else to have him and the frat.

In another lifetime, maybe. The romance I shared with Savion was like nothing else I had experienced. Yet the love I had with Isaiah was different. It was strong. It was complicated. It wasn't perfect. But we worked at it and made decisions which allowed us to be nothing more than ourselves, not an illusion with unrealistic expectations.

Someone tapped Isaiah on the shoulder from behind. He turned around and leaned down as a dark skinned guy said something in his ear. In the dark, I couldn't tell who it was at first.

Isaiah shook the dude's hand and stepped away. He mouthed "I'll be back" to me and headed up the stairs to where they were playing House music.

When my eyes adjusted, I saw who it was: Eugene, the Alpha I met last summer in DuPont Circle and had almost called for a one-night stand last fall.

"Oh lord," I said.

"No, not the Lord," he said. "Just Eugene. May I dance with you?"

I rolled my eyes and let him step to me.

"Whatever," I said.

"I appreciate it," he said. The song changed to something more down-tempo. He held me on my sides and rocked back and forth.

"I see you still with the light-bright," he said.

"Yup, sure am," I replied. "Does that bother you?"

"Why so combative?" he asked. "I just want to be your friend."

"I've got friends," I said. "And I got frat brothers."

"That's right," he said, black skin shimmering under the club's few lights. "You're in that made-up frat. Theta Pi Chi?"

"Beta Chi Phi, ass," I responded. "What do you want?"

"I'm only dancing," he said. "I don't see you out a whole lot."

"I'm pretty busy," I said. "I'm still in undergrad, you know."

"I know," he said. "Listen, I just wanted to say hello, dance with you for a bit, and let you know something."

"What?"

"That I ain't mad at you," he said. "It looks like you got a good thing going."

"You think so?" I asked. "How would you even know?"

"I get around," he said. "Plus, you can just tell. That man loves you. Hold on to him."

"I will," I said. "It was... good seeing you again, Eugene. Seriously."

"Thanks, Adrian. It was good seeing you, too." He gave me a hug and went on his way.

Isaiah came back with two more drinks. I took one and began to sip it.

"Why you leave me with that jerk?" I asked. "You don't even like him."

"To prove to you that I'm not jealous of him," he said plainly. "Last time he came around, I acted a fool. Just wanted to make it up to you. Plus, he asked nicely."

"That's sweet," I said.

"So," Isaiah continued. "You gonna let me smash tonight?"

"Perv," I replied.

The night went on and the drinks flowed. More and more people filled the club and it seemed like nobody left. I lost count of how many drinks I'd had, but I thought I was being pretty responsible.

Before we knew it, the club was shutting down. It was four o'clock in the morning! That was crazy—I'd never been to any club that stayed open so late. As the lights came on, Isaiah kissed me deeply.

"Work it, bitch!" a young queen said. "You betta get that big gangly nigga! Work bitch!"

I laughed through Isaiah's kiss. He gripped my hand, half from devotion and half for support, and we left the club.

We met Cat and Samirah at the car.

"You have a good time?" Cat asked.

"Hell yeah!" Isaiah said. "This was the motherfuckin shit right here."

"Good," Cat said. "Get up front, baby," she told Samirah. Isaiah and I got into the back. He immediately began kissing my neck—one of my "spots."

Cat and Samirah didn't seem to mind as me and Isaiah made out in the back seat. In fact, I may have been too drunk to even know what I was doing at the time.

About 30 minutes later, Cat had pulled up to the front gates and let me and Isaiah out. I think she had hopes on getting a little back seat action of her own.

"Bye girl!" Isaiah yelled to Cat as she drove away.

I laughed. Damn, I was a happy drunk.

Before I could even fix my eyes on Isaiah's dorm, he had grabbed me and tossed me against the iron gates. Gripping me by the shoulders, he thrust his tongue deep into my mouth, the slurping noises punctuating the quiet on the yard.

I wasn't much of a moaner, but that night, all bets were off. I grabbed his ass in my hands and squeezed it as hard as I could.

"Oh... shit," he said, grinding into me while he held the iron gate with both his hands.

Maybe it was the alcohol in my system or maybe it was just that I was focused on the task at hand, but neither me nor my boyfriend heard the giggles and footsteps behind him.

"Mmmmm-hmmmm," one of the voices said. "Somebody is caught out there!"

"I know, right?" the other voice said. "Nasty ass basketball players!"

They giggled some more. Isaiah smiled at me and kissed me on my forehead. He hugged me, burying me in his coat while he turned partially around to greet the girls.

"What's up Angela? Sup Tracey?" he said.

Lord, not Angela and Tracey—the two hugest gossips on campus.

"Hey boo," Angela said. "See you're kind busy there, buddy."

"Mmmm hmmm," Tracey added. "Who's the girl?"

I giggled inside his coat, knowing their minds would be blown if they could see me.

"Don't try to hide her, boo," Angela said. "We know it ain't Taina!"

"That's right," Tracey said. "You put it on her so bad, she couldn't even come back to campus when you broke up with her!"

They both laughed hysterically, obviously drunk themselves.

"Go on home now, ladies," Isaiah insisted. "Y'all ain't ready."

"Ain't ready?" Angela asked. "Nigga, you act like whoever you got under that coat look better than me or some shit. Unveil the bitch if she so bad."

I tapped Isaiah on the chest, letting him know it was okay with me if he wanted to.

"Aight," Isaiah said. "You want to see who I'm with now?"

"Hell yeah!" the said in unison.

"Just remember this moment—you asked for it," he said. He

let me go and I emerged from his coat with the biggest shit-eating grin on my face.

What I saw before me was two women holding their heels in their hands, obviously on their own walk of shame from whoever had fucked them and kicked them out of their dorm room. They were pretty girls, if not too done up in make up and hair. Tracey had on her "fuck me pants" while Angela wore a halter and hot pants.

"What the fuck?" Tracey said.

"Wait a minute," Angela said. "Was you just... kissin'... Adrian?"

He nodded.

"I don't believe this shit!' Tracey said. "You a goddamn lie! You are not telling me you was fuckin Taina all this time and now you fuckin a nigga?! What the hell?!"

"I don't believe it," Angela said. "He's joking."

"No bullshit," Isaiah said. "This shit right here is real."

He kissed me again, square in the lips, long tongue and all.

"Ewww what the fuck!" Tracey exclaimed. "Are you fucking kidding me!"

"Don't trip ladies," Isaiah said. "This my nigga."

"Adrian motherfucking Collins," Angela said.

"The one and only," I replied.

"And all this right here..." I said, grabbing Isaiah's dick through his jeans, "...is mine. Ya dig?"

Whipped into a frenzy, Angela and Tracey hurried off and I grabbed Isaiah's hand.

"Well played, Mr. Aiken," I said.

"Indeed, Mr. Collins," he replied, leaning in to kiss me once more. "Indeed."

Chapter Ten:
February 15

I was livid.

"You aight, frat?" Aaron asked me. I slowly nodded, too enraged to speak.

Just Aaron and I rode in the front seat of his car with three of our nine pledges in the back seats. We were heading to our so-called "secret destination" for a milestone event in the pledge program, but the pledges didn't know that.

As far as they were concerned, they were about to get the shit kicked out of them for their disrespect of me at the set we just left.

"I cannot fucking believe you guys did that," Aaron genuinely said. "Adrian has been the best fucking big brother to you guys out of everybody, and you fucking did what you did?"

I said nothing.

"Permission to speak, Big Brother Aaron," pledge number three said.

"Granted," Aaron said.

"We really, really sincerely apologize, Big Brother Adrian. It was not our intention to disrespect you or your relationship in any way."

"Shut the fuck up," I said. "You fucking shitbirds disrespected me more than I ever thought possible. What were you thinking? Who the fuck does the shit that you did?"

"Chill, bro, it wasn't them," Aaron said.

"'All for one and one for all,' right?" I asked. "I don't give a fuck who popped out and did it, all nine of them are responsible."

In the rear view mirror I could see each of the three pledges had their heads hung low. Served them right.

Aaron's phone rang.

"Hello? Hey, what's up bruh?" he asked. "Yeah he's here. Hold on." He gave me the phone.

"It's your LB," he said.

"Micah?" I asked.

"Bruh, what the fuck is going on?" he asked.

"You heard what happened?" I replied.

"Calen called me and told me they disrespected you and you went the fuck off," he said.

"That's pretty much it," I said.

"I mean, what did they say? It was like a song? A skit?"

"I'm not even trying to get into it, bro."

"You ain't hurt him too bad, did you?"

I was silent.

"Hello? Dude, you ain't kill him did you?"

"Naw," I said.

"Adrian, what happened?" he repeated. "What did you do?"

"Dude, we're at the spot. I'll call you back later. B Chi."

"Chi Phi, frat."

I hung up the phone.

"Get out and get in formation," I said. We all closed the doors of the car and walked to the grassy field at the edge of Fort Slocum Park. The other brothers' cars quickly followed and parked. The pledges hurried out and got in their formation.

"March," Tommy instructed. The pledges locked their arms and marched into the woods to their destination.

Tommy stood still while the other brothers walked alongside the pledges—some of them taunting while others were uplifting. It was the schizophrenia of the process: many voices at once, all of them intended to help in some way yet there was always one or two that actually didn't give a shit whether you stayed or dropped.

Right now, I was in the chorus of those who didn't feel like being inspirational or uplifting.

"Adrian," Tommy said. "Hang back a second. You, too, Ed."

My line brother and I waited while the rest of the chapter descending up the hill into the woods.

"Adrian, I need to know that you're gonna be good after what happened," Tommy ask.

"That depends," I said. "You gonna let him get away with it?"

"I think he's paid for it after dealing with you, don't you think?"

"Yeah, whatever," I said. "I don't have shit to say to him. Ed, that's about to be your special, and I'm sorry but I don't fuck with that dude."

"I ain't mad at you," Ed said. "He was out of pocket. And I will talk to him about it. I don't want you to hate him, but I can't make you like him."

"Aight then," I said. "Then we good."

"We'll talk about it some more," Tommy said.

"I'm done talking about it," I said. "Can we go get our speshes now?"

In silence, Tommy began walking toward the rest of the group. He clicked his flashlight on at the tree line, as did Ed and I.

We entered the woods as one but we ran out without any order whatsoever—the somber ceremony became a raucous celebration. After two weeks of hard pledging, our boys finally had been assigned their personal big brothers.

My perse, or spesh, was Christopher White. I liked him a lot and could see that he wanted Beta for the right reasons. He didn't rock the boat, did most of his tasks well, and seemed to truly believe in the brotherhood.

Aaron, whose car Christopher and I were walking back to, was the only chapter brother with two personals. Several factors contributed to his luck (or misfortune, depending on who you asked)—his status as chapter president, his seniority as a brother, and the fact that there was one more pledge than there were active brothers. His personal little brothers were my housemate Orlando Ford and Angel Rosario from his school.

All three of our guys were among the five "chosen" pledges. Even though I tried hard to treat all of the nine the same, I had a natural affinity toward the ones I had known before the process began and who had actually demonstrated their worthiness.

"Pledges, welcome to the best spesh families in the chapter," Aaron said. "Relax, it's just us, we chillin. You trying to hit up the Diner?"

"For real?" Orlando said, looking at me in the rear view mirror. I smiled and nodded. "Hell yeah!"

Aaron smiled back.

"Alright, we're going to The Diner in Adams Morgan."

"So, like, we can talk freely right now?" Christopher asked.

Aaron and I looked at each other and paused.

"Yeah," Aaron said. "You can speak freely."

"Oh my God dude, I am so mufuckin hungry," Orlando exhaled.

"*Coño*," Angel said. "Me too."

"So..." Christopher continued. "This whole 'spesh' thing... like... I still don't get it."

"For Beta, your personal and your spesh are the same thing because the chapter is so small. Christopher, Adrian is your personal because Tommy felt like your personalities match and that he can help you out during your process. Same with me, Orlando, and Angel. Your personal is who you go to when you have problems and need some help, need somebody to intercede on your behalf to the chapter, all that. Tommy plans and implements the process, and you can trust him to be neutral, but your personal is the one who has your back from this point on, no matter what."

"Oh," Christopher said. "Does our personal give us our line names?"

"That's not for you to worry about, unless you want a really fucked up one," I smiled.

"I'm good," Christopher said.

The boys chattered among themselves and Aaron joined in every now and again offering some words of wisdom. He was a great chapter president, all things considered. I was ambivalent toward him when I first pledged because of some homophobic remarks he made during rush, before he knew I was gay. Over time, as we got to knew each other, I forgave his comments and got to see him as a Beta and a leader. He was a far better diplomat than I could ever be and knew how to keep the chapter balanced.

It was true what they said about the real pledging beginning after you crossed. There was no way for me to know the "real" Aaron while

I was pledging. I would get to know his personality through chapter meetings, service projects, and impromptu fellowship like a late-night meal.

We were able to find a parking space right across the street from The Diner because it was so late and a weeknight. We had a seat at a corner booth and quickly placed our orders. As was customary, the brothers paid for the pledges' meals any time we were together.

We laughed a lot. The pledges were "on" so much, both literally and figuratively, that it was hard for them to just unwind. But this night, one of the most special of the process, they could just let loose for a while.

They were very careful not to speak ill of each other or the brothers. They did vent about the volume of information they had to memorize and having to live with each other in one apartment. That was one thing I actually missed about the process, for I was an only child and was a little too used to loneliness. Having six other guys always around for help or entertainment was a plus.

On the other hand, having Orlando out of the house while he was pledging us, and Brad supposedly pledging Kappa, I enjoyed the quiet moments for myself and for my date nights with my boyfriend.

We laughed our way out of The Diner after two o'clock in the morning, maybe even two thirty, and we noticed some shady looking dudes leaned up against Aaron's car.

"You know these dudes?" Orlando asked.

Aaron peered across the street.

"I think so," he said.

Two of the guys were standing stoically against the brick wall of the closed hardware store we were parked in front of. The other two guys were practically sitting on the hood of Aaron's car. One of them was twirling a cane. The red and white stripes on the cane portrayed who these guys were.

"Yo, Aaron," Orlando said. "I mean, Big Brother Spesh or whatever… we gonna let these niggas lean on your ride like that?"

The Kappa turned around and smiled.

"What's up, Aaron?" he asked.

"Kindly get off my ride, Mario," Aaron instructed. Otherwise ignoring the guys, he unlocked his door and opened it. Orlando and I walked around the car to the passenger side, where the second Kappa was blocking the back door.

"Move it," Orlando said.

"Aaron, why aren't your pledges greeting me properly?" he asked. "Don't fellow Greeks get deference anymore?"

"You've got one more second to get the fuck off my car," Aaron said.

Orlando pushed past the Kappa as he grasped the car door.

"Who the fuck you touchin', son?" he said, slamming the half-open car door. I glanced up at the Kappa pledges and noticed that one of them was Brad, my housemate.

Needing no further reason to get into some trouble, Orlando swung on the Kappa, who by the grace of God took enough of a duck to narrowly avoid being clocked in the chin. He did, however, stumble backward into me and I pushed him away.

Mistaking my deflection for an act of aggression, the other Kappa shoved me from behind.

The next thing you know, all you heard was car doors slamming, boots scuffing the ground, and raised voices. Arms flailed, elbows were thrown, and shirts were grabbed. Pledges were helping out their big brothers and roommates pushed roommates.

It was over in thirty seconds or less.

We got in Aaron's car quickly and after a quick head count, he sped off.

"Anybody hurt? Anybody hurt goddamit?" he asked, breathless.

"I'm fine," he said. "You all good back there?"

"Yeah, we good," Orlando said. "That shit was all right! Let's do it again!"

"Lord Jesus, help the boy," Aaron said.

One thing about those Betas... if you hung around us long enough, there would be a story to tell your grandkids.

Chapter 11:
February 25

I gripped my blue tray with both hands as Isaiah filed behind me in line in the cafeteria. We rarely got the opportunity to eat together due to our schedules, so it was quite a rare occurrence for the both of us to be seen together during "prime time"—the seven o'clock hour.

That was the hour when most of the students of color ate dinner, whether to people-watch or to be seen themselves. It was also usually when the basketball team ate dinner, right after practice.

I was finally putting on some weight for the first time since high school. Pledging did nothing for skinny brown boys like me. Luckily, having a good man who liked to eat helped out. He was slowly but surely getting up to his ideal NBA weight and trying to keep up with him put weight on my bones, too.

I had a plate of spaghetti with meat sauce, a salad, and a tall glass of orange juice. Isaiah had pasta and a salad as well, but also had a small plate of baked chicken. Protein was the name of the game. Although I couldn't eat as much as he did, I could tell he was eating healthy.

We walked through crowds of people, not unusual for prime time, though it seemed like more people were staring at Isaiah than normal. He certainly got looks, simply for being a tall black man. He was also attractive, which accounted for other stares. And yes, he was a basketball player, which damn near put him up there with Jesus. But today was different. Today, they stared at me, too.

My Potomac chapter brothers were eating on the other side of the cafeteria, at the far wall. I nodded at them as Isaiah and I walked with trays still in hand to the tall windows overlooking the river.

We sat down and Isaiah quietly said grace.

"How was practice today?" I asked as we dug into our meal.

"Tough," he said.

"You alright?" I asked. He nodded.

"It hasn't been the same since I came out to Coach K," he admitted.

"I'm sorry," I said.

"It's not your fault," he said. "I just really thought... of all people, he'd just... I dunno..."

"You thought he'd just accept you and get over it?" I asked.

"Yeah," he said sadly. He gripped his cup tightly as he gulped his water, the veins popping from his forehead and his hand. He put the cup down and picked up his fork, aggressively attacking the food on his plate as he spoke. "I don't know why I would be so fucking... stupid... arrogant."

"Or hopeful?" I asked. "There's nothing wrong with hope. You love this guy. He's teaching you everything you need to know to become a pro baller. He'll come around."

"I don't know, babe," he said. "It's been... Wait, here come your boys."

I looked up and saw all of the Potomac half of our pledge line waiting to properly greet me. My boys were sharp in their crisp khaki slacks, black shoes, and black pea coats. Their black berets were firmly in their left hands while they stood at attention.

"Excuse us, Big Brother Adrian," Mark began. "May we please greet you?"

"By all means," I smiled.

"B...C...P!" Mark shouted.

"Greetings, Big Brother Adrian, that ferocious and phoenix-like number four of the Upsilon Line of Sadistic Sigma Chapter of Beta Chi Phi Fraternity, Innnnnnncorporated!"

"Thank you, pledges," I said. "Please greet your other big brothers on the other side of the room and enjoy your dinner."

"Thank you, Big Brother Adrian," they said in unison. Mark, an adequate ace who was growing on me, led the remainder of the line with precision through the cafeteria. For the moment, all eyes were on them: Mark, the precise and persistent ace; Rick, the introspective number four; Alex, the volatile number five; track star Joshua, the number seven, eager, but often-absent; and the boisterous number nine and tail, my housemate Orlando. My boys were sharp.

"You like them," Isaiah observed.

"I do," I said.

"Even the ones you didn't know at first?" he asked.

"Yeah, it's true," I said. "They grew on me. But back to you."

"Yeah, it's just been hard, you know? Like, this coming out thing is tough. On one hand, you got folks who are supportive. Then you got those who don't give a shit either way, like most of my teammates. But to have coach like… he's just being so cold to me, yo."

"He's not fucking up your playing time, is he?" I asked.

"No, not at all," he said. "You know I'm still starting."

"So what exactly is he doing?" I asked sincerely.

"Like, I always felt like before, after practices or games, I could just talk to him. You know, on some man-to-man shit. But after I came out to him… he just…"

"Tell me," I said. "This happened a week ago. You waited until the time was right and you told him. But you haven't told me what he said. Was it that upsetting?"

"He said a lot of shit, Adrian, but I don't want to repeat it word for word. If I told you what he said, you would get upset. But it's not personal, it's just how he is. Just how he talks. He doesn't mean it."

"So why don't you paraphrase?" I asked. "I can take it. For real."

Isaiah exhaled deeply.

"He asked me who you were, and I told him I had introduced you two at the New Year's party. Then he asked if you had me strung out on drugs."

"What the hell?"

"I think he thought I 'turned gay' from ecstasy or something. You know he's old, Adrian."

I stifled a laugh.

"Then what happened?" I asked.

"Then he told me I was just going through a phase and nothing was wrong with experimentation, but I had to cut out all this 'love talk' because it was going to ruin my career."

I frowned.

"I told him that you and I had talked about all that and that I was fine with whatever happened. He told me I was throwing my life away by following you and that I'd have to work twice as hard if I was still going to play for his team."

"Wait… you think he'd throw you off the team for being gay?" I asked.

"I don't know," he answered. "All he's done so far is work me harder in practice, single me out a lot, call me some choice names, you know."

"Has he called you a faggot?"

"Hell no, never that," Isaiah quickly replied. "He knows thems fighting words. He does call me 'sugar britches' now."

"'Sugar britches?' How old is this guy?" I scoffed.

"Old," Isaiah replied.

"Baby, I'm sorry this hasn't been smooth sailing for you. But try to remember, he's only known for a week and he's still processing everything. I'm sure he's never had a player come out to him before, so he's figuring out how to deal with it. You wanna know the good thing?"

"What?" Isaiah asked.

"You're still playing. He hasn't benched you. And he's not gonna. You are a damn good player and he knows it. He won't do anything crazy."

"I hope you're right," he said, holding his head in one hand and twirling his fork in the spaghetti with his other hand.

I reached out for him, leaving my open palm on the side of his tray. He took his hand away from his head and placed it in my palm. I squeezed it and smiled at him.

"It's gonna be okay," I said.

At that moment, Ashley Thompkins' wide hips brushed against our table as she walked by. Isaiah and I looked up to meet her icy glare.

"What a waste," she said, still walking.

"Excuse me?" I said. She kept walking. I jumped up and walked quickly behind her.

"Adrian, don't, she ain't worth it," Isaiah called to me. I looked back briefly to see him stand up and extend his hand to me. I wasn't ready to back down.

"What did you say, Ashley?" I said. She turned around, long braids whipping around her.

"Did I stutter?" she asked. "I said 'what a waste.'"

"And what is that supposed to mean?" I asked.

"You know what I mean," she said. "You know how hard it is for a black woman to find a good black man? It's bad enough we losing them to white women—now we losing them to other men."

I stared at her, slowly cocking my head to the side.

"This is where you're mistaken," I said slowly. "Good black women aren't losing good black men. But good black men are turned off by you because you're an evil b-"

Isaiah stood in my line of sight before I could utter an "itch," giving Ashley the chance to walk away.

"Come on baby," Isaiah whispered while trying to turn me around. "She ain't worth it. She is not even worth it. Let's go."

I struggled to get loose from him but he wasn't having it.

"I wish you would, Adrian," Ashley said.

"Get out of here, Ashley," Isaiah demanded. "Now!"

She turned up her nose and walked away.

"She is such a fucking bitch," I said. "Made me lose my appetite."

"Let's get out of here," he said. "I'm not hungry anymore either."

We got our coats and walked our trays over to the conveyor belt. Aaron jogged over to us before we hit the door.

"I saw what happened. You good?" Aaron asked.

I nodded.

"I'm good."

Isaiah and I exited the cafeteria and made the slow walk up the hill to his dorm room. I felt bad for Isaiah. I felt bad for us.

"Why the fuck did we have to be gay?" I said out loud. "This shit is really fucking hard sometimes."

Isaiah stopped dead in his tracks, hands still thrust deep inside the pockets of his leather jacket.

"Hey," he said. "Come here."

I walked over to him with my head lowered and my eyes looking at his size 18 Adidas.

"Look at me," he commanded. I raised my gaze until I locked eyes with him. To my surprise, his eyes were filled to the brim with tears.

"Don't ever let nobody make you feel like you're less-than," he demanded of me.

That was the last straw for me—the waterworks soon followed.

"I don't want people to look at you differently because of me. I don't want your coach to be treating you bad. Why does everything have to change just because you love somebody?" I asked these questions in between my silent sobs.

"Everything has to change… because it just does," Isaiah said. "I'm okay with that. Change is change and it's coming whether we're ready or not, whether we ever came out or not. Baby, if I was another man, a woman, or an acorn, or a rock, I'd still be in love with you and I'd do my best to get next to you. This shit with Kalinowski ain't gonna stop me from being with you. That bitch Ashley ain't gonna stop me from being with you. I don't care what comes next, I'm gonna be here."

"I know," I said. "It just hurts."

"Let it hurt," he said. "But be strong because of it. We ain't got long to be here. Let's just be. Aight? Just be."

I nodded. He wiped my eye with his hand. Damn, I hated crying in front of him. As he wiped the last tear, we heard the click of high heels coming toward us.

"Here's the happy couple Coach Kalinowski has been telling me about," she said. Rebecca Templeton had a way about her that was just sexy—sarcastic and damn near aloof; she could rock the hell out of a strand of pearls and stilettos.

"Jesus, what do you want, Becky?" Isaiah said, calling her by the name she wouldn't stand for.

"Rebecca. Listen, I just had some late meetings with some Jesuits and I'm walking to my car. Not trying to interrupt your moment," she said.

"Thank you," Isaiah said. "I'll see you at practice tomorrow."

"Are you okay, Adrian?" she asked me, ignoring Isaiah.

I nodded.

"He's not beating you, is he?" she quietly asked me.

"Who, Isaiah?" I asked. "Shit no!"

"Rebecca?" Isaiah asked. "Are you serious?"

"I was actually joking, but I see my brand of humor is lost on college kids."

Then I laughed.

"There we go," she smiled. "Listen. It's tough being a basketball player's boyfriend, isn't it?"

"Not your business, Rebecca," Isaiah interjected.

"Potomac basketball is my business. Literally."

Rebecca dug into her purse and took out a gold business card holder. She opened it up and handed her card to me.

"Adrian, take this," she said. "In case you want to talk. I understand this more than you know."

I took her card.

"Rebecca J. Templeton, Esquire?" I read aloud. "You're a lawyer?"

"Among other things," she said. "Harvard Law, Duke Undergrad."

"Nice," I said.

"We'll be getting home now," Isaiah said. "Be safe, Rebecca."

"You too," she said. "And Isaiah? Just because the gender changed doesn't mean I'm going to be any more sympathetic to bullshit. You got that?"

"Yes ma'am," he said.

"I'm 30," she shot back over her shoulder as she walked away. "Calling me ma'am is worse than calling me Becky."

"I like her," I said.

"That makes one of us," Isaiah smirked.

Chapter 12:
February 28

After a solid six hour study session in the library, I was on my way to Isaiah's place for some rest and relaxation. On the way, my phone rang.

"Hello?" I asked, not recognizing the number.

"Hey stranger," my dad said.

"Hey dad, is this a new number or something?"

"Yeah... got tired of Verizon and switched over. Upgraded to a BlackBerry."

"You know they let you keep your old number now."

"Really? Eh, that's fine. I got too many women calling me anyway, gotta change it up," he joked.

"Got any more kids out there?" I asked, only half kidding.

"No," he said. "Not that I know of. You're still an only child."

"So what's up, dad?"

"Nothing... I haven't talked to you in a while. How's school?"

"Not bad," I said. "My major is pretty laid back. Doing mostly research this semester. I'll be doing more fieldwork senior year."

"Son... exactly what kind of job do you hope to get with a degree in Anthropology?"

"I dunno. I haven't thought about it too much."

"Don't you think you should start?"

"You sound like mom," I groaned.

"As well I should," he said. "Neither of us want you to graduate and not be able to get a job."

"I'll find a job, dad."

"Doing what, playing 'Gorillas in the Mist' someplace?"

"All anthropologists don't study apes, dad," I said.

"I'm just joshin', boy."

"Oh..." I said. "By the way, dad... thank you for the check this month. It really comes in handy. But it's way too much! What am

114

EPIPHANY

I supposed to do with five grand every few months? Five grand dad? Really?"

"I'm blessed," he said. "And guilty. So deal with it. Save it. Buy a house one day. Or just save it for a rainy day. I don't know too many wealthy anthropologists, so I suspect you'll need that money."

"Thanks dad," I said. "I really do appreciate it. I don't want for anything."

"Good," he said. "So how's the chapter?"

"We're doing really well," I said. "We got nine boys on right now. They are all pretty strong, too. I kind of didn't like one of them at first, but he's grown on me."

"That's good!" he said. "I really should get active again. There's no alumni chapter out here in Jersey, though. Closest one is New York City, but that's two hours away."

"Yeah, nobody wants to make that kind of hike for an alumni meeting. You should come down and visit one weekend. See the boys before they cross."

"I don't know about that. I've been so busy lately," he said.

"Can't you just fly down one Saturday? I think you'll get a kick out of them," I pleaded.

"Maybe another time," he said. "You guys don't pledge how we did. It's more… it's just too much."

"Come on dad, we're not terrorizing these guys," I said.

"Do you give wood?" he asked pointedly.

"Everybody does it, dad," I said. "These guys are no different from my line and the line before us."

My dad let out a long sigh.

"I know your mother didn't raise you to be beating people," he said.

"Dad, come on. We're not fighting these guys. They've never had to go to the hospital. We just-"

"Don't tell me anything else about it," he said. "I'm not interested. Just be safe, for God's sake, and don't end up on the news."

"Okay, dad. Listen, I'm almost at Isaiah's place."

"Isaiah's your friend on the basketball team?"

"Yeah... my friend." I said.

"That's good. Tell him I said good job this season and I'm looking forward to the conference tournament on ESPN."

"Will do. Love you, dad."

"Love you too, son."

I sat down on the bench across from the doors of Isaiah's dorm. Within minutes, he came out, still looking as somber as he had the night before.

"What's wrong?" I asked.

"That damn Rebecca wants to have a meeting with you, me, and Coach K to 'mediate' our situation," he said.

"Me?" I asked. "What did I do?"

"Corrupted me with your sinful lifestyle," he deadpanned.

"Shut up," I said. "Are you nervous about it?"

"Coach K can talk to me any way he wants to. I can take it. But he can't play that shit with you. I ain't having it."

"Dude, don't worry about me," I said. "There's nothing Coach K can say to me to make me mad unless he says he's kicking you off the team. And that's not going to happen."

"You don't know Coach K like I do," Isaiah said. "He can be one nasty bastard when he wants to be."

"And so can I," I said. "Isn't that why you like me?"

I lightly pinched him through his coat.

"And a whole lot more," he said. I looked up to the top of the building in the night sky and stuffed my hands in my coat. We sat in silence for a few moments.

"What's wrong?" he asked. He folded his arms.

"Nothing. Just looking at the sky."

"Something's on your mind. Is everything okay?"

"I'm fine, man. Seriously."

A few more moments passed.

"You don't really ask me a whole lot about the frat," I said. "You're always okay with me being out late. Doing my own thing with the bros."

"The frat's your thing. I never knew I was allowed to ask questions."

"You can ask me anything you want."

"What is it you all say? 'Discretion is key?' I would never step into fraternity territory. Unless you wanted me to."

"Oh, okay."

"Do you want me to?"

"I dunno."

"Why you being all sketchy?" He laughed.

"I know you joke about it sometimes...but do you think I really be beatin' my pledges?"

Isaiah frowned.

"You want my honest answer?"

"Of course," I said. He sighed.

"Some really bad stuff happened to you when you were on line. And I think it made you tougher. And maybe the guys after you...well, maybe they need to be tougher too. I don't ask no questions. But I know you wouldn't do anything stupid."

I leaned back on the bench, looking upward into the trees above the bench.

"I did something stupid," I admitted.

"Uh oh."

"I'm not a hazer."

"I believe you."

"But...things happen."

"You want to tell me more?" I shook my head.

"Not right now. Maybe not ever."

"Are you in trouble?"

"No."

"Well...you know you can tell me anything, right?"

I nodded. Sighing, he uncrossed his arms and stared at me. I wouldn't look at him. I was trying hard to focus on us, not the lunacy of this pledge program I was wrapped up in. It was changing me. I tried to fight it, but this image I was portraying was threatening to crack under the pressure. I secretly loved that Isaiah let me have the frat to myself.

I could explain to an outsider no better than one could understand it if he saw it for himself.

He lightly tugged my arm and coaxed my hand out of my pocket. Without looking at me, he held my hand in the darkness.

Chapter 13:
March 5

It was a long walk to the gymnasium at the back end of campus. Over the past few days I had a lot of time to practice what I wanted to say to Rebecca and Coach K. They could be asking me anything at all and I had to be prepared to represent myself—and Isaiah—very well. I mean, this was my boyfriend and he was practically on trial for his sexuality here.

I was hoping it wouldn't be too adversarial. Hell, maybe they would surprise me and give me the blessing of the basketball program.

If I closed my eyes, I could imagine Rebecca Templeton smiling and giving us her blessing to pursue our love affair as out and as proud as we wanted to. She would march with us on the National Mall for marriage equality. She would offer to be a surrogate mother for me and Isaiah's child.

Coach K would arrange our big gay wedding in the campus chapel, convincing the campus Jesuits, and indeed, the Vatican itself, to approve me and Isaiah's big gay wedding *just this once*.

They would throw rice at us as we left the chapel in our matching tuxedoes. In the quad, my Beta brothers would surround us and sing the sweetheart song—and the solo part would be sung by my dad.

Our moms would wear beautiful pastel dresses with carnations pinned to them. And we'd light a candle in memory of Isaiah's father. We'd drive off across the 14th Street bridge with tin cans tied to our bumper and a sign saying "Just married, bitches!"

Yeah, in my dreams.

I was wearing plain black slacks, a cream colored button up shirt, and a charcoal gray sweater. The weather was getting a little warmer, but the trees on campus were still spare. I went without a jacket for the first time since last fall.

For good measure, I put a fraternity pin on my collar. It wasn't a frat event, but somehow I felt better letting Coach K and Rebecca know that even though I was dating one of their players, I was still a man's man when I needed to be.

Our gym had been erected in the 1950s and its façade definitely had a Streamline Moderne style. It was the only Art Deco-era building on campus filled with tall and ornate buildings in the Romanesque style. The gym was absent of spires and gargoyles, instead giving you an impression that over 50 years ago, Potomac thought that *this* looked futuristic.

I pushed through the front doors and turned left toward the basketball office. Toward me came several of the men's basketball team members, freshly showered after a long practice.

"Sup, Adrian?" Hodari asked me, shaking my hand and pulling me toward him in a light hug.

"Chillin' man," I said.

"Heard you got a hot date with Becky T and Coach K," he said.

"Yeah," I said. "Got any advice?"

"Shit man," he said. "I ain't never been where you are. Good luck, though."

"Thanks," I said. A few of the other players said hello to me as they passed by. They were familiar with my face now from seeing me with Isaiah at parties on campus. I wasn't sure if they knew the drama that was unfolding, but to their credit, there was no teasing or even a sideways glance.

Maybe it was true that most people in general didn't give a damn who was fucking who. The people in my life who love me never gave me a hard time with it. The people who gave me a hard time—like my prophyte Jamal—weren't in my life anymore. And sure, I had a pretty bad experience with him last fall—he tried to beat me up one night behind my apartment, but Isaiah literally rescued me and made short work out of Jamal.

Damn, I had a good man. I just had to defend my relationship with him to Rebecca and Coach K so we could all go on with our lives.

But shit, Rebecca is a *lawyer*. How do I argue with a lawyer? My stomach began to flip.

I opened the door to the basketball office and told the

receptionist that I was here for a meeting with Rebecca Templeton and Coach Kalinowski. She told me to take a seat.

Around me were posters of Potomac Pirates past, from all the way back in the 1960s. The office itself was clean, small, and filled with mahogany furniture.

From a side door emerged Rebecca. Always stunning, she had on a charcoal gray pinstriped pants suit, a gold brooch of a grasshopper on her lapel, and black stilettos. Her long red hair was pulled back in a ponytail. With her heels on, she was a good two inches taller than me.

"I'm glad you came," she said, lightly smiling at me.

"I wasn't aware that I had a choice," I replied.

"There's always a choice, Adrian," she said. "Don't forget that. Come on in."

"Nice suit, by the way," I said.

"Thanks," she replied. "Yeah, I noticed that we do match today, don't we?"

I smiled. Entering the small conference room, I saw Coach K on one side of the round table and Isaiah on the other. Neither man stood.

I extended my hand to Coach Kalinowski and told him it was nice seeing him again.

"We've met?" he asked.

"You met at the New Year's party at Renard's," Isaiah said, visibly annoyed.

"Oh," Coach said, shaking my hand.

"Have a seat, Adrian," Rebecca said. We sat across from each other at the table.

"Gentlemen," she began, pushing her horn-rimmed glasses up her narrow nose, "Make no mistake about the purpose of this meeting. I called it. My job is to protect the Potomac University basketball brand through the protection of its players. I don't work for Coach Kalinowski and I don't work for the members of the team. I am paid by Potomac University to make sure it looks good. Does everyone understand that?"

We all nodded.

"So what's your job title, if you don't mind me asking?" I said.

"I'm actually an independent contractor," she said. "Consultant to the President, if you will."

"You report directly to the president of the university?" I asked. She smirked and looked at Coach K.

"And no one else," she said. "That said, let's begin."

I folded my hands on the table and sat upright, waiting for someone to start talking. Isaiah and Coach K shifted in their seats.

"I'll start," she said. "The first mission of Potomac University is to educate the total—mind, body, and spirit. Before the basketball, before anything extracurricular, there is the education of brilliant young minds. Is this something we can all agree on?"

We nodded.

"Then we can also agree that Potomac has many unique traditions which make it special. What are some traditions you like about Potomac, Coach K?"

The gray-haired man looked at Rebecca and slightly rolled his eyes, clearly annoyed by her approach.

"Winning basketball championships," he answered.

"Good," she said. "What about you, Isaiah?"

He thought about it for a moment, then spoke. "I haven't participated in this myself, but I like the tradition of graduating seniors sitting in the lap of the St. Ignatius statue."

"That's a good one!" Rebecca said. "I forgot all about that one. And you, Adrian?"

"I like Potomac's tradition of inclusion, like basically how it had admitted black people before any other non-HBCU in the city."

"Somebody knows his history," Rebecca said. "Very good. One of my favorite traditions is the heroes' wall by the hospital. Have you ever seen it?"

Isaiah and I shook our heads.

"If you walk behind the student center and go way up to the last hospital building on campus, there is a wall with all sorts of plaques on it. Each plaque has a name inscribed on it. It's the name of every serviceman lost in World War II who went to Potomac. You should visit it. It's very beautiful."

I looked at Isaiah and we both nodded at each other.

"So why do I bring up traditions?" she asked us. "I bring them up because each of us at this table is here because we, at the very least, like being at Potomac. We might even love some aspects of it. Regardless of who we are and what we bring to the table, Potomac is the only reason we know, respect, and love each other. That's pretty fair, right?"

"Yeah," I said. There was still tension between Isaiah and Coach K, but as far as I was concerned, Rebecca was on the right track.

"Isaiah," Rebecca said, "I've been at Potomac for almost five years now and I am not exaggerating when I say you are far and away the most interesting player I've met. You've always been humble, respectful, quiet, and introspective. But when somebody really gets to know you, they see that you're funny, passionate, and protective of the people you love. And I know that's not many people. Am I wrong about anything I've said?"

"No, you're right," he said. "I can count the people I love on one hand and I'd do anything for them."

"I know," she said. "I can tell by the way you look at your boyfriend, even now."

He tried not to look at me, but I saw him glancing.

"See, you're blushing," she said.

"Aww dammit, Rebecca," he said through a grin. I smiled as well.

"And Adrian, I know we don't know each other well," she began. "But I did my research. Big man on campus. Active in Beta Chi Phi. Used to be active in the NAACP. Everybody likes you. I like you."

"Thank you, Rebecca," I said.

"You're welcome," she said. "And I think it's safe to say that you're scared shitless for Isaiah, right? This coming out thing was hard for you, but you think it will be even harder for Isaiah because he's a semi-public figure with a lot riding on him right now."

"You're right," I said. "I really, really care for him but I'm so scared I'm going to be the reason his chances at a professional career are ruined."

"And they will be ruined if you don't leave him alone!" Coach K exploded. "I don't care about this freaky deaky love fest you two are doing, but Isaiah has an excellent shot at being a first-round draft pick, kid! You can't keep leading him down this path—he's gonna end up in a gutter with a needle in his arm with the rest of these junkie queers down in Southwest!"

"You will not speak to Adrian like that, Coach K," Isaiah interjected. "I told you before, you save that crazy talk for me, but if you even raise your voice at him I swear to God I will quit this fucking team."

"Isaiah, allow me," Rebecca said. "Coach Kalinowski, shut up for a second. Listen to what one of your best players is saying. He loves this guy that is sitting in front of us. Adrian is a good kid. He's not on drugs. He's not a hustler or a prostitute. He is a Potomac University student who fell in love with his classmate. That's it, in its barest possible terms."

"Rebecca, I don't care about all that. I make superstars and win games. That's what they pay me to do."

"And they pay me to make sure that the pressure doesn't drive them crazy," Rebecca continued. "Coach K, you are a legend. Your boys come to Potomac for *you*. The first-class education is truly secondary. You have been head coach for over 35 years. You are not only the most respected person on this campus but the highest paid, too. And you deserve it. The university overlooks your style and focuses on your substance. Seven national championships? Twenty-one first-round draft picks? And you've won over half of all your conference tournaments? Coach K, you're awesome."

"I know," he said.

"But it's also 35 years later. You have here a young man who will be a captain of your team next year and will be drafted in the first round. This I know. You cannot control the personal lives of your players now any more than you could twenty years ago when they were freebasing cocaine with Victor Charles."

Whoa, I thought.

"Not fair, Becky," Coach K said.

"Rebecca," she said. "And no, it's not fair. These boys are absolutely nothing like your team from back then. The worst they do is drink and we can help them with that. But what I need for you to do as a man, as the eldest in this situation, as the coach of a legendary basketball program, is to give Isaiah a break. He is a good kid. He has a future. Him loving Adrian is not going to land him in prison or dead in a gutter. I won't allow it, his mom won't allow it, and he won't allow it. Promise me you can start fresh from this moment."

Coach K folded his arms and remained silent.

"Isaiah and Adrian," she continued after a few moments of silence. "I have to address you together because I know you're a set. And it's cute. No really, it is."

Isaiah loosened up and smiled a bit.

"You have to understand a few things about Potomac basketball," she began. "This team has never had a player who was openly gay. And no matter what Coach K has to say about it, on this campus, Isaiah is openly gay. That's done. You can't un-ring a bell."

Isaiah slowly nodded.

"I've read the books, I've seen the Oprah shows. I know you don't want to be on the DL anymore. I get it. Truth be told, I never even liked Taina."

"Why does everyone say that?" Isaiah asked me. I shrugged.

"Let's face it, the girl is about as interesting as wet piece of bread," Rebecca said.

"Yeah, pretty dull," Coach K said. "And a little weird if you ask me."

"Nice though," I added hopefully,

"Regardless," Rebecca continued, "I can understand why, after two years, you were ready to be yourself and not who you thought everybody wanted you to be. I am so incredibly proud of you for that."

"Thank you," Isaiah said.

"But guess what?" Rebecca said.

"What?"

"Are you crazy?!?! There are no openly gay NBA players! You really want to be the first? You are driving us insane over here!"

Isaiah frowned and held his head down.

"Raise your head high when I'm talking to you, Isaiah!"

Isaiah sat up straight and raised his head while he looked at Rebecca in the eyes.

"Isaiah, I know you were born this way. Nobody is challenging that. And everybody in this room loves you. That hasn't changed and it won't change. But listen to me and listen well: you have the opportunity to play a sport at which you are amazing and get paid for it. We are talking NBA. You could make more money than you have ever seen. You could move your mom out to a nice neighborhood like you always wanted. Why do you want to risk all that?"

Isaiah's mouth tightened but his stare never left Rebecca.

"Is it love?" she asked. He looked at me.

"Look at *me*, Isaiah," she demanded. "Is it a cause? Is it social justice?"

Isaiah looked from me to Coach K.

"Look at me, Isaiah!" she shouted. "Why do you want to risk giving up so much just to live as an openly gay man?!"

"Because I can!" he shouted back. "Because I can! Nobody in my life has ever asked me what I want. They look at me and assume what I am. They see my height and assume that I love basketball. I must be a dumb basketball player. I must be a whore that sleeps with a bunch of women. I must love hip-hop and gold chains and basketball. I must love basketball, right? Nobody has ever stopped to ask me what the hell I love! Rebecca, how do you think it makes me feel that I play the same sport that my father was playing the day he got shot and killed right in front of me? I think about my father every time I pick up a basketball, every time I put on a uniform. Hell, sometimes when I put on white socks I think about him. And you know what? I put on white socks every single day.

"I like basketball. I'm good at it. But I love other things a whole lot more. I love being at Potomac—unlike many folks you're used to dealing with, I did come here for the education first. And I like Coach K—Coach, I love you. I like your style. I get you. And I know you want the best for me.

"I know you guys think I should just shut up and keep working hard so I can go to the NBA. And for you guys, I can still make it a goal. I'm not giving up on basketball. I can play through the pain of missing my dad. I've done it for this long, I can keep going. For you. For him. For my mom.

"But this man? This man right here? He is my future. He is my best friend. He has seen me at my best and at my worst and he loves me anyway. He is the reason I believe I can be whatever I want to be, because I saw him do it first. Do you understand the drama, the torture he had to go through because his fraternity found out he was gay? And now, a year later, he is still on top. Yeah, it wasn't easy. But he shows me daily that I can be exactly who I am despite what corner anybody else paints me in.

"I know he will be there whether I go pro or whether I join Teach for America. Coach K, Rebecca—I will stay in this because I am good at basketball. But I am not compromising my integrity, my friendship, or my life. Not for money. Not for fame. If I can't get drafted because they know I'm gay, then I don't want to play."

Isaiah was beet red and breathing hard.

"Now that's my boy," Rebecca said, smiling and folding her arms.

I was blown away. If I didn't know before, I now knew two undisputed facts:

One: Isaiah was head over heels for me more deeply than I had ever imagined.

Two: Rebecca J. Templeton, Esq., was the baddest bitch.

"Isaiah, Adrian, Coach Kalinowski... I want you all to consider the following things. First, Isaiah is out on this campus, but he doesn't have to be out off campus. Isaiah, I'm not suggesting that you revert your status in any way. Nor am I suggesting that you stop going out. But we need to make sure that you are going out to places that Potomac University trusts will protect you. VIP access only. No media. Don't answer now—think on it."

Isaiah nodded.

"Adrian, nobody is going to ask you to go back in the closet, either. But we need for you to understand and think about the inevitable media attention that will follow Isaiah. You need to know that anything and everything you say—including your Facebook statuses—can be used to prevent Isaiah from excelling. You're a smart guy. You know that the media is only your friend if you own it."

I nodded.

"So just think about the gift you can give to Isaiah—merely silence if anybody asks you about your relationship with him. I can help you. I can coach you. It's my job. Think about it."

"I will," I said.

"Coach K," Rebecca continued, "You've gotta stop riding him so hard in practice and afterwards. Forget that he ever came out to you. You're not dealing with it well and you're taking it out on him. Just think about it. Know that he's not nearly the same as your problem players of the days of yore. Think on it."

Coach K nodded in agreement.

"Gentlemen, we've got a lot of work to do, but don't rush into any decisions. All we want here is to maximize Isaiah's options. If he wins, we all win. Understood?"

"Yes ma'am," I said. Rebecca raised her eyebrow.

"Miss," I self-corrected. "Never ma'am. I remember."

"I like you," Rebecca said. Turning to Isaiah, she instructed: "Keep him. He will never embarrass you. Because if he does, he'll have me to deal with."

We all stood up simultaneously to leave the meeting.

"Coach K," Isaiah said, extending his hand across the table. "Thank you for taking the time to hear me out. I appreciate that."

"You're welcome," he said, grasping Isaiah's hand. "Kid, I know I'm an asshole. But don't let it be said I never tried to look out for you."

"That, sir, could never be said about you."

They both smiled at each other for what would be the first time in weeks. Rebecca also smiled. She never stopped smiling, even as she picked up her purse and left the room with a fling of her hair.

The baddest bitch, I repeated. *Yes, indeed.*

Chapter 14:
March 8

"Dude, how come these bitches won't come over here and twist my locks?" Hodari said, snapping his phone shut and throwing it on his bed. He was wearing a towel around his waist and his long locks were still moist from a fresh shampooing. His tall, brown body was thick and chiseled from his muscled thighs to his perfectly symmetrical chest, broad shoulders, and arms that were hard as steel.

"If you stop calling 'em bitches, maybe they'll want to come over," I laughed.

"I don't call 'em bitches to they face!" Hodari stressed.

Isaiah laughed from his bed, reclining in his baggy sweatpants and hooded sweatshirt.

"I'm going to the store, y'all want something?" Isaiah asked.

"No thanks," Hodari said. "Unless you can convince one of these chickenhead freshmen to come back here and do my hair."

"Nut. Just twist it your damn self," Isaiah suggested.

"I hate twisting my hair!" Hodari said. "It takes forever!"

I shook my head. "I'll see you when you get back."

"Aight," he said, leaving the room and letting the door close behind him.

"Adrian," Hodari said.

"What up?" I replied.

"Come twist my locks," he asked.

"No," I said.

"Please?" he pleaded.

"Dude, I don't do hair," I said.

"Ugh, you are the sorriest gay dude ever! What can you do gay?"

"Uh... what?"

"You don't dress trendy. You don't be knowing the gay slang. You don't do hair. What's the point of being gay if you ain't no fun?"

"You are an idiot," I laughed. He laughed with me. He slowly opened his dresser drawer and pulled out some hair clips, a white towel, a few thin hair bands, and a tub of holding gel for natural hair.

He sat on his bed with his legs crossed and began applying the gel to the roots of his locks. After he did that, he took the lock in the palms of his hands and rolled it until it was tight against his scalp. He used a clip to hold the lock down as he moved on to the next one.

"Is that all it takes?" I asked.

"Yeah," he said. His big brown eyes looked up at me as he twisted the next lock.

"I mean, I can try that," I said. "But… you really need to put some clothes on first."

"I got a towel on," he said.

"Clothes," I repeated. "I'm not trying to have Isaiah come back in here and find my fingers in your scalp like something's going on."

"Lord, that jealous ass nigga," he said. He finished the lock he was working on and stood up. "You are a real outgoing dude. Do a lot of shit on campus. I ain't asking what you see in him, cuz that ain't my place. I'm just saying if somebody asked me, I wouldn't have pegged you and him to be compatible."

"Who knows why things work out the way they do," I said. Just then, Hodari dropped his towel to the floor and let the family jewels out. I got an eyeful of probably the biggest penis I'd ever seen. My eyelids fluttered, then I turned my head slightly to the side, avoiding Hodari's gaze.

"I mean, you know how it is," I continued. "Before last summer, I didn't even know he liked dudes. Now here we are."

"Yeah," he said. "Here you are." I didn't turn my head back around until I could hear him moving about the room. When I looked back up, his back was too me. The back view wasn't any more G-rated: nothing but long, black dreadlocks cascading down a muscular back, stopping about halfway down to make an arrow pointing to the small of his back and the crack of his high ass.

What was with basketball players and high asses? Whatever the reason was, I thanked God for it!

He reached into his bottom drawer, bending all the way over at the waist. He pulled out a pair of boxer briefs, slipping them all the way up his legs until they fit snugly around his waist. He turned back around and looked in another drawer, getting out his basketball shorts and a tank top. Before he put them on, he locked eyes with me and smiled.

"Lookin' ass nigga," he said.

"Whatever dude," I shot back. "Sit in your chair and give me the gel."

He sat down and handed me his tools. I applied the gel to an area of his scalp and began to twist.

"Too tight?" I asked.

"Nope," he said. "Just right."

He sat in silence as I twisted away. Hodari was definitely an attractive dude. I didn't think he was gay, just a jokester. Then again, I was never one to catch on to flirtation, subtle or otherwise.

"You ever had a dude do your hair before?" I asked.

"Nope," he said. "First time."

"Cool," I said.

"Adrian," he asked a short time later. "Why do you think Isaiah doesn't like us?"

"Us, who?" I asked.

"The rest of the basketball team," he said.

"I don't get the impression he doesn't like y'all," I said.

"He act like he don't," Hodari continued. "He and I been on the team two and a half years now, and I feel like I didn't really get to know him until you came into the picture."

"You think so?" I asked, pinning back a row of his dreadlocks. "Because, on the real... I always assumed that you all would know him best. Y'all and Taina."

"Her ass," he said. "I was so glad they broke up. She was always just around. And in the way. I mean, that's his business but damn he coulda done better."

"Nice girl, though," I said. "But still, I always kinda viewed Potomac basketball as this elite brotherhood. You all hang out together.

Eat together. Practice together. I assumed it was inevitable there would be friendships."

"See, that's the difference between a sport and a frat. Yeah, we choose to play basketball. We all enjoy it. And we all hope to go pro, at least play overseas for a few years. But the brotherhood is what you make it. We got chosen because of a skill, not because we have the potential to be life-long friends."

"True," I said.

"Betas, man... y'all don't realize it, but you choose to be around each other. Choose to go through the shit you go through to call each other brothers. We chose basketball, but the end result is a career move—not brotherhood."

"I feel you," I said, gelling up another section of locks.

"In the end, I think we all like being around each other because we know each other, but there's also this feeling that it's... eleven of us, plus Isaiah. Not twelve of us."

"I think I know why that is, well part of it," I said.

"Whatchu think?"

"Well, you're straight... right?"

"Yeah. 'Straight but not narrow' is what I saw on a t-shirt one time," he said. "Got no problems with you being yourself if you let me be me, too."

"Cool," I said. "But because you're straight, you don't have to think about certain things, you know? You don't have to worry about not getting a job because people know you like women. You don't have to think about marriage equality because it's already legal for you. It's a lot of stuff you just don't have to worry about because you're part of the majority."

"Yeah," he said.

"Maybe Isaiah was never that close to you all because he didn't want to lie to you. Maybe he didn't want to get close, then come out to you and have you guys be angry at him because he didn't tell you he was gay first. I don't know man—these are just guesses."

"No, man, those are actually good points. I never thought about it from the other side."

"The other thing about Isaiah that I've learned… he's not a big group person. He thrives in one-on-one situations."

"Yeah, that's definitely true. He's a good dude, though. I'm not trying to say it's anything wrong with him. I hope you know that."

"I understand totally. What you say is between us."

"Isaiah told me the meeting y'all had with Becky and Coach K wasn't too bad. Intense, but not too bad."

"That's accurate."

"How did you like Coach K?" he asked.

"Like is such a strong word," I replied.

We laughed.

"He was out of pocket at times," I admitted. "But there's a lot more going on there than I thought. I know Isaiah is cool with him, so he's cool with me. He ain't my coach."

"Yeah, you either love him or hate him," Hodari said. "I haven't decided yet."

"So what about you, man?" I asked.

"What about me?"

"People are talking like you might leave early and go pro," I said.

"Just rumors," he said. "I'm with your boy. I'm not leaving here until I get that degree, ya heard? The hell I'ma do leaving early and get a shitty draft pick—or not get drafted at all? I'd rather get that business degree finished first then make it happen. More respect that way. And a bigger net in case some shit goes wrong."

"Well, whenever it does happen, I'm hoping for the best for you, man," I said.

He looked up at me with a wide smile.

"I appreciate that, homeboy," he said.

I did a few more rows and in no time, Isaiah was back in the room.

"Oh jeez," he said. "This nigga got you doin' his hair? How the hell did that happen?"

"It's a long story," I said.

"Man, yo nigga was all over me dawg!" Hodari lied. "He was all 'Oh Hodari, let me play in your locks, 'mmkay?' and I was all 'naw

man, you know Isaiah gonna act all funny and shit if he catch you doin'
that.' But he practically rubbed his dick on me beggin', so I was like shit,
what up?"

Isaiah stared at Hodari.

"You a goddamn lie," he laughed. We all had a hearty laugh at
that one. Hodari was truly one of a kind—a comedian in every sense
of the word.

"You heard from ya girl?" he asked me as I continued to twist
his locks.

"Not in about a week. She stays pretty busy over there," I said.

"Tell her to holla at me, for real," Hodari said. "I'm kinda really
feelin' shawty."

Just then, the thundering boom of a frantic voice and fists
against wood shattered the peace of the dorm room.

"Yo, Isaiah!" the voice said. It was Calen.

"Isaiah, where's Adrian? I need Adrian! It's Calen, man, open
up!"

Isaiah tossed his bag from the store to the bed and quickly
opened the door. Calen spilled into the room, out of breath.

"Adrian, man this is bad!" Calen said.

"Dude, what's wrong? What happened?" I asked.

"The chapter got snatched! Somebody dropped dime and we're
all suspended!"

My heart and stomach sank to my knees. Calen continued his
hysterics as I sat down on the bed, trying to listen, but it didn't work.
All I heard was the rush of white noise as I tried to process just how
bad this situation could get.

We were fucked.

Chapter 15:
March 9

Calen was a complete wreck. I should remind Aaron not to call Calen first with bad news—he only seems to take it well from me.

At Aaron's request, Calen and I got on the phone and called brothers to meet at our place for an emergency meeting. It couldn't wait and we needed everyone there. Unfortunately, it couldn't start until after midnight as Ciprian was in Baltimore for a debate tournament and Mohammed was with him.

When they finally arrived at our apartment, minutes after midnight, Aaron began the meeting. The whole active chapter was there: Aaron, Tommy, and my entire line except Micah.

"Brothers, this emergency meeting is called to order," Aaron began. "There will be no notes and no mention of this meeting to anyone outside of this room. Is that understood by all?"

"Yes, Brother President," we replied in unison.

"Then *let brotherly love continue*," he said, quoting our secret motto from the Book of Hebrews.

"Brother President, Brother Pledgemaster..." Ed began. "Aaron, Tommy... what the hell happened? All I was told is that we were on suspension and we're not allowed to even talk to the boys. What's up?"

"We have received both an email and a hand-delivered letter from the Region Director stating that Sigma Chapter is immediately suspended from any activity in the name of the fraternity—including pledging—pending an investigation of hazing. If we are to touch, meet with, or speak to any of our pledges, we risk an immediate disciplinary suspension as a chapter."

"What?" Calen said. "Hazing? We haven't hardly done anything to them! Which of them would drop dime?"

"Calen, we can't jump to conclusions just yet," Tommy said. "All the letter says is that there are allegations of hazing. We don't know who reported this. It could have been a pledge. It could have been the advisor. Technically, it could even be one of us. We don't know and we may never know."

"So we get screwed and we don't even get to face our accuser?" I asked. "That fucking sucks, yo!"

"Wait," Mohammed asked. "What's going to happen to the pledges?"

"The letter says that the pledges will continue on with the official pledge program—basically the Monday night meetings and the official ceremonies—without us," Tommy explained.

"What?!" Ciprian shouted in his drawl. "How in the pure hell is grad chapter going to cross our boys and we can't even be present! That's some bullshit!"

"It happens all the time," Aaron said. "A chapter doesn't keep shit tight, the region director will snatch them and let the boys be paper. When a pledge complains about hazing, he's not doing it to make a statement. He's not going to press charges. He just wants to be a Beta. Even if he's crossing just to be inactive in a suspended chapter, all he wants is to cross."

"That's crazy," Calen said.

"And even worse," Tommy said, "is that if our boys don't really finish this process and cross the way they are supposed to—the Sigma Chapter way—they are never going to get respect from our old heads."

"We gotta figure out who snitched," Ed said.

"Damn right," Calen said. "We did nothing to those boys that didn't happen to us."

"What difference does it make who snitched?" Mohammed asked.

"What do you mean?" Peter asked. "We need to know who the weak link is, and-"

"And then what? Make him drop?" Mohammed asked.

"Yeah!" Peter said.

"Do you know how crazy you sound right now?" Mohammed asked. "We are already being investigated. How will it look if we force out the one who was brave enough to speak out?"

"Brave?" Aaron repeated. "Are you serious right now? If any

of them had a problem with what was going on, they could have gone to their spesh, their dean, or even me. But not a single one of them came to me, not one! Whoever did this is a coward. We could have handled this like men."

"Aaron, when are we going to take responsibility for what we did to those men as a chapter?" Mohammed asked sincerely. "It's not like our hands are clean in this, are they?"

"You know who snitched, don't you?" Calen asked.

Mohammed slowly turned his gaze toward Calen.

"If I knew who it was, I wouldn't tell you," Mo continued. "Look at how you're acting, you're practically foaming at the mouth. Look around you. Each one of us has either done something to a pledge directly, planned on it, or been in the room when it happened."

"He's right, brothers," Tommy said. "Like it or not, we're in this together. We are going to be investigated together, and depending on how well we arm ourselves, we will all be suspended together."

"Real talk, Mohammed hasn't done anything to those boys. Why would he get suspended?" I asked.

"Because I was there. And I did nothing," he said.

"But nobody got hurt," I said emphatically.

"Nobody?" Ciprian said. "Adrian, really? Let's not talk about how you carried on that night."

There was suddenly a rap on the door. Calen rose to answer the door.

"Who is it?" he said.

Several more raps followed. Calen rapped back, and the people on the other side of the door responded. Whoever it was, they were brothers—they knew and responded to the raps of admission.

Calen opened the door and greeted our chapter alumni: Micah, from my line; Stacy Briggs from Aaron and Tommy's line, Terror Squad; Deji, Craig, and my spesh and Dean Steven from Sankofa; and Maurice Taylor, Kymani Simpson, and Christopher Baynes from the line called Revelations. We took time to properly greet everyone with the fraternity grip. There were a total of sixteen of us in the room now.

"I didn't know you were all coming," Aaron said.

"We assumed our invitations were lost in the mail," Deji said. "How are you going to have a meeting about something this serious and not tell your alumni?"

"We're handling it," Tommy said. "We still don't have all the facts, like what they think we did."

"Fuck the facts," Craig said. "These dudes have been on for five weeks already. We got brothers that took off work to see them this weekend—shit, me and Steven drove down from Philly. What the hell, now we can't even see them?"

"We can't help that," Aaron said. "I have the cease and desist right here in my hand."

"Fuck a cease and desist," Craig said. Although I no longer feared him as I did when I was a pledge, Craig never failed to live up to his line name: "Psycho."

"Listen," Steven said. "I really do respect each and every one of you in this room. I believe in you. There's not a single one of you who I voted "no" on. But you have to fix this. Sigma chapter cannot fall, not now."

"We know," Tommy said. "We just need to figure out who snitched so we can figure out what the problem is."

"What would they have to snitch about?" Steven asked. He was always the most level-headed of all my prophytes.

The current members of the chapter were all silent.

"Have they taken wood yet?" he asked.

"Yes," Tommy said. "We avoided it for as long as we could."

"What's the most any of them have taken?" Maurice asked.

"In a night?" Tommy asked. "I don't know, like forty?"

"Forty?" Craig said. "Is that all?"

"Isn't that a bit much?" Kymani said simultaneously. They both looked at each other with a shrug.

"What else?" Steven continued.

"You know, the usual," Aaron said. "Same stuff we've been through."

"The Chair?" Deji asked.

"Yeah."

"Thunderclaps?"

"Yeah."

"TV?"

"Yeah"

"Bubble ups?"

"Yeah."

"Six inches?"

"Yeah."

"The Scorpion?"

"Yeah."

"The Iron Maiden?"

"What's the Iron Maiden?" Tommy asked.

"I don't know, what's the Scorpion?" Deji said.

The brothers laughed. Just a little, though.

"Alright," Steven said. "Next question. How many of you have personally given strokes to a pledge?"

All of us raised our hands except for Mohammed and Tommy.

"Damn," he said. "Okay. Have any of you ever lost your cool in set? Has anything ever gotten out of control?"

Silence fell over the room.

"Tell the truth, brothers," Chris Baynes said.

"There was one time," Aaron began slowly, "the night that we got our personals. One of the pledges did a song that was disrespectful to the brother it was intended for."

"Who was the brother?" Steven asked.

"I'd rather not say?" Aaron replied.

"Well what was disrespectful about it?"

"I think that brother should explain why, if he wants to." Aaron turned his eyes to me.

"Spesh?" Steven asked.

"I'm not getting into it," I said.

"Adrian, if you did something to this pledge that he complained about, then you're gonna have to get into it."

I exhaled.

"It's pledge Dexter…" I began. "The dude from Rock Creek. He messed up my greeting."

"On purpose," Calen added.

"Yes," I said. "It seemed like he purposefully kept messing it up. So to punish him, we asked him to pop out of line and sing a song."

"Not unreasonable," Steven said.

"He started singing 'Chi Chi Man' and directed it toward me."

"Oh…" Steven said.

"What's the big fuckin deal?" Craig asked. "Isn't Chi Chi Man that cartoon from the 80s?"

"That's Mon Chi-Chis," Deji whispered to Craig.

"Oh," he said. "Well what the fuck is a Chi Chi Man?"

"A Chi Chi Man is a derogatory term for a gay man," Mohammed explained.

"Oh… oooooh," Craig said. "So… you fucked him up after that, right?"

"I went up to him," I continued. "And I asked him if he thought I was stupid. And I asked him if he thought I didn't know what it was supposed to mean. And before he had the chance to answer, I grabbed him by the throat and jacked him up against the wall."

Brothers sat in silence with their mouths open.

"Adrian Collins," Craig said. "I didn't know you had it in you! Whattup, bruh!"

"I'm not proud of it, Craig. I lost control."

"But I bet you he won't disrespect you anymore," he said. "I don't play that shit. After what you and I went through, I came to respect and understand you. As a man. As a gay man or whatever. You my frat now, and I'll be damned if I let anybody disrespect you. You were a lot easier on him than I would have been."

"Was he hurt?" Steven asked. "And how did it get broken up?"

"For the few seconds I had him by the throat, I guess he couldn't breathe well. And I guess I banged his head against the wall when I jacked him up. But nothing seemed serious or permanent. No bruises that anyone could see. Tommy and Aaron got me off him."

"That could have gone a complete different direction, bro," Kymani said. "He could have hit his head the wrong way, got knocked out or worse. Or you could have squeezed his throat too hard."

"It was very dangerous, Adrian," Steven said.

"I know," I said. "I shouldn't have done it. I'm sorry."

"Fuck that, don't apologize," Craig insisted. "Anybody who will disrespect a brother needs to be dropped from the process."

"We didn't exactly choose him," Tommy said.

"He's a fucking add-on?" Kymani asked.

"Pretty much," Tommy said. All the alumni groaned.

"How many of the nine were ones that you actually wanted?"

"Five," Aaron said.

"So four of these bozos are add-ons?" Deji asked. "You all let nationals almost double your line?"

"Deji, these guys were good candidates," Tommy said. "Emeka has a 4.0 GPA. Josh runs track—people are calling him America's answer to Usain Bolt," Aaron explained.

"And what about this jerk Dexter? And the other one?" Kymani asked.

"They interviewed really well," Tommy said.

"This some bullshit," Maurice said. "Back when I was in the chapter, we didn't even let people know when rush would be. You picked who you wanted, told them about the rush. Then you found some buddies to show up to fill like five or six more seats. Then when it's over, only the ones you want pick up an application. How hard is that?"

"These aspirants talk to each other," Ed explained. "Mark Ferguson practically stalked Adrian—he might have known about rush before some of us did!"

"And the smoker didn't shake anybody out?" Steven asked.

"Not everyone," Ciprian said. "Brothers, listen… I know I wasn't one of the chosen last year. That's cool with me. But I worked hard, got in, and serve the chapter to the fullest. I had the same process as everyone else did. Who's to say that the process doesn't change people for the better?"

"Or at least change pledges into people who can respect the frat and each other," Calen added. "Listen, we hear you, and we respect what you're saying, but in the past five weeks, we came to like all nine of these dudes, regardless of whether we knew them before or if they started proving themselves. And don't jump on Adrian for losing his cool—he is one of the most fair and kind brothers to these fools. He didn't deserve the disrespect he got. And he ain't got no beef with Dexter now. It's over. Dexter is not the snitch."

"I can attest to that," Ed said. "Dexter wouldn't do it. He knows he was wrong and he had to write a paper about 'murder music' to make up for his disrespect. I don't think any of the add-ons would snitch."

"So maybe it's a mother?" Steven asked.

"A girlfriend," Deji added.

"A father?" Maurice posited. "There are more and more legacies coming through and their dads are not feeling the chapters like they used to."

"It could be anybody," Aaron said. "I don't think the most important thing is who it is, but how we're going to respond."

"You gotta get the boys together so they can close ranks and keep it tight," Kymani said. "Let them know that they can't say anything about what happens in sessions. That all they do is the national workshops and the ceremonies."

"You want them to lie?" Mohammed asked.

"I want the chapter to not get de-chartered," Kymani said. "Listen, if the region director interviews you—and he will—do you plan on telling him everything?"

Mohammed remained silent.

"Say something," Kymani demanded. "Are you going to snitch when he comes down here? In fact, did you snitch in the first place?"

"Listen, motherfucker!" Mohammed exploded. "I am sick and tired of all of you perpetuating this stupidity! Do you understand what is going on here? We have been hitting grown men and telling them it's in the name of brotherhood! And you know why we do it? Because we think it teaches a lesson. We think that we're teaching them things about black history and Africa and slavery when we torment them. You know what? If they don't know where they came from at 19 or 20, how in the hell can we teach them?"

"Look, I'm just-" Kymani tried to continue.

"No, you look!" Mohammed went on. "I come to each and every session to look out for Emeka. He's my personal. When I look at him, I see a version of myself. I am Algerian, he is Nigerian, but what's the difference? I'm light, he's dark, but we're the same—we're not from here. We go through this process and struggle to sometimes understand the language, the slang, even the concepts that are taught. But somewhere in the back of my mind, I know this isn't right. I know this isn't how you teach brotherhood."

"Yo, Mo..." Craig said. "On the real, did you snitch on the chapter?"

"No, I didn't," Mohammed hissed. "And I know Emeka wouldn't, either. I don't think any of the pledges did—they're dumb, just like we all were. They will never tell. And if you tell them to keep their mouths shut, they will."

"Well that's good," Craig said.

"If you really ever cared about this chapter," Mohammed continued, "you will come to your senses and stop what you're doing. I can't participate in this anymore. Aaron, you are the leader of this chapter. I have respect for you. I know you're doing the right thing. Tommy, you're a good Dean of Pledges. But we can't keep doing this. Everything that we went through was not good. We know it wasn't. It's time to stop."

"So what are you suggesting?" Steven asked.

"I'm suggesting that we abide by the suspension and let the pledges finish the national process."

"Abso-fuckin-lutely not!" Craig said. Several other alums vigorously shook their heads and expressed their opposition.

"The best thing for the chapter," Deji said, "is to take the five chosen boys underground all the way, and finish the process. Let everybody go legit with the national process, but only the five you had from the beginning get the real shit. No other way."

"You want half the line to be paper?" Peter asked.

"I want half the line to not even exist," Deji said. "Them niggas will never be Sigma Chapter to me. Ya heard?"

"Take the five underground, ignore the rest," Craig concurred.

"And do everything the same," Maurice added. "Don't sanitize the process just because some of them couldn't take it."

"I don't know how I feel about that," Tommy said. "These dudes have bonded. It's been five weeks."

"Fuck em," Deji said. "This is for Sigma. Sigma Chapter comes first."

"I will leave the chapter if that's the solution we choose," Mohammed said.

"Then bye, nigga," Craig said.

"Stop," Aaron said. "Everybody be quiet."

"Dude, I'm just sayin'..."

"Enough!" Aaron shouted. "Alumni, we respect your opinions and will take them under advisement. Now, please leave."

"What?" Deji asked. "Negro, did you not hear us say that some of your prophytes came from out of town?"

"Yes," Aaron said. "And we appreciate that. We need you. And even though you won't be seeing any pledges this weekend, I want us to hang out, go eat or something. But right now, we need to be alone. Thank you for coming."

"Man, fuck this! I'm going over to Jamal's house. At least he had the goddamn sense to go inactive this semester rather than coming back to this bullshit." Craig said, quickly rising. Angered, all of the visiting brothers stood up and filed out of my apartment.

Micah lingered behind to whisper in my ear: "I wish I could stay and support you, but I'm an alum now, too. Yet and still—you know I got your back."

I nodded and gripped him.

Steven was the last brother to leave. He addressed us when he was at the door.

"I made all of you," he began with a sigh and a head-scratch. "And you made it to this point for a reason. I hope we were able to teach you something. I don't know how I feel about all this. But I trust you. I truly do."

With that, he left.

"Who invited the alumni?" Aaron asked.

"I didn't know they weren't invited, Aaron," Tommy said. "I'm sorry."

"It's cool," he said. "I just wanted to talk among ourselves first."

He buried his face in his hands. In deep introspection, we remained silent.

"I don't think we should take any of them underground," I said. "I know my role in all this, and taking half of them under will only make it worse."

"We can't let them have five weeks of pledging and then just stop without all the traditions," Peter said. "They'll know nothing. They won't have the bond that we do."

"They definitely won't have a bond if we only continue with half of them," Tommy said.

"Brothers, the priority here is keeping the chapter alive," Ed said. "We want that. The pledges want that. We don't know who snitched and we don't know what they snitched about."

"We can't talk to the pledges," Tommy said. "If we get seen talking to them, it's curtains."

Silence.

"Spring break is starting," he said. "For Potomac, at least. Rock Creek is next week. Just leave the pledges alone. No contact. The region director is coming to town on the 18th. Nobody talks to anybody about this. You understand?"

We all nodded.

"We might have to take the loss on this one. The chapter might get suspended, depending on what they have on us."

"What do we do if the pledges call us?" Mohammed asked.

"I don't know, ignore them," Aaron replied. "Refer them to Tommy."

"But what about Orlando?" Calen asked. "He lives with us. Is he coming back? What do we say?"

"I don't know, dammit!" Aaron said. "Just let me think. I need to think."

"Brothers... let's just go. Get some rest. It's been a long night," Tommy said. "I'll tell the pledges to lay low. And they'll lay low."

Somberly, Ciprian, and Mohammed left my apartment without saying goodbye. Ed and Peter left next, nodding to each of us. Tommy touched my shoulder as I stared off into space. Calen went downstairs to his room and closed the door.

I stood up and walked over to my president, whose head was still in his hands.

"You're doing the right thing," I said.

He looked up at me and I noticed that his eyes were threatening to burst with tears.

"I killed our chapter," he said. "All this shit goes down on my watch."

"Aaron, none of this is your fault," I said, kneeling down on the floor in front of him. "If you want problems, we got plenty, but none of them are your fault. We're gonna get through this, aight?"

He nodded. Slowly, he reached his hand out to me. I reached back, gave him the fraternal handshake, and took him into my arms. Silently, he cried on my shoulder until no tears were left. He spent the night on my couch, mostly laying awake in quiet contemplation. I sat in the chair near him, sleeping only intermittently until the sun rose.

We didn't know it for certain, but we held on to the belief that somehow, some way, everything was going to be alright.

Chapter 16:
March 11

The university chartered buses to take students to the conference tournament in New York City. It would happen all week during spring break. Potomac University was not short on school spirit. Every year, hundreds of students would come to the conference tournament, eschewing more exotic spring break locales like Cancun or Jamaica. They'd spend a lot less on the dirt-cheap bus trip and staying in hotels that the university practically filled to capacity with students.

The players, the basketball staff, and the families would ride in ritzier buses, of course, and in a hotel with slightly better amenities.

I sat toward the back of the family and friends bus while the team and coaching staff rode ahead in another bus. I didn't know these families or these friends very well. I had seen a few at the New Year's party at Renard's, but truth be told, I was too wasted to remember anyone.

Potomac paid for people on "the list" to travel and stay in New York for free. In the larger scheme of things, it was a small price to pay to keep the players happy. They worked hard all season and deserved to have their people supporting them, especially while having to endure the sometimes erratic personality of Coach Kalinowski.

On the bus, there were some parents, some grandparents, some girlfriends, some baby mamas, and some babies. With the exception of a few teenaged boys who might be siblings of players, I was the only unrelated man traveling.

I sat near the back, still in deep thought after the events of a few days ago. I wasn't used to nights without pledge sessions. I also wasn't prepared for the sudden severed ties from my personal. Christopher White had done nothing but be a good pledge—there was no reason that he should be punished.

In my heart, I truly didn't believe that any of the pledges would have complained about the process. None of the five chosen ones were taken by surprise at the intensity of the process and the four additional pledges adapted well. They were so close to the end—to have the most important weeks of the process taken from them was a nightmare for everyone.

Yet and still, I hadn't decided if I would be truthful about my role in the whole mess. I didn't want to be suspended from the fraternity.

"Hey handsome," Rebecca said. I looked up, awakened from my daze, to see Rebecca in a tight-fitting black sweater and jeans. Her hair was in a ponytail and her glasses rode low on her nose.

"Hi there," I smiled. "I didn't know you were on this bus."

"I like to ride with the families sometimes," she said. "Being around the boys all day can wear on my nerves. Plus, it's good business to make sure the families are happy."

"I can see that," I said.

"Anyone sitting next to you?" she asked.

"Nope, I'm solo," I said. "Wanna sit?"

"Sure," she said. I moved my bag and gave Rebecca the aisle seat.

"You looked sort of lost in thought," she said. "Is everything okay?"

"Yeah," I said.

"Don't lie," she said quickly. "Not only is it written all over your face, Isaiah told me that you were having some troubles."

"Yeah, something like that," I said.

"So what's really going on?" she asked again.

"Rebecca, there's so much going on. My frat… my chapter… we've been put on suspension pending an investigation into hazing allegations."

"Whoa," Rebecca said. "Adrian, I have to tell you something. You know I'm a lawyer. And I work for Potomac University and the basketball program. Whatever you tell me has to be as a friend—I'm not your lawyer."

"Never mind then," I said.

"Adrian, please don't be mad. It's just that whatever you tell me can be subpoenaed. If it's incriminating, I could be forced to testify against you. Not to mention the potential conflict of interest since I work for the university."

"I said never mind then, damn." I looked out the window as we rolled down the highway. Rebecca rose from her seat and left me alone.

I leaned my head on the window and watched the Maryland countryside roll by. I nodded off to sleep.

I didn't really dream. I was aware of the low chatter of the others on the bus. But my mind kept replaying the pledge process from my perspective and all the things I did wrong. I couldn't turn it off.

I had been nasty to prospects when I could have been friendly.

I helped weed guys out who we could have given a chance.

I had deviated from what my fraternity mandated.

I had paddled pledges.

I had assaulted a pledge who disrespected me.

And I felt bad about it. No, I didn't feel bad about it as it was happening. And I didn't quite feel bad about possibly getting caught.

I felt bad that I didn't feel bad.

No matter what Sigma chapter put these guys though, it still didn't compare to the fear I lived with day in and day out during my process. I had to deal with homophobic comments from men I loved and wanted to be like. I was myself assaulted by Craig and Jamal and I hadn't even done anything to deserve it other than being myself. And even after I crossed, I was attacked by Jamal.

I didn't feel bad for them because I knew I had had it worse. And I felt bad for myself that I just didn't have the empathy of Mohammed or the level headedness of my Dean, Steven.

I fell into a deeper sleep.

In my mind's eye, I was being interrogated by my region director and chapter advisor. The room was white, practically empty, and illuminated by fan unknown source. They knew everything and they tried to force me to admit it. I wouldn't.

My father was there. He was angry with me. I couldn't hear him, but he was shouting, getting in my face. Out of the corner of my eye, I saw my mom standing with her arms folded.

I blinked slowly, and when my eyes opened again, Steven, my

Dean, was there, standing next to Christopher, my spesh. They were my family tree, my past, and my future. Their faces were somber, yet hopeful. I couldn't tell if they were proud or disappointed.

I stood up from my chair, but I realized I was being lifted up. My hands were behind my back and I couldn't move them. I was handcuffed.

Police officers were taking me away.

With a gasp, I woke up. I wasn't sure how long I had been asleep.

I got up to stretch my legs and relieve myself in the restroom at the very back of the bus. When I got out, Rebecca was waiting for me in the aisle by my seat.

"Lawyers can be obnoxious sometimes," she said.

"You're just protecting yourself," I said as I sat down. She rejoined me in the empty seat.

"Adrian, I guess I didn't realize how serious it was," she said. "I called Isaiah and he gave me some more details."

"Oh yeah?" I asked, unimpressed.

"Yes," she said. "Adrian, if you ask me, you're going to need a lawyer."

My heart sank, but not unexpectedly. I nodded.

"Do you want a lawyer, Adrian?" she asked.

"I can't afford it," I told her.

"Do you know what *pro bono* means?" she asked.

"Free, right?" I asked.

"Pretty much," she said. "Look. I work for Potomac first and foremost. Taking you on as a client is a huge professional risk for me. So please keep this quiet. I don't need the university administration having a cow because I'm representing a student in a hazing case."

"You're really going to represent me?" I asked.

"Adrian, let me tell you something," she began. "I believe, based on what I know of you and what I know of this situation, that you are a good man. I also believe, based on friends in fraternities and sororities, that these investigations are usually based on flimsy evidence that will never stand up in court. We'll go over everything, but you're not going to say anything to anyone, got it?"

"Got it," I said.

"One more thing," she continued. "I don't lose."

"Somehow I didn't think that word was in your vocabulary," I said.

"Now do me a favor," she said. "I want you to smile. Everything is going to be alright. Your man is on a team that has 24 wins and only 5 losses in the regular season. Potomac is paying for you to come see your man play this week. And you get to stay in a hotel for free. You might be going through a rough patch, but damn it, aren't perks nice?"

She cracked a smile, which I returned.

"Rebecca, I think you just made my day," I said, extending my hand to hers. She clasped my hand and blushed.

Chapter 17:
March 15

The Salem University Stallions punished the Potomac University Pirates in the first half of the conference championship game. Our boys were behind by 18 points. The starting line up seemed to be plagued by foul trouble and random injuries. Hodari and Isaiah were both getting angry with their teammates and it showed. I could only imagine the conversations that must have been occurring in the locker room at the half.

The school had arranged some fun excursions for the families while the team was sequestered in practices before the games at Madison Square Garden. On the first day we visited Ellis Island and the Statue of Liberty. On the second day, we visited the Museum of Modern Art and then caught a revival of *Cats* on Broadway, during which I fell asleep. On day three, I took a break from the field trips and went exploring on my own. I visited Columbia in the hopes of running into the Betas there, but I never did find any.

Isaiah's mom had come up to the championship game. She had wanted to come up to enjoy the rest of the trip, but she just couldn't take the time off work. I knew it annoyed Isaiah that she couldn't be around as much as he wanted her to be.

My personal, Chris, had been texting me all week but I couldn't respond to him. Not only had Aaron told us to have no contact with the pledges, but Rebecca also strongly suggested against it. I knew that Christopher was from New York, but his spring break wasn't until next week.

During halftime for the game, I received one more urgent text from Chris:

SPEC, PLEASE CALL ME! I AM GOING CRAZY OVER HERE. MEET OUTSIDE OF MADISON SQUARE GARDEN AFTER GAME. OK?

I wasn't supposed to respond, but I wrote back.

OK

The game resumed with an explosive intensity from the Pirates after halftime. Hodari and Isaiah were like new men. Their game was flawless and their points just racked up. Better still was the Potomac bench. Coach K had made good use of his freshmen for a change and their thirst for minutes translated into a powerful defense.

With three seconds left, the boys had eked out a tie game. As the clock counted down, Isaiah launched the ball from half-court, hoping to end this thing once and for all without going into over time.

The shot was good and the arena exploded! Every Potomac student, alum, and family member screamed and ran past the security and to center court, crowding around the champion team. Swept up in the moment, I was right in the thick of it. Gloria was right next to me, acting a damn fool as we all were.

The pep band fired up the Potomac victory cheer, which I had come to know well, considering we were winning games.

> P-O-T-O-M-A-C
> Who's the best university?
> Potomac, Potomac, rah-rah Potomac!
> Who's a purple pirate? I'm a purple pirate!
> Goddamn right! And all the pirates say…
> Arrrrrggggggh!

Filled with emotion, the basketball players all clung to each other, some in tears. I followed the crowd, surrounding the team, slapping them on the backs and offering high-fives. When Isaiah turned around and saw me, he lit up like a kid on Christmas day. He hugged me, picked me up, and turned me around, sweat and all.

"Congratulations!" I yelled over the crowd.

"Thank you!" he shouted back.

Before either of us could say anything else, the crowd was separating us. I wasn't upset—this was his moment to shine and there were hundreds of people here celebrating this moment with him and for him.

I'd have him to myself when it mattered most anyway.

I didn't linger at the arena because I had promised I would see Christopher after the game.

He was exactly where he said he would be. To my surprise, he was wearing his daytime pledge gear: beret, pea coat, khaki slacks, and black shoes and socks. He also had the identical black book bags that his line brother had.

"Why aren't you in street clothes?" I asked. "And why are you here? It's not your spring break yet."

"Greetings, Big Brother Adrian, that ferocious and phoenix-like number four-" he began.

"Chris, stop, please..." I begged. "It's just you and me."

"Adrian, what is going on? Why have we been dropped? What did we do?" he asked.

"What did Tommy tell you?" I asked.

"He called the ace and told him to tell us that the chapter process has stopped but to keep attending the cluster workshops," he said. "But Adrian, we don't want that. We want the whole experience!"

"Okay, okay, calm down," I said. "You are buggin' out, yo!"

"I'm sorry," he said. "Is there any place we can go that's more private?"

"My hotel is a few blocks from here," I said.

"That works," he said. "Let's go."

We began walking up the street and around the corner.

"I can't believe you wore your pledge gear up here," I mused.

"I don't know about y'all, but we're still pledging," he explained. "We're studying. Making up greetings—better greetings. Trying to guess what else there is left to learn. Nobody wanted this, Adrian, I promise you."

We walked a few more blocks and we were at the hotel. I brought

Chris up to my room on the tenth floor, turned on a lamp, and threw open the curtains to reveal as much of New York as was available: another huge gray building and a glimpse of the busy street below.

"Not bad," Chris said.

"Yeah, considering it's free," I said.

"How'd you manage that?" he asked.

"You know who I'm dating, right?"

"No, who?"

"You really don't know?"

"Nope."

"I'm dating one of the basketball players from my school."

"Oh. Which one?"

"Isaiah Aiken," I said.

"Oh. He's good," Chris said. "So you really are gay, huh? Like, no bullshit, for real, for real?"

"Yup," I said. "That's how I got the room. Friends and family got to come free. I'm like… a little of both."

"Dude… for real?"

"I know, right? I didn't even know shit like this existed before this year."

"Big bro, you 'bout to have it made! Isaiah is so gonna get drafted, if not this year, then next! Tell that nigga to put a ring on it!"

I laughed at my little bro.

"I'm not even thinking about all that," I said. "I do know this: I really miss being around you and your line brothers. I'm really sorry we had to stop the process."

"But why, man? Tommy just said the chapter process was over. No why, no explanation. Then we all got these letters warning us to stay away from you guys and not engage in any underground activity."

"We got a letter from the region director telling us that the chapter is suspended pending an investigation into hazing allegations."

"Hazing? But who would say that?" Chris asked.

"You tell me, lil bro," I said. "You all were going through it. Any one of you could have said something to the frat and we'd never know who it was."

"But none of us did," Chris said adamantly. "We all sat down and talked about what we were going through every night before bed. And nobody was even close to that point."

"What about Dexter? The night that I jacked him up?"

"Man, we got into his ass about that! We told him he was dead ass wrong for disrespecting a prophyte. And he admitted he was wrong and thought it would just be funny. But after he wrote that paper, he definitely started to appreciate just how wrong he was. And he told us as soon as this was all over, he was going to apologize to you, for real."

"Wow," I said. "So you really don't think any of you complained?"

"I really, really don't think so," he said.

"Then they must be making it up," I deduced.

"They who?" Chris asked.

"The chapter advisor," I said. "Has to be. He's the only one who has been trying to catch us. He reported us because I played him after the pledge ceremony. Remember?"

"Yeah, I do," he said. "You know, at the workshops, he would always try to take us to the side and ask us if everything was okay. And we always said we were fine. Every time, all of us—we said we were fine and that nothing was wrong."

"But he came after us anyway," I said. "Yo, Chris, thank you. You helped me put the pieces together."

"You're welcome, big bro," he said. "So when can we get back online?"

"I don't know, man, it's not my call. I'll talk to the bros. But there's some other things you need to know."

"What?"

"All the shit you're doing, some of it is legitimate. Like the stuff you gotta memorize? That's for your benefit. The lessons, the oral traditions. We want you to know that. And yeah, you all take wood, just like we did. But why? Why really?"

"The four elements—the wood is the earth, the knowledge is air, the sweat and tears are water, and the pain is the fire," Chris explained, as it had been explained to us and the generations before us.

"In your heart, do you believe that?" I asked.

"It's what you taught us," he said.

"But do you believe it?" I asked. "Do you believe in fables about why we hit you, or do you believe in the principles of Beta Chi Phi?"

"I... I guess I believe both," he said.

"Think about why that's problematic, lil bro," I said. "I don't have all the answers, but we gotta start thinking harder about the questions."

He nodded.

"I can dig it," he said. "I just want to be done, though. You know? I want to just get past all this so I can be on the other side."

"I feel you," I said. "You will be."

My phone went off, alerting me of a text message.

VICTORY DINNER IN THE BALLROOM. BE MY DATE. 8PM. LOVE YOU

I smiled.

"Your man?" Chris asked.

"Mmm-hmm," I said.

"I'm telling you man, make him put a ring on it so you can be livin' that high life!"

"Crazy! I ain't thinking about all that. I'm just enjoying the ride."

"That's what he said."

I slugged him in the arm.

"See, all that hazing right there..."

"Man... thank you for tracking me down. I'm glad we talked."

"Me too, big bro."

"But you never told me. Why are you up here? You know Beta wasn't about to give you no spring break."

"My line decided that we were going to be put back on, no matter what," he explained. "And they told me I needed to find you. I guess everybody felt we had a good relationship. And truth be told, I just plain wanted to see you. We heard you'd be up here. We used some of the pledge treasury to get me a bus ticket up here. And I'm gonna head back down in the morning."

"You wanna crash here for the night?" I offered.

"Nah, going to my girl's place down at Wagner College. In fact, I need to head down there now. If my mom knew I was in the city and didn't see her, she'd kill me."

"I'd kill you too, man—don't do moms like that. At least go see her in the morning."

"I'll do that, then," he said. "Bro… thanks for everything, for real."

"No doubt," I said, giving him a big hug. "Be safe."

He let himself out of my room. I threw myself down on the bed while my mind whirled with different thoughts, ideas, and emotions.

I needed to call my chapter bros and tell them what I could piece together. I needed to tell Tommy and Aaron that everything was going to be okay.

More importantly, I needed to call my lawyer and tell her all that I knew. I had an interview with the region director to get ready for and she would be preparing me on how to respond.

"*Potomac Universitas—pro mens, somes, quod animus.* This is the motto of our dear university. Tonight, we celebrate the conference victory of our men's basketball team and salute them as they begin the NCAA tournament. Straight to the top, men! Cheers!"

The president of the university toasted the team and we raised our glasses of champagne along with him.

The banquet was a sumptuous meal—shrimp and lobster bisque, baby spinach salad, and a combination entrée of filet mignon and sea bass with asparagus and carrots on the side. Desert was a crazy delicious tiramisu.

At the head table sat the university president, the head coach, and the co-captains of the basketball team. The rest of the players sat at their own table while about three dozen family members, friends, and important alumni of Potomac filled the rest of the tables.

Rebecca sat with me at a table toward the back of the ballroom.

"They look great, don't they?" she asked. The team really did look awesome. Just hours ago, they were sweaty, angry men thirsty for a victory. Right now, they were clean-cut young men in suits. And in the coming days and weeks, they'd be back to the thirsty athletes they were before. Potomac intended to take this thing all the way.

"They do," I replied. I noticed another familiar face toward the front, near the table of honor—Renard Charles.

"Mr. Charles is here," I said.

"The Charles family have all been major supporters for years," Rebecca said.

"What's up with that?" I asked.

"I'll tell you when you get older," she quipped.

After the dessert course, the players all got up to mingle with their guests. It was a well-choreographed ballet. They fanned out into the crowd and crisscrossed the room, meeting each guest two at a time. Rebecca never once left her chair, though her eyes followed the team even as she chatted with me.

She had trained them well indeed. Separate them, make the fans believe they were untouchable for the majority of the meal, then send them out into the crowd by twos. Overwhelm the crowd while graciously saying thanks for their support. Then quietly join the families so the boosters could see that above all else, family was most important.

Rebecca earned her pay, that's for damn sure. Every rich alumnus in that room was in awe of these well-spoken, courteous black men.

Hodari and Isaiah were a team, of course—the gregarious one and the quiet one. Hodari was a hand-on-the-shoulder talker, while Isaiah stood with his hands clasped in front of him, bending slightly at the waist.

"Why do you do this, Rebecca?" I asked.

"Do what?" she asked back. "This job?"

"Yeah," I said. "You've got a law degree. Where's the law in this?"

She smiled.

"This is the law, Adrian. It's the law of the land. This school has specific rules of order. If we can maintain order in this basketball program, them Potomac can do what it needs to do as a university. In case you didn't know, Potomac rises and falls based on basketball. If it weren't for Coach Kalinowski, Potomac would be a third rate Catholic school living in Georgetown's shadow. Now look at it."

"But don't you miss the idea of being in a court room?" I asked.

"If I do my job well in this room, then Potomac doesn't have to end up in a court room. Listen," she whispered. "Twenty years ago, Coach Kalinowski almost ruined Potomac because he couldn't control his players. It was all over the news. His boys fraternizing with Victor Charles openly at clubs, Victor buying the players gold chains and rings. It was a public relations nightmare. And when Victor went to jail—oh boy."

"So they brought in consultants like you to make the school look better?" I asked while she sipped her wine.

"Bingo. I'm only the third one. But I'm itching to do more. All this... this is babysitting. I can't wait to talk some more about your situation with these asshole Betas of yours. I think we have a strategy that will leave you on top, but you've got to trust me."

"If you can keep these guys out of the news, then I trust you."

"Good," she smiled. "We can do this."

Gloria finished hugging her son and posing for pictures with the university photographer and walked over to Rebecca and I.

"I gotta get back on the road, y'all!" she announced. "Gotta get to work in the morning."

"Gloria, won't you stay the night and take a morning train back?" Rebecca asked. "I feel bad that you can't spend more time with the rest of us."

"Chile, that work on my desk ain't gonna do itself. It ain't too late. Adrian, good to see you baby!" She hugged me tight.

"Miss Rebecca, good to see you, too," she said. Rebecca gave her a hug and a kiss on the cheek.

"You take care, Ms. Aiken," she said. As Gloria walked out, she caught Isaiah's eye one more time. She waved at him, beaming with all the pride due to him. He smiled and mouthed the words "love you" while wrapping up his conversation with Coach K.

A few more moments passed and Isaiah walked to us.

"Why didn't you come over, I could have introduced you to some people?" he asked.

"Rebecca briefed me," I said. "I know the game. This is your show."

"Yeah, you right," he said. He looked like a big kid tonight, apple-cheeked and still giddy from the win. His hands were in his pockets. He looked like he wanted to say something, but couldn't.

The university photographer quickly walked over to us and took our picture. It must have been a lovely candid shot, with Isaiah and I looking at each other and longing to touch.

"No," Rebecca said to the photographer. "Delete it."

"What?" he asked. "Look at this, one of my best shots of the night. Look at the emotion."

"Delete it," she said without looking. Immediately, he complied, but not without giving Rebecca a contemptuous look. I was disappointed, but I understood. This was about his future. It wasn't personal.

"Sunday morning, meet me for brunch on U Street," Rebecca said. "Strategy. Got it?"

"Got it," I said. "Have a good night, Rebecca."

"You too," she said. Looking up at Isaiah, she added "Be safe."

The room was thinning out, yet the key players remained.

"I can't wait to get out of here," he said, attempting to loosen up his tie.

"Wait, here comes Renard," I said.

The older, chocolate brown skinned man sauntered over to us. His short hair had only a hint of gray at the temples. He wore a smart charcoal gray suit with a purple handkerchief and tie. He was sharp.

"Adrian, right?" he asked.

"Yes, Mr. Charles, I'm surprised you remember me," I said, extending my hand to him. He shook it firmly.

"I couldn't forget you," he said. "I'm glad you like my clubs—all of them. Never thought I'd see the day that a Pirate and his... friend would frequent my 'other' club, if you will."

Isaiah blushed and looked down.

"We enjoy the music," I said quickly. "Maybe my fraternity can borrow the DJ for a party we're having later this spring."

Renard winked. "I'm sure something can be worked out. Isaiah?"

"Yes, sir?" he replied.

"Keep him," Renard instructed. "He won't let you down."

Isaiah grinned and nodded as Renard walked away.

"Dude, did Renard totally just clock us?" I asked.

"Man, I feel like Renard knew the deal since New Years," he said. "I can't figure that dude out. His family is sketchy, but he's the nicest dude you'll ever meet, with all kinds of legitimate businesses and philanthropy and shit."

"You think he's family?" I asked.

"I'm thinking so, but I don't know. This whole world is so crazy."

"But you're sitting on top of it," I said. "I'm proud of you."

"Thank you, Adrian," he said, still yearning to reach out to me as I was to him. We looked around and still saw alumni and family members mulling about. In the far corner, Isaiah noticed Hodari talking to a young lady. When they caught eyes, Hodari gave what I thought was the peace sign with his fingers.

"Can we go to your room?" he asked. "That nigga gave me the 'do not disturb cuz I'm finna fuck' sign."

"Of course you can come to my room," I said. "I thought you'd never ask."

We walked to the elevator of our hotel and pushed the button. As we waited, I silently prayed that we'd have the elevator to ourselves. I hadn't even held my man's hand for a week, much less had any alone time with him.

The elevator opened and it was empty. We stepped inside and nobody joined us. We were alone.

I grasped his hand in mine and looked up at the ceiling. I didn't hug him, I didn't look at him. I just held his hand.

He didn't let go when the doors opened. We walked hand in hand down the hallway to my room.

I slid the card in the slot and the door unlocked. I grabbed the handle and gently pushed the door open. As reached for the light, Isaiah stopped me.

"Don't," he said. The door closed behind him and the room turned pitch black.

He reached out for me and touched my shoulders. Slowly and carefully, he pushed me against the wall. I felt him move closer to me. He pressed the entire length of his body against mine. I could feel his belt buckle press against my torso.

In the darkness, every sound was an exclamation point. Our suit jackets swished as we peeled them off and threw them to the floor. He loosened my tie, the silk swoosh against the cotton sounding much like bodies against bed sheets—precisely where we would end up in a few moments.

Our hands crossed each other as we simultaneously fiddled with each other's belt buckles. Mine came off first and my pants slid down to my ankles. I stepped out of my shoes and pants in one smooth motion. Moments later, Isaiah did the same, his belt buckle hitting the floor with a thud.

He kissed me and the smack of lips against lips pierced the dark room like a dart. One, two, three… infinity. His hands gently peeled my shirt away from me one button at a time. His hands explored every inch of my chest, lightly brushing my nipples and my stomach.

Even in the dark, I knew every inch of his body. My mouth quickly found his chest and I sucked each nipple until he moaned. My hands found the waistband of his boxer-briefs and I pulled them down to the floor.

We stood there naked in the dark. His light skin practically glowed as my eyes adjusted in the dark. My brown skin on top of his, caressing him as we stood, was a ghostly contrast.

He slid his arms around me and down my sides. Nearly kneeling now, he picked me off the ground and cradled my naked body as though he were carrying me over the threshold.

He gently laid me on the bed and kissed me.

Like a champion.

Chapter 18:
March 18

Sigma Chapter was scheduled to meet with the investigation team at 7:00 p.m. at the Embassy Suites in Chevy Chase, on the DC and Maryland line. Scheduled to be present were the region director, John Carver; chapter advisor Michael Spector; the grad chapter president Kwame Brooks; and the assistant to the region director, Calvin Cates.

We were ready for the fight of our lives. All eight members of the chapter sat in the lobby of the hotel, just outside of the salon in which we'd be interviewed. The benches on which we sat were soft but backless, so our slouching made us appear to be deeper in thought that we actually were. In reality, we tried to clear our minds and focus on nothingness—much like that plain white room that I daydreamed about a few days prior.

We were sharp in our crisp shirts, neckties and fraternity pins. Nervous as hell, but we looked good.

"Y'all good?" Aaron asked us. We all nodded.

"Listen… Sigma chapter stands *united*," Tommy emphasized. "Adrian gave us good advice, yo. Just stick to the script."

"It will work," Calen added. "Rebecca said all we gotta do is show up, shut up, and listen. Don't admit to shit."

We sat in silence for ten more minutes, waiting for one of the investigating brothers to emerge from the conference room. Calvin Cates, a young brother fresh out of undergrad at Johns Hopkins, finally emerged.

"We're going in randomly, brothers," he said sympathetically. "Brother Adrian Collins?"

"That's me," I responded.

"You're first," he said, holding the door open for me. I sighed but I stood up confidently, straightened out my tie, and entered the room.

Brother Region Director, John Carver, sat in the middle of a medium length table, flanked by the insipid chapter advisor Brother Spector and the stocky grad chapter president, Kwame Brooks. Each had a notepad and paper in front of them, as well as three identical manila folders. Not exactly thick with papers, I still wondered what was in them.

"Hello, brothers," I said.

"Hello Brother Collins," Brother Carver said. He was an older man, about my dad's age, with big glasses, dark skin, and coarse salt and pepper hair.

"Please have a seat in this chair in front of you," he said.

I sat down and placed my hands in my lap. Brother Cates sat in a chair next to the door.

"Brother Collins, do you know why you're here today?" he asked.

"A letter was sent to my chapter suspending us from all activities and contact with our pledges, pending an investigation of hazing allegations," I said mechanically.

"That's correct," Brother Carver said. "So what do you specifically know about the allegation?"

I was sure to sit up straight in my chair.

"I am aware that your letter states there is a hazing allegation. I'm here to learn more information about it."

Brother Spector was already annoyed.

"Let's try this again," Brother Carver said. "We want to know why someone would make a hazing allegation against Sigma chapter."

"Brother Carver, with all due respect, the best person to ask would be whoever made the allegation. I don't know what was said to you or who said it. I am here to learn more," I said.

Brother Carver looked over his glasses at me then looked at the brothers to his right and left.

"Adrian, come on, work with us," Carver said. "Your father helped to build this fraternity."

"My father is not part of Sigma chapter and he is not a member of this investigation process. I'd appreciate it if he was kept out of this discussion. I am here to learn more about the specifics of the allegations against my chapter. Once I learn more about them, there is a chance that I can provide more insight or an explanation, but right now, you're telling me nothing."

"Wait a minute," Brother Spector said. "Why are you acting like you're doing us a favor? Don't you understand that your chapter has been suspended? It's on you to provide information about the mess that your chapter engages in so you can save your chapter—it's not on us to save you."

"Brother Spector, with all due respect, if there is an allegation, then it's your duty to investigate it. I am here waiting patiently to hear what the specific allegations are against my chapter. If you tell me what the allegations are, I might be able to help your investigation. So brothers... what has Sigma chapter been accused of?"

"Hazing, obviously," Brother Spector said.

"What are the specific incidents?" I asked. "And when did they occur?"

"Get this asshole out of here," Spector said, gesturing to Brother Cates.

"Brother Spector, please," Brother Carver said. "Adrian, we are giving Sigma chapter the chance to come clean, to walk away from this with a short suspension—maybe even 'time served' so to speak. You've missed two weeks of the process, don't you want to actually be there to initiate your pledges when they're done?"

"I would love to help you, but I am not answering any questions until you tell me the specific charges against my chapter, including the incidents themselves and their dates and times."

"Adrian, does Sigma Chapter pledge?" the previously silent Brother Brooks asked.

"Sigma Chapter participates in the standard membership selection and education program," I answered. "If Beta still calls that 'pledging' then yes, we participate in it."

"Do you do anything outside of that process?" Brother Carver asked.

"Don't answer that!" a booming female voice said. Rebecca had entered the conference room, startling Brother Cates who was to be guarding the door.

"And who the hell are you?" Brother Carver exclaimed, standing up at his seat.

"My name is Rebecca J. Templeton, and I am counsel for Mr. Adrian Collins." she said. I turned around to see my attorney in a smart black suit, stiletto heels, pearls, and her raging red hair pulled back into a severe bun. Her black glasses couldn't hide the intensity in her eyes.

"Young lady, this is a private fraternity meeting," Brother Brooks said.

"Actually, it looks like an interrogation where you planned on asking my client to violate his Fifth Amendment rights."

"What?" Spector said. "Get out of here."

"I won't," she said plainly. "But what I will do is ask you once and for all what the allegations against my client are."

"Ma'am, this is fraternity business," Brother Brooks asserted.

"Do you know what hazing is, sir?" she asked.

"Of course," Brother Brooks said.

"Well then, you freely admit that this meeting is held with the intention to cause mental discomfort, harassment, and ridicule. You have not once told my client what you are accusing him of, instead trying to use mind games to violate his Fifth Amendment rights. You have suspended him, separating him and his chapter brothers from the rest of the fraternity, causing social isolation. And while they are already members, you are forcing them to endure this harassment in order to maintain their membership. That, gentlemen, is textbook hazing."

"Ms. Templeton, I am the region director, John Carver. This is not hazing, this is an investigation. We don't want any trouble."

"Oh, you're John Carver," she said, feigning surprise. "I was hoping I could meet you." She turned around to face Brother Cates.

"Excuse me, can I please have a chair?" she asked him.

Cates looked for the okay in the face of Brother Carver, who nodded slightly and took his seat. Brother Cates quickly grabbed one of the chairs lined up against the wall and sat it next to me.

"Mr. Carver, can you please tell my client what the allegations against him are?" she asked, simultaneously opening her briefcase and pulling out an accordion folder.

Brother Carver sighed and began.

"Ms. Templeton, Brother Collins, we received an anonymous email stating that on the very late evening of Thursday, February 15, a group of Betas and pledges got into a fight with members of another fraternity in the city."

Oh my God, I thought. They heard about that altercation we had with the Kappas. How the hell did that happen?

"Who were the members and pledges named in the allegation?" Rebecca asked.

"Adrian Collins and Aaron Todd were the only brothers mentioned. The pledges were Orlando Ford, Angel Rosario, and Christopher White."

"So... this doesn't sound like hazing to me," Rebecca said. "It sounds like a fight between two rival fraternities."

"Because there were pledges there, we had to investigate it as a potentially improper pledging situation," Brother Spector said.

"Gentlemen, this is absurd," Rebecca said. "I shudder to think how much money Beta has lost in the investigation of this fight. A conference room for you, Mr. Carver? A plane ticket from your hometown of... Boston, is it? Another room for Mr. Cates? Food? Ground transportation?"

"Excuse me?" Brother Carver said.

"I'll get back to that in a moment," she said. "Adrian, you've now heard the one and only allegation against the chapter. Do you have anything you'd like to say to your brothers? You can do that now."

I inhaled deeply and exhaled. It was now or never. I could only guess what Rebecca thought I should do, but I knew that above all else, she trusted me to do the right thing.

"Yes, I was involved in a scuffle with several Kappas in Adams Morgan on the night in question," I began. "I was at a very late dinner with the other brothers you mentioned and the Kappas had assembled around Aaron's car. We were trying to get back to campus, but the dudes wouldn't move. One thing led to another and we were scuffling. It was over in less than 30 seconds. Yes, I should have found a way to walk away from the fight, and I apologize for not doing that. But I have to say that I wasn't hurt, nobody I was with was hurt, and none of the Kappas looked hurt, either. It was truly just a scuffle... some pushing and shoving. That's it."

"Are you taking sole responsibility for this situation?" Spector asked.

"Yes," I said without hesitation.

"So this means Sigma Chapter as a whole is off suspension, correct?" Rebecca asked, not missing a beat.

"Ms. Templeton, not that it's any of your business, but Sigma chapter has long been suspected of bending and breaking the rules of this fraternity," Spector said.

"But because you had no proof, you intended on bending and breaking the rules yourself in order to have my client—or any of these other fine young gentlemen—incriminate themselves."

"Who the hell are you, Superwoman?" Spector asked.

"Please be quiet," Brother Carver hissed at Spector.

"I'm not Superwoman," Rebecca said.

"So what do you want?" Brother Carver asked. "Brother Collins has confessed to the fight with the Kappas and he knows how damaging that can be to our reputation as a fraternity. He faces a suspension from the fraternity, at least until his graduation."

Rebecca smiled.

"I don't believe that's going to happen," Rebecca asked.

"What makes you so sure?" Brother Carver said.

"Mr. Carver, as I said before, I was looking forward to meeting you. See, when Adrian divulged his problems to me, I did my best to research every aspect of this fraternity so I could provide him the best possible defense. And what I uncovered was pretty astonishing," she said. She pulled a stack of papers out of her accordion file.

"Let's see, you were initiated into Beta about 20 years ago down at Florida State—Xi Chapter, is it? That's a very respectable length of service. I'm not Greek, so I can't say I always know how these things go. But Xi Chapter has been inactive for the past ten years... seems as though the state director for Florida turned his own chapter in for hazing. Didn't make you very popular down there, did it, Mr. Carver?"

He sat silently.

"You've been region director for the past six years—three terms! Might even be a record in the fraternity. And word on the street is that you plan on running for national vice president soon. On the other hand, since you've been RD, at least one chapter per year gets suspended under your watch. Beta Beta at Lincoln... Alpha Theta at St. John's... Eta Chapter at Cornell. Makes you wonder if you're really a friend to the collegiate chapters at all."

He continued his silence.

"What's most interesting, in my opinion at least, is not the squashing of the collegiate chapter voice, but the benefits you receive in your position. The free trips in the name of the fraternity. Nice lodging. More than adequate transportation. It's a nice life, isn't it? But what about your credit card expenses from four years ago, Mr. Carver?"

He slowly closed his eyes.

"Before any one in Sigma Chapter was even in college, you used the Eastern Region credit card to make personal purchases. We're talking a trip to Las Vegas... leather jackets... jewelry. You were living the high life on the eastern region's money, weren't you? Sure, you were put on a repayment plan and allowed to keep your position—a pretty stupid decision to keep a thief in office, if you ask me, but hey, I'm not the fraternity's general counsel. But it's just not a good look for a man with this sort of controversy to seek such a high office in the fraternity. Tell me, Mr. Carver, do you really think you can win an election nationally if the entire Florida district still hates you and you silence the voices of the undergraduates in the eastern region?"

"What... the hell... do you want?" Brother Carver fumed.

"It's not what I want," Rebecca said. "It's what will happen."

"Then say it, dammit," Carver said.

"My client will take responsibility for the scuffle and will agree to nothing stronger than probation. No one else in the chapter will be disciplined behind these charges."

"Is that it?" he asked.

"No. The other thing that will happen is that you will leave Sigma Chapter alone."

"You can't come in here and threaten us!" Spector exploded.

"Mr. Carver, I'm not asking you to ignore your duties as a region director," Rebecca said, ignoring Spector. "What I am asking you to do is be mindful that the eight members of Sigma chapter and their nine pledges are among the best and brightest in this entire fraternity. If this chapter is suspended, you can guarantee it will be the nail in the coffin of your political future in the fraternity. But if you let them be, then you can be assured that everything said today will remain in this room. All I'm asking for you to do is end the harassment and hazing of my clients and control your graduate advisor. That's all."

"Are you going to let her talk to you like that?" Spector growled at Carver.

"Shut up, Michael," he shot back. He closed his eyes and held his hand against his eyelids, sitting still for a full minute.

"Brother Cates," he said softly.

"Yes, sir?" he asked.

"Please send in the rest of the chapter."

Cates rose quickly, opened the door and beckoned that the chapter come in. They quickly entered and made a semi-circle around Rebecca and I. She rose, allowing Aaron the chance to sit. He did and Rebecca retreated to a corner.

"Brothers," Carver began slowly and quietly. "I regret that so much of your personal time has been spent defending yourselves against allegations for which you had no details. So that you all know, Sigma chapter was reported for an altercation that several of you had with Kappas in Adams Morgan in February."

Aaron's eyes opened wide for a split second, then he remembered himself and regained his composure.

"You know that Beta Chi Phi Fraternity, Incorporated, frowns upon any public displays of disunity, aggression, or any other behavior not becoming a gentleman. We were saddened to learn today that Brother Adrian Collins was involved in this fight."

I could sense the brothers gazing down at me but paying attention to the region director.

"Today, Brother Collins has accepted full responsibility for his actions and has accepted that he will be the sole brother from Sigma chapter punished for this offense to our creed."

Several brothers scoffed at the notion of me being the sole holder of any blame.

"Because of Brother Collins' exceptional loyalty to Beta Chi Phi and a promise to uphold the principles of the fraternity, I have decided that these few weeks of isolation from the rest of the fraternity and your pledges is punishment enough. From this point forward, Brother Collins and the rest of Sigma chapter are returned to good standing in Beta Chi Phi. You may resume normal chapter operations, participate in the education program, and function fully as members of the fraternity."

We all breathed sighs of relief. Several brothers patted me on the back and shoulders.

"You're all dismissed," he said. "I'll see you at the national convention this summer."

Brothers gripped each other and began leaving the room happy, though Brother Spector snatched his belongings and stormed out the room. My chapter began to leave.

"Ms. Templeton, Brother Collins, a moment please?" Brother Carver asked. We rejoined him at the table, where Brother Brooks also remained with a smirk on his face.

"In all my years as a brother of this fraternity, I've never had a brother bring a lawyer with him," he said. "I can't be mad, Adrian—you played the game and you won. I'd certainly rather have you as an ally than as an enemy. But promise me two things."

"What's that, Brother Carver?"

"You keep the promise your lawyer made—nothing you heard in this room gets out to anybody, you understand me? You do that, and Sigma Chapter is as good as gold. But if you run your mouth, I will come for your chapter so hard…"

"I intend to honor our agreement," I said.

"Good," he said. "Secondly… and more importantly… if you ever bring this woman to another Beta meeting, I won't be nearly as kind as I have been today. I don't want to see her ever again in my life, you got that?"

"Don't worry, Mr. Carver," she said. "It is not my intention to have to deal with you ever again. I'm quite certain you'll leave this chapter be."

"Good night, Ms. Templeton," he said. "Good night, Brother Collins."

He and Brother Cates departed, leaving just me, Rebecca, and Brother Brooks.

"Well played," he said with a smile. "It's nice to know that the younger generation knows what's up with that scumbag."

"Why do you keep re-electing him?" I asked sincerely.

"Because brothers are stupid," he said. "They vote for the best posters and the hippest campaign slogans. You know, we used to be a real, grassroots nonprofit organization."

"What happened?" I asked.

"The founders pledged their first line. All went downhill from there," he said with a smile. "You take care, brother. Keep fighting the good fight."

He gave me the fraternal grip, nodded at Rebecca, then walked away. When the room was empty and the door closed, I finally let out a squeal of delight.

"Oh my God, Rebecca you were fucking awesome in there! How the hell did you get all that dirt on Brother Carver? I had no idea he was such a sleaze ball!"

She smirked.

"I'm not just a lawyer, Adrian. I make sure an entire basketball program looks good so that the university looks good. And sometimes, in order to make something look good, you've got to uncover just how ugly it is. In Carver's case, it wasn't too hard. People had posted gossip about him on blogs and message boards. I followed the leads... then I followed the money. You want to get somebody good? Follow the money."

"You found all this out on the internet?" I asked.

"Most of it," she said. "But some things I had to call in some favors about. It's probably better that you just don't know, okay?"

"I got you. And I trust you. Thank you so much Rebecca."

I hugged her. What she did for me on that day was among the most selfless things anyone had ever done for me. She placed a lot on the line just to help my chapter and risked great personal and professional embarrassment if Brother Carver hadn't caved to her demands. In reality, she had no right to waltz into our meeting and start spitting legal jargon and mumbo jumbo—but she counted on my fraternity brothers not knowing the difference.

In this case, the gamble paid off. She gave me a coronary in the process, but I could see that she was a damn good litigator.

"Adrian, there's something else you should know," she said as we walked out of the room.

"What's that?" I said. The rest of the chapter was just outside the room, waiting for me.

"Gather around me, guys," she said while she took a seat on a bench. Some of us sat next to her while others sat on the floor below her.

"I'm no sorority girl," she began. "But you have to know that these men would not have attempted to suspend you guys on a hazing charge if they didn't believe they could trip you up and get you to confess. And that leads me to suspect that something is indeed going on. I don't want to know what it is, if anything. But if you're hazing your pledges, you have absolutely got to stop. There won't be a second chance—because you guys were victorious this time, the next time they are going to go for the jugular. And you know what, after today I wouldn't blame them. For the love of God, keep your noses clean."

We remained silent and looked down. She was right. Absolutely right. Even though we won this battle, we were still dead-ass wrong in what we were doing. We couldn't keep living from hazing allegation to hazing allegation. We had to do better—and fast.

Chapter 19:
March 20

"Please bring the pledges in," Tommy instructed me. I opened the door to Ciprian's house and beckoned the pledges in. The shades were drawn and a single candle was lit in the center of the room. It was a thick, white candle that you had to grip with both hands.

"Pledges, have a seat wherever you like," Tommy instructed. Ciprian had dragged his dining room chairs into the living room, ensuring that all eight members of the chapter and our nine pledges had a place to sit if they wanted. No leaning on walls, no sitting on coffee tables. Tonight, we were equals.

The pledges entered our circle and saw that only two chairs were side by side and every pledge would have to sit next to a brother. Momentarily confused, they took seats. Christopher—my personal— sat next to my left. My housemate Orlando sat to my right, next to his personal Aaron. Once all the pledges were seated, Tommy took the candle from the center of the room and took it to his chair.

Once the candle was moved, all we could see in the room was the person holding it. The rest of us sat in the dark, not knowing who was sitting where, save the men we saw sitting next to us.

"Brothers... both brothers who are initiates and brothers who are still pledges... this is something that we've never done before. This meeting is just for us to talk everything out. We've gone through a lot in these past few weeks, but we've made it through. And I'm proud of all of you for still being here. But we've all got a lot on our minds and a lot to say. So at this meeting we're all equals. We sit on the same level, nobody rising above the other, neither brother nor chapter officer. I will pass the candle to my right. If you have something to say, you can speak when you get the candle. If you don't, pass it along. But don't be afraid to speak. Whatever we say stays in this room. We are all equals."

Tommy passed the candle to Rick Brown, the silent and trusted number five of the pledges, who passed it to his spesh—my ace—Peter Grant. Peter paused with the candle and then passed it to his number

Mark Ferguson. Mark said nothing and passed the candle to his spesh, Ciprian. Ciprian put the candle on the floor in front of him.

"I pledged this fraternity because I wanted to be my own man," he began in his slow southern drawl. "If I had pledged Alpha, I would have been a third generation legacy. But I didn't pledge Alpha. I pledged Beta. I knew that I'd never hear the end of it from my father. And I know even though he still loves me, he's disappointed I didn't go that way.

"I say that to let you all know that I choose to be here. I *choose* to be here. I know that I wasn't well-liked by my prophytes. Hell, I wasn't even wanted—they made that clear every step of my process. I worked hard every week to prove myself to the brothers. And after I crossed, I never missed a meeting. I love this fraternity, but sometimes I feel like I'll never be treated the same as everybody else, even though I went through the same process. I feel like because of the loopholes in the process, I was allowed to have a chance that the brothers never really gave me. But still, I choose to be here."

He passed his candle to Dexter Rodgers, who immediately passed his candle to his spesh, my line brother Edward Jones. He held the candle in his hand while he spoke.

"I feel the same way as Ciprian sometimes," he said.

He paused, then passed the candle to Joshua Robinson, the slim Potomac track star, who passed it to his personal, Calen. Calen said nothing and passed the candle to my little brother, Christopher. He placed the candle in front of him.

"I guess I have to be the first pledge to speak," he said. "First, I want to say that this is hard for me, speaking as an individual and not as part of a group for the first time in weeks. I'm not a shiner, I swear.

"The weeks that we were not part of the chapter pledge process were really hard on us. We sorta missed set, in a way. I think all nine of us really like being around each other and gain strength from each other. And... I don't know... that's what I guess the process is all about, right? We endure things together and get stronger as a unit because of it.

"The hardest part wasn't really the absence of the process—sure, we were scared that we'd be paper and not accepted by the rest of the chapter. But what really hurt worse was the complete lack of contact and communication. Do you all know how badly it hurt us that you all wouldn't even speak to us when we walked past you on campus? That's the kind of shit that we would go home and be depressed about.

"I still don't understand exactly what happened. I'm glad you've asked us to come back, but I'd still appreciate some answers."

He picked up the candle and handed it to me. I saw that when I held the candle, the glow from the flame obscured my vision and I couldn't see the faces of the people around me. This candle-pass not only illuminated the speaker, but hid his audience. It was almost as if you were speaking to yourself.

"I can't speak for the rest of the chapter, but I know that I was just as hurt not talking to you guys, either. I missed the greetings and being able to whisper 'stay strong' to you when you were on your way to class. I was so proud of all of you guys.

"So it really hurt when we found out we couldn't have any contact with you. That wasn't our decision. That came straight from the region director. But on top of that, there was no way for us to be sure that one of you hadn't dropped dime on the chapter. We didn't want to believe it, but there wasn't anything we could do to find out that wouldn't put us all at risk. We had to make the decision which protected the chapter in the long run. I'm really sorry that we couldn't handle it any better than that."

I had more to say, but I wasn't ready to share it yet. I passed the candle to my housemate Orlando.

"I don't have much to say," he said. "I guess I was upset that you guys thought one of us could have snitched on the chapter. I mean, some of you live with us outside of this process. You know us. You know we're down for the get down. Fuck the process, I thought we were friends. And at the end of the day, y'all never did trust us. That sucks."

He gave the candle to our President, Aaron.

"This activity is not supposed to be a conversation, but I'm going to respond to what you said. You're right; we didn't trust you and we should have. You already know why we couldn't talk to you. We wish it hadn't been that way, but it was. All nine of you need to know that I would trust you with my life. I know you wouldn't betray me or the chapter, and I hope you know I wouldn't betray you.

"Ciprian and Ed's feelings are valid, too. The way our selection process works is inevitably going to breed contempt for people who gain admittance fair and square but might not know the members of the chapter very well. It sucks and I don't know how to change it. But I do know how to change me. For anybody in this room I may have been cold or aloof to during this process or the last—I'm sorry."

Aaron passed his candle to Angel, his other little brother.

"Since we're talking freely, I definitely have some things I need to get off my chest, too," he began. "We're talking circles around this big ass elephant in the room but I need to say it: I resent people who didn't work as hard for this as I did. I love and respect all of you, but it doesn't seem fair that all I had to do was have good grades and interview well. Five of us on this pledge line showed up to events, got to know the brothers, and really understood the principles before we even submitted. Then at the last minute, we got four more. What kind of sense does that make? Why do they get to pledge now? Why couldn't they wait until the fall? And it's hard for me to even say this because I really do like the four guys I'm talking about, but it's really fucking up our unity. And I see that this isn't new to Sigma chapter, either. So what the fuck are we doing to do to make things better now and in the future?"

He passed his candle to his number three, Emeka Mbanefo, who quietly placed it in front of him.

"Like Big Brother Ciprian, I was not one of the chosen," he began. "I appreciate how some of the other big brothers would reach out and try to get to know me anyway, but some of you never bothered. Even when I reach out to you with open arms, your arms are folded. You look at me with contempt.

"I make no excuse for the mistakes I made in pursuing membership. I didn't know I could come to service projects. I didn't know I should be going to programs. Maybe my mistake was in being too discreet. But I can't apologize for making it. I can't apologize for a selection process that you're not happy with."

He passed the candle to his big brother, Mohammed.

"Adrian probably knows me best out of everyone in this room, so nothing I say tonight will be a big surprise to him. I've always felt like an outsider in Sigma Chapter, even though I was one of the 'chosen' so to speak. I came to events, did what I had to do, got picked, pledged hard, and crossed. But I still feel like an outsider. Sometimes I chalk that up to being foreign to you. But recently I began to think maybe it's not because I'm foreign, but because I fundamentally don't believe in the pledge process.

"There's no way to say it other than this: hitting people doesn't make better brothers. I will not use my hands on any of you except to lift you up, to grip you, and to embrace you as my brother."

Mo passed the candle to pledge Alex who briefly held it.

"I say fuck all the talking, I want to pledge again." He passed the candle to Tommy, completing the circle.

"I don't know how I would feel if we suddenly stopped giving wood to pledges," he admitted. "We have years and years of alumni who wouldn't be feeling that. And do we really want to hear them tell us how wack we are for stopping? I'm afraid of that day. I don't want to alienate them. We need them."

He passed the candle to Rick, who opted to remain silent a second time. He passed the candle to Peter.

"I'm still a neo, at least for another few weeks, but I'm graduating at the end of the semester," he started. "Look, you all know I'm practically engaged to my girl and we both live Christ-centered lives. Or at least we try to. There's a lot about Beta that I love and a lot that I am trying to understand. I will never understand why we think physically harming another man is okay. It's not. We need to stop. Everything else we can work on over time. But when I graduate, I will not be one of those alumni who complain because we stopped brutalizing people."

Peter passed the candle to Mark, who once again declined to speak. He passed it to Ciprian, who passed it to Dexter.

"I think I should take this time to publicly apologize," he began in his Jamaican lilt. "Adrian, I really was disrespectful to you, and I really had some nerve, especially because I'm trying to be where you are. I never really thought the rumors about you were true. I just sang that song, that homophobic song, to get a reaction. Hell, I didn't even think most people understood the lyrics. But I apologize, sincerely this time, and from the bottom of my heart. I hope we can move past this and I can call you my brother one day—and mean it."

He passed his candle to Edward, who passed it to Joshua. Surprisingly, Joshua spoke.

"None of my line brothers have said anything specifically about the paddling yet, but I will," he began. "I know that I, too, was not one of the chosen ones. And I've explained why you never saw me to everybody twelve times over. I feel like I'm doing what I have to do to prove myself, and for the most part, I can take it. But real talk—all this hitting shit needs to stop. I have a future as a runner—I'm going to the Olympics. I'm claiming that. You all put my career at risk with this shit. And if the region director had interviewed me, I can't tell you that I would have protected the chapter. I'm looking out for me first. And I would expect that from anybody else in a similar situation."

He handed his candle to Calen.

"Yo, I'm blown that my spesh really said that," Calen said. "My line had it so much worse than y'all! If you can't deal with it, you can drop. Nobody is making you pledge. Get the fuck out of here with all that. Paddling won't kill you."

He passed the candle to Christopher, who gave it to me.

"Dexter… thank you for apologizing, and I accept it. I can also admit that I was wrong for how I handled it. Sometimes… I hate to say it… the fraternity can bring out the worst in us. I was never a physical person before this experience. It's crazy to me that my first response to what you did was to jack you up. I don't know what it was. The anger. The moment. The fact that I knew I could jack you up and as a pledge you couldn't do anything back—whatever it was, it was wrong of me and I'm sorry.

"You know, many of you don't know the story of how I came out to my chapter. I was dating a dude on campus when I pledged, and he was well known to my prophytes. Two of them put the pieces together and outed me at a set. They didn't talk to the other brothers, they didn't even talk to me—they told everybody that I was gay and then tried to beat me off the line. That was just about the worst thing that could have happened to me.

"It caused a lot of friction in the chapter and on my line—and I know there are people on my line who don't exactly approve of me being gay, but for better or for worse, we all accept each other. I made a promise to myself that I wouldn't become the brothers that did those things to me.

"But I see that I have broken that promise a year later. I don't know how it happened. But I apologize—to you, Dexter. To the rest of your line. To my line brothers and my prophytes. I'm sorry. I don't know what happened to me, but I became something I said I wouldn't.

"If we—as a chapter—decide to change or eliminate certain parts of the pledge program, I wouldn't mind. I think we can teach the lessons we need to in a way that doesn't put us at risk. This is our chapter and we've got to make sure it lasts for generations to come."

I passed the candle to Orlando, who spoke.

"This process changes you," he said. "I just want to be done and get to work. I want my life back. And I want the respect of everybody in this room. I can take the wood. But I also feel like taking wood is the coward's way out. Hold the standards high first instead of resorting to the paddle when we don't know our information. At least, that's what I would do if I was a brother."

He passed the candle to Aaron.

"We need to become whole again. The chapter is running on fumes now. We have a lot of talent in this room, but we're squandering away our talent by getting caught up in who was chosen and who wasn't; who is in favor of wood and who isn't. Fact is, we have to make some tough decisions if we're going to survive—Rebecca Templeton isn't going to be able to bail us out next time we get in trouble. And please believe that if we don't get our shit together, there will be a next time. Brother Spector will make sure of it."

He passed the candle to Angel.

"I just want to pledge, cross, and be a Beta."

He passed the candle to Emeka.

"That's all I want, too. I want to pledge and be able to respect myself and all of you."

He passed the candle to Mohammed.

"I want you to finish pledging and know all the information you need to keep this chapter alive."

Mohammed passed the candle to Alex.

"I want to pledge," he said.

He passed the candle to Tommy.

"I want you all to pledge and get the same respect the rest of us received."

He passed the candle to Rick, who this time, sat the candle in front of him. He rubbed his hands over his frayed cornrows and began speaking.

"You all know I'm not much for words. I hate public speaking. I panic when I think about our probate show—if we're still having one, that is. But I want everyone in this room to know a few things.

"First, I have wanted to be a Beta since I was twelve years old. The only teacher I had in middle school who gave a damn about me was a Beta. He was young, fresh out of college and determined to save young black boys in Shaker Heights. He taught English all three years I was there, and he was so successful that they just kept looping him up with the classes.

"Because of him, I knew what to expect out of the process. I knew it wouldn't be easy. So I stood there and I took it. I took the verbal shit with no problem. I knew it was a game and I could take it. And I took the physical shit, too. I knew that just because I took it didn't mean I had to be that kind of brother if I crossed.

"But now I see there is no end to it. No matter what, I'm going to do the same things that were done to me. I survived, so why not, right? It's just the way things are, right?

"I don't think so. My teacher, Mr. Nelson, taught me better than that. I know that much of what we were going through was wrong and didn't make any sense. We weren't getting to know you all like we should—hell, half the things we were learning in set were neither accurate nor universal. What's the point of learning 'Excuses' when every chapter does it differently? What's the purpose behind these challenges if they are specific to Sigma chapter? It's like I'm not even pledging Mr. Nelson's fraternity at all.

"I was going to drop the day that our process stopped. I really wasn't feeling this anymore and I would rather not be Greek at all than to be a hypocrite. I took my vows as a pledge very seriously and my duties as a man even more so. So that day, rather than make a big deal, I was going to turn in my pin and my pledge gear and get my life back.

"Then, as you know, we got dropped. And I think, for us, that's when the real pledging started. The nine of us talked every day and every night about what Beta really meant to us, and what we would do if the chapter couldn't finish pledging us. We went to our official workshops with pride. I don't know if anyone told you this, but Sigma chapter's pledges were the sharpest pledges in the cluster every week.

"If you didn't know why, you can thank Christopher White for that. He personally brought me back from the brink of dropping and promised me that things would get better, and they did. He promised us that he would hold us together, and he did. He told us he'd reach Adrian, and he did—and yeah, we all had to put money together for a bus ticket for him, but we did it. We were ready to be Betas with or without you.

"I mean no disrespect by any of this. And I stand with my line brothers when I say I want to continue and that I want to pledge. But I will not move forward if it's not a process that maintains my dignity and self-worth. That's it."

He exhaled slowly and passed the candle to Peter.

"That's my spesh!" he exclaimed. "The doors of the church are open."

He passed the candle to Mark Ferguson.

"I don't have much to say," he said. "I agree with what everybody has said on both sides. I want to finish this process, but I want the respect of the old heads. I don't know how to do that, but I am going to stick with the process until it happens."

He passed the candle to Ed, who passed it to Josh, then Calen.

It stopped with Christopher.

"I just wanted to say thank you to my line brother Rick," he said. "I just did what anybody else would do in the same situation. We start with nine, we end with nine. And we keep working hard until the chapter picks us up again. And if they don't, then hell, we'll just be the most thorough paper-ass Betas the world has ever known."

He passed the candle to me.

"Ain't nobody in my chapter gonna be paper," I said. "Believe that."

I passed the candle to Orlando, who passed it to Aaron.

"Never will Sigma chapter be paper," he echoed. "And never will Sigma chapter skate. We might have to change the game a little, but only to make Sigma chapter stronger."

He passed the candle to Angel, and it went to Emeka, Mohammed, Alex, and back to Tommy.

"The candle will continue to go around the circle until everyone has said what's on their mind that they want to say," he said. The candle went around the circle once, twice, and a third time without stopping.

"Brothers, we've got a lot to think about," he said. "But it sounds like everyone wants to move forward. This night starts a renaissance for Sigma Chapter. We are strong and will become stronger. We are wise and will be wiser. Sigma chapter stands united."

He blew the candle out.

"Brothers... pledges," Aaron said in the darkness. "Make one circle—one big circle—and sing the pledge hymn."

We felt around in the darkness for the shoulders of the person next to us. I felt Christopher on my left—he grasped my right shoulder hard and pumped it twice, letting me know he was there and everything was okay. Orlando did the same on my right, practically towering over me. We swayed to the right, then the left, and in unison began singing the pledge hymn of Beta Chi Phi:

> *...the Faith of our fathers, our brothers and sons*
> *Uplift our brotherhood until our days are done...*

Chapter 20:
March 22

I peered around the corner of the smoky room with my weapon in my hand, ready to pull the trigger should I see my target. I made sure I was below his waist level so that I could aim upward, unnoticed by my victim.

The fog was thick and only strobe lights illuminated my path through the labyrinth. Secondary lights were built into the floor to show me where it ended and the padded wall began. I hadn't seen my victim for at least five minutes now, but I was determined to shoot him square in the chest as often as I could to collect my prize.

Me and Isaiah's date night of laser tag was, of course, his suggestion. I had never played before but within five minutes, I was an old laser war veteran. The fire burned inside me and I was hungry for a "kill."

He paid for our admittance fee, and the guy who outfitted us with our weapons and chest plates told us the place would be pretty empty because it was a week night. That was fine by us.

I jogged through the maze-like pit, looking for my target, carefully turning any corner by crouching down low. Finally, I saw my victim creeping in the wrong direction.

"Hey, light skin!" I called out. He foolishly turned around, exposing his chest plate and I shot three times, quickly turning around and running away. The weapons made futuristic sounds with each pull of the trigger.

"Aww dammit, again?" he exclaimed. I heard his heavy footsteps chasing me around the corner from which I had come, this time unrelenting. I had to get to the second level of the open pit so I could have a more clear shot at him. Only one more to go before I won.

I made it to the padded stairwell and jetted to the mezzanine level. By the time I made it to the top, Isaiah was already at the bottom step. I couldn't get a good shot at him—coming up to the next level was now futile. I was a sitting duck if I couldn't get that last shot.

I ran as fast as I could to the other end of the mezzanine through the fog. Isaiah was gaining on me. Before I knew it, he was on me.

"Hold it right there," he said. I held my gun close to me and waited.

"Now we can do this the easy way or we can do it West Baltimore style. Now I suggest you gone ahead and turn around real slow, put your weapon in the air, and let me pop off these last three shots."

"Aight, you got it," I said. I raised my hands in the air and slowly turned around to face him. When I got him in my sight, I dipped low at my waist, covering my chest plate and shooting wildly at Isaiah's exposed chest.

"Aww fuck!" he said. "You got me!" His chest plate glowed a ghostly red, signifying his loss and mine turned gold as the victor.

"Good game!" I said. "This was fun!"

"Yeah, it's fun when you win," he pouted.

"Ha! Don't be a sore loser—at least you've got basketball!" I said.

He smiled and grabbed me by the waist as we walked out of the smoky pit.

We turned in our equipment and meandered out of the laser tag facility in the Foggy Bottom section of DC. The place was right next to George Washington University in a mini-mall.

"You wanna catch the bus back to school or catch a cab?" I asked.

"Let's sit down for a minute," he said. "I want to talk to you about something."

"Okay," I said. We found a bench overlooking a triangle of grass adjacent to the mini-mall. The street was busy with cars going both ways, but the pedestrian traffic was light, allowing us to talk to each other in virtual privacy.

"Everything good with you and the frat?" he asked.

"Yeah, it's going okay," I said. "We had to make some changes to the process to make up for lost time, get ready for the probate, and to just get the boys ready to meet all the old heads. But they are good dudes. And Rebecca really told us what we needed to hear to get our asses in gear. We came too close to being suspended from the frat."

"Yeah, I was worried about you for a minute there," he said.

"For real?" I asked. "You seemed pretty low key about the whole thing."

"Can't let you know how much I worry," he said. "Don't wanna look like a bitch or nothin'. You know."

He was especially cute when he was trying to be a tough guy.

"I appreciate that," I said. "And I'm glad you gave me the space to work it out on my own."

"I know how much Beta means to you and I just wanted to support you without smothering you, 'cause that's what you do for me."

"I try," I said.

"And that's what I wanted to talk to you about," he continued. "I've been thinking a lot about what Rebecca said in our meeting. And as much as I think she's irritating, she's really had my best interest at heart the whole time I've known her. And she really didn't have to help you out, but she did. That really proved to me that she cares. Not just about me, but about us. I've never really had anybody in my life who was that selfless, besides you."

"I think she's a good woman. And a good friend," I said.

"Right," Isaiah continued. "I've been thinking about whether we've been going too fast, or getting too careless with our relationship."

"You want to take a break?" I interjected. My heart seemed to skip a beat, and I coughed, playing off the panic which was creeping in.

"What? A break? Like break up? Hell no, do you?" he asked.

"No," I said. "I was just bracing myself for bad news."

"No, baby, not at all," he said. "It's definitely not like that. It's just that Potomac is a small campus. And it's a liberal campus. Everybody knows about us but nobody cares. Aside from the few chicks that give us the side-eye, I haven't heard a whole lot of gossip about us. And I want to thank you for that. In a lot of ways, I just wanted that respect that you have. Nobody really fucks with you. And I see now that nobody really fucks with me, either.

"I think you're pretty hard to fuck with in the first place," I said.

"True," he said. "But I've been thinking about the future, you know? And what if I do have a shot at the NBA? If these cutthroat scouts are out here trying to see what I'm all about, I don't want to give them a reason to not draft me."

"That's what I've been trying to tell you," I said.

"I know! You were right the whole time and I've just been so happy that I wasn't thinking straight. We've been together almost a year now…"

"Here you go with your fuzzy math again," I said.

"Shut up," he said. "Anyway, we've been together long enough where I am starting to see all the possibilities. Not just shacking up with you indefinitely and living off wine and sex. But like… the future-future. What happens if I do get drafted? What having that kind of money will do to my life. Who I'll be able to trust. Kids, a family, all that shit. I guess what I'm saying is that if I want the kind of future that NBA money can buy, I do need to make smart decisions now. I'm not going to be judged just on how well I play ball—I'm going to be judged on everything, and so will the people I love."

"That's all true," I said. "I'm glad Rebecca sent you that message. A dude like me—I'm going to be okay. I've got nothing to lose. But my biggest fear is being the reason that you lose it all."

"And that's the thing," he said. "I think I figured out a way to have it all. But it's not going to work without you."

"Alright. Let's hear it," I said.

"Well, the first thing I want to know… right here, right now… do you see us together after we graduate?"

I closed my eyes for a moment and visualized our graduation day, posing for pictures with our parents, and driving off into the sunset.

"Yes," I answered. "I definitely see us together after graduation. Where and how? I don't know. But you and I feel right together. Everything has been just as it should be, so I don't see why we wouldn't be together."

"Good," he smiled. "Now, do you think you could handle being in a discreet relationship with me?"

I remembered my life with Isaiah when nobody—not even Nina—knew that we were together. I didn't like it.

"Isaiah, if you're talking about going back in the closet and taking me with you, then I'm not feeling that. I like my life right now," I said.

"No baby, that's not what I mean. On campus, we're good. People know. Fine. We can manage that. What I mean is can you handle me being interviewed for magazines and newspapers and not acknowledging that I'm in a relationship with a dude? Would you be fine with people assuming that I'm straight, even if I'm not?"

"If it's for your career... then of course. You lead a different life than I do, so I understand that you have to do what you gotta do. Rappers do the same thing. It's cool."

"What if we stopped going to gay clubs together?"

"I go maybe once or twice a year at best," I said. "I can go with Morris or Cat and them. Now the question is are *you* cool with that?"

"Yes, for now," he admitted. "I don't look at it as a permanent solution, but I think it's something I can put off for now. What about rallies and marches and political stuff? Are you okay if I don't go to those things?"

"Dude, have you seen me at a gay parade?" I asked. "I mean, I'd go, but again, we don't have to do everything together to still *be* together. I'd just feel bad if it's something you'd want to go to and couldn't."

"Like I said, boy, this is temporary for me. I want to do all those things—and I'm getting the feeling I want to do them more than you do," he laughed. "But what's important is that I get to where I want to go first, then figure things out when I get there. Rebecca said there's never been an openly gay NBA player. Well, what if I became the first?"

"That would be hot," I said. "And a lot of responsibility as well as stress."

"Right. But I can't be the first until I make it there. So Rebecca was right—I need to just chill for a while and make smart decisions until I get to that point. If you're down with that, then I think we can make it happen."

"I'm down with it," I said.

He exhaled and hugged me tight.

"I'm glad," he said. "I really do like basketball and I think I have a shot. Thank you so much for supporting me."

"I love you," I said.

"Love you more," he replied letting go of me. He tried to kiss me on the lips, but I pushed him away.

"We're in public," I said.

"Oh goddamn it," he said. "Can we rethink this?"

"You're such a horny bastard," I said.

"I am," he smiled. His hand rested on my knee and slowly inched its way up my thigh. I closed my legs and pushed him away. He smiled even more.

"Adrian, now that we have that out of the way, I want to ask you one more thing," he said.

"Okay, what?" I replied.

"I want you to live with me this summer—and for senior year."

I blinked once.

"Say what?"

"I want you to live with me again," he said. He grinned like a kid, as he always did when he tried to charm me.

"Wow, for real?" I asked.

"Yes, for real! Listen… I have a lead on a couple of brownstones off campus, right on the bus line. Coach and Rebecca let us live off campus if we show we're responsible. And Rebecca feels like it might be best for us."

"She thinks living together is better than us being discreet?"

"No, she thinks that if we live off campus—together—we can be more discreet. And she's right, when you think about it. No more creeping across campus from dorm to dorm. No more making out at the front gates and getting caught by these chicks. We could just… you know, be together. Like it was last summer. But in our own place with our own shit."

"One bed?" I asked.

"King sized if you want," he said. "No more twin beds to cram into."

"One room?" I asked.

"We can get two bedrooms if you really want," he said.

"Wow," I said. It made perfect sense. I was ready to live off campus. I liked living with my housemates, but I valued my alone time a lot, too. Dating a varsity athlete ensured that I had time alone.

But was I ready for that step? Actually shacking up with my boyfriend?

"Come on..." he pleaded. "We've already lived together before. This is nothing new. More privacy for us. Fewer distractions for you, if you want. And you can have Beta meetings and shit there. Our own spot."

"Yes," I said. "This is a fucking crazy idea, but I'm willing to try it out!"

Isaiah stood up tall in jubilation.

"Yeah!" he shouted. "Yes, yes baby, this is going to be amazing, I promise you!"

He pulled me up off the bench and hugged me, picking me up slightly off the ground.

Everything felt right. Every single thing about this moment and about my entire life since meeting Isaiah felt like it was meant to be. As he placed me down on the ground, I took a good look at his face. In it, I saw the fears of our past finally allayed. Here stood a man who had put so much on the line because he believed in me. I was no longer worried about the future, as we had found a way to just be us without fear, but also with responsibility. I knew that I wouldn't lose him to Taina, who hadn't returned to campus and had all but disappeared from the collective consciousness of the community.

We weren't perfect and there was much to learn about each other. But never before had I ever been part of something that felt so right. We were daily working on our relationship, keeping communications open at all times, and daily striving to be more than our previous relationships, both those we had been in and those we had seen through our parents.

Everything was right and I deserved it. Finally.

Chapter 21:
March 25

I sat in the library with our pledges as they had their normal study hours. I needed this time as badly as they did. My stats class was kicking my entire ass. I would be glad when the ordeal was over. It wasn't technically in my major, but my academic advisor said I should take it if I wanted to go to grad school later.

Calen walked sternly through the study carrels while the pledges worked.

"Frat," he whispered.

"What up?" I replied. He beckoned me over to the corner so that we could speak without disturbing our boys.

"What are you doing?" he asked.

"Studying, duh," I said sarcastically.

"Your man is playing right now! On TV! Why you not down at the pub watching it?"

"Because I have to study, man."

"Dude... Potomac is in the second round. They are saying we could go all the way this year!"

"Yeah man, I know. I'm kinda sleepin with one of the players, remember?"

"Dude... you don't even like basketball, do you?"

"I do!" I exclaimed. "Kinda."

"Adrian, homie, bro... I am relieving you of study duty. Go down to the pub and catch the second half of the game!"

"I mean, we're winning, right?"

"It's too close to call, man! That first round game was against Bethune-Cookman. That was nothing. But this game against DePauw is kinda crazy. Go. Now!"

"Okay, okay!" I grabbed my coat and put my things in my bag.

"What would Isaiah say if he knew you were missing the games? Would he miss a step show you were in?"

"You right, bro, I gotta watch this."

I hurried out of the library and walked the block to the pub in the brisk night air. I couldn't believe Calen had guilt tripped me into watching this game. It wasn't that I didn't like basketball—it was cool. And I did enjoy seeing my man play. But it was never one of my favorite sports to watch. I guess I liked football better. Then a little tennis and some track and field. Basketball was a little too ubiquitous for me to care a great deal about it.

I couldn't tell that to the two hundred people packed into the campus pub to see Potomac play DePauw. I can't lie, once I was into it, I loved basketball as much as every other Potomac student. But it wasn't the sport; it was the energy, the atmosphere, the purple and silver t-shirts and paraphernalia.

The crowd at the pub was about half male and half female, mostly white, with pockets of black people. I made my way as close to the television as possible and quietly looked on as Isaiah shot a three-pointer.

The pub cheered and I joined them. As the game went to a timeout, the black folks sitting closest to the screen turned around and noticed me. I pretended not to notice them.

"Hey, it's Adrian," one of the guys said. Their eyes seemed to widen with excitement as though I was a celebrity. I knew them, yet I didn't know them. Had this been my freshman year, or even my sophomore year, I might have made it a point to know who they were by name. But now, being wrapped up in Beta and in a serious relationship, black life at Potomac was passing me by.

"Come sit down, man," the guy said. "Yo, make some room." His lady friends scooted over and gave me a place to sit. I had never been deferred to like this in all my time at Potomac.

"Thanks," I said, sitting on one of the hard benches the pub was known for.

"You rooting for number 42?" one of the girls asked me. That was Isaiah's jersey number. I smiled but said nothing.

"It's all good, boo," she said. "We got you."

I continued smiling and turned my attention back to the television. They knew. They all knew. And it was okay.

DePauw had a very strong defense but Potomac was simply outscoring them. By the end of the game, Potomac had won by a margin of eight points.

I was glad to have spent at least some time enjoying the game. The Pirates were advancing to the Sweet Sixteen and I could tell Isaiah that I had watched the games and even followed along.

There was no need to tell him about the girl who knew I was rooting for number 42, or that the community seemed to just know about our relationship. The important thing was that weren't treated any differently because of it. I had a duty to protect him, to keep him focused, and to safeguard his future. Our future. I understood better than ever what Rebecca was trying to teach us.

This sort of life might not exist in the real world outside the gates of Potomac University, but it was the life we had, enjoyed, and would get used to for a while. There were great privileges, both tangible and intangible, but the responsibilities were far greater.

Chapter 22:
Friday, April 7

"We're marching across those burning sands
Marching 'cross the desert to Beta-land..."

Not only was the campus electrified with the energy of an unstoppable basketball team who had made it to the Final Four, but the communities of color were also energized by the season of probate shows. The rumor mill was popping with all types of stories about black and Latino Greek life. It seemed like every organization was having a line, and it was a big guessing game to see who would come out.

We had heard the rumors about our own organization, from the true (our temporary suspension) to the outlandish (we put somebody in the hospital). Luckily, because our pledges were so bent on continuing the process, they never reverted to street clothing even when they weren't technically pledging.

When we resumed their process, we jumped right back into things with a lot of catching up to do. We stayed true to our word and never hit them with paddles again.

Our boys had actually been officially initiated a week before their probate. It was a huge change for our chapter—my line had probated on the very same day that we crossed, as was the custom for all Beta chapters. But due to the suspension, our boys were behind schedule, so we gave them the option to just be finished or to have a hell week and probate.

They chose the probate. They opted in to hell week. They wanted everything we had had. We still took care of them, didn't revert to all we said we were giving up in terms of hazing. But they still wanted memories. So we made them. And the only way to a probate was through hell week.

Hell week was no walk in the park, though, for even though we collectively decided not to hit our boys, they still needed to go through the chapter's traditions, if for no other reason than their legitimacy in the eyes of our alumni. They received their line names, visited the important monuments and gravesites in the fraternity, were pelted with water balloons galore, and ate the same "Beta food" that we all had. It was hell week, after all, not heaven week.

One of the most treasured traditions we had was the Death March, which was a grueling, slow, two and a half mile march from Potomac to Rock Creek College which culminated in a long, affirming, pre-dawn session with all of our chapter's alumni. When I went through it, it seemed like it lasted all night long. When our boys went through it, we had to modify it so that it was less public—gone were the days where we could bring the boys out at a late night party and let the campus see them one last time before the probate.

We did everything in reverse, and if you ask me, it worked a little better—different, but better. We began the march at Rock Creek and allowed the alumni to inspect and uplift the boys in private. Yes, some of the alumni were pissed and tried to take it out on the boys. But most of the alumni understood and gave their usual affirming messages.

The boys still marched, this time to Potomac, and not with the usual obstacles and challenges the brothers put before them. I was torn. So much had been modified for these guys, and though we knew it was for the good of the chapter, I couldn't help but feel disappointed that the changes had to happen on our watch.

By the time we got to campus, a sizable crowd was already waiting in The Square. Me and Mohammed jogged out to the center of the crowd and fanned everyone out, making a circle for the line to enter.

"Back up, please!" I instructed. "Everybody can see if you all take three giant steps back."

The crowd complied for the most part and started to spread out for us. Our pledges—rather, our new brothers—stomped in wearing the standard black work suit that all previous lines had worn.

The line, sharp as always, was finally in formation and the many brothers and alumni who had come to support formed a large circle around them, maintaining crowd control while enjoying the show.

"B-C-P... Greet!" Mark, the Ace, said.

"Greetings, most illustrious Big Brothers of Beta Chi Phi Fraternity, Innnnnncorporated! The men of burgundy and gold: not very old, wisest in spirit, biggest in heart, the brotherhood destined for greatness from the start. May we continue, dear big brothers?" the pledges greeted in unison.

"Proceed!" Tommy shouted.

"B-C-P... Greet!" Mark commanded.

"Greetings, most illustrious Big Brothers of Beta Chi Phi Fraternity, Innnnnncorporated, Sigma Chapter!" the pledges greeted.

"B-Chiiiii!" Aaron called.

"Chiiiii Phiiii!" we responded.

"B-C-P... Greet!" Mark shouted.

"Greetings to the Brothers of Tau Line, better known as Terror Squad! Greetings, Dean Big Brother Tommy, better known as that Destructive Deuce of Terror Squad, Big Brother Watergate! Greetings, President Big Brother Aaron, better known as that Triumphant Tres of Terror Squad, Big Brother Bruce Wayne!"

"B-Chiiiii!" Aaron called again.

"Chiiiii Phiiii!" we responded. The neos then went into a song from the old rap group also called Terror Squad, in a nod to Aaron and Tommy's line.

"Greetings to the Brothers of Upsilon Line, better known as Uprising!" the neos greeted. My line gathered in front of their line to get a better view and truly feel the greeting.

"Greetings to the Audacious Ace, Big Brother Peter, also known as The Martyr of Uprising! Greetings to the Devastating Deuce, Big Brother Ciprian, also known as Smooth Operator of Uprising! Greetings to the ferocious four, Big Brother Adrian, also known as Lazarus of Uprising! Greetings to the fascinating five, Big Brother Mohammed, also known as Protocol of Uprising! Greetings to the studious six, Big Brother Edward, also known as The Inquisitor of Uprising! Greetings to the terrifying tail, big Brother Calen, also known as Gibraltar of Uprising!"

"B-Chiiiii!" Calen called with enthusiasm.

"Chiiiii Phiiii!" we responded.

"Greetings to all the alumni of the Sadistic Sigma Chapter of Beta Chi Phi Fraternity, Innnnnncorporated!"

All of our alumni did the fraternity call in acknowledgement. The greetings went on and on for quite a while. Even though we instructed the neos to give brief greetings, there were still a lot of Beta chapters and other organizations to get through.

After the greetings, they recited all kinds of fraternal information that they had to memorize while they were pledging—poems, songs, previous lines, past presidents, founders. A probate show was like an "everything you know" show. The point was not just to introduce the new members to campus, but to show the Greek community just how hard they had pledged. The name of the game was respect, and with our bump in the pledge process being well known to fellow Greeks, we had to prove that we still ran the yard.

To the credit of the neos, there were no mistakes made in any of the greetings. The sorority women loved their tributes and signified their approval with choruses of coos and sorority calls. There wasn't so much as a stumble over any of the information. The boys were tight.

"Probates, I am not feeling this show," Tommy said after the greetings were done. "We spent a good 20, 25 minutes just saying hello, twenty more minutes spitting information. It's getting late, I'm getting tired, now show me something good!"

"You want to see something good?" the neos responded in unison.

"Excuse me while I whip this out," Dexter quipped, on cue.

Simultaneously, the neos unzipped their work suits to the waist to show their brand new burgundy fraternity t-shirts with gold letters. Absorbing the cheers from the crowd and the call and response of the fraternity brothers, you could see each new brother practically inflating with confidence. Christopher, the number eight of nine, and of course my spesh, seemed to be the proudest of all. Or at least, I was the most proud of him.

"Ladies and gentleman, I am proud to introduce you to Sigma Chapter's twenty-first line—the Phi Line—better known as Phantoms!

And why do we call you Phantoms, brothers?" Tommy asked.

"We...are...the..." Mark began with a slow step, clapping his hands beneath his legs and behind his back.

"Phantoms of Sadistic Sigma Chapter of the mighty Beta Chi Phi," the neos began mimicking Mark's step. "We're ordinary men in the day, but ghosts in the night. You think you've got us figured out? Well let me whisper in your ear... you really don't know what's going on so watch us disappear."

It was a fine public explanation for why we had named them Phantoms. We traditionally picked a word or phrase which began with the same letter or sound as the corresponding Greek letter that the line was named for: Tau for Terror Squad, Upsilon for Uprising, and now Phi for Phantoms. But the real reason for Phantoms was because the line had been suspended and like ghosts, they still pledged anyway, disappearing and reappearing sporadically.

"Who the hell are you, neos?" Aaron shouted after the step was over.

"We are Betas! We pledge through the pain!" they responded. "Sadistic Sigma, bring it back again!" One by one, each new brother popped out and introduced himself.

"Mark Ferguson, sophomore, Potomac University. I'm the ace of this line, holding it down for my line brothers known as the Phantoms. Because I lead this line, I was given a name that proves my discretion, determination, and my inevitability. I am Dark Shadows."

It wasn't all that—we just named him that because he was creepy and stalked me before rush. But we came to like him.

"Angel Rosario, junior, Rock Creek College. I am the deuce of this line and burgundy and gold flows all up and through my veins. I was given a name that also carries the weight of my fellow Phantoms—I am the god of dreams, the precious dream of brotherhood. I am Morpheus."

Which was true, he really did dream of brotherhood. He also had the uncanny ability to sleep standing up in set.

"My name is Emeka Mbanefo, sophomore, Rock Creek College and I am the tres," he began in his Igbo accent. "When there is a complex problem that needs a solution, I'm the first one my brothers call on. When you need someone to look at all the angles, call me. I am Pythagoras."

He was truly a smart guy, but even after all this time, we didn't have a particular affinity for him. But that was Mohammed's spesh and he was determined to give him a good line name.

"Mi name Dexter Rodgers, junior, Rock Creek College. Mi bring tings unexpected to the dull and ordinary. Mi bring fiyah to the ice, and wetness to the dry. Mi name now and forever be Chaos Theory… the ferocious numbah four… and don't forget it."

Dexter turned his accent on and off when it was convenient for him, but even through his recovering homophobia, I could find some attractiveness to him. He wasn't exaggerating about his line name—he definitely brought the chaos wherever he went.

"I am Rick Brown, junior, Potomac University, and I am the nickel of this line. I speak only when I need to. I am… The Thinker."

More importantly than only speaking when he had to, everything he said was deep.

"I am that sensational six, Alejandro Cristobal Valenzuela, sophomore, Potomac University. I have wanted this moment all… my… life! My enthusiasm for this is combustible. That's why my brothers call me… Nitroglycerine!"

That and we could never predict whether he was having a good day or a bad day.

"Joshua Robinson, lucky number seven, sophomore, Potomac University. I am that brother who you can depend on to make a good impression. I don't need to be in the spotlight to do the work of this fraternity. That's why my brothers call me… Special Guest Star."

That was a true statement, though it was more a testament to his absenteeism due to his track and field responsibilities.

"Christopher White, elite number eight, sophomore, Rock Creek College. My brothers saw a natural leader emerge in me. When it mattered most, I was there for my line to lead them the way, the same as I will for my entire life as a man of Beta Chi Phi. That's why my brothers named me… Moses."

A spot-on description of the man who traveled through the wilderness to lead his people home.

"Orlando Ford, junior, Potomac University. I am the tail and the nasty, naughty, notorious number nine of this line! They called the last tail before me Gibraltar because he was an unmovable rock. But you see these?" He lifted his fists in front of him. "These rocks move. That's why my brothers know me as... KABLAM!"

More accurately "Kappa Alpha Blam!" for the scuffle we had gotten into with the Kappas which lead to all the drama during their process.

"B-C-P!" Mark led.

We came to bring some soul to your life
With steps and rhymes so smooth and so out of sight
We are the Phantoms on the scene with a style so divine
Men of burgundy and gold, we are nine of a kind

"Now let's give them what they came for!" Chris shouted. Our neos tore it down—I had to admit they stepped more precisely than my line had. These boys had practiced into the wee hours of the night for weeks, giving the campus a twenty minute step show unlike that which they had ever seen before.

They knew all the steps that we knew and had made up their own. They flipped, they jumped, they damn near stomped holes into the ground.

By the end of the show, they were almost too out of breath to sing:

Calling all brothers to the floor, of Beta
We got some here but we need some more
Calling all brothers to the floor, of Beta
We got some here but we need some more

When we assembled into our big circle, Tommy went to the middle and pulled several brothers forward: me, representing my line,

Deji and my Dean Steven, and a few older brothers. We were our chapter's song leaders—the men who could sing the best and knew how to direct the rest of the chapter in song. The step masters and pledge masters always deferred to the song leaders after all brothers were "called to the floor."

After singing just about every song we knew, we sang the hymn, with the familiar refrain:

> *And before he takes his final breath*
> *He is glad he chose Beta for his life*

On the final lines, I noticed our neos beginning to break down in tears. In true Beta fashion, the tears were contagious and we could barely finish the song. A round of fraternity calls drowned out any of the sobs and we all embraced each other.

My personal came over to me, tears glistening in his eyes.

"Thank you," he said, bottom lip quivering.

"I love you man," I said. "I am so proud to call you my brother."

We embraced, forgetting to even perform the fraternal handshake. We held each other for a while and I felt my shoulder get damp from his sweat and tears. I patted him on the back and pulled away.

"You frat now," I said. "And your public awaits you."

He turned around to face the hordes of people waiting to congratulate him. Aaron and Tommy had the honor of giving the boys their crossing jackets in the chaos—burgundy jackets with burgundy and gold Greek letters on the front with all of their relevant crossing information on the sleeves and back.

I took a few steps back just to observe the scene. I was happy for the boys, but I think most of all, I was glad that it was all over.

I felt a tap on my arm, turned to my right and saw Mohammed.

"Congratulations," he said.

"For what?" I asked.

He smiled.

"Not only did you save the chapter and help us stop the madness that almost drove me away… but you're not a neo anymore!"

I returned his smile.

"Oh yeah," I said. "And congratulations to you, too."

I gave him the grip, held him tight, and exhaled.

Chapter 23:
April 8

"Your spesh is mad intent, son!" Calen said to Christopher.

"Wouldn't you be, too?" Christopher replied.

I sat on our sofa with my hands clasped in front of my face, studying the game closely. Potomac's appearance in the Final Four was not going well at all.

I was surrounded by of the brothers from Potomac: my housemates Calen and Orlando; my chapter President Aaron; my line brother Ed; my neos Mark, Rick, Alex, and Josh; and of course my spesh Christopher, who still couldn't get enough of being at Potomac even though he was free to roam as he chose now that he was off line.

The chapter felt huge now that the boys were done and it was nice having a huge presence on the yard. Being chartered on multiple campuses took its toll on us sometimes. There was so much service to be done and twice the number of campuses to do it on. As a younger fraternity, it was also important to be seen doing the work. We didn't have the luxury of a name brand like other fraternities. We had to set ourselves apart in our members—if people knew us, they liked us. And if they liked us, the legacy continued.

Between studying, helping the boys with the probate, and keeping up with the so-called Big Dance, I was now beside myself with anxiety. Kansas was whipping Potomac's ass—we were down 15 points well into the second half.

"Aye, we can still make this happen," Aaron said. "This is the furthest we've gotten in four years, I believe in them."

I slowly nodded.

"Why they keep giving Billy Abbott the ball?" Mark asked. "They need to just give it to Hodari and Isaiah and call it a day."

"They give him the ball because he's a shooting guard. That's what he's supposed to do. Always giving Hodari and Isaiah the ball ain't gonna work," I said, not taking my gaze from the screen.

"But he's fuckin' up," Mark said. "He's a freshman, he can't take this pressure."

"Listen, do you see how they are gunning for Isaiah every time he gets the ball?" I asked.

"Yeah, man," Ed said. "It's like they trying to end his career out this motherfucker."

"Thank you!" I said. "If they play like a fuckin' team they might have a chance."

"I dunno, bro," Josh said. "I think Kansas is just a stronger team."

"Maybe," his line brother Rick said. "But they can do this."

Hodari passed the ball to Billy. Billy shot the ball and missed.

"Fuck," I said.

"That nigga is shootin' bricks!" Alex said.

This pressure was getting to be too much for me. I cursed Calen for making me be more proactive in following the games. Not only was I now fully invested in the games, but I was freaking out anytime a player from the opposing team even looked at my man wrong.

Kansas took the ball to their hoop and attempted to shoot another two-pointer. Somehow, in his efforts to block the shot, Isaiah collided with a Kansas player and ended up sprawled on the ground.

"Fuck!" I rose to my feet along with the other brothers.

"He's okay," Orlando said. "He's okay, he just got tripped up."

"Then why ain't he moving!" I said.

"He is moving!" Orlando said. "Look."

Hodari and Coy Newman, a freshman guard, grabbed Isaiah's arms and lifted him up. Isaiah rubbed his eyes, shook his head, and got back in the game.

I exhaled.

"Yo, this nigga cannot be allowed to watch basketball any more!" Calen exclaimed. We all laughed and sat back down. He was right—I couldn't deal with the excitement now that I had a personal stake in the whole thing. That was my man. I wanted him to be a success. He had my back, now I was gonna have his.

Even as the clock ticked down the final seconds and Kansas

had beaten us by a margin of 20 points, I knew everything was going to be okay. Isaiah had once again played one hell of a game and had helped to take the team further than it had gone in the previous few years. Coach Kalinowski was bringing the team back to glory.

Christopher whispered to me as the game ended:

"You sure you can deal with this for another year?"

I turned to him and nodded.

"It's all good," I said. "Takes some getting used to. But I think I can do it."

"And when he goes pro?"

"Shit... I don't even want to think about that one, little bro."

He laughed and playfully punched my shoulder. We were all pretty bummed that the team wouldn't be going all the way to the top, especially after such a bad blow out, but what could you do?

Late that night as I slept, my phone rang.

"Hey," I said groggily. I knew it was Isaiah, but he didn't say anything.

"Y'all back?" I asked.

"Yeah," he said.

"I saw the game. I'm sorry you didn't win this one."

More silence.

"Are you okay?"

"Can you come see me?" he said.

"Yeah, you want me to come to your room?"

"Naw. Esplanade."

"Aight."

I slid on some sweatpants over my shorts and my crossing jacket over my t-shirt, hoping it would be enough in the still-cool nighttime air. The esplanade, a grassy, park-like area on the roof of our student center, was a favorite spot for me and Isaiah's when it wasn't too cold. I knew it was a pretty serious matter if he wanted to meet there.

I was there within minutes and Isaiah was already standing there waiting for me. As he heard the click of the metal doors opening, he turned around. Under the ghostly florescent glow of the esplanade lights, I could see something different about his eyes.

"You been crying?" I asked. He nodded.

"We lost," he said, a sob getting caught in his throat.

"Aww, baby," I said. I embraced him and he hugged me back tightly.

"It's okay," I said, patting his back. I always knew that Isaiah was an emotional dude—he never hid it before—but I suppose I underestimated just how profoundly this loss would affect him.

"I never thought we would make it this far," he said. "And we blew it."

"No you didn't," I said. "Kansas is a really, really good team. And they really studied you guys."

"We should have come harder," Isaiah said. "I could have done more."

"Yeah, maybe you could have. But you can only learn from what happened. You can't beat yourself up about it. Hey, look at me."

Isaiah released me from his tight embrace and looked down.

"No, look at *me*," I said, cupping his chin with my hand. His brown eyes focused on me.

"You are Isaiah Christopher Aiken and you are gonna be alright. Ya heard?"

He nodded.

"I'm serious! Yes, this shit fucking sucks, but you can hold your head high because you helped take this team to this point. Yeah, the championship eluded you—this year. But next year? Please, you are going all the way. Billy Abbott is gonna be a better athlete. Rashad Johnson is gonna step up in leadership to replace Geoffrey Jones. And if you ever play Kansas again... Please! They will know better than to try to hotbox you."

"You really have been watching the games... that's kinda sexy," Isaiah said.

He leaned down, kissed me, and hugged me tightly again.

"Thank you for having my back," he said. "Love you, baby."

"Love you more," I said.

"Can I spend the night with you?" he asked.

"'Course you can," I said. "You don't want to be alone tonight?"

"Well… I kinda got sexiled," Isaiah laughed. I smiled back at him.

"Hodari and his harem strike again," I said.

"You know this," he said. "But starting this summer… we won't have to worry 'bout none of that. We gettin' our grown man on."

"Still can't believe we're gonna be shacking up," I said. Isaiah led my by the hand to the doors leading back down into the student center.

"And you know this," he said. "Adrian Edward Collins. Hey, we get married? It's gonna be Adrian Edward Aiken. That's a lot of vowels."

"Here you go again," I said with a smirk. "And who says I'm taking *your* last name, Isaiah Collins? I don't even have no ring on this finger."

"Yet," he said. "Just you wait."

There was never any middle ground with this dude. Black or white, hot or cold, love or hate. But I loved every single passionate moment of our relationship. Neither of us would have it any other way.

Chapter 24:
May 12

The sky over Washington was a deep blue, with pure white, fluffy clouds spread out over the city like balls of cotton spilled on a tile floor. My last paper was completed and my last final had been taken that morning. I still had a few more boxes to pack before I left my apartment in Hurley Village at noon.

It was a busy day, as all my birthdays usually were. I was finally turning twenty-one—perfectly legal in every state. I felt much older than that, though. I had my first taste of alcohol as a teenager but never drank to excess. I was in a serious relationship. I had pledged. I had one more year before I was done with college. Hell, I was a grown-ass man already. Twenty-one was just a number.

I dumped out the contents of my desk: pens, pencils, notes, spare change, condoms, lube packets... things that summarized my junior year. My Beta ritual book. The leather journal that Isaiah got me for Christmas. The light brown teddy bear with the purple "Somebody at Potomac University Loves Me" t-shirt. These things would never see the inside of this or any other dorm room again.

We were moving to a newly renovated brownstone in Dupont Circle, about two miles from campus and easily accessible by the public bus which went past the edge of the Georgetown neighborhood and right to the front gates of Potomac University.

Our house was about a block away from P Street. We could still see the action but were far enough away where we couldn't hear it. It was Isaiah's first choice, but he was open to others.

The property manager showed us the building one evening a week and a half ago. Hodari came along, as he was also looking for a spot and the building's owner was renting out two units.

The front of the place looked like something out of Sesame Street—perfect stone stairs leading up to a beautiful set of wooden doors with a brass knocker. There were clean bay windows as clear as crystal to the left of the door.

"The first floor and basement make up one apartment," the manager said as we entered the small foyer. "The second floor and attic make up the second. The owner could have easily made this four apartments, but he figured an upscale young family might appreciate the innovative design."

"Nice paneling," I said. The manager smiled.

"This is just the entry," he said. "Here's the key to upstairs. Why don't you two go on up and look around while I show Hodari downstairs?"

"Thank you," Isaiah said, reaching for the key. While Hodari and the property manager entered the apartment from the door to the left of the entry way, Isaiah and I climbed the long staircase straight up and back to what would be our new home.

The door had a simple brass number two bolted to the front. Isaiah slid the key inside and slowly opened the door.

He reached for a light switch and illuminated the small hallway we walked in to. Shiny wooden floors greeted us everywhere we went. Turning the short corner, a wide living area greeted us.

"Whoa," he said. Almost the entire second floor of the house was wide open, with a long, red brick wall extending from where we stood to the back of the room. A kitchen with all new, stainless steel appliances opened up into a living room and dining area. A bathroom was behind us. I walked across the hardwood floor in silence, hearing my own footsteps as I traveled.

"Wow," I said. "This kitchen..."

"The floors... and look how high this is," he said, reaching upward. His fingertips barely scraped the ceiling.

"Now that's tall," I said. "What's in this room?"

We walked toward the front of the house and pushed the door open to reveal a cozy bedroom, or perhaps even a den. The windows overlooked the tree-lined city street below.

"This is nice," Isaiah said. I looked around the room, inspecting the closet.

"Lots of space," I said.

"Let's check out the attic," he said. We left the bedroom and walked up a second set of stairs, just off the main living area. He turned the doorknob and one large room was revealed to us.

"This could be... our bedroom?" I asked.

"Yeah," Isaiah said. "The ceiling is a little lower, but I can walk around okay. It's comfortable." He walked over to the low windows overlooking the street.

"We can put some chairs right here," he continued. "And look back there, baby, we can put a bed, the TV, a throw rug. This whole big ass room can be our bedroom. Just us. We can entertain downstairs and then have it be just the two of us up here. Our own little spot."

I looked around. It was certainly an attic. But it was a big attic, with lots of space for anything I had collected over the past three years. There was a second bathroom and more closet space. The views were just as good up here, even though the windows were smaller.

I liked it.

"Baby?" I asked.

"Yeah?" he replied.

"This is it," I said.

He smiled.

"You like it," he said. "I knew you would. Come here."

I walked over to him and put my hands around his waist.

"Ooh, you know better," he said, grabbing my hands and placing them on his ass.

"I love you," he said, kissing me. "Welcome home."

A week and a half later was today—our big day move in day and my birthday. I hadn't even gotten the chance to think much about it since that day, but Isaiah handled most everything for me. He said he wasn't going to have me worried about movers and whatnot during finals. Of course, he was having finals too, so I didn't really get how he was going to handle the arrangements, but I trusted him.

A few minutes after noon, I got a knock at the door.

"Movers," the man on the other side said. I opened the door and welcomed the uniformed men in.

"Everything's all boxed up in the downstairs room," I said. The three men walked past me to my room. My bags were packed and sat by the door.

My housemate Brad walked in the wide-open door and we locked eyes.

"This is it?" he asked.

"Yup… this is it." I replied. I eyed his crisp white fraternity shirt with red letters. His coming-out show for Kappa was about a week after the Beta probate.

"Hey man, I really enjoyed living with you this year," he said. "And I gotta say man… I'm sorry about the fight my prophytes picked with you this semester. It was really uncalled for and I'm sorry it got out of hand."

I nodded.

"It's whatever," I said. "Listen… now that it's all over, I really just need to know something."

I paused and looked at Brad directly in the eyes.

"Did your prophytes report us anonymously? Are they the reason we got investigated?"

Brad looked down to the floor.

"Man… I don't know," he said. "I mean… it's possible, but they never told me one way or another. Look man, I was just trying to be a Kappa, you know? I wasn't thinking about what they were doing. I just wanted to be down. Now that I'm in, I'll make sure the beef is squashed. Aight?"

"Yeah, sure Brad," I said. I extended my hand to him. "Congratulations, again."

"Thanks man," he said, shaking my hand.

The movers started walking between us to take my boxes outside and to their truck.

"Hey, have you seen Orlando or Calen?" I asked. "I'd like to say goodbye before I leave."

"I haven't seen them," he said. "I think they had a final."

"Oh... okay." It would be really annoying that I wouldn't get to see my frat brothers before we parted ways for the summer, but I supposed most of us would still be around for graduation.

Within moments, the movers were ready. It wasn't like I had a whole lot of boxes and bags to take with me.

"We have space in the truck for you, Mr. Collins," the mover said.

"Thanks, but I have one more thing left to do on campus," I said. "The property manager will let you in when you get there. These boxes are all for the upstairs apartment."

"Yes, sir," the mover said. "We're on our way to Mr. Hudgins and Mr. Aiken's dorm next."

"Great," I said. "Don't forget that the Aiken boxes are going upstairs, too."

"Yes, sir," he said. He exited the apartment and I left the door cracked a little while I glanced around one last time.

These were my last moments in my apartment and in any campus housing. In this living room, I watched DVDs and ate take-out with my man. In that old brown chair, I sat while we all got ready for Halloween. In my room, at my desk, I rifled through scraps of paper looking for phone numbers of men who might replace Isaiah or Savion when I was in need of affection. And in my room, on my bed, was where I had tried several times—each time, unsuccessfully—to allow Isaiah to penetrate me.

Now I was moving out and moving on to walk the grown man's path with a man that I had loved for nearly a year, from the moment he turned around to face me in another dorm room one muggy summer day. I didn't know it then, but I loved him and would only love him more with each passing day.

"Bye, Brad," I called out. He didn't hear me. I left our now-sparse living room and locked the door behind me.

After I dropped my key off and signed out at the residence hall office, I made my way to the last appointment I'd have on campus for a while: coffee with my attorney in the student center.

"Are you really wearing jeans?" I asked.

"Why yes, I am," Rebecca replied. "Jeans and a t-shirt. Can you believe it?"

"Barely," I said. She had her hair in a simple ponytail. She wore gold hoop earrings, a crimson Harvard Law t-shirt, slim jeans, and wedge-heeled sandals. She was pretty whether she dressed up or dressed down.

"Why so casual?" I asked.

"That's why I wanted to see you," she said while sipping her smoothie. "I don't know how to break this to you, so I'll just say it."

"What? Oh my god, what happened Rebecca?"

"The University President let me go," she said. "I don't work here anymore."

"They fired you?!" I said. "What the hell, Rebecca? Why?"

"It's okay, Adrian," she said. "I made some choices, I took some risks. And you know what? I don't regret a single one."

"Wait…" I paused, thinking about what she just said. "You got fired because of me, didn't you? They fired you because you represented me to the frat? That's it, isn't it?"

My heart sank and my stomach began to cramp. I took a sip of ginger ale.

"Adrian, I don't regret a single second of representing you, so please don't feel bad that this happened. I knew from the moment I took you as a client that I was violating my agreement with the university. And I knew that I put the school at risk. Listen… They were paying me to make them look good, not defend a non-basketball player against hazing allegations. I tried to spin it, to explain that you were a close friend of Isaiah's and that it was best for Potomac if you prevailed. But they weren't having it. So, yesterday was my last day."

"Rebecca, there has got to be something I can do," I said. "Let me talk to the president. Me and Isaiah. Me, Isaiah, and the coach. Please, something. He'll listen to us."

She shook her head vigorously.

"Rebecca, please, a petition. We can get the players and their parents to write letters. Alumni, too. Don't you have some friends who are donors?"

"Adrian, no," she said. "It's over. I took a gamble and I lost."

I exhaled and placed my face in my hands.

"This can't be happening," I said through my palms.

"It's okay," she said. "Look at me. Come on, look at me."

She grabbed my hands and lowered them to the table.

"It's okay," she repeated. "I've been here for five years. It was time to move on."

"But it's my fault," I said. "I got you fired because of some fraternity bullshit."

"It wasn't bullshit," she said. "You were in serious danger of being compelled to confess to things you didn't have to by a man who is hell-bent on throwing chapters under the bus for his own personal gain. Adrian, if you were going to get busted, it had better be for a damn good reason. And that scuffle you had in Adams Morgan wasn't a good enough reason to be suspended from the frat."

I nodded.

"You're one of the good guys," she said. "You're here to enjoy college. You make your mistakes sometimes, just like the boys I worked with. You fall down, but you pick yourself up and brush yourself off. Sometimes you don't need help, but sometimes you do. And this time, I was there to help. That's what I do. That's all I've ever done."

"It's not fair," I said. "What are me and Isaiah supposed to do without you?"

"No, it isn't fair" she said. "But it is what it is. You and Isaiah will be fine."

I looked away from her and into the trickle of people studying for their last remaining finals in the lounge beyond the coffee shop.

"Let me tell you something," she said as I stared. "When I started at Potomac, I was 25 years old. I wanted to do something that helped make student-athletes more savvy and aware of the many ways they could get taken advantage of: rogue boosters, shyster agents, and even the girls around here trying to get knocked up so they can have a lifelong meal-ticket, whether he marries her or not. And I did that for five years.

"Before then, I clerked at the DC Superior Court and volunteered at the Pro Bono Foundation. I had a law degree but no direction. Now I have more direction than ever before. Maybe even for the first time."

"Why did you even go to law school if you didn't know what you wanted to do with your life?" I asked.

"Did you know I was engaged?" she asked. I shook my head. "Well, I was. I spent all four years at Duke with the love of my life, Ronnie Campbell. He was a star wide receiver. Smart. Sexy as hell. Black guy. I met him during freshman orientation. By fall break, I knew he was the one."

"He was your Isaiah," I mused. She blushed and smiled.

"You could say that." I smiled knowingly.

"I know people thought I was some sort of gold-digger. Here I was: some random white chick who had snatched up one of Duke's few NFL prospects. But hey, we were in love. What can you say to that?"

"I'm sure the sistas had a field day," I chuckled.

"Oh, you know they did," Rebecca continued. "But I always had my own plan, regardless of what people thought. No matter what, I was going to Harvard Law. Ronnie could follow me there if he wanted."

"Whoa, he had NFL aspirations and you thought *he* was supposed to follow *you*?"

Rebecca laughed. "I had tangible goals! I couldn't put them on hold. But a funny thing happened, Adrian. Even though I was with him all four years of college, I wasn't convinced it was going to last after graduation. Until he actually got drafted."

"Really?"

"Yup," she paused, sipping her drink. "The man got drafted by the New England Patriots. He was really going to follow me to Boston."

I chuckled some more. "That's awesome," I said.

"Obviously, he couldn't have known for certain that's where he'd end up. But when that happened, we both sort of just knew."

She sighed and looked down for a bit.

"Anyway, about a month later, Ronnie took me down to his family home in Virginia, a town called Arvonia. I thought we were just visiting, but as it turns out he proposed. It was crazy! I said yes, of course."

I knew I wasn't tripping, but I also knew I had never seen Rebecca wear a wedding band before. I knew this story wouldn't end well.

"The next night, Ronnie went out with some of his high school friends to some local bar. There were like six of them in this pickup truck. I mean, they were country boys. They always did things like that. But something in my gut told me that something awful was going to happen. I begged Ronnie not to go. Figures…. the worst argument of our relationship would happen on the day we got engaged."

"What happened? Did he go?"

"Yeah, he went… after he called me a bitch—I'm sorry, he said 'Why don't you stop acting so bitchy, you're gonna marry a pro baller.' I shut up and let him go. He went to the bar, had a great time. He called me from the bar to apologize later that night. Then… well, then their truck flipped over on the highway. And nobody was hurt seriously… except for Ronnie. He was killed instantly."

My heart sank to the pit of my stomach.

"Rebecca… I'm so sorry."

"Thank you," she sighed. "It was ten years ago. It still hurts, but you have to keep living life. Ronnie's family was good to me. They knew all I ever wanted was for him to be safe and to stay out of trouble. I stayed in town for the funeral, then came home. I started law school soon after that. For a while, I floated through. I passed my classes, made connections and all. But I was different. I was empty. I dated, but nobody like Ronnie ever again.

"Three years later, I was done with law school and started clerking for a judge down here in DC Superior Court. I passed the DC bar and did some pro bono work on the side when I could. Usually copyright and trademark law. Nothing huge. Then I met the President of Potomac at this reception during Congressional Black Caucus weekend."

"Uh, no offense… but what were you doing there? Hell, what was he doing there?"

"Just networking," she said. "The judge I clerked for was a well-respected African American jurist and he always got invited to these things. So I went."

"Gotcha," I said.

"Well I happened to meet this guy and we talked for a really long time. He was telling me how the school really aimed to protect and uplift its black men, particularly the basketball players. People were well aware of all the controversy from the 80s when Victor Charles had a hold over the players. You already know what a train wreck that was."

"I've definitely put the pieces together," I responded. "I can't imagine what it would have been like to have players fraternizing with known drug lords."

"A hot mess is what it was," Rebecca said. "And the President knew the program still had a long way to go. My predecessor was leaving and he wanted to take my position in a new direction. He wanted a woman. Not just a mother to these guys, but a strong woman who they would respect and trust. As soon as my clerkship was over, I was hired by Potomac. That was five years ago."

"And you did it because of Ronnie?" I asked. She nodded.

"Ronnie was gone. I couldn't stop him from getting in that truck. I'm at peace with that. But never before had I seen a university president so keenly interested in protecting his basketball team. Sure, it's a business decision. Preserve the brand, preserve the school. But it was more than that. Dealing with the basketball team is like having a bunch of ball bearings on a wooden labyrinth. Some of them you can only guide down the path for so long before they fall off—getting a gold-digging girlfriend, having a baby way too early, entering the draft too soon. All of these are things I would try to help the program avoid. Every now and then, you guide one of those ball bearings to the end of the labyrinth. Barry Branch. Kahlil Salaam. Isaiah Aiken. These are guys that I helped steer in the right direction. These are guys that I'm proud of. Yes, I'm sad to be leaving my players, but I know I did a damn good job."

I slowly nodded.

"You did, Rebecca. I don't know what else to say. You've done so much for me and so much for Isaiah. Thank you so much."

I hugged her, long and hard.

"You're welcome," she said. "You know, Isaiah is really lucky to have you. I am so serious."

"He was lucky to have you, too," I said. "So what do you do now? Where do you go?"

"I take some time out for myself," she said. "I've got savings, I'll be okay. Potomac firing me won't kill my career. I've still got CBC connections. Maybe I'll work for the NAACP."

"You love you some black folks," I laughed. She smiled.

"I love good people, no matter what color they are," she said.

"Fair enough. Rebecca, I think I need to get going. I'm moving today, and... well, it's also my birthday."

"Happy birthday!" she exclaimed! "Are you finally 21 yet?"

"Hells yeah!" I said, standing up. "No plans though. I'm just glad to have my own spot now."

"Do you need a ride there? Or anywhere?" she asked, gathering her purse.

"Uh... well, now that I think about it, I could use one. I'm done with finals. Seems like my people are nowhere to be found. Guess I should go... home."

"Sounds weird, right?"

"A little bit," I said as we walked. "A little bit."

In about fifteen minutes, Rebecca's shiny black Mercedes pulled up to our brownstone.

"Definitely a fine pick," she said, eyeballing the property.

"Thanks for linking us up with the owner," I said. "And, you know... the free rent."

"Now I didn't do all that," she said. "Isaiah has free room and board. This is all courtesy Potomac University."

"Yeah, I know. Still feels like my fairy godmother hooked me up, though."

"Maybe a little."

"So... are you sure the school is okay with me living with Isaiah? Like, no bullshit?"

She sighed.

"Don't get all huffs and puffs on me," I whined.

"Okay, okay," she said. "Listen, as long as you stick to the script, everything will be cool."

"What's the script?"

"You and Isaiah are best friends. He was given the privilege of off-campus housing for his academic performance this past year and as a bonus got to take along a friend. And that's you."

"I can dig it. So why didn't anybody tell me the damn script before now?"

"Oops."

"Oops? What the hell, Rebecca?"

"Well sorry, babe, I was sorta busy getting fired!"

"So who knows the real deal?"

"Well, you, Isaiah, all your friends..."

"No, I mean up the chain... like, who really made this happen?"

"The only people who know about it are the only ones who need to—Coach K and the university president. I imagine my successor will inherit this as well."

"Wow," I said. "The president of the school knows who I'm sleeping with."

"Please believe it," Rebecca said. "He knows a lot more than anyone thinks. So be careful, Adrian. He does trust you. And if he knew you, he'd like you. I convinced him that you're on the same page as the rest of us. You know, keeping the program smooth."

"Yeah," I said. "I'm with the program."

"You love it," she said, matter-of-factly. I smiled.

"You know what, after all the drama? I do love it. I really do. But it's because I know Isaiah is worth it."

"You know what, Adrian?"

"What?"

"If the shoe was on the other foot, you'd be worth it, too. Don't forget that."

"Thanks, Becky," I grinned. She didn't correct me.

"Boy, if I was nine years younger…"

"And a man," I added. We laughed. "Would you like to come in and see the place? I mean, it's just boxes, but, you know…"

"I'd like that," she said.

In minutes, we were walking up the stairs to the front door. I glanced behind me and noticed a car slowing down and idling in front of our house. I tilted my head slightly to peer inside the open window.

Rebecca looked around just as the car sped off.

"You know him?" she asked.

"I think so," I said. "It looked a little bit like one of my fraternity brothers you never met. His name is Jamal. He and I got into a fight."

"Oh, the guy Isaiah beat up?" Rebecca said.

"Yeah, him," I replied.

"Well thank God he told me about it after it happened," she said. "We were all set for a lawsuit from that guy, but it never happened."

"Thank goodness," I said. "That guy was bad news. If that was him, I guess he just wanted to see if it was really me. Loser."

I let us in to the house and we walked up more steps to our apartment.

"They really did renovate this place nicely," she said. "I love the hardwood."

"Me too," I said, opening the door. "Well, here's the living room with the kitchen. Sorry for the boxes everywhere."

"It's okay," she said. "I like the granite counter tops."

"Thanks. Oh yeah, we have a back door to the patio and a small backyard. Wanna see?"

"Sure," she said. I walked to the rear of our apartment and swung open the back door.

"Surprise!"

I was stunned. Everybody was here. Everybody.

"Happy birthday to you!" they sang, Isaiah the loudest of them all. "Happy birthday to you! Happy birthday, dear Adrian... happy birthday to you!"

"Oh my god, you guys!"

Isaiah was there, standing in between my mom and his mom. My entire chapter was there, including my spesh family and most of my line brothers. Cat and Samirah were there, as was Morris. Hodari and several other basketball players were there, too.

"You knew about this?" I asked Rebecca. She smiled.

"Yup... Came together great, didn't it?" I nodded my head vigorously.

I walked around the patio greeting everyone assembled there, shaking hands and offering the fraternity grip where appropriate. But the best surprise was yet to come.

I hugged Isaiah tightly and thanked him for the surprise.

"I've got one more," he said. I looked at him quizzically. He stepped to the side.

Nina was here. I screamed. We hugged each other tightly. My best friend was back in the country.

"How you been, boo?" she asked.

"Great! Everything's great! I can't believe you were able to keep this a secret from me!"

"Isaiah and Hodari were about to bust!" she said.

"Hodari knew?"

She nodded.

"Y'all been..." I whispered.

"I'll fill you in," she giggled. I hugged her again.

I looked around at the dozen or so people assembled to celebrate me. My frat. My family. My best friend. My man. This was my life.

"Welcome back, Nina," I said.

"And happy birthday, Adrian," she replied.

Part Three: Summer

Chapter 25:
June 25

One of the great things about living in DuPont Circle in the summer months was our ability to walk to everything we wanted and needed. Nina and I decided the afternoon wasn't too hot to walk to Books-A-Million before she had to head to campus to work her night gig as a student guard. I would be working as a part-time research assistant for my favorite anthropology professor, Sally O'Bannon.

Nina wore a long sundress in an orange and black West African print. Her hair was in two big afro puffs on the sides of her head. I simply wore cargo shorts and a plain t-shirt.

"You never did tell me how your grades turned out last semester," she asked me as we walked back to my place from the bookstore. Each of us had a bag filled to the brim with books and magazines. Summer was about the only time we had to read for pleasure.

"Not too bad," I said. "I got a 'C+' in statistics, but just about nobody in that class did better than a 'B,' so I felt okay with it. I got a 'B' in that black women writers class…"

"And…?" Nina asked.

"And I got 'A's in all my other classes! 4.0 in my major so far!" I beamed with pride.

"Work, bitch!" she exclaimed. "You have come so far!"

"Thanks, bitch," I said.

"So what's the secret?" she asked. We paused on the stoop before entering the house.

"It's no secret," I said bashfully.

"Lord, here we go again," Nina groaned through a smile.

"Come on," I said. "I went through a whole lot last year. I devoted all my free time to things I wanted, but not things that helped me keep my focus on school. Beta changed my life, but it ain't finding me a job. And you know I loved me some Savion, but with him I lost all types of focus. It was all about the romance—not reality. What I got with Isaiah is different. We're a team, you know? We work together. He makes sure I have my eyes on the prize, just like he wants me to do for him. I mean… it sounds crazy, but wherever he goes after college, maybe he's taking me with him. And maybe that's what I want. And if I go with him, I can't be that dude who barely graduated from Potomac. I got to stand tall on my own. To complement him—not live in his shadow. I guess he just lets me shine the way I need to."

"Wow. That's deep," Nina said. "And probably the most mature thing I've ever heard you say." I smiled.

"Thanks, girl. And thanks, also, for letting me shine. You're the best friend a boy could have."

"Shut the fuck up," she laughed. "Ain't nobody got time for your 'thank you for being a friend' love fest bullshit. Let me in this house so I can get some water."

"I love you too, bitch," I said. I unlocked the front door and we walked up the stairs, shooting one-liners at each other, playing up our sarcasm each step of the way. It was funny how with some friends—or lovers—you had to say exactly what you felt to convey a point. But for others, you could say "I hate you," mean "I love you," and never be misinterpreted.

"So, you and Hodari…going pretty strong?" I asked as I placed my key in the door.

"Yeah, I'm enjoying him," she said.

"You make him sound like an appetizer," I said.

"We have fun," she said. "He likes me. I like him. I don't know how serious it's going to be, but whatever. We'll see."

I opened our apartment door at the top of the stairs. We entered. The apartment was silent and stagnant. I couldn't put my finger on it, but I knew something was wrong as soon as I felt the air.

I closed the door behind Nina and looked up. Isaiah rushed toward me—his face was beet red and his eyes glistened. Nina quickly stepped to the side, looked beyond Isaiah, and froze.

I looked from Nina back to Isaiah. His lip quivered.

"What's wrong?" I asked softly. He shook his head and closed his eyes, grabbing both of my hands with his.

"It's not true," he whispered. "It's not true."

"What's not true?" I asked.

Isaiah stepped back. As I looked into our living room, I saw a familiar fair-skinned woman with long brown hair sitting on our sofa. I knew who she was instantly.

"Taina!" I said with a start. Isaiah's ex-girlfriend. The one he wasn't quite broken-up with when we started dating last summer.

"Taina, girl, you look…" I began. She balanced her weight on the arm of our sofa and stood herself up.

She was huge.

She was… pregnant.

"You look… good." I said.

"Thank you," she said coldly. "Hello Nina."

"Hi," Nina replied. "So… where you been?"

"I was at home in Rochester," Taina said. "I was busy having a challenging pregnancy, not that anyone in this room bothered to reach out and see where I was."

"I'm sorry to hear that," I said.

"Mmm-hmm. I bet you are," Taina replied.

"Taina came by…" Isaiah began, "to… uh… she's pregnant."

"Yeah, I gathered that," I said. My heart raced at a speed equivalent to the clamp contracting around my stomach. I put my bag on the floor. Taina seemed to smirk while Isaiah continued to cringe.

"How far along are you?" Nina asked.

"Eight months," she replied. "I got pregnant in late October, early November. In case you were wondering."

"Okay," I said. "Well. That's… yeah. How about that?"

"How 'bout it?" Taina taunted. I looked at Isaiah, whose eyes still glistened in anguish.

"Adrian," he said softly. "Taina… she came here to tell me…" He trailed off and looked away.

"Just fucking tell me," I whispered. He walked up to me and touched me on the shoulders with both hands.

"Taina says the baby is mine," he said in one exhale.

My heart was ready to explode in my chest. My stomach felt as though it would rip in two. My sinuses were on fire.

"Is it?" I asked.

"Of course it is!" Taina interjected. "Why else would I be here?"

"Will you be quiet for a second?" Isaiah asked, dropping one of his hands.

"I've been quiet for eight months, baby," Taina retorted.

"Baby?" Nina scoffed. "Seems like he hasn't been your baby since he dumped you. And what kind of woman get pregnant and waits eight months to tell the daddy—if he's even the daddy in the first damn place."

"Oh," Taina said, inching toward Nina. "Should I presume you're invested in this conversation because you've been fucking my man, too?"

"Stop it!" Isaiah demanded. "Taina, you can't just show up here causing all this chaos! We broke up, okay? And then *you* disappeared. You can't just show up like everything is cool."

"You're right." She turned around and headed back to the sofa. "Everything isn't cool. See... this is your baby. You're about to be a father whether you like it or not."

Isaiah turned to me and Nina. "Nina... I think you better leave."

"Oh hell no," she replied. "You think I'ma leave y'all in here with this lyin' skank?"

"Nina, please. It's complicated," Isaiah said. I snatched my shoulder from his grip.

"I'll be fine, Nina," I said while I walked into the living room. "I'll call you later."

"Aight, boo," she called back to me. "You better fix this!" she hissed at Isaiah before she turned heel and slammed our door.

I leaned against the brick wall in my living room and stared at Taina's belly. It was covered by the fabric of a bright yellow sundress. She noticed me staring.

"You know, I always thought you were one of the good guys," she said.

"Oh yeah?" I asked. Isaiah walked into the room and stood by me. She nodded.

"I thought you were the kind of guy that Isaiah needed to be around. The kind he needed to be like: popular, friendly, outgoing. Into everything. Passionate about so much."

"He still is one of the good guys," Isaiah said, reaching out to my shoulder. I walked away before he could touch me.

"How did you find out... about us?" I asked.

"How did I find out?" Taina laughed. "Oh, so you think somebody texted me when they saw you two making out at the front gates of campus? Or that somebody emailed me when they saw you out in DC, hugged up and holding hands? Or hell, that I got sent a Facebook message when they saw you creeping out of his room?"

She laughed some more. It was an insincere, maniacal cackle.

"Yes, all those things happened. All the women on campus who envied me, who were jealous that I had Isaiah from day one couldn't wait to tell me that my man was with another man. And not just any man... my man was with Adrian Collins. Oh yes, that Adrian Collins. The Beta. Used to date Savion Cortez. My motherfuckin man was gay. And they couldn't wait to tell me under the guise of sisterly concern, from one black woman to another."

"I'm sorry that happened," I said.

"Save your apologies," she said. "They told me these things, but I already knew. I knew it the day I saw you two kissing on the espalande."

"When did you see us on the esplanade?" Isaiah demanded.

"Last December," she said calmly. "The last night of classes."

"After my chapter's party," I said, remembering the evening well.

"The night we made it official," Isaiah said. "And you told me..."

"That he loved you," Taina completed. "Yeah, I saw the whole thing. I saw you pick Adrian up, spin him around, and kiss him. Oh yes, you kissed him, Isaiah. The same lips that used to kiss me, suck on my titties, and eat my pussy were on a man. My man was fucking a man. That was my man, Adrian. That was my fucking man and you lied to my fucking face, Adrian! You acted like y'all were the best of friends!"

"We were, Taina!" I shouted back. "I never expected to fall in love with my best friend, but I did. I didn't make him gay. I didn't turn him out. Shit happens, damn! The fuck you want me to do about it now?"

"You can fall the fuck back while I handle business with the father of my child," she said.

"Don't talk to him like that," Isaiah said sternly.

"Oh, now you decide to open your mouth and be a man? To protect your little boyfriend from a pregnant woman? Boy, bye."

"You can't even prove that's my baby!" Isaiah shouted. "You walk in here trying to fuck up the best thing I *ever* had in this world because of a hurt ego. Taina, look, I am sorry these chicks are clowning you. That ain't right. And yes, I was wrong as hell for not breaking up with you sooner. But that has nothing to do with Adrian and everything to do with us. We didn't work, Taina. I was with you because I liked you and because you were my chance at a normal life. But I didn't love you. I never loved you. And you claiming that's my baby you're carrying? That's not going to make me love you. I love Adrian. You got that?"

Taina smirked, stood up, and gathered her purse, straw hat, and sunglasses.

"If you loved him so much, you wouldn't have been sleeping with me last October. And November."

Isaiah was silent.

"Look, you don't know what the hell I've been through. I'm having a gay man's baby. How do you think that feels? I came close to aborting it. Hell, on Christmas day, I tried to kill myself. But I didn't. I'm stronger. I'm not the same person you knew. Shit, I thank God that I will never be her again."

"What do you want from me?" Isaiah asked.

"I don't want anything," she said as she put on her hat. "I am giving you the opportunity to be part of your child's life. I'll be staying with my girls in Georgetown for a week or so. After that, you won't have to worry about me anymore."

She put her sunglasses on.

"But know that this is your child and I'd like for you to know it. I may have disappeared for a few months, but it took me that long to woman up and get over your shit. Hopefully it won't take you as long."

She walked to the door. Noticing that neither of us was exactly rushing to open it, she said simply "I'll let myself out."

I walked across the room, past Isaiah, and picked up my bag of stuff from the bookstore. I then walked toward the stairs leading to our room.

"Adrian, stay and talk to me," Isaiah asked. I ignored him and started walking up the narrow stairs.

"Please don't walk away," he called out. I kept walking. When I reached the top of the stairs, I heard him follow.

"Baby, talk to me," he pleaded. I looked out the window, bag still in my hand.

"Please," he said, touching my shoulder.

"Don't fucking touch me," I snarled.

"Baby, please," he said, stepping close into my space.

"I said don't touch me!" I snapped, turning around with my books in hand, shoving them at Isaiah. He deflected the bag and it fell to the floor, magazines and paperbacks spilling out.

He bent over and started picking up my stuff. I kicked off my shoes and peeled off my shirt, standing in the heat of the attic. He turned on the air conditioning.

"I'm sorry this happened," he said.

I lay down on my side of the bed, face up, staring at the ceiling. He lay down next to me in silence. I turned my body away from him.

"I know you don't want to hear it right now... but I love you. Always have, always will. This won't break us. I won't let it," he said.

A single tear, undetected by Isaiah, rolled down my face.

Chapter 26:
June 26

Perhaps out of the self-defense of my own heart, I slept the afternoon and the evening away. By the time I woke up a little after 2 a.m., Isaiah was sound asleep.

I had slept off and on for ten hours.

I checked my phone and saw missed calls and texts mainly from Nina. She wanted to know what happened and if I would be okay.

I went to the bathroom and then came downstairs to quietly watch television. I turned the sound down and turned on the closed captioning so I wouldn't wake Isaiah. Not that he deserved a good night's sleep—I just didn't want to be bothered with him in my face trying to apologize and make up for the scene Taina caused. And, you know, getting her pregnant.

So much had happened that I didn't know what to feel. I was too angry to be sad, too sad to be angry. I hated that I loved him; I hated what he did. I hated myself for loving him. Why did I sleep with him when I knew he was technically still with Taina? Why couldn't I have waited?

Above all else, though… Why was he still sleeping with her as late as November when he was saying he loved me?

3 a.m.

4 a.m.

5 a.m. Still no answers, still no clarity.

6 a.m. I texted Nina back.

I'M COOL. IT'S PROBABLY HIS KID. I'LL BE FINE.

6:15 a.m. I crept back up to our room where he was still sleeping. I stood there in the darkness and stared at him as his chest rose up and down.

I gathered a pair of underwear, a shirt and shorts, deodorant, a book bag, and my cell phone charger.

I looked at him once more. At the last minute, I grabbed my journal.

I left.

6:30 a.m. I walked to the bus stop on P Street a block away from our apartment. The day was already warm—muggy even. I looked down at my phone and scrolled down to my dad's name.

Shortly after I clicked on his name, he answered.

"Adrian?"

"Hey, dad," I said somberly.

"What's wrong?"

"Nothing," I lied.

"Then why are you calling me so early? Did something happen? Is it your mom?"

The G2 bus pulled up to the stop and I got on board.

"No dad, nothing like that. Listen, uh, can I come see you?" I asked.

"Today?"

"Well… yeah."

"Um… well, son… sure. Yes. I'm working all day, but I'm free tonight."

"Thanks, dad," I said as I sat in the back seat of the bus. "I'm on my way to the Greyhound station to get a bus ticket now."

"Bus?" my father asked incredulously. I laughed.

"What do you want me to do, fly to New Jersey?"

By 10:30 a.m., I was in a Delta Shuttle heading to the Philadelphia International Airport. My dad was so ridiculous. I could have caught the Amtrak to Philly and been there in two and a half hours, tops. Two hours flat on the high-speed train. But my dad insisted on putting me on a plane to Philadelphia so I could have lunch with him in Camden, New Jersey.

I hadn't been on a plane since my senior class trip to Puerto Rico, but I wasn't anxious. I had my journal in my hand, the leather-bound book that Isaiah had given me for Christmas, but I still hadn't written anything in it. Every time that I opened it, I froze and my mind went blank.

It hurt too much to write it all down. Everything that had happened was too much. I just wanted to get away to someplace that nobody knew me. I didn't want to write. I wanted to forget.

When I turned my phone back on in Philly, I saw missed calls from Nina and Isaiah. I called Nina back.

"Boy, where are you?" she asked.

"In Philly, about to go see my dad in Camden," I said.

"What? How the hell did you get to Philly?"

"Flew," I said.

"Stop lyin'," she said.

"Dead ass," I said. "I told my dad I wanted to see him and he made it happen."

"Damn, he loves his son," she said.

"Guilt will make you do things," I said.

"Is there anything you need me to do?" she asked. "You need me to go beat up Taina?"

"Nina, you can't fight a pregnant woman."

"Watch me," she said.

"Nina, no. I don't know what I want."

"Isaiah's already been blowing up my phone trying to figure out where you are. I told him I didn't know."

"Good," I said. "Keep it that way."

"You gotta talk to him at some point," she said.

"I know. But not right now. I'm too blown by this whole thing to even think about it."

"Are you going to tell your dad?" she asked. I looked around and found myself in the pick-up area outside of baggage claim, waiting for the ride that my dad promised.

"I don't know what I'm going to tell him," I said. "I just want to see him. I need my dad right now for some reason. I don't know why."

"Okay," she said. "Well… good luck, I guess."

"Thanks," I replied. "Nothing can be worse than what I'm going through right now."

A driver held a sign up with the name "Collins" in bold print.

"I'm Adrian Collins," I told the older, white gentleman in the suit.

"Pleasure to meet you, Mr. Collins," he said while firmly shaking my hand. "Do you have any luggage?"

"Just my book bag," I said.

"Can I take it for you?"

"No thanks, I can hold on to it."

"Very well, sir," he said. He led me to the black town car and opened the door for me. We were on the road to Camden shortly thereafter.

I quickly remembered to call Professor O'Bannon's office. I wasn't scheduled to come in, but I had no clue when I'd be back in the city.

"Hi Professor O'Bannon," I said when she answered.

"Hello Adrian, how are you?" she asked.

"I'm okay. Listen, I really hate to have to ask you this, but I may need a few days off this week, if that's okay with you."

"What's going on? Is everything okay?"

"It's a long story, Professor O'Bannon. I'm going through some things at home. Well, not home-home, but where I live now off campus. With my… partner."

"Oh," she said. "Oh my. You're not in danger, are you? Do you need me to come pick you up?"

"Oh, no, nothing like that Professor O. But I'm on my way home to New Jersey. Well, not home, but to my dad."

"Wow, Adrian," she said. "It must be pretty serious for you to go visit with him."

"Yeah. It is. I was really hoping that you'd understand my need to be away for a little while."

"Adrian, you're a superstar," she said. "The work will be here when you get back. Please just take care of yourself."

"Professor O, you're awesome. Thank you so much. I promise I'll be back soon."

"No problem. Be well."

I sighed. I didn't even have a chance to take in the scenery around me as we left Philadelphia and headed into downtown Camden. Not that there was much to look at.

My phone rang again. It was Isaiah. I looked up to the ceiling of the car and answered the phone.

"Hello?" I said.

"Adrian, where are you?" he asked.

"Out."

"Where?"

"New Jersey."

"New Jersey?! What the hell are you doing there?"

"Wait a minute, who do you think you're talking to?"

"I'm sorry, I'm sorry. I'm just worried."

"You should have been worried when you were getting Taina pregnant."

"Adrian, I'm sorry. I fucked up."

"Yeah, you did."

"Can you please come home so we can talk about it?"

"Don't you listen? I'm in New Jersey. I just got here."

"Is Nina with you?"

"No, she's not, and what's up with all the questions?"

"I don't want to lose you, Adrian. Can you blame me for fighting for you?"

"Nigga, please. Don't fight for me."

"You got me messed up, Adrian. Everything I ever said to you was true. I am not going to give up."

The car slowed down in front of a large office building and my driver stepped out.

"I have to go, Isaiah, I'm at my... I'm where I need to be."

"Baby, please-"

I hung up. The driver opened the door for me.

"You can check in at the reception desk, sir," he said.

"Thank you very much!" I said. I looked up and saw a twenty story building as black as an iron skillet reaching up into the sky. It shined like a chunk of obsidian with perfect silver rectangles forming the windows.

The revolving doors led me to a wide open foyer decorated with huge granite statues which looked like Oscars or Emmys. Everything around me was huge and gray. The center island was a security and reception hub. You had to visit the island before passing through the metal detectors to the elevators.

"Welcome to the Concord Building," the black lady guard said. "Can I help you?"

"Yes, I'm here to see Adam Collins," I said.

She stared for a moment.

"You're his son," she said. I smiled and nodded.

"Y'all look just alike. Sign in for me right here, baby," she said, picking up her phone. She dialed an extension, and I once again looked around the cavernous room.

"Mr. Collins for Mr. Collins," she told a voice on the other end. "Thanks."

"Come on through here and take the elevator up to the 18th floor," she said.

"Thanks!" I said. "Have a good one."

"You too," she said.

I walked to the elevators, which looked like big toasters built into the wall. Two conservatively dressed woman patiently waited behind me. I turned around and smiled.

"Oh my… you're Mr. Collins' son, aren't you?" the elder of the two women asked.

"Yes, I am," I responded. "Adrian Collins."

I extended my hand to theirs and they happily shook it.

"You really do look like him" the younger woman said.

"So everybody knows him around here?" I asked as we got on the elevator. They pressed floor 18 for me while they hit 12.

"Of course," the younger said. "He's Managing Director for the Corporate Finance Division."

"Okay…" I said. "Whatever that means."

The women looked at each other with some sort of amazement that I wasn't catching on to.

"What?" I asked as the doors opened on their floor.

"Nothing," the elder said. "The similarities are only skin deep. That's all. You're probably majoring in the liberal arts. That's good. Have a great day!"

"You too," I responded, puzzled. The doors closed and I imagined that a Managing Director must be a pretty good thing, and perhaps that kind of salary allowed my dad to drop a few thousand into my bank account every so often.

The 18th floor was decorated totally differently from the foyer. There was burgundy carpeting and drapery everywhere, with gold accents and goldenrod furniture. This would be heaven for my frat.

A young Asian woman approached me with her hand out.

"Mr. Collins! I'm Susan, your father's assistant. How are you?"

"I'm great Susan, nice to meet you," I said. She was a beautiful young woman.

"I'll take you to his office now, follow me."

She took me down the hall where I saw more yards of burgundy fabric interposed between modern wood office cubicles and doors. The offices had frosted windows with the names of the executives etched on them. The cubicles were nothing to shake a stick at either—they were spacious and neat and everyone I saw seemed busy, but happy.

We came to the corner office, and as the women on the elevator said, there was my dad's name and title: Managing Director, Corporate Finance Division. She tapped on the door and opened it slightly, letting me in.

My dad's office was huge! It wasn't like any office I had seen before. There were windows everywhere, giving the dark burgundies and golds a fresh look under the summer sun. His desk seemed like it was ornately carved from one huge log. There was a laptop on his desk and a few inconspicuous file cabinets, but otherwise, this looked more like the chamber of a king, complete with with ornate rugs and drapery.

"My boy!" he said, standing up and approaching me. I smiled.

"Hi dad," I said. He extended his arms around me and gave me a huge hug. I hugged him back.

"How are you? How was your flight?" he asked.

"It was fine—quick. I still don't know why I couldn't just take the bus, or Amtrak," I said.

"Two reasons," my father said without missing a beat. First, you're a Collins. Second, because you obviously need me."

"Fair enough," I said.

"So why don't we have lunch and talk things out, okay?"

I nodded.

"'Preciate you, dad."

My dad drove me to a decent place nearby called 20 Horse Tavern. It was a weird little building with exposed brick and golden paneling. It apparently used to be a stable. Now we were having lunch there. Dad ordered a bacon cheddar burger and I had an angus burger. We each had a beer and made chit-chat while I avoided my real reason for visiting.

"I'm glad your grades were pretty good this semester," he said. "Very good work."

"Thanks," I said quietly.

"But now we're going to stop avoiding the issue. What exactly is wrong? Seven hours ago you called me at the crack of dawn asking if you could see me. Now everything is okay. What's happening?"

I inhaled, sipped my beer, and tried to find the words.

"Dad... I know we've never been close. And this relationship we have, well, we're still trying to make it work. And it's tough because we live in two different places. And you're busy and I'm busy. But, there's a lot more going on with me than I let you know. A whole lot. It's like... I wish I could share it with you when it's happening, but I don't know if you want to hear it. Or if you need to hear it. And sometimes I'm just scared of what you'll say or how you'll react."

"You never need to fear my reaction. I'm your father. You have to be able to trust me and your mother."

"I know, but dad... this is pretty major. And it's like not just what I need to tell you, but everything else. Like, the collateral issues."

"Son... is this about the hazing allegations your chapter went through?"

"What?"

"I know all about it. Son, everybody knows you're a legacy. There's nothing that you do that isn't on somebody's radar. When I heard the chapter was in trouble, I wanted to reach out to you, but I left it alone. You're a man. You'd figure out what to do and how to do it. So I stayed away. I never imagined that you'd solve it by getting independent counsel for the chapter, though. When I heard how that white girl busted up into that interrogation and started throwing around constitutional rights... I just laughed. I said 'that ain't nobody but Adrian setting these fools straight.' And I was proud of you because you handled it."

"Wow, you knew all that?" I asked.

"I found out bits and pieces," he said. "I might not be active but I've still got friends who look out for me and for you. No worries."

"Oh." I said.

"Nothing else has happened with the frat, has it? That region director coming at you again?"

"No, not at all. Dad, that's not why I wanted to see you."

"Oh, it isn't? Well, that's fine. What's on your mind? What's bothering you?"

"There's no really easy way to say this. For a while now... since I was in high school, really, I've known I was different. And when I got to college, I was able to finally be myself. Because of it, I think I became even more emotionally distant from mom than I was before. But now, she and I are good. We like each other again. And I'm happy. Dad, I'm so happy. Well, I was until yesterday. But in general, I feel like I am the man I am supposed to be. And I'm glad you're in my life, and I want you to stay in my life. I hope that you can accept me and understand that I am the same person you know and love. What I tell you in the next moment will only change your understanding of me—I don't want it to change our relationship. Dad... I'm gay."

"You're gay?" he echoed.

"Yes. I'm gay."

My dad wiped his mouth with his cloth napkin and then chugged the last bit of his beer.

"You don't like women at all?" he asked.

"Just as friends," I said. "Soon as I hit puberty, everything just started getting screwy. Crushes on boys and everything. I knew I was different. I didn't want to put a label on it, but I was pretty sure I was gay. I thought once I got to college, it would just be easy to come out and live my life. But it wasn't that easy at all."

"I can't imagine," he said quietly.

"Freshman year, I dated this lacrosse player from Maryland. Kept it quiet. Didn't last long though. Sophomore year, fell in love with this dude named Savion. Dominican dude. But when I pledged, it all fell apart. But the summer after I pledged, my whole life got turned upside-down. That's when I became roommates with Isaiah."

"Uh-huh," my dad said.

"And like, well... Dad, we're together now. By his count, we've been together for a year. By my count, it's been official since last December. But either way, we're together. And it's pretty serious, dad. Like... we moved in together and everything."

"Wow," he said.

"Dad... I know it's a lot... but there's one more thing..."

"Okay," he said.

"Isaiah's ex-girlfriend showed up to our house yesterday. She's pregnant and she says it's Isaiah's. And I think she's telling the truth."

My dad blinked.

"So... you're shacking up with a bisexual baby daddy?"

"Dad!" I began to laugh. Hard. That my dad could summarize all this information so quickly and succinctly was astounding. We were not similar in that regard. He was to the point, I had to tell a story. But as sharp as a tack, he boiled down my relationship to a simple sentence.

"I'm shacking up with a bisexual baby daddy?!" I repeated through the guffaws and tears.

All the months of work I had put into my relationship boiled down to this. From the minute I saw him in my dorm room last summer to the night we cuddled each other to sleep. The first night we made each other climax to the first time we were seen in public together. We snuck around yet we hid. We came out. We faced the drama of our mothers, his coach, and Rebecca Templeton. We had weathered everything together. But it all came down to his ex-girlfriend anyway.

No matter what happened, he would be connected to her. This baby was his, I knew it was. And he had drawn me deep into his baby mama drama. Even my dad recognized it. If I stayed with him, there would always be drama, confrontations, and child support craziness.

She would always be there.

My guffaws now turned into sobs.

"He turned my life into a Jerry Springer show!" I wailed. "What the hell did I do to deserve this?"

"Oh, son," my father said. He stood up and came over to me, placing his hand on my shoulder. "You didn't do anything to deserve it, I'm sure."

"Then why is this happening? We had everything, man. Dad, you're the last person I even had to come out to. Like, that's it. Mom likes him. His mom likes me. It was all perfect. But then he fucked it up. And the thing is he fucked it up eight months ago when he was sleeping with her while he was telling me he was breaking things off."

"That's not your fault," Dad said. "Listen, go to the car. I'll handle the bill. We're going home."

Through tears still running down my face, I hurried to his car. A few minutes passed and he came outside. Soon, we were on the road to his house in Franklinville, a 45-minute drive from Camden.

"Dad, I'm sorry if this overwhelms you. I just needed to see you and talk about it. I don't know why I couldn't just call you," I said, finally calm from my breakdown in the restaurant.

"Never apologize for needing your father. I failed at that for so long. I'm just glad you feel like you can talk to me. And for what it's worth, boy, I'm not upset that you're gay or anything like that. Yes, it's shocking. I never knew. And maybe deep inside I feel like you not having a father figure has something to do with it."

"No, not at all. I mean… you can't teach me how to be sexually attracted to a woman. I just am or I'm not. And I'm not. Never have been. I love women as friends. But that's it."

"I understand," he said. "I think. Still, I wish you didn't have to go through what gay black men have to go through. It can't be easy."

"You're goddamn right it's not easy, but I'm strong. Trust me."

He nodded. The rest of our trip to his house was spent in relative silence, save the phone conversations he took relating to his work. In the meantime, I texted back and forth with Nina.

JUST CAME OUT TO DAD. HE'S COOL SO FAR

STFU! OMG!

YEAH GIRL. A MESS. WHY DID I BREAK DOWN?

LOL. PUSSY

I KNOW RIGHT?

ISAIAH STILL ASKIN BOUT YOU. WANT ME TO SAY ANYTHING?

NOPE.

WANT ME TO PUSH TAINA DOWN THE STAIRS?

NO!!!!

LOL JK

My dad lived in a huge house on a grassy hill somewhere out in the boonies of Franklinville. It was a really classy place. I couldn't believe my dad had all that space for just him.

We pulled into the garage next to his vintage '67 Super Ford Mustang. It was a huge red and black toy compared to the BMW my dad drove to work every day.

"Sweet," I said. "Where do you drive that thing?"

"Anywhere I want," he said. "Usually just to take my dates in. They love it."

"Dad, when are you gonna settle down?"

"Never, hopefully," he laughed.

We walked into his house through a door from the garage. His place looked something like a ski lodge on the inside, with a two-story ceiling and exposed wood at its height. Stairs led to the second story of the house. We sat on his huge white leather sofas.

"Your place is pretty awesome," I said.

"Thanks," he said. "You're welcome to visit any time. Seriously."

"Thanks. So dad... what do I do?"

"Hell if I know!" he said. "I mean, really, what can you do?"

"I could leave him," I said. "I could walk away and say fuck it, this is your drama. You slept with this girl and you made a baby, so take care of it and leave me out of it. I mean, that's what I feel like saying to him."

"So why didn't you last night when you found out?" he asked.

"I don't know, dad. I was shocked. And... I love him. I'm not afraid to admit that."

"So if you love him, why don't you stay with him?"

"I don't know. I just don't know if I can do it, dad."

"Well, I don't know if I could do it either," he admitted. "But son, no matter what, I love you and I support whatever decision you make."

I smiled and nodded.

"Thank you. Thank you so much."

"Now make yourself at home," he said. Wander around a bit. Take a nap. Whatever. I'm going to do a little work from my office. But just give a yell if you need me."

"Will do," I said. I watched my dad walk up the stairs and disappear to the second floor.

"Bisexual baby daddy," I said again with a laugh. I reclined on the sofa and before I knew it, I was asleep.

I woke with a jolt. It was a few hours later. My dad came back downstairs and saw that I hadn't moved.

"What time is it?" I asked.

"Oh, about 4:30," he said. "Took a nap?"

"Yeah, I did. Dad... I think maybe I should go back home. To DC."

"Why?" he asked. "Don't you want to hang out here for a while? This is your home, too, you know."

"I know... it's just that... I can't solve anything here. I can't deal with my issues here. Maybe I do need to get away for a while, but not like this. I've got to see him first."

My dad nodded.

"I thought about that while I was upstairs working. Let me tell you something. Becoming a man isn't just about turning 18 or 21. It's not about voting or driving or drinking legally. It's about coming into your own, making grown-up decisions without your parents' prior approval. I know Elizabeth Collins did a fine job raising you on her own. I can see the fruits of her labors right here before me. And you've already made a bunch of significant decisions all by yourself.

"But becoming a man... We all have one defining moment in our lives where we can look back and say 'That's when I became a man. That's when I did what was right.' Not what felt good. Not what was popular. But what was simply the right thing to do.

"We have valleys. We have our darkest days when we don't know what's next. We don't even know what's on the other side of that valley. But you've got to have faith that there is another side and that you will make it there. This is your odyssey, Adrian. You've got to go through it. You've got to face it. And you've got to come out on the other side a stronger man for it.

"I believe in you, boy. And I trust you. Whether you stay with him or you leave him, you will be fine."

My face turned as red as it could through its shade of brown and I hugged my dad. I could see his eyes starting to water as I let go of the hug.

"Thank you so much, dad," I said.

"One more thing," he said. "And I swear I'm going to be kicking myself 20 minutes after you leave here. But I want you to have these—for now."

He reached in his pocket and gave me a set of car keys.

"The BMW?" I asked. He shook his head.

"The Mustang???" I said. He nodded.

"Dad, are you telling me you want me to drive the Mustang home? All the way home? To DC?"

He nodded.

"Oh my God, dad, I don't know what to say!"

"Get your ass on the road before I change my mind. By the way, you are borrowing this car—borrowing it, I say! I want it back. Keep it as long as you need to. Enjoy your summer. But take your odyssey. Don't just stay in DC. See the east coast. See the world. Create some memories for yourself. Become the man you want to be."

"Dad... wow... I promise, I will not so much as give her a scratch! And I'm a safe driver, I promise."

I hadn't driven a car in two years at least.

"Have fun, Adrian."

I went to the bathroom, took a piss, washed my hands and face, and got ready to go. In the garage, my dad once again admonished me to be careful.

I typed in my destination into the GPS system my dad had installed in the Mustang and saw that I would have quite a trip ahead of me, but I should be back in DC before it got too late.

"I love you dad," I called out as I pulled out of his garage. He threw up the fraternity sign as I drove off.

***

I couldn't believe this was actually happening. I had a vintage car to myself on the highway and just the clothes on my back, as though that was the normal thing an average 21 year old college student should be doing.

I drove for about two hours and finally stopped at an Arby's to grab some dinner. I brought the journal in with me, but I still couldn't bring myself to write anything. I had only just started dealing with the emotions that I had uncapped in front of my dad and things were too raw for me to go any further.

My mind was an empty slate for the majority of the trip. I tried to enjoy the ride as much as I could, but it was tough. I should have had my girl Nina with me, or my frat brothers, or Isaiah.

Isaiah. And Taina. And their kid.

I erased them from my mind and kept driving.

I made a stop in Silver Spring, Maryland instead of heading straight to the brownstone in DuPont. I parked in my mom's driveway and walked up the path to her door. I rang the bell, even though I had a key.

"Adrian? Well come on in, what are you doing here? And where the hell did that car come from!" my mom asked.

"It's a long story," I said. I stretched my arms out in front of me and waited for my mom to come give me a hug.

"Oh," she said. "You must be having a crisis if you come needing hugs! Come here, baby."

I hugged my mom so tight.

"Oh mom," I said. "So much insanity."

"I bet. You need to stay here tonight?"

"I think I'd like that," I said.

"Well, it's getting late. I'll go get us some cheesecake and we can talk for a bit. But you know a sister needs her beauty sleep."

I laughed.

"A slice of cheesecake and twenty minutes is all I need, ma."

She smiled.

It was good to be back home.

Chapter 27:
June 27

I woke in my own bed, in my own room of my mother's house, to the smell of freshly cooked bacon and a light rapping on the door.

"Come in," I mumbled.

My mom entered wearing a blouse, slacks, heels, and pearls—ready to tackle another day at the office.

"I'm heading out," she said. "I cooked some bacon. You can pop some waffles in the toaster if you want to. Are you going to stay here tonight?"

"I dunno," I mumbled.

"Well, you can if you want to. And you can move back here for the summer if you want—you are not trapped in this relationship with Isaiah. Free rent is a perk, not a necessity of being with him."

"I know."

"And remember what I said last night. You are better than baby mama drama. You understand?"

"Yes, mother," I said, flipping over in the bed.

"I'll see you tonight I guess," she said.

"Have a good day," I said. Within seconds, I was asleep again.

By the time I had slept the morning half away, I got up and fixed myself those waffles and ate the bacon my mom left on the oven for me. I relaxed and watched some television before growing restless. Before *The Price is Right* was over, I had already gotten my things together and left for my place.

I wasn't sure if Isaiah would be home. He had his summer league stuff to take care of. I hoped to avoid him as I packed my bags.

My prayer went unanswered as I heard Isaiah talking into his cell phone.

"Listen to me," he said firmly. "Joint custody is all I will accept. And if you can't deal with that, maybe you can talk to my lawyer about it… Rebecca Templeton. Yeah, she remembers you, too. And she doesn't like you. So if you try to pull some old bullshit with me and my child, I got Rebecca to light your ass up. So I suggest you watch yourself. Yeah, whatever."

He looked up and saw me staring.

"I gotta go," he said, hanging up the phone.

"You're back," he said.

"I'm just here for…" I began. He rushed toward me and hugged me, smothering my face with his chest before I could say anything more. I stopped trying to talk and just let him hold me.

I missed this.

I hugged him back.

"Baby, I'm glad you're back, because I need your help. See, I've been looking up websites on fatherhood and child custody and… umm… I think, I think I'm ready for joint custody of my child. I think I can convince her to let me raise it. Like maybe, she can have it during the week and I can have it on the weekends. Or, you know, something like that."

"How are you gonna raise a baby on the weekends during the basketball season?"

He smiled.

"Aww man, I don't know. But we can work something out. See, I was thinking we could put a crib upstairs in our room. We have enough space. Babies are tiny. And by the time we graduate, we'll be ready to move anyway, so we can get a place with another bedroom."

"Isaiah…" I said.

"No wait, for real. Listen. So maybe… maybe we could make our living room into more like a studio and put the baby upstairs. Yeah, you like that better, right? You don't want to have a baby all up in your space all the time."

"Isaiah… I don't know if I want a baby at all."

Isaiah continued his spiel.

"I know, I know, I get that. So maybe… maybe Taina raises it most of the time and we can see it on the weekends? It'll be like… fun, you know?"

I shook my head.

"I don't want this," I said.

"Baby... come on, sit down on the couch with me," he said, taking me by the hand. I followed him.

"Come on, get next to me. Get all comfy like we used to."

I begrudgingly sat next to him and rested my head in his chest. I listened to his words reverberate through his body as he tried to convince me that his thrown-together plan would actually work.

"This is the thing Adrian... All I know is I got a baby coming. Like soon. Soon, soon. And I'm not ready at all. And I don't like my baby's mother. Can't stand her. But I know the one thing I have is you. And I cannot do this without you. So please, please say you'll work with me on this. Please tell me that you'll be there for me. I don't know how it's gonna work, but I know it will work if you've got my back."

Silence.

He rubbed my arms slowly and kissed the top of my head.

"I love you, Adrian," he said. "Please stay."

I turned to him and kissed him on the cheek.

"I can't," I said. "I can't do this."

"No," he said, pulling me back into his arms. "It's not going out like that, Adrian. We can work this out. I swear to God we can."

"We can't work this one out, baby, it's too much. I can't be some... stepfather for this child. I never thought about kids before. Now I have to decide whether I want to deal with a child and its mother. You see what's happened?"

"Mmm-mmm, no," he said. "We can do this. We can get through anything, don't you believe that?"

"Anything but this," I said pulling away from him. "Isaiah, from August to December of last year, I waited for you. I've never waited on a man. But that's how I thought I knew this was for real. I was patient. I gave you your space and time to tie up whatever loose ends you had with Taina. And you know how much it hurt me to see you two together. You didn't break up with her until December, man! But I stayed. Because I knew this was your journey and you had to do it your way. But you were fucking her. And it would be different if you had already had this baby before you and I got together. Maybe I could have lived with it, learned to accept that I fell for a dude who happened to have a kid. But you were fucking her while you were saying you loved me. And I knew it, but I just didn't want to admit it to myself. That fucking hurts me to my core. I've accepted everything else to this point—why do I have to accept this too?"

I got up and walked to the refrigerator, getting myself a bottle of water. I chugged half of it while Isaiah sat in silence.

"Because I know what it feels like," he said.

"How what feels like?" I asked, setting my bottle on the counter.

"That the person you love slept with somebody else. Even if it was just once. I know exactly what that feels like."

"What are you saying?" I asked.

"I know that you slept with Morris last fall," he said.

I looked down at my bottle.

"It was only one time," I said. "And I felt like shit right after it happened."

"I know it only happened one time," he said. "And I know that if I had been there for you like I should have, it wouldn't have happened at all. If I had taken care of business with Taina, I wouldn't have kept up this charade with her and she wouldn't have gotten pregnant. Adrian, I'm not mad that you slept with Morris. How can I be? I was sleeping with Taina. But I just really hoped you would see that this sorta puts us at square one. All the creeping and hiding and lying—that's in the past. We can move forward together, right?"

"Are you trying to tell me that because I slept with Morris once that everything is fair and square now? We're even-stevens because I had a fling with some freshman I didn't even have a connection to? You have truly lost it," I said.

"That's not what I'm saying at all, baby," Isaiah said. "I'm just trying to tell you that I'm sorry. Eight months ago I fucked up big time and I'm going to spend the rest of my life living with that mistake. I just don't want to lose you over it."

He cupped my face with his hand and leaned down to kiss me. A small peck on my lips at first, then a longer one. By the third kiss, my mouth opened to taste his lips again. He hugged me while he kissed, pulling me back to the sofa. We lay there, me on top of him, kissing each other for as long as it took to keep this moment frozen in time.

"Stay with me," he whispered between kisses. I said nothing in response, but continued to kiss him.

Suddenly, I felt a vibration between us. His phone was going off. I took it out of his pocket and gave it to him without looking at it.

"Thank you," he said. He looked at the number and exhaled as it rang.

"Hello?" he said. "I told you I would call you later... none of your business. Yes, that's what I said. Don't worry about who I'm with, what do you want?"

I got up from Isaiah. He grabbed my belt loop to prevent me from getting up.

"Don't go," he said. "No, Taina, I wasn't talking to you. Listen, I will call you back. Later, damn!"

He hung up the phone and slid it back in his pocket. He looked at me with the most pitiful, longing eyes.

"It's time for me to go," I said. "Let me go."

Isaiah slowly dropped his hand from my belt. I walked up the stairs, half-expecting to hear his footsteps following me. They didn't.

I grabbed a few more t-shirts, shorts, underwear, and a pair of jeans and threw them into a gym bag. I wasn't sure what else I would need or where exactly I was going, but I had to be prepared for anything.

I came back downstairs with a full bag. I placed it by the door and came back to Isaiah, now sitting in the plush chair which matched our sofa. He stared off into space.

"Where are you going?" he said.

"I don't know," I said. "But I'll have my cell phone with me."

"It's okay if I call you?" he asked.

"Yeah... I don't hate you, Isaiah. I hate the situation."

"I do, too," he said. "Look, isn't there anything I can do?"

"No," I said. "This isn't about you now. I have to figure this out on my own. I literally don't know what to do next. But when I know... you'll know."

He nodded. I squeezed his shoulder and kissed him long and tenderly on his forehead. He looked up at me, then I walked away, toward the door and my bag.

"Isaiah," I said, turning back to face Isaiah as he sat slumped in the living room chair. "For what it's worth, I'm sorry I slept with Morris. I know we weren't officially together, but still. I know it was a lot for you to deal with, whenever you found out. And I'm sorry."

He nodded.

"I'll always love you, Adrian. Whether you come back to me or not. There will never be anybody in my life with a light that shines like yours."

I smiled through my quivering jaw and quickly turned my head. I picked up my bags and headed out the door, closing it quietly behind me.

By the bottom of the steps, the tears flowed freely. At the stoop, I could barely see to walk safely, yet I somehow made it to the sidewalk. I stopped at the curb, next to the tree box and dropped my things to the warm pavement. I sat on the curb, my face finally resting in my hands in an attempt to hide the tears.

"What's wrong witcha, nigga?"

I wiped my eyes, sniffed, and got myself together before I looked over my shoulder to see Hodari towering over me.

"God, does anybody work during the day anymore?" I said.

"Nigga, do you work?" Hodari retorted. "I'm the one coming home from a job. You sittin' on the curb lookin' like a broke-down Oliver Twist."

I laughed with him.

"What's up, man?" I greeted him, shaking his hand while still seated.

"Chillin'," he said. "I'd ask how you are, but uh… by the looks of it, this whole shit with Taina and your boy got the best of you."

I nodded.

"Mannnnn, fuck these tricks," he said dramatically. "I ain't gay or nothing, but I know what you and Isaiah have works. For y'all, at least."

"Please don't try to make me change my mind, Hodari," I pleaded.

"Change your mind? Nigga, I don't even know what you're talking about. All I know is that if a dude gotta be gay, he needs to be like you and your boy. You're just fuckin' normal. You ain't no sissies. You just dig each other."

"Thank you?"

"Son, you trippin'! Listen to what I am saying. I don't have no gay friends. You and Isaiah—that's it. And if I gotta have a gay couple in my life, it needs to be y'all. You're good, regular people."

"I appreciate you saying that man, but I'm tryin' to tell you... I'm not with Isaiah no more."

"What?! Quit playin'. Over this bullshit with that crazy bitch?"

"Please don't call her a bitch, man. She's about to be somebody's mother."

"She ain't my mother," Hodari said. He had a seat next to me on the curb.

"Yo, this curb is kinda toasty."

"I didn't really notice, what with the breakdown I'm having over here."

"Awwwww," he said, throwing an arm around me. "It ain't gotta be like this. You know some other dudes on the team already got kids. And at least one isn't with his baby's mother. I mean, you not in bad company."

"Hodari, I'm not trying to hear that. I'm only 21—I don't want to be no step-daddy. Or Uncle Adrian. Or whatever the fuck I'm supposed to be."

"You don't have to," he said. "Just be Adrian. Period. Isaiah doesn't want any more or less than that. Even I know that."

"I know. I just need time to think. It's too much happening at once."

"That's life, my nigga," Hodari said, suddenly standing up. "It happens. Sometimes it happens for you. Sometimes it happens against you. And sometimes it happens in spite of you and your plans. God's always got it under control."

"So you a preacher now?" I asked while I stood. He laughed.

"Ain't no preacher," he said. "I got a relationship with God.

Everybody has a valley to pass through. And I'm telling you man… If Isaiah having a son or a daughter is the worst life has to offer you… Then damn, that's a good ass life."

I pondered what he said for a moment, not wanting to agree, but also not finding any reason to argue.

"I'm 'bout to shower and get my grub on, man. I know you don't want to see your boy right now, but you're welcome to come have some lunch with me if you want."

"I appreciate that, Hodari, for real. But I want to just get on the road. Get away for a bit."

"Will I see you again? You know, any time soon?"

"Maybe," I said. "You might."

He shook my hand and pulled me into a quick hug.

"You'll work it out," he said.

I smiled and turned toward my dad's Mustang. I threw my bag into the back seat and was shortly on the road again.

I drove until I hit Georgia Avenue down by Howard. I pulled into yet another McDonald's and brought my journal with me. This time, I was determined to write something.

I had a filet-o-fish, fries, and an orange soda. The journal sat next to me, patiently waiting for me to finish my meal.

I opened it to the first page and put my pen to paper.

I got this journal for Christmas. It's been over six months and this is my first time using it. June 27. I'm sitting in the McDonald's on Georgia Ave. My boyfriend got his ex-girlfriend pregnant and now I have to decide whether to stand by him.

This fucking sucks.

I closed the journal. I couldn't do it.

I picked up my phone and saw a bunch of random texts from people asking how I was. Apparently, word had gotten out that Taina was back.

It's funny how, for two years, everybody knew them as Taina and

Isaiah. They were like a supercouple. Inseparable from the moment they met, so it seemed. A chick daren't even look at Isaiah for too long. It was well known that he belonged to Taina.

Taina wasn't even a bitch about it. It was just a fact. She was the bubbly, friendly one. He was the shy athlete. They just sort of worked well together.

But when it slowly seeped out that instead of Taina, it was me in that spot... sure, there was shock. There was resentment. But by and large, Taina bore the brunt of that. It was as if everybody on campus could breathe a sigh of relief because they never truly liked her—never truly accepted the Taina and Isaiah mythology. Somehow, it seemed that the campus accepted me and Isaiah and quietly unified to make sure we were protected.

It was weird. Taina had done nothing wrong in this situation but people were dying to tell her that her man was gay. Me and Isaiah had done everything wrong, from lying to our friends to making out in public. But people cared about us. His teammates looked out for him and me. My gay friends liked him.

Nothing can be that perfect, can it? For two dudes to be so totally in the wrong and have this innocent girl get her heart trampled and get pregnant by her gay ex.

This shit was crazy.

I could think about it, but I couldn't write it down.

I could cry about it, but I couldn't talk about it.

I felt guilty. I felt like every fucked up thing I had ever done in my life was finally being repaid. Nobody can have a life as perfect as me and Isaiah's for long. Not how we had come by it. It wasn't right.

I needed to go. I picked up my things and walked back to the car. As I hurried, I walked past a group of young dudes. I didn't really pay attention to them.

"Excuse me," one of them asked. While I kept walking, I turned back and said "Yes?"

"I was just wondering... do you have a brother named Daniel?"

"Indeed, I do," I responded, squinting my eyes so I could see the group more clearly.

"Where did you meet him?" he replied.

"I lifted him out of the lions' den without a scratch on him."

"My brother," he replied. I put my keys back in my pocket and approached my brothers of Beta Chi Phi. I knew they looked familiar, but I wasn't sure how I knew them.

The group of three were dressed casually with no Beta gear on to speak of.

"Hey Brother Collins," began the brother who initiated our challenge, "You probably don't remember us, but we're neos from Mu Chapter, Howard University."

"Oh yeah, I remember you all now! How have you been?"

"We're good, bruh," he said. "My name is Henry Wilson, this is my front Patrick Lyle, and that's our tail Joey Oates."

I gripped each of them and patted them on the back.

"Whatchu doin over here, bruh?" Joey asked.

"Just riding around, grabbed something to eat."

"I feel you," he said. "You was lookin' mad intent."

I shrugged. "Yeah, kinda. Got some things going on."

"That Region Director ain't still gunning for you, is he?" Patrick asked.

"Oh, y'all heard about that?" I asked. They all nodded.

"I mean, it's none of our business," Henry said, "But we like Sigma Chapter, namean? And that RD is always going after undergrads. But yo, we heard how you handled his ass, too."

"Oh really?" I asked.

"Yeah, son, we heard you was kickin' tables and throwing chairs!" Joey exclaimed.

I laughed hard. "So that's what people are saying?"

"It's not true?" Patrick asked.

"I did not kick over any tables or throw any chairs... nor was anything about that meeting supposed to be public."

"Well... we won't ask any questions," Henry said. "But it's kind of clear that you were the hero in that situation."

"Thanks, bros. Seriously, I'm glad you all are hearing good things."

"Much respect, bruh," Henry said. "Hey… you doin anything tonight?"

"Nope," I said.

"Why don't you roll with us up to Gaithersburg and kick it?"

"What's in Gaithersburg?"

"Just chillin' with some bruhs. Mostly Mu chapter, some old heads. Come on, we're headed there now, you can follow us."

"A midweek chill session?" I asked. "Yeah, I can dig it. One of y'all needs to ride with me though, make sure I don't get lost."

"I can," Joey said. "You got ID, right? We should probably stop at a liquor store."

"No doubt," I said. "Let's hit the road."

This was exactly what I needed—a random, chill night with the bros. Plenty of liquor, laughs, and opining about the good old days, even if they were only last year.

I knew none of these brothers well, but we saw each other often at cluster events like intake and founders' day celebrations.

They knew me through my work as a Beta. It was nice to know that people noticed the work I did, even if they assumed I was a menace to our Region Director.

No one from Sigma Chapter was available to come through to the apartment in Gaithersburg where we hung out—understandable, as many of us scattered to the four winds over the summer.

There were five of us left in the apartment by the end of the evening: me; Joey and Patrick, two of the three neos I had met; and their two prophytes, Sonny and Kenya, who had recently graduated.

"Y'all going to convention, right?" Kenya asked.

We all nodded.

"Are y'all registered for convention?" he asked.

I looked around at my brothers and scratched my head.

"Lord Jesus, help the children," Kenya said.

"Y'all gotta understand that the frat is not just about kickin' it and community service," Sonny said. "There is serious business that gets done at these conventions. Don't get left behind because you didn't know."

"Word," Kenya added. "I heard they still don't have any candidates for national second vice president."

"The undergraduate position?" I asked. "Nobody is running for that? That's crazy, who wouldn't want to run for that?"

"It's a lot of work," Sonny said. "But it opens doors. You get to go to the national board meetings twice a year, represent the frat at shit like Congressional Black Caucus Weekend, NAACP conventions, sorority conventions—that's the best part."

"Wait, that's your position, isn't it?" I asked. He nodded.

"Why didn't you say something before?" I laughed.

"Shit, nigga, I been second vice the whole time you been a brother."

"Yeah, true... I definitely did learn that when I was online. I guess sometimes you just don't make the real life connections unless somebody connects the dots."

"It's all good," he said.

"So how come nobody in Mu Chapter wants to do it?" I asked.

"That's a lot of work," Joey said. "I'm trying to keep my grades up."

"It's not that bad," Sonny said.

"But you hardly get to go to chapter shit when you have that position. You can't be up in set hazing up pledges and you're a national board member," Patrick said.

"True," Sonny said. "Not a good look. But all that networking I was able to do while I was in that position got me a job on the Hill this year."

"Word?" I asked. "But how do you deal with the niggas like John Carver who try to throw chapters under the bus?"

"It's a lot of people on the board who don't like him, and believe me, he gets put in check when it's his turn. You know, Beta has a lot of good brothers around the country. We're still a small fraternity and a young one, too. So I get to see all the good work we're doing. And yeah, there are a lot of challenges, but it's worth it. One day, we're going to have the brand recognition of A Phi A or Omega Psi Phi. We're earning it every day."

"That sounds really cool, bro," I said. Sonny laughed.

"Sigma Chapter be killin me with the 'bro' shit—it's bruh!" I laughed along with him.

"Whatever man. You know, my dad has pretty high hopes for me. In general, but even as a Beta. He wants me to enjoy it but to work hard for it. I'm glad to see we're doing good things outside of the chapters."

"Yo!" Patrick exclaimed. "Adrian needs to run for national second vice!"

"You buggin'." I said. "I don't know shit about being on a board. I'm just trying to graduate next year."

"Dude," Joey interjected, "Do you know how well liked you are? How many people respect your chapter? Especially coming off the investigation without so much as probation. And everybody knows that was because of you."

"It wasn't just me," I said.

"He's right, you know," Kenya added. "I've kept my eye on y'all for a while. Sigma has what it takes to be real power players in the frat, but y'all never come out of your shell. Why is that?"

"I didn't know we were in a shell," I said.

"We all are," Sonny said. "I guess it depends on how you look at it. But seriously bruh, Beta needs leaders. You know, people who get what this is all about. And I know you get it. I know you work hard for Beta."

"I'm not even a chapter president," I said. "I only just got elected secretary this past May."

"So? You don't even need to be a chapter officer to run. You have to be mentally prepared to be on a board of directors. You've got to be able to plan for the future, not necessarily know how to lead a chapter."

The future. I was an anthropology major with no clear options after graduation. I wasn't sure about grad school and I definitely wasn't sure what kind of job I wanted or would even be good at. But I loved service and I loved Beta. Maybe running for this position could give me the skills I needed to make my life into something other than school and being someone's boyfriend.

"I see you thinking about it." Kenya said. "With your thinkin' ass."

I laughed.

"Can I just think about it some more?" I said.

"Convention is at the end of July," Sonny said. "Think about it all you want, but I'm telling you, this is the move you want to make."

"We'll see," I said. "It's getting late, though."

"Yeah man —but um, you've been tossing em back kinda hard tonight. Why don't you crash here instead of getting back on the road?" Kenya suggested.

"Really? You know, I appreciate that. Thank you."

"No doubt man," Kenya said. "You family. All of you can stay. We got blankets, pillows, all that shit. Just kick it. You home."

Even though my fraternity was small, it was great to have brothers no matter where I went. Men who looked out for you and saw behind chapter letters and reputation. This was exactly why I had pledged Beta Chi Phi—for the promise of an enduring and sincere brotherhood.

It had been a very long and trying day. The sofa was calling my name. Before I crashed, I took one last look at my phone.

No calls. No texts.

Finally, the universe had given me space to breathe.

Chapter 28:
June 28

Me and the Howard bros got up crazy early and had breakfast at IHOP so that our hosts could get ready for work and their neos could get back into the city. As for me, I was heading north to Baltimore. I was determined to enjoy this new-found freedom to do exactly as my father said: to get out there and have my own adventure while I didn't have any significant family or personal responsibilities.

I decided I was going to be a tourist all day, to see all that Baltimore had to offer someone with nothing but time to kill. I'd take in the zoo, the inner harbor, and whatever else I felt like doing. I had wheels, a bank account full of guilt money from my dad, and no attachments whatsoever.

After getting a little lost somewhere outside of Cooksville, I finally made it to Baltimore, Druid Hill Park, and the Maryland Zoo. I spent a lot of time just wandering around and looking at the animals, as an anthropologist in training should. Even though my specialty wasn't primates, I did enjoy them the most. Watching them interact, take care of each other, lounge around—it fascinated me. I was truly Sally O'Bannon's prize pupil, making an academic moment out of what should have been "me" time.

After the zoo, I head down to the inner harbor for lunch and more sight-seeing. I hit up Harbor Place and the aquarium primarily, but again, I spent a lot of time just sitting around, watching the water and watching the people.

As I gazed out in the harbor, my phone rang. It was Nina.

"Hey," I said.

"Hey boy, where you at?" she asked.

"I'm chillin'," I replied.

"But where are you?"

"I'm out and about. What's up?"

"Why are you being secretive?"

"I'm not being secretive, I told you I'm out and about."

"Well, whatever. Look, I need to tell you something about Taina."

"I really don't want to hear about Taina."

"But you really need to hear this."

"I don't want to hear it. I am having a good day. I have been by myself, thinking, chillin', doing me. You notice I haven't called you?"

"I mean, I noticed, but I didn't think you were intentionally not calling me."

"I haven't called anyone. I'm doing me."

"Oh." There was an awkward silence.

"So what else is going on?" I asked.

"Are you serious right now?" she replied. "You're asking me what else is going on?"

"Uh, yeah."

"Negro, there is nothing else going on! You broke up with Isaiah, who happens to be having a child with his ex-girlfriend, and you disappeared. You really think there's anything else to do or think about?"

"Actually, I would hope there is. You have a man, Nina. His name is Hodari Hudgins. Remember him?"

"We're just dating. What is wrong with you? Why do you sound so... mean?"

"I'm mean because I want to have one day, just one day, to myself, to not have to think about all the bullshit I just went through. And here you come wanting to tell me some gossip about Taina that just can't wait? I don't want to know about it. Focus on your own shit, your own dude. Leave me and mine alone."

"But you need to know..."

"No the fuck I don't! Now leave me the fuck alone so I can get some peace!"

I hung up the phone.

Wow, did I really just cuss out my best friend?

The phone rang again. It was Nina calling back. I sent the call to voicemail.

A wave of depression finally came over me. It was the feeling

I had subconsciously tried to avoid for days while I processed all that had happened. My anger clouded everything, made me feel like I was walking through a fog. Prior to this moment, it was as if I was living someone else's life and I was reciting lines. But now, it was different. Now I was angry at people invading my space as I tried to heal. I was trying to get my "grown-man" on and just separate from everything, but people wouldn't let me. Nina wouldn't let me. I just wanted to grow, to move on, to decide what to do next on my own.

Right then, because of Nina, because of everything, I had broken my concentration. All I wanted to do now was to call Isaiah. I wanted to hear his voice. I wanted to bitch to him about how Nina was pissing me off, but I couldn't because I was still pissed off at him. I was trying to get over him, but I was relapsing.

My eyes began to water right there as I stared out into the harbor.

"Mmm-mmm, hell no," I said aloud. "Not today. Get it together, Lazarus."

I stood up, looked to the sky, and walked to the car.

I drove around Baltimore for a good thirty minutes, just looking around. I wasn't sure where I was going or if I was going to go home that night or not. I hadn't yet found what I was looking for. I wasn't even sure what I was looking for.

I found myself on North Warwick Avenue for the third time that day. For some reason, I kept finding myself there. It started to look familiar to me, but I wasn't sure if that was because I had seen it so many times that day.

It hit me suddenly that I was very near where Isaiah's mother lived. It was close to six o'clock in the evening and she'd likely be home from work if I stopped by. If I could find the place from memory, that is. I for damn sure wouldn't call Isaiah to get the address.

I drove slowly down North Warwick, certainly looking as suspicious as a drug dealer to the locals. I knew I was on her street... if I could only remember which house it was... They all looked the same.

I crossed Westwood Avenue and knew I was in the right block. I glanced down a ways and saw the school and park where Isaiah's dad was killed. I slowed the car down more and looked to the right.

Taking grocery bags out of her small sedan was Ms. Gloria Aiken herself in a cream colored linen suit, fresh from her job. I slowed down and idled next to her.

"Need some help, pretty lady?" I asked. She turned around and peered into the car.

"Boy!" she said as she beamed. "You better park that big old car and come here and give me a hug!"

I smiled and quickly found a space near her house. I was sure to put the club on the steering wheel and turn the alarm on. If anything happened to my dad's car, I am sure I would spontaneously combust. Then my dad would bring me back to life and kill me again.

"Look at you looking all rugged!" Gloria exclaimed. "Got a little hair on your face and everything!"

I rubbed my chin and smiled.

"I guess I forgot to shave," I said.

"It looks good, boy," she said, giving me a hug and peck on the cheek.

"Whatchu doin up here?" she asked.

I shrugged.

"Just hangin' out," I said. "Decided to come up here for the day. Maybe longer. I don't know."

"Yeah..." she said. "I know you know about the baby." I nodded. "Mmmmmm-hmm. A mess. Trying to make me a grandmother, good as I look!"

She laughed her usual, loud corner-girl laugh and patted her hair.

'It's something, isn't it?" I said.

"Mmmmm-hmm. Mmmm-mmm-mmmph." She shook her head.

"Can I help you take your bags in the house?" I asked.

"Sure you can! It's not a lot, though. Just grab those two, and I'll grab these."

We got ourselves situated and walked up the handful of steps to her front door. Once we got inside, I was flooded with memories from the last time I was in her house. It was like Christmas all over again, but with less anxiety. Strangely, I felt like I was at home.

"Stay for dinner, will you?" Gloria asked.

"That sounds good to me," I said. "I mean, if I'm not imposing."

"Of course not," she said. "I save all my hot dates for the weekend." She winked.

"You a mess," I said.

We soon sat down to a meal of crab cakes, tossed salad, and fruit salad on the side—a great meal for the summer. We chatted a little bit about the upcoming football season as Gloria was a sports nut and I was still finding my way around the basketball court. I found out that she comes to the Potomac football games sometimes, even though Isaiah doesn't play.

"You know he used to play three sports," she said. "My baby was in football in the fall, basketball in winter, and track in the spring. Yup, all the way until high school. Then he stopped and focused on the two Bs: basketball and books. Which is fine because he was really a bum in track."

"That's funny," I said.

"Oh, he knows! That's why his grades were so good. When his dad died, I knew I had to stay on him like white on rice. He was not going to be out in the streets, know what I mean? Shit... sorry, I mean 'shoot.' Because these niggas out here are trifling. And I know because I know their families."

"Isaiah always talks about moving you out of here," I said.

"He been saying that since he was eleven. I don't know, it's rough but it's not horrible. It's home, you know?"

"If he starts making the kind of money where you could move out to the county, would you?"

"I guess... I mean truth be told, I could probably move right now if I wanted to. We ain't poor, you know. I work full-time. I'm not an old lady. Isaiah act like we on skid row."

We laughed together.

"Yeah, you have a cute house," I said. "It feels... just right."

"My brother Gregory used to live in the basement when me and Isaiah's father first came here. Did you know that?"

I shook my head.

"Mmmm-hmmm," she continued. "Me and Tony bought this house right out of high school. Dirt cheap. Our parents pitched in with the down payment and we got a good mortgage rate. I had a job with the government and Tony was doing security at night and going to Coppin part time. We asked Greg to move in to make things even better. You know, help with the mortgage, utilities, all that. It was fun. We were all young and dumb and having a lot of fun in our early twenties."

"Gregory is your brother who passed, right?"

"Yeah. He got that HIV. He never told us how he got it, but I always sorta knew. He never did no drugs, never got no blood transfusion... Anyway, this was way back in the day before they had all them good AIDS drugs. Now, it's like you get HIV and can live fifty years, but diabetes will kill you. I miss him a lot."

"Gloria, you said you always sorta knew how he got it... What do you mean?"

"Greg was a tall, good-looking dude. Pretty boy. Loved partying. Always had a lot of friends. Usually guys. Adrian, I'm saying I think my brother was gay. And I think he got AIDS from having unprotected sex and thinking he was invincible. He died just like a lot of gay men in the 80s: living fast and thinking AIDS couldn't happen to them. But it did happen to Greg. By the time he was diagnosed, it was too late. He died about six months after Isaiah was born."

"Wow, that's crazy! I am so sorry!"

"Thanks, baby. It was twenty years ago, but I miss him like it was yesterday."

"Does Isaiah know this?"

"Yeah... I mean, most of it, I guess. We never sat down and talked about it like you and I are. He knew Greg passed. He knew it was sudden. And I told him I thought Greg was gay when he came out to me. Adrian, to be honest, when Isaiah told me he was gay, all I could think about was Greg and how he died. Now, I know every gay man don't have AIDS. But I know how it is out there. Y'all don't get the same kind of messages about safe sex like straight people do. Y'all are so preoccupied with staying physically safe that you forget about being sexually safe."

"You mean... Trying to hide who we are so people don't treat us differently?"

"Exactly. See, I knew my baby wasn't gonna choose no dummy."

I looked down at my plate and played with my last bite of crab cake.

"Anyway, how are *you* doing?" she asked me. I continued to poke at my food.

"You know how I'm doing, Gloria."

"Not good?"

"No."

"Awww, baby. I can't imagine what you goin' through right now."

"It's bad. Really, really bad. I feel like... like somebody ripped out all my organs and put them back in the wrong places, like it ain't even my body anymore."

"Damn, baby," she said. "Now, you know that's my son, so you know I'm biased. But I'ma tell you like it is. That boy loves you. His life with you has made him into the man I knew he was born to be."

I shook my head.

"Gloria, I understand, but that's not helping."

"Now just hear me out for a second. Like I said, I know he loves you. But he fucked up. And I don't know what I would do if I were you. I didn't raise him to make no dumb mistakes like having a baby at his age. Especially with so much at stake. But that baby is coming. He has no choice but to be a father. And I got no choice but to be a grandmother."

She shivered.

"Can you believe that? A grandmother. At my age!"

I smiled.

"But you have a choice, Adrian. You don't have to be a father.

You don't have to be a play-uncle, a godfather, or even a friend. You can walk away from all of this and not be bothered. And if you did, I wouldn't blame you."

She stood up and cleared out plates while I contemplated what she said.

"I'd be real sad to lose you, though," she continued. "Just when we're getting to know each other."

I stood up and went to the kitchen counter with her.

"We can always be friends," I told her, giving her an unexpected hug. "Thank you for dinner, Gloria."

"You not leaving, are you?"

"Well... I'm just on the road. I've got no place in particular I'm going."

"Why don't you stay the night? Get some rest and head out in the morning? Where you going next, Philly? The Eastern Shore? New York?"

I shrugged. "All of the above?" She rolled her eyes.

"Boy, take off your shoes and relax. You are home. You will not be driving that big old Mustang all up and down the east coast without a game plan. If something happens to you, how is your momma gonna know where you are? In fact, have you called her to let her know where you are?"

"Uhh..."

"I thought not! Call her. Now. Then decide where you going next. And tell her where that will be in the morning. Hmph. Driving around willy nilly like this is a game."

She disappeared to her back porch to smoke a cigarette.

I walked back to the car to grab my bag and called my mom while I did so. She was surprised I was being so adventurous, but she was supportive, even as she begged me not to wreck my father's car.

Gloria let me sleep in Isaiah's room for the night. She told me that she would have offered the basement, but she felt it might be a little too chilly down there. I had no problems staying in Isaiah's room, though I watched television until late in the evening down in the living room.

I walked up the stairs, quietly, after Gloria had retired for the evening. I passed by a photograph of Gregory Aiken, the spitting image of Gloria, just male. He was, as she described, a pretty boy, with round features and curly hair. He practically glowed with life. It was hard to believe that this man had been gone for twenty years.

I had a small family. I had no idea what it might be like to have a gay uncle, much less one who had died from AIDS. The disease was so unreal to me. I didn't know anybody with it and never considered myself at risk. I got tested once or twice, but never really thought about whether I was truly at risk.

Isaiah and I had done things but never had penetrative sex. I wasn't a woman; I had no vagina. Hell, everybody knows that anal sex hurts. I guess it's no wonder that he'd sleep with Taina if he couldn't get ass from me.

He hadn't actually betrayed me. He slept with his girlfriend. That's what boyfriends do. I was not his boyfriend. I was the other man.

I also saw a picture of Tony Aiken on the wall. Even though Isaiah looked like his mom, it was his dad who truly spat him out. The only real difference was that Tony had a coarseness about his face that suggested he was a little more worldly, a little more hardened. Isaiah, as much of a man's man as he could be, still looked the part of a child. After all, he wasn't 21 yet, though his birthday was coming up.

Bet he never expected the gift of a baby for his birthday.

I opened the door to Isaiah's room.

Can't believe I'm here. I said to myself. *Without him.*

I peeled my clothes off in the dark until I was down to my boxer-briefs. I wanted to look through his drawers, his closet, under his bed. I wanted to know him without him knowing I was here. I wanted to find something, anything that would let me know if I needed to stay with him or leave him. Some clue, some miniscule, overlooked clue that would tell me that Isaiah was the one.

I opened his drawer and found a plain white t-shirt, size extra-large. I picked it up, smelled it, and rubbed it in my face. It didn't smell like him at all—just smelled like the cedar chest that I got it from.

But it was his. His shirt, his room, his mother's house.

I slid out of my underwear and was naked with his shirt still in my hand. I thought about all the other times we had seen each other in various stages of undress. Now I was naked, in his room, without him.

I put on his shirt and crawled into his bed face down. He would have thought the scene sexy, his man wearing his clothes, lying face down on the bed with his ass barely peeking from underneath the bottom of his shirt.

Had he been there, he would have crawled on top of me and enveloped me in his warmth.

I fell asleep, imagining what he would be thinking if he could see me now.

I woke up, disappointed that I hadn't dreamed of him.

Chapter 29:
June 29

After a few morning phone calls, I decided to head to New York to visit my spesh and the other brothers I could find. It was Friday and it was time to find some focus for my weekend. No more weepiness and reminiscences—it was time to go to the city that never sleeps and party it up with my brothers.

I said farewell to Gloria, who let me know that she didn't envy my position but she was glad to have seen me.

I had seen a lot of New York the last time I was there during the basketball tournament, but I didn't really kick it at the clubs and lounges. It was more of a family trip. This time, it was gonna be all about me and the boys.

On the road, a strange thing happened. I started remembering the trip we took to Philadelphia when I was a pledge. During hell week, we always went to visit the grave of the first deceased Beta, Richard Ellis Dawkins. We took our pledges there to tell them the legend of his life, how he could have been a founder, but chose to wait a semester to honor other obligations. How he became a teacher and track coach in New York, and later Philadelphia, and started new chapters everywhere he went. How he had a love of music and wrote most of our songs. How he had a propensity for social action and chaired many of our programs. How he did all of these things for fourteen years and somehow never became national president. How he tragically died after a bout with pneumonia.

My dad later told me that he knew Brother Richard and that in hindsight, it was pretty clear that he had died of AIDS. He told me that he was sure that Richard was gay, but that nobody had a problem with it. It just wasn't discussed.

As I saw more and more familiar landmarks, I decided that I had to visit his grave and spread red and yellow rose petals over it, as was the Beta custom. At least once in my life, I needed to do this during the daylight hours as a regular visitor, and not leading pledges through broken fences in the middle of the night.

After getting lost somewhere on the outskirts of Philadelphia, I called a few brothers and finally got better directions to the cemetery. Steven knew the way, but asked me why I needed to get to the cemetery.

"I'm on my way to New York and I just feel like I need to pay my respects. It's on the way, no big deal."

"Everything okay?" he asked.

"Yeah, why?"

"You know you can talk to me, bro."

"Yes, I know. But why, what have you heard?"

"Rough breakup."

"Oh. That. Steven, I dunno man. I'm just playing it by ear. But in other news… I kicked it with Mu Chapter a few nights ago."

"Word? Mu Chapter? I didn't know they liked anybody but Mu Chapter."

"Dude, they are mad cool. Real down to earth. Their neos and some of their old heads had a get together and invited me over. And we talked all night practically."

"That's good, man."

"And… they kinda put a little idea in my head."

"What?"

"They suggested I run for national second vice."

"I'm sorry, what?"

"You heard me, fool! They want me to run for national second vice president at convention in August. Down in Atlanta."

"Why?"

"Why not?" I said. "First, word on the street is that nobody that tried to run could get certified. I don't know if it was grades, finances, whatever. So I might get down there and there's no competition. Secondly, one of the dudes that was there has that position currently-"

"Sonny Hudson?" my Dean asked.

"Yup, him." I replied. "He said it's not too bad, and from what he heard, I had the right temperament for it."

"I don't know, Adrian, that's a lot of work. And your

temperament… Well, you know I love you like blood, but you be acting out of pocket sometimes."

"Ahhh, whatever. I'm gonna do more research, but I'll let you know what I decide. But I appreciate you being honest with me."

"Always, Frat."

"I'm at the cemetery, bro. Talk to you later."

Across the street from the cemetery was a flower shop. I stopped in and purchased a single red rose and a single yellow rose from the old, gray lady behind the counter. I thanked her and she wished me well.

I walked quickly through the cemetery gates, certain of where my brother's grave was in relation to the street on which I'd parked. There was nothing to me which was un-creepy about a cemetery, even in the daylight. The silence of the grassy knolls, headstones, and statues wasn't serene to me. It was eerie.

I finally found the grave, which still had remnants of red and gold candles along the headstone. There was no need to light them as the summer sun illuminated the entire grove with its midday rays. I felt a little calmer now that I had reached my destination. Since I knew the deceased, in a sense, I felt more at ease.

I grabbed the petals of the red rose, symbolizing the blood of our ancestors upon which the fraternal legacy was built. I tore the petals out as one and reverently cast them before me. They fell over Richard's grade in a quiet cascade. I then grabbed the yellow rose, symbolizing the golden light of knowledge and hope. From Beta in the blood, the literal, breathing legacy of my brother, to Beta in the infinite, unknown knowledge of the after life. I completed the silent ritual.

"Relax in paradise, dear brother," I said aloud. I sat down on the ground in front of the grave and just stared at the headstone.

"I've never really lost anyone before," I said. I wasn't sure if I was speaking to Richard, to God, or just to myself, but I continued. "My grandmother died when I was like three, and my grandfather died before I was born. My mom was an only child and so was I. So I don't really know what it means to lose somebody. Not like this. I guess the frat introduced me to what it means to grieve. Kinda weird. We all have this collective sorrow when we hear your story, and we feel like lesser people because we didn't know you. Yet this legend tries to teach us to be more like you. To not focus on the accolades, but on the joy in the work of serving the fraternity. I still feel like a neo sometimes, you know. I knew my role. I just shut up and do the work. I don't complain. I wasn't an officer the first year. I really didn't want to be an officer this year, either, but I guess they needed a Secretary. Heh... Give the sissy the Secretary gig. But it's okay, I was happy to step up. Somebody's got to, right? And I guess that's how you lived your life, too.

"You know... I wish I had known you. My dad said he knew you. He said... he said everybody knew you were gay, but everybody loved you just the same. I think that's cool. That's really cool. I feel like maybe I'm headed in the same direction. I mean, yeah, I've had my issues in the frat, but nothing too major. Nothing like what you probably faced. Damn, I wish I could really talk to you, pick your brain, see what it was really like for you.

"When we talk about you, they never mention if you had a partner. They just say what you did for the frat and for your day job. And then you died. And I'm no dummy—I know that no healthy man drops dead from pneumonia of all things. Not in the 80s for Christ's sake. We all know pneumonia is code for AIDS, or AIDS-related illness. Which really sucks because I used to think I didn't know anybody who was HIV positive. Now I know two people who probably died of AIDS. That really fucking sucks

"I don't... I don't want to die alone. I don't want people to remember me just because I was an active Beta. I might not act like it, but I do want a husband. Or a partner. Or whatever the fuck I'm supposed to call it. I want somebody to call my own. And I want kids and a house and all of that. I want it all. I don't want to be alone."

"He didn't die alone."

"Whoa, what the fuck!" I leaped back from my seated position and almost rolled right on out of that grove.

"Who the hell are you and did you really just sneak up on me dude?!" I shouted.

"I'm sorry!" the man said. He wore a plain black suit which had to have been burning him up in this hot June sun.

"Wait a minute," I said. "I know you."

I focused on his face. Underneath the wire-framed glasses and the gray goatee were unmistakable brown eyes and a thin-lipped smile.

"Founder Wade," I gasped. He nodded.

"Please forgive my cursing," I said, approaching him with my hands outstretched. "I didn't know anyone was here."

"Do you have a brother named Daniel?" he asked.

"Indeed, I do," I responded.

"Where did you meet him?" he replied.

"I lifted him out of the lions' den without a scratch on him."

"My brother," he replied, taking both my hands and greeting me with the grip of the fraternity.

"I'm Adrian Collins, number 4, Upsilon Line, Sigma Chapter," I said.

"William Wade, number 2, Alpha Line, Alpha Chapter."

"If I didn't know that already, my Dean would kill me," I laughed.

"It's nice to finally meet Adam Collins's son," he said.

"Wow, you knew my dad, too?" I asked. He nodded.

"Knew him, pledged him—might have shared a girlfriend or two. Who knows? The 70s were a blur," he deadpanned.

"You're funny, Brother Wade," I said. "What are you doing here?"

"Same thing you are," he said. He looked down to his hands. I noticed he was carrying a single red rose and single yellow rose just as I had. In silence, he performed the same ritual I had, scattering first the red rose petals and then the yellow. I watched, humbled, in silence.

"Like I was saying before you freaked out, he didn't die alone. He was loved by his fraternity and his family," he said.

"I know that," I said. "I just meant... Well, you know, it was a personal moment and all... I'm just saying, Brother Wade... Oh hell. Brother Wade, I'm gay. And I don't want to live this screwed up life that has me chasing after some ideal man who doesn't really exist. And dying alone in the process."

"Brother Collins, there are no perfect men. There is no Mr. Right. We're all flawed in some way, some of us more deeply than others. All we can do is our best. That's exactly what Brother Dawkins did. I told you he didn't die alone. The love of his life was right at his side."

"I apologize for assuming, then. I didn't mean to make him seem like some tragic hero."

"He was a hero. He was my hero—nothing tragic about him. And yes, he was gay. Very openly gay. The fraternity doesn't mention that. Not because the fraternity is ashamed. But the fraternity wants to respect Richard's partner. His privacy. His wishes."

"I understand," I said, looking down at Richard's grave again.

"Do you?" Brother Wade said. "Do you really understand, Brother Collins?"

"Uh... maybe?" I replied. He smiled and sighed.

"Richard was my lover," he said.

"Oh," I said. "Wow. I'm... sorry."

"Don't be sorry for me, young one. I've made my peace with his passing. I miss him every day, but I know he belongs to heaven now. I come out here sometimes and talk to him. And every time, I see that the brothers have made sure his plot is neat and clean. I love that about Beta."

"Coming to visit this place during hell week really changes the pledges," I said.

"I know," he replied. "I'm glad you all do it."

"Brother Wade... How did you know that Brother Dawkins was... you know... the one?"

"I don't think I really knew until it was too late," he said. "I was stubborn back then. And afraid. Scared of what people would think. I still liked women, so my feelings for Richard really frightened me. We were on-again and off-again for years. But that last year he was alive? It was all about us. Maybe I always knew that he was the one but just didn't want to admit it."

I nodded in agreement.

"How have you been able to go on this long without him?"

"Life goes on. What else can I do?"

"Yeah, you're right," I said. "Do you… want some time with him?"

"No, thank you. I should probably get back to work."

"Where do you work?"

"I'm a professor at La Salle University. It's nearby. I'm directing the pre-freshman enrichment program this summer."

"Sounds fun," I said.

"I suppose," Founder Wade said. "Listen, Adrian… you're not going to find the answers to life's burning questions in a cemetery. If you want to know if somebody in your life is the one, ask yourself. If you want to know if you're doing the right thing, then pray. Don't lose sight of the gifts you already have to find your way."

"Thanks, Brother Wade," I said. "There's just… so much going on. And I don't know what to do exactly. So many questions."

"I know," he said. "And not every question has an answer. Just live your life. Don't make the mistakes that I made. If you love somebody, tell them now and tell them often. They won't always be there."

I extended my hand to my brother.

"Thank you, Brother Wade."

"I'll see you at Convention?" he asked.

"I'll be there," I replied.

I watched my Founder walk away from the cemetery and down the street to his car. I walked to my own car and thought about everything he said.

Even though he was at peace, there was a profound sadness about him which was palpable. He had lost the love of his life and wasn't the same since.

I sped away from Philadelphia and promised myself that his story wouldn't be mine. I had to live, laugh, and love—and I would be damned if anybody held me back.

A few hours later, I was in New York, parked in front of my neo's house and fed the meter. Every fraternity brother knew the significance of hospitality to our fraternity. The notion was all throughout our ritual and even in our motto *Let Brotherly Love Continue.* Every Beta's house was my house and every Beta's mother was my mother. Christopher's mother was especially happy to have me spend some time with her son. I was glad to finally meet the woman who bore my little brother.

Some places our mothers couldn't go, however, and that evening we departed for a massive fraternity party. We took the subway up to the Hudson River Café in Harlem. The place was packed with a line going down the block.

"Holy shit," Christopher exclaimed. "This is how the New York bros roll?"

"Apparently so," I said, my mouth slightly agape. Beta was truly a big deal in New York. Christopher got in line.

"What are you doing?" I asked.

"Getting in line. How else are we getting in?"

I shook my head.

"Foolish neo," I mocked. "Our brothers are the hosts. We go to the front." I took him to the front of the line and explained myself to the bouncer. After he frisked both of us, we were in.

"Damn," Chris said. "How was I supposed to know that?"

"You watch. You learn. Now you know." He marveled at my class and sophistication. I was just glad the bouncer didn't embarrass us.

The interior of the club was classy and spacious. Reds, whites, and blacks decorated the open space as dozens upon dozens of revelers crowded the way. Floor to ceiling mirrors made the whole place seem at least twice as big as it really was. Toward the front of the room I noticed the New York Betas who were hosting.

The music was so loud that it was impossible to hear anything, though I comically tried to introduce myself over the throbbing bass. All I could ultimately do was throw the fraternity sign, make a Sigma with my fingers, and place it on my sleeve to signify which chapter I came from. Once they realized what I was saying, they hugged and gripped me and my spesh.

We acclimated ourselves to the bar first and foremost. I was still not much of a beer drinker, preferring the strong tropical drinks when I was out. Christopher, on the other hand, started with a shot of vodka and a beer.

The music was off the chain. People were wall to wall and the dance floor expanded well beyond its planned limits. We decided to go out there and just dance. I did my usual two-step while Christopher did his New York thing. It seemed like all New Yorkers fancied themselves great dancers though whether that was true or not remained to be seen, at least in Christopher's case.

An hour or so later, it was pretty clear that we were both drunk. Christopher drank like a fish and I knew I was personally past my limits. But damn, the drinks were so good.

We were approached by two Latina chicks wearing red and black lettered tikis. They tried talking to us, but it was so loud and I was so drunk that it didn't matter what they said because I couldn't comprehend it. All I knew was that I had seen their organization's letters before someplace, but not on Potomac's campus.

Next thing we knew, these chicks were grinding their asses on us. Christopher was in heaven. As for me, well, although it did nothing for me physically, it was nice to be able to pass for straight every now and then.

The girl that was dancing with me turned around and tried to tell me something in my ear as she danced. It was no use—couldn't hear her.

I smiled and shrugged. Then she kissed me. I was stunned. She laughed.

"I've got somebody," I said in her ear. Then I grabbed her and kissed her back. Hard.

Yep, I still got it. I thought.

***

It was at least 4 a.m. by the time we got back to Christopher's mom's place. We tried our best to whisper while we tipped into the apartment. We slithered into Christopher's messy room.

"Yo, I can't believe how drunk we are," Christopher said.

"Did I really make out with that girl? Right there on the dance floor?" I asked

"You sure did, big bro," he said as he unbuttoned his shirt.

"I am such a bad gay," I said. "Very, very bad."

"You ain't a bad gay, nigga," he said. "You da best gay I ever met."

"Really? You really mean that spesh?"

"Hell yeah!" he said, slipping his belt off. His pants fell off his slender waist and he stood before me in his black boxer shorts.

"Spesh, do you know any other gay people?"

"Nope!" He dove onto the bed. I laughed and slid out of my clothes.

"Well, I guess I know Isaiah," he said. "Why'd you break up with him? And why you tell that girl you were seeing someone?"

"I don't know why I told her that. I guess habit. And I told you already, Isaiah got his ex pregnant. I'm not feeling that."

"But you love him, don't you?" He turned the light out after I got in bed next to him.

"What's love got to do with it?" I asked.

"Now that was gay."

"No… gay is laying in your bed half nekkid with your frat brother."

"It's a queen-size bed! Whaddya want, to sleep on the floor?"

"Nope. Just sayin'."

"Yeah, thought so, nigga. Anyway, I'm just sayin, if you love him and he loves you, shit… Ain't nothing else to say. He doesn't do drugs, does he?"

"Naw."

"He don't beat you, do he?"

"Hell no."

"So he loves you and he treats you good and the only thing that's the problem is the baby?"

"And the baby's mother."

"Okay, and the baby's mother. Man, this is not a problem. Stay with that dude."

"But I got doubts, bro. This whole relationship jive like started out with a lie. First, he didn't tell me up front that he was gay. Or that he was crushing on me. Then, when shit started poppin off, he stayed with Taina. He didn't break up with her. And I should have cut it off then. But I stayed. I waited for him. Now he's about to have a baby by her. Who's to say he's gonna stay with me? Maybe I don't know the real him after all. Or maybe he's not really ready for all this. He says he is, but I don't think so. Not the baby, but definitely not a relationship."

I looked at my brother. He was knocked out.

"Man…" I let my thought trail off. Better to just go to sleep and try to have a more coherent conversation in the morning. The longer I stayed out here on the road looking for answers, the less I really knew.

Chapter 30:
June 30

Christopher and I spent a leisurely afternoon getting our lives together, cursing alcohol, and promising never to drink again.

Where did we end up that night?

A lounge.

He had wanted to go see this Saturday night poetry showcase down at the Nuyorican Poets Café. I had never been there before, but I was eager to check it out. I hadn't heard good poetry in a very long time.

For as much as I had heard about Nuyorican, I thought it would be a lot bigger than it really was. A lot about New York was like that. Nevertheless, it was a nice spot with small tables and a stage at the far end of the room.

We got there pretty early, so of course we had some drinks to go with our meal. I was glad I had chosen Chris to be my personal little brother. Our relationship only got better with time. He was just so real. Eager to learn more about Beta everyday, he kept his mind and his heart open to all possible experiences. This was a great feeling for a man with no siblings. I had finally gotten the big brothers I always wanted by pledging Beta, and now I got the little brother I wanted, too. This was shaping up to be a really good weekend so far, even though it was capping off one of the worst weeks of my life.

Tomorrow was Sunday. I had no clue where I would go next. Maybe further into the northeast to Boston. Visit the homeland of my fraternity. Alpha Chapter. Beta Chapter. Boston Alumni Chapter. Maybe I'll find some more guidance about this whole national second vice president proposition. I mean really, me? A national board member?

Or maybe I'd go Midwest. Or further. Maybe I'd just keep driving west until I hit the Pacific and then decide what to do.

I wasn't ready to go home. I wasn't even sure where home would be once I got back to DC.

"Hey, Earth to big bro… the first act is coming up."

I snapped back to reality and began paying attention to the hostess, a tiny Filipina woman with a booming voice.

"Ladies and gentlemen, welcome to the Nuyorican Poets Café! I am Sunfire and I will be your MC for the evening. I might grace y'all with a little somethin' somethin' later on in the evening, but I promised I would bring up your opening act without hesitation. Y'all already know who it is. This young brotha has been tearing up the scene ever since he came back home from college. DC loves him, but New York needs him more. Y'all give it up for Savion!"

Time froze.

My entire life with Savion flashed before my eyes, from the night I met him at a poetry reading the Deltas sponsored to our first night together. From our first date to the night he told me he loved me. From the day I started pledging Beta until the day I lost him because of Beta.

He was my boyfriend. My first grown-up love.

Time started again and in slow motion, a beautiful Dominican boy with his hair impeccably cornrowed took the stage. He wore yellow lensed sunglasses, a plain white t-shirt, khaki cargo shorts, and New Balance sneakers. A plain gold chain adorned his neck.

He looked good.

"Yo, what up y'all?" he asked the audience, which still applauded for him. "Y'all know what time it is. I'm gonna hit y'all off with some old stuff, some new stuff, then I'm out. And to my kids in the audience—go home, it's past your curfew. But your daddies can stay."

The audience erupted with laughter.

"I'm just playin, y'all… Anyway, check it:

> *Scratching out words*
> *Like DJs scratch beats*
> *Swallowin' my enemies*
> *Because I got to eat*
> *Biting off heads*
> *Like Diddy bit the 80s*
> *I ride my consciousness*

Instead of a Mercedes
Don't need no fakers and
Don't need no thugs
Don't have to rob a bank
To show my mom some love
I won't rape my people
I won't abuse the race
I won't sell out the culture
In front my father's face
Cuz I respect my sisters
And I love my brothers
I praise only God
I believe in no other
What is consciousness?
Is it who, what, or where?
Can you tell I'm saved
Under this nappy hair?
Saved by my mind and
Saved by my self-"

Our eyes locked. He froze. The crowd, which had been into his performance, started to buzz, unsure what was happening.

"Keep going," I mouthed while I nodded. Christopher looked at me.

"You know that guy?" he asked.

"That's my ex-boyfriend."

"Wooooooooow!"

"Saved by my mind, and saved by myself..." Savion continued. "Shit, y'all."

"Take yo time!" Sunfire said from the audience.

"See, y'all know me... I'm an angry gay Latino kid. And y'all love that about me, and I love y'all for it. But yo...on the real... the game just changed. I need to kick a little remix of something for y'all... I remember most of it, but I think it needs the Savion treatment real quick... Sunfire, give me a beat... downtempo. Something sexy."

Sunfire clapped her hands and beat her fists on the table alternately while the audience looked on.

Savion began his new piece:

> *"the other men*
> *came and took him*
> *the other men*
> *stole him*
> *forty days and forty nights ago*
> *they took his soul*
> *but… but…*
> *forty seconds ago*
> *he came back.*
>
> *forty one seconds ago i was*
> *playing the role*
> *like i was billy bad ass*
> *tough guy poet*
> *wanna be a star*
> *but forty seconds ago*
> *i was reminded of who i used to be*
> *of who i was*
> *and whose i was*
> *and i am reminded that*
> *my life was good*
> *and i don't have to be so…*
> *tough.*
> *sometimes.*
>
> *the other men took him*
> *but i am now*
> *the other man too*

Thank you."

The crowd went crazy. I couldn't believe how much he changed, yet remained the same. He was confident and humble all at the same time. He also had a little bit more of a swagger about him, which I had to admit was sexy. And the cornrows…

Savion hit his stride and ended up giving a full set of his work, about five or six more poems. I could tell by the reactions of the crowd that he was a local celebrity, much like he was at Potomac when I first met him.

When his set was over the crowd rose to its feet, clapping and cheering furiously. He acknowledged the cheers, bowed a little, and stepped down. He hugged Sunfire and then walked toward us.

"Oh my God, he's coming over here," I said through my teeth as I smiled at him.

"Be cool bro," Christopher said.

It seemed with every few steps, Savion was stopped by people congratulating him on his set. I couldn't figure out whether they were friends or strangers—Savion had a way of treating everyone equally. He looked at them in the face, shook their hands and hugged them, and touched them on the shoulder.

I loved that about him. It's exactly what first drew me to him. At Potomac, so many guys were stuck on personal space, machismo, and aloofness. That's why I hadn't known Isaiah intimately for the whole two years before we first got to know each other. But with Savion, the attraction was instant. There were no boundaries to speak of.

He got closer. Was that sweat breaking out on my forehead? I stood up.

"Hi," I said.

"Hey," he replied.

"Nice poems," I said with a smile.

"Nice to see you," he replied. We hugged each other for the first time in well over a year. I had all but forgotten how his small frame felt in my arms. The stubble on his cheek tickled mine.

"Why you can't call nobody?" he joked. "I miss you."

"I've been… busy. You know how it is."

He nodded. "Isaiah."

I nodded back. "Yeah, Isaiah. But not anymore."

"Say word?" he asked.

"Yeah. Oh, I'm sorry, Savion, this is my frat Christopher. He goes to Rock Creek."

Chris stood up and shook Savion's hand.

"Can I get you a drink?" Savion asked us.

"Sure," Chris said. "I would like..."

"We're fine," I said. "Why don't you just sit with us a while?"

"Thought you'd never ask," he smiled. He pulled a chair up and we began to chat quietly.

"So I'm not gonna lie to you, Adrian... You know I was pissed when I heard you hooked up with Isaiah. I was like damn, I thought we could work this shit out after a while. But I heard y'all was like for serious and shit."

"You shouldn't have been pissed," I said. "Isaiah's a good dude. We had a good run."

"So it's over? For real, for real?"

"Some things happened very recently... I'm not thinking it's going to work out."

"So you're still with him?"

"Right now, no. I guess we're on a break."

A break. I had heard that before. Isaiah was on a break from Taina when he and I got together.

"Oh Adrian... So much drama."

"What? I didn't ask for this drama, you know."

"But you thrive on it," he said. "Woe is me, I hate my mommy. I hate my daddy. I hate the white man. I hate college. I hate pledging."

"Fuck you, man," I said, my tone getting serious. "You know you never heard me say any of that."

"I'm just fuckin' with ya, baby," he said. "Don't worry. I loosened up in the past year."

"I can tell," I said. "For what it's worth, I missed you. A little bit."

"I missed you a little bit, too."

We talked more and more throughout the evening. The more

we talked, the more I felt a void was being filled that I had neglected in the past year. Savion was my heart during sophomore year. He gave me nothing but his love and raw emotions from day one. He was romance personified. Whatever I wanted from him, he gave to me gladly. I never had to wait on him. His love was loyal, steadfast, and ubiquitous.

I only lost him because I had lost my own way. So often, I considered the hazing to be the worst part of my pledge process. Indeed, I had suffered bruises and inflicted them on others. But the worst part of my process was what I had to choose and how much I had to lose.

Selfishly, I blamed Savion for not standing by me as I endured the process. But what man in his right mind would stay with someone who would allow himself to go through what I had been through?

Savion made the right choice. Life went on. For me, that meant a life with Isaiah, which had led me to the crossroads I was at now. For Savion, that meant graduating and becoming a middle school English teacher by day and a rising spoken word poetry star by night. It was exactly the sort of life I expected him to lead. No surprises, just good work and good words.

Where the hell did I go wrong?

I noticed Christopher yawning while watching the performers. Savion excused himself to use the restroom.

"You're not enjoying yourself, huh?" I asked.

"It's okay. Not really what I expected, but it's cool. I'm glad you're having a good time."

"Thanks. I am. Listen, if you want to leave, we don't have to stay."

"And have you miss your reunion with your boo? Naw, I'm cool. I can stay as long as you want to."

Savion soon came back.

"Hey, why don't we all come back to my place and kick it for a bit? I think you'll see that I've upgraded a bit from my last spot."

"Oh," I said. "Where do you live?"

"Three blocks from here, across the street from the subway."

"Sounds good to me," Christopher said. We stood up and quickly left the Café.

After a quick walk, we were in front of Savion's building.

"You know what y'all," Christopher said. "We're right here at the subway. I'm pretty tired. And I know y'all want to catch up some more. Adrian, would you be okay getting back to my place on the subway?"

"Yeah man, it's on the same line. No problem."

"And if it gets too late, you can just go back in the morning," Savion added. "I mean, we're friends, no big deal."

"Aight, bet," Christopher said. "Savion, it was nice meeting you man. Keep up the good work with the poetry and shit."

"Thanks, man. Nice meeting you, too."

"Frat, be good," he said, offering me the fraternal grip.

"I will," I said. "Thanks."

As Christopher strolled away, Savion snorted.

"Hmph, you ain't never hug me like that."

"That was the grip, fool," I said. "Show me this apartment of yours."

We went up an old elevator to the eighth floor of his building. He led me down the hallway to a corner apartment. It was perfect for him. Not too big, but had a nice little living room filled from top to bottom with nothing but books. He always had a lot of books. The kitchen was tiny, but cute, something straight out of the fifties. His bedroom was fairly large and had a nice view of this corner of the city. He led me to the window and started pointing out the landmarks that I should know.

"So, which way is New Jersey?" I asked.

"Behind us," he said, standing close behind me.

"And Brooklyn?" I asked.

"That-a-way," he said. His hands reached around me and he hugged me from behind. I held his hands and exhaled. He rested his head on my shoulder.

"I missed you," he said.

"The phone works both ways, you know," I said matter-of-factly.

"I was giving you space," he said. "Guess I gave you too much."

I let go of his hands and turned around to face him.

"You gave me what I needed," I said. I leaned close to him and we kissed. I closed my eyes and absorbed every ounce of passion in this moment. Our mouths made small circles as our heads slowly tilted in alternating directions. We were planets colliding into one another.

I inhaled him and I recognized his scent, a mixture of his cologne, the moisturizer he used on his skin, and the cream he used in his hair.

He began unbuttoning my shirt as he kissed me. I undid my belt buckle and unzipped my pants. He pulled his white t-shirt over his head and kicked off his tennis shoes. He quickly resumed kissing me again and we fell into his bed.

Our hands discovered our bodies as though it was our first time. It may as well have been—he had gained weight and had been working out. There was definition in his abs and chest that I didn't remember.

"You still look good," he said in between kisses.

"You look even better," I said.

"I try," he said. He straddled me and touched my face. His hands were strong, but gentle. I quickly flipped him over and laid him on his back.

"A little more aggressive these days, eh?" he asked.

"Shut up," I said lunging at his lips with my mouth and thrusting myself into him. His hands reached for my underwear while I tasted his neck for the first time in so long.

"Is this what you want?"

I sharply inhaled and opened my eyes.

"What?" I asked, frozen. His voice sounded like Isaiah's for split second.

"I said 'is this what you want?'"

"Oh," I said. I continued to kiss him and he pulled my underwear all the way down. He flipped me so he was now on top, taking off his shorts. I looked down at our naked bodies and then up at Savion's beautiful face.

"I see the way he looks at you. It's like… when you're not looking, he's longing."

Nina's voice rang in my head. When I first heard those words, it wasn't Savion she was talking about.

I brought him close to my body and hugged him. I couldn't let go. I stroked his hair and lightly kissed his forehead.

"I do love you, I really do. But I'm… scared at how deeply I do feel for you."

Isaiah's face flashed in my mind. He was a vision of earnestness and humility when he spoke those words to me just a year ago.

"Savion… I can't," I admitted as I stroked his hair.

He looked up at me.

"What do you mean you can't? You are. We are."

"I can't do this to you," I continued. "Or myself."

He broke away from my hold and looked at me from his side of the bed. I couldn't look at him.

"Do what? Come back here to my place and get down like old times? Why? Are you afraid?"

"I'm not afraid… I'm just not…"

"It's him," Savion said. "You're not over him."

I shook my head.

Disgusted, Savion stood up and turned the light on. He gathered his clothes and began getting dressed.

"Savion, I'm sorry."

"Shut up. Put your shit on and get out of here."

"Savion, I love you and I'll always respect what we had, but…"

"I said shut the fuck up! If you really loved me you would have left me the hell alone, Adrian! I was doing just fine. You hear me? I was fucking amazing. And actually I had the audacity to think that you had come back into my life through some divine intervention. Like you happened to come into the Nuyorican because somehow the stars aligned and we were meant to be together again."

"I didn't mean for that to happen. It was really just a coincidence."

"You and your excuses," Savion said. "Well what the fuck are you waiting for? Put your clothes on."

I did as he said, feeling sorry I had ever chosen to come back here. This evening had gone horribly wrong. The last thing I wanted to do was hurt my ex-boyfriend. He was a beautiful person who I had hurt too many times.

"I just want you to know," I said while buckling my belt, "That I only want what's best for you. I didn't mean to mislead you by coming here with you. I just wanted to see you. I've been going through so much this past week and I really did think I was meant to see you. But maybe not for the same reasons you wanted."

"And what's that supposed to mean?" he asked.

"I understand that he is hurting you. If he has the balls to walk around campus hand in hand with this girl, right in front of you, then he doesn't care about you!"

"He does. I know he does. Nina, you just don't understand… I love him"

"It means… that I needed to see you one more time so that I would know."

"Know what?"

"Who I love. Who I want to be with."

"And now that you've been with me once more, you know that it's Isaiah?" I nodded slowly.

"I'm in love with him. And I want to be with him."

"Then why are you here with me? Hmm? Tell me that, Mr. Lazarus? You couldn't even stay in a relationship long before you let a bunch of your peers beat you down in the name of brotherhood. And you go from one freak show to the next—you get into a relationship with the most down low of them all. And then what happens? You come running back to me."

"Is that how you really feel?"

"Yes… It is. I gave you all that I am, Adrian. I couldn't be no more real with you if I tried. I gave you everything I had and you still couldn't decide what you wanted. Even now you don't know."

"That's where you're wrong," I said. "I do know."

I walked to him and touched him on his shoulders.

"I love you. And one day I want to be your friend, but-"

"You don't love me. You don't love him. You only love yourself. Now get out."

I frowned and let my hands fall from his shoulders. I patted my pockets to make sure I had everything I came with.

I walked out of his bedroom. He followed close behind me until I was out of the front door. He watched me as I walked toward the elevator.

"Adrian," he called out.

"Yeah?"

"I... uh... I hope you find what you're looking for. But please... forget about me. I don't want to see you again."

"Savion, I'm-"

He slammed the door. I heard the deadbolt lock and the chain slide.

I took the stairs down to the street below. I couldn't believe that I had hurt my first love yet again, this time irrevocably. I felt horrible inside. Yet, I still remembered another.

"But you have to admit, Adrian... Isaiah left her for you. He must really care for you to turn his back on everything he knows."

And I turned my back on the only love I knew before Isaiah—quite possibly the only other man who knew the real me.

"Don't you realize you are the only man I've ever said those words to? The only one! How many ways can I say it before you start believing it?"

I believed.

Finally, I believed.

It was time to go home.

Chapter 31:
July 1

Early Sunday morning, I bid farewell to my gracious host and got on the road to Franklinville, New Jersey to return my dad's car. We had had a lovely odyssey together, but it was time to return her to her rightful place. I now knew who I was and where I belonged.

I tried to reach Isaiah intermittently all morning, but it kept going straight to voicemail. I really wanted to tell him I was on my way home—where I belonged. Whether that was at my dad's house, my mom's house, Gloria's, Potomac, or my brownstone, it didn't matter. Home was where my heart was and it existed in all of those places.

I was still uncertain about Taina and this baby. I didn't know what I would think about it when it finally got here, or what sort of role I was to play in its life. But Isaiah was my man and I would stick by him.

Around noon, I arrived in Franklinville and drove up my father's driveway. As I parked outside of the garage, I tried calling Isaiah one last time.

"Hello?"

"Baby," I said. "It's me."

"I know," he said. "Where you at?"

"I'm at my dad's house about to go inside," I said as I closed the door.

"I've got something to tell you," he said.

"Okay..."

"Taina had the baby last night."

"What?!" I exclaimed. "It's too early! She had another month to go. Is the baby okay?"

"Relax, the baby's fine," he reassured me. "I was there. I saw the whole thing."

"Whew," I said, sitting down on my father's porch.

"You really care, huh?"

"Of course I do. That's your child."

"Yes, he is," he said. I heard the door slowly open behind me. I didn't turn around, but raised my hand up to wave hello to my father as he checked on me.

"It's a boy?" I asked.

"Yeah... it's a boy. She named him Zion."

"Zion? That's... different."

"Yeah...I had no say. But I can live with it. Zion Anthony Aiken."

"She gave him your last name. Can she do that?"

"We're doing a DNA test to be sure, but Adrian... I know it's mine. I know she wasn't with anyone else."

"Does he look like you?"

"He looks like... a baby. They all look alike."

I laughed.

"I want you to come home, Adrian. I want you to meet my son."

"I want to come home, too," I said. "That's why I was calling you all morning. I'm tired of running from this. I want to make it work."

The phone went dead.

"Hello?"

I looked at my phone to see what went wrong.

"Then let's make it work," Isaiah said. I turned around and stood up.

He was here. He came to me.

My eyes flooded with tears.

"Don't cry, baby," he said.

I collapsed in his arms and we both slid back down to the floor of my dad's porch.

"Sssshhhh," he said. "Why are you crying?"

"Because you came," I said simply.

"I never gave up on us," he said. His voice cracked.

"I know you didn't," I said.

"I knew the minute you packed your bags and left that I had

to fix this. That I had to make things right. This past week has been hell. I only ever wanted you to have the best and I gave you the worst possible situation you could ever have. We've been through too much to fail. I wasn't going to give up on us. Not for one second."

"Wait a minute," I said in between sniffs. "Taina had the baby and you left her?"

"I was there with her through the whole labor. I saw my son being born. I held my son. Then I put my son down and drove all morning to come get you. You and my son—you both come first. I would lay down my life for either of you. And I don't know how it's going to work out. I don't know where he's going to stay when he's with us. But I want him with us. Together. You are both my family. Now, I know you weren't hardly thinking about children, and I respect that. But I just want you to meet him. Just look at his little squishy face once and see what I see."

"How did you know I was here?"

"Your mom told me you might be here. She told your pop and he said it was cool. And he said I could stay here as long as I needed to."

"My dad... my mom... wow..."

"My mom told me you had stayed with her, too. And I'm glad you did. She loves you, too. And I don't think she'd forgive me if I let you go."

"Your mom is the coolest."

"Ain't she bad?" he laughed.

"Isaiah, listen. I left because I needed to find answers. I needed to find myself again. I spent a lot of time thinking, soul-searching. Talking. Getting advice. But in the end there was nothing that anybody could say to me to sway me one way or the other. I had to look inside myself, man. And when I looked inside... I found you."

I felt his cheeks expand into a smile as he rested his head against mine.

"I saw Savion when I was in New York," I continued.

"Oh yeah?"

I nodded. "Isaiah..."

"Don't… I don't want to know. You have a history with him. All I need to know is… Well, I already know. Because you're back here in my arms."

I slowly nodded my head.

"That's ancient history," I said. "All that's left is us. That's all I want. I don't want nobody else, do you understand me?"

I release myself from his embrace, stood up, and looked at him.

"Isaiah, I don't want to be with anyone else. Ever. I'm choosing you. I choose us. Now. Always. I love you. And I know now that loving you is never going to change. I don't care if you had Zion, Zephaniah, Zachary, and Zoom-Zoom-Zoom. I would still love you. We ain't perfect. We ain't the Huxtables. But what I have with you is like nothing else in this world. And if there's anything else like it, I don't want it, because loving you is good enough for me."

"Baby," he said, eyes now red from the constant stream of tears. "Sweet, sweet baby. I know I've fallen so short of everything you deserve. And you deserve it all. You're right, we're not perfect. And we're going to stumble and make even more mistakes. But I would rather stumble toward a life with you than with anybody else. I love you so much. I want to spend the rest of my life with you. Will you? Will you be part of my family? Be my mother's son? My son's protector if I'm not there?"

"Will you be protected by me?" I countered. "Will you let yourself be vulnerable when you need to be loved? Will you let me carry your burden when you get tired sometimes? Will you trust me when I say that I will stay?"

"I will," he said.

"And so will I," I replied. I leaned down and kissed him softly on the lips. In that instant, I knew why I had gone through everything I had been through in the past week.

He was the one.

We stood up as we kissed and Isaiah lifted me up off the ground like he did the day I first told him I loved him.

"Did we just get engaged?" I asked him as he placed me back on the ground.

"Fuck that," he laughed. "We just got married!"

I laughed.

"Mr. Collins! Mr. Collins!" Isaiah yelled into the house. "What? Oh, you're back," Dad said. I had my arm around Isaiah's waist. "Everything all worked out?"

"Yeah, Dad," I said, wiping the last tear away. "Dad, this is Isaiah. But I guess you knew that. Well, anyway, I'm kind of in love with him and I hope you're okay with that."

My dad smiled.

"I'm okay with that," he said. "More importantly, how is my car?"

Isaiah beamed at me. I tossed my dad the keys.

"She's fine," I said. "Thanks for letting me borrow her."

"Anytime," he said. "And by anytime, I mean never again. I nearly had a stroke after I realized how much that car is worth!"

Me and Isaiah laughed in unison.

"Mr. Collins, if it's okay, I'd like to take your son back home with me to meet... my son."

"Be safe, fellas," my dad said. I loosened my grip on Isaiah and ran to my dad, hugging him with all my might.

"You, sir, are coming to Atlanta for convention," I said.

"Am I?" he asked.

"Yup! Because you need to see your son get elected to national office."

"Oh lord, here we go," he said. "I swear you are definitely your mother's son. Always the overachiever."

"And you know this!"

"I'd hate to cut this short," Isaiah said. "But we've got to go. Mr. Collins, a pleasure sir." They shook hands. Isaiah then looked at me.

"Ready?" I nodded my head vigorously. The next thing I knew, Isaiah scooped me up in his arms and carried me down the stairs and around the other side of the house where he had parked.

"Nice van," I said. "Who is the previous owner, the Teenage Mutant Ninja Turtles?"

"Shut up, niglet," he said, placing me on the ground on the passenger side. "That's the best rental I could do at 5 a.m.!"

"Well fine," I said. "Let's go meet a baby named Zion then!"

Isaiah quickly put the van in gear, backed out from my dad's house, honked the horn once and sped away. My dad waved from the porch as we hauled ass out of Franklinville.

Hours later, we were in the parking lot of the Georgetown University Medical Center, where Taina had the baby. The sun was just starting to set on the horizon as Isaiah called Taina from his phone.

"Aye, I'm back," he said. "I told you where I was going. To Jersey to bring my man home."

He looked at me, smiled, and grabbed my hand while we walked. All that coaching from Rebecca had gone out the window—this boy was happy.

And so was I.

"Of course he came back," he continued as we walked. "He wouldn't miss meeting my son... Yeah, yeah, *our* son. Well we're coming up... Excuse me? Nah, playa, we're on our way right now. Ain't gonna be no games. No more. I'm happy, girl. You need to be happy, too. Aight? Hello? Hello?"

"Lost the signal?" I asked.

"I think she hung up on me," he laughed.

Minutes later, we were on the shiny silver elevator to the maternity ward.

"You nervous?" he asked.

"A little," I said. "I mean, clearly Taina doesn't want to see me."

"Well she better get used to seeing you," he said. "This is a package deal."

"And you definitely got the DNA test done?" I asked as the doors opened.

"I insisted on it," he said. "Results will be in soon, maybe a few days. But like I said... I know it's mine."

"I know," I said. "But Rebecca taught me well. Get that shit in writing."

He touched my cheek with his fingertips.

"I love having you in my corner," he said. We approached the nurse's station where we signed in. As the father, Isaiah was given a special bracelet. Apparently it had some sort of chip in it which matched a chip in a similar bracelet that Zion wore. It acted as a subtle tracking device to make sure the right babies were released to the right parents.

"Wait here," Isaiah instructed as we passed a clean waiting area on the corner of the ward. "I don't want Taina to upset you. You know, she might have post-traumatic depression and say some shit she regrets."

I laughed. "Post-traumatic? I think you mean post-partum depression."

He laughed with me as he walked down the hall. "You know what the hell I mean, nigga."

I sat down in the '70's era chairs with orange leather cushions with my hands in my lap. As expensive as Georgetown's tuition was, you'd expect the décor to be a little classier. This was truly no Potomac University.

A few minutes later, Isaiah emerged with a small bundle in a blue blanket and a huge grin. Isaiah was so big and the bundle was so small that it almost didn't seem real.

He careful sat down next to me and held the baby out in front of him.

"Hey little boy!" he said to Zion. "It's Daddy."

"Well, take the blanket from over his face so I can see him," I said. Isaiah readjusted his kid and removed the cowl-like blanket from the baby's face.

Underneath was the most beautiful child I had ever seen. He was fair-skinned like both of his parents, with a tuft of smooth, jet black hair already on his head. His eyes were closed but he was still gurgling as though he wanted to be heard.

"Wow," I said. "He's... a baby."

"No shit," Isaiah said.

"Don't cuss around the baby!" I exclaimed.

"He don't understand cuss words yet!"

I groaned.

"He's handsome though," I said. Isaiah held him up to his face and kissed him. The action caused Zion to open his eyes and look in my direction.

"He opened his eyes!" I said.

"You see him?" Isaiah said to Zion. "That's Adrian. Adrian Collins. He's your... well, he's special to your daddy. And that means he's special to you, too. Aight?"

Zion gurgled.

"You want to hold him?" Isaiah asked me.

"Can I?"

"Of course you can. Just watch his head." Isaiah handed Zion to me. I held him out in front of me with both hands and watched him, praying he didn't somehow leap from me and fall to the ground.

"Adrian, come on. He's not a bag of flour. Hold him to you, like against your chest. You know... like a baby."

Isaiah repositioned my arms and placed Zion in them as he should be held. I looked down on him as he looked up at me, gurgling the whole time.

"This is awesome," I said. "I'm holding a baby."

"You're holding my son," he added. "Hold on, stay just like that."

He produced his camera again and stole a quick snapshot of the moment.

"Did you just take my picture, dude?" I asked.

"Yup," he said. "My man and my baby. Don't get better than that."

Just then, a nurse walked by.

"Would you like me to take one of all of you?"

"Oh, you don't have to..." I began.

"Yes, please!" Isaiah exclaimed, practically knocking his chair over to give the nurse his camera phone.

"On three," she said. Isaiah placed his arm around me and his free hand under the baby as I held it.

"One," she began.

"First family picture," Isaiah said.

"Two…"

"Oh, Jesus," I said.

"Three!"

I looked at the image on Isaiah's phone again when we got back to the brownstone. I lay on my stomach across our bed on the plain brown comforter.

"You know, this is a nice picture after all," I admitted.

"Ain't it?" he said as he unlaced his sneakers and slid them off. "I'ma put it on Facebook."

"You cannot put this on Facebook," I said. "Too many people will see it and ask questions."

"Baby, I have exactly 32 Facebook friends and not even all of them can see everything. My privacy settings are like whoa. Anyway, I gotta show it to your mom."

"You're Facebook friends with my mom?" I asked.

"Uh, yeah."

"Wait a minute… My mom is on Facebook?"

"You mean to tell me I'm friends with your own mom and you're not? Ha! Yo momma don't wanna be your friend!"

"Shut it up," I said in between chuckles. "I'ma have to talk to Elizabeth about that one."

"But naw, I know all about the risks of social networking. I will not let you or Rebecca down."

"Good," I said. I slid his phone back over to him, closed my eyes, and laid my head down on my crossed arms.

"So what happens with Zion next? Where is Taina gonna go?"

"Back to Rochester for now," Isaiah said. "She claims she's not coming back to Potomac for school, but we'll see about that. She needs to just finish up here, or at least stay in the area. That's my son, I need him near me."

"I understand."

"And, well… Rebecca also recommended a good lawyer to me. She handles custody cases really well. I talked to her briefly this week and we're going to start the process for joint custody and child support immediately. We're not going to wait on Taina to get the ball rolling."

"That's good," I yawned. "I don't want her to try no funny business. I mean, shit… it would be to her advantage to make this an amicable situation because after next year… Well… We'll see what your salary will be like after next year."

"Yeah," Isaiah said. "We'll see." He turned the light out in our room.

It was getting late. I stood up and peeled my shirt off as Isaiah got on the bed.

"You still look good, boy," Isaiah said. I smiled.

"I was only gone a week," I responded.

"Still… felt like longer."

"Yeah, it did," I said. I pulled my socks off and got on the bed next to Isaiah in just my boxer shorts. He put his arm around me and I rested on his chest.

"I'm so glad you're home," he said.

"Me too," I said. "I'm glad I know where I belong."

"Me too."

We sat in silence for a few moments. Our hands casually roamed each other's skin, as though with minds of their own they were navigating new territory.

"Baby?" he asked.

"Yeah?"

"I have something I want to give you," he said.

"What is it?" He leaned over to the nightstand and opened the drawer. He pulled out something small and square and put it in my hand. I held it in front of me so that I could see it in the light.

"A condom?" I asked. He nodded. "Well how is that a gift? You always wanna fuck."

We laughed together.

"Baby… The condom is for you."

I looked at the condom again. I inched away from Isaiah and stared into his face.

"Are you for real?" I asked. He nodded.

"So you're saying… You want me to…?"

"Yes, baby," he said. "I want you."

"Awwwww, shit!" I growled. I pounced on Isaiah with an instant, rock-hard erection and showered him with the best foreplay we'd ever had. I was aggressive, pinning him down and tonguing him down simultaneously. Before too long, we were both down to our skin and Isaiah was on his stomach.

"You ready?" I asked. He whimpered a yes.

"Now don't act all scared," I said. "And don't you run from it, either."

"Okay, I got you man… oh… yeah… yeah, Adrian… ah… oh yeah… oh, God… Adrian… yes… yes… *oooh yeah, baby!*"

Epilogue:
One Year Later

Things were never really the same between me and Nina. After the day I cursed her out for trying to talk to me about Isaiah when I was trying to forget him, a switch was turned on (or off?) in both of us that signaled a turning point in our relationship. We would always be friends, but I couldn't accept that she didn't give me the one thing I needed at the time: space. Even Isaiah had given me space.

We spoke after Zion was born and she finally told me what she had been dying to tell me. Taina's new boyfriend was Jamal—my gay-bashing prophyte. It was no coincidence that I had seen him driving down P Street the day of my birthday barbecue. As it turned out, he was Taina's reconnaissance here in DC while she was in Rochester.

All things considered, it didn't matter. I didn't have to deal with him. I didn't even technically have to deal with Taina if I didn't want to. Once paternity was officially established, Isaiah's attorney negotiated a great custody agreement. Taina acquiesced to moving to DC again, where she finished up her coursework at Howard University. Jamal was always on the periphery, but to his credit, he left me alone. Although Isaiah and I remained uneasy about having Jamal around Zion, we had to let go and let God deal with it. Taina was in love with him and we could keep Jamal away from Zion no easier than Taina could keep me from him.

I grew to love the little bugger, too. Except for when I was traveling on behalf of Beta Chi Phi in my role as national second vice president, I was extremely happy to hang out with my man and his son. I even got him a Future Beta onesie. I was constantly amazed by how quickly he seemed to grow, from his bushy black hair to his height. He would definitely be a basketball player like his dad.

My dad did indeed attend his first fraternity convention in about twenty years to help my last minute campaign for national office in the frat. Even though it wasn't a position which I had ever dreamed about,

I realized the more that I researched that this was a position I needed to have. We had to bring some transparency back to the fraternity—to return it to the roots of the founders and their dream. And since our founders were all still living, it should be easier for us to get back there.

My dad proudly stood by while Founder William Lucas Wade administered the oath of office. It was my proudest moment as a Beta thus far.

My next proudest moment was supporting my line brother Mohammed as the best Dean of Pledges that my chapter had ever seen. I was proud also to pin my second special in the chapter. Even though he was a one-time fling, Morris and I put our past behind us. He became the first openly gay aspirant to ever pledge our chapter. I was proud to have helped lay the foundation for that moment.

Throughout the year, my mom and Isaiah's mom made quite the pair spoiling Zion. Between all of us, Zion was the most stylish baby in the DC area. Although Zion wasn't really my mom's grandson, I think we all knew this was as close as she would get for a while. She loved doting on him. Gloria felt the same. When Taina came, we made an interesting extended family when we all attended basketball games during Isaiah's senior season.

Isaiah and Hodari had another phenomenal season. For a while there, it didn't even seem that Potomac could be beaten at all. We made it all the way to the finals again, and this time we didn't choke. This national championship assured Hodari and Isaiah's place in the NBA draft. Hodari ended up second pick overall. Isaiah was a very respectable ninth pick.

Hodari went to the Washington Wizards. Isaiah went to an expansion team called the Brooklyn Empire. They were a newer team looking to rebuild their squad after previously taking a gamble on a too-young draft pick who wasn't up to the rigors or athleticism of professional basketball. Isaiah was eager for the challenge and glad to be remaining on the east coast.

I hadn't yet found a job in Brooklyn, but I was determined. I believed in my relationship with Isaiah, but I refused to let him carry me. I thought something in education might be nice. Maybe I would work for an after school program for a while, or some other nonprofit which dealt directly with people. I had made some good connections through the fraternity and I knew that a great opportunity was right around the corner.

My mom and Gloria were sad to see us leave the DC/Baltimore area, but they were happy we were still together. My mom often complimented me on how good I was with Zion. I didn't think I was doing anything special—he was Isaiah's son and I'd do anything for him. He was just a kid. He didn't ask to be born into drama, so I protected him from it, often being the voice of reason in Isaiah's tirades about Taina.

On our last day in the brownstone, movers carefully carried our boxes away. Isaiah and I stood in our old bedroom, which was now totally empty save for the light fixtures. Isaiah held Zion in his arms.

We stared at the room in silence, wistful and reminiscent about all that happened there and thankful we had come through it all even stronger.

"Hello?" a voice called out up the stairs.

"Up here," Isaiah said. The clicking of high heels got progressively louder as Nina entered our room.

"Hey, girl," Isaiah said, walking toward Nina and pecking her on the cheek.

"Hey, boy," she said. "Hi, Zion! How are you?!"

Zion smiled, then bashfully hid his face.

"You so silly!" she cooed. "How are y'all doin'?"

"Good," I said, giving her a hug.

"I'm glad I caught you before you left," she said. "Can I talk to you real quick?"

"We can go downstairs," Isaiah said.

"Thanks," I said. They left, leaving me and Nina alone.

"Adrian, look. It's been a year. And I know we've been talking off and on, but it's nowhere how it used to be."

"Yeah," I said. "I kinda miss being best friends."

"I know we can't go back and undo the last year. And listen, I totally understand why you reacted how you did last summer. I wasn't listening to what you were telling me. All you wanted was space. And you know... I sit back and wonder how you made everything work between you and Isaiah. I realized... you actually listen to each other. And that's a beautiful thing."

I smiled. "Yeah, I guess so. We listen. Nina, I think that we had been so close for so long that we did forget how to listen to each other. We're so busy telling each other how it is that we forget to just stop and listen for what we want. You know, your brand of medicine is a bitter pill. And people don't always want to hear it, but you're usually right."

"But is being right more important than just being there? I don't think so."

"You're right," I said. "In any case, I am glad that you told me about Jamal. Well, I'm glad I eventually listened long enough for you to tell me. I would have gone nuts if that kind of news took me by surprise."

"I still can't believe out of all the nutcases in the world, he and Taina would find each other," Nina said.

"And they're still going strong," I said. "Jamal's been quiet though. So I guess all we can do is wait it out. They won't last."

We sighed simultaneously.

"So, I guess this is farewell," I said.

"Seems like it," Nina said.

"Nina, I'm sorry I let this year go by without trying to fix this distance between us. It should have never happened."

"Aww, sweetie," she said hugging me. "This is just another step in our lives. You'll be back down here for homecoming and I'll come visit you at the loft in Brooklyn."

"You better," I said. "And you and Hodari...will I be getting some good courtside seats to see the Wizards play?"

She laughed. "I don't know about all that. Hodari is still... himself."

"At least he's serious about playing ball and getting paid," I said.

"Better that than nothing," she sighed. "You know me, though. My options remain open."

"Don't I know it? I can't wait to meet the man who will sweep you off your feet."

"Me too!" she laughed.

"Hey…you knock 'em dead at that advertising agency on K Street."

"I will," she said. "Be safe on those roads, okay?"

I nodded and hugged her one last time. She bounced off down the stairs.

I spent another few moments looking at my empty room. As a tear threatened to form in my eye, I looked upward and fought it off.

"It's been real," I told the room. I turned the light off and walked downstairs. Isaiah was still holding Zion.

"Hey, you take him," he said. "I'll lock up."

He handed off the baby to me and immediately Zion lit up. Maybe what my mom said was true, that I really was good with Zion. He took a real shine to me for some reason. He was just about a year old but hadn't said any real words yet. I secretly dreaded the day when he'd learn to call me something. Isaiah was desperate to figure out a good word for step-father, even though we weren't married and had no immediate plans to be. I personally thought Adrian was a good enough word for Zion to call me if he could ever say it.

I walked Zion outside. He loved grabbing onto my face and somehow seemed to think that my goatee was his for the taking.

Taina and Jamal stood outside waiting for us so we could hand the baby off to them. I knew better than to attempt to even talk to Jamal—after all this time, he wouldn't look me in the face. Taina and I had grown civil. She even cracked a smile when she saw Zion grab my chin.

Jamal got into his car and waited. Isaiah locked the door behind him and came to Taina and I.

"We'll be back down in two weeks to see him," he said.

"Cool," she said. "He's going to miss you."

"I'm going to miss him, too," he said. "Once you finish at Howard this winter, we gotta make some better plans. You moving to New York, maybe."

"I don't know," Taina said. "We'll see."

"Bye bye, baby," I said to Zion. "We'll see you soon, okay? Love you."

I kissed Zion on the cheek and then handed him to his dad.

"I love you, little boy," he said. "Daddy will see you real soon, okay? Me and Adrian are gonna bring you so many presents from New York! Daddy loves you, Zion."

He gave his son kisses and hugs and then handed him back to Taina.

"You're doing good, Taina," he said to her. She paused, taken aback by the compliment.

"Thank you," she said, regaining her icy façade. "Be safe out there. You too, Adrian."

"Thanks, Taina."

Taina strapped Zion into his car seat and then sat on the passenger side of Jamal's ride. Soon, they were off and away. Our movers, too, drove off. We'd meet them in Brooklyn late that night.

Isaiah and I would be driving my graduation gift to New York— my dad's 1967 Mustang. He decided it should belong to me. He said I'd earned it, after having my own adventure and not wrecking it. Besides, he bought himself two more vintage cars to replace it.

"Well, this is it," I said, fastening my sear belt.

"You sad?" he asked, clicking his own belt into place.

"I'm a Son of Potomac. What do I have to be sad about?"

He smiled.

"I love you so much."

"I love you, too. Now let's go. Which way, Mr. Aiken?"

"North, Mr. Collins" he said. "And don't stop 'til you get to Brooklyn."

"No doubt," I said, pulling the Mustang out of the parking space.

"Wait!" Isaiah said.

"What?!"

He leaned over and kissed me. His mouth tasted as good as it ever had.

"Our last kiss in DC," he said.

"For now," I quickly added. We pulled out of the space in front of our brownstone and drove away from the block. Everything behind us got smaller and smaller until everything—our house, our school, our challenges—faded into a distant memory.

One day we'd tell the story to our son and he'd laugh at us for ever being so young and in love.

Rashid Darden is a novelist living in Washington, DC. *Epiphany* is his third novel.

Thought it was over, didn't you?

There are two sides to every story.

While Adrian and Isaiah ride off into the sunset,
take a glimpse into one of the lives they left behind.

THE LIFE AND DEATH
OF SAVION CORTEZ

Available now

www.oldgoldsoul.com

–

Made in the USA
Charleston, SC
03 March 2012